THE ETERNAL BETRAYAL

CURSEBREAKER

BOOK SIX

JT LAWRENCE

FIRE FINCH

FIRE FINCH

Copyright © 2024 Fire Finch Press

www.jt-lawrence.com
All rights reserved.

About the Author
JT Lawrence

JT Lawrence is a USA Today bestselling author of 30+ books, and a Kindle Unlimited All-Star. Mother to a menagerie of chaos, voracious reader, gin fan, and urban farmer.

*Stay up all night
with USA Today bestselling author
JT Lawrence.*
www.jt-lawrence.com

Sign up to her **VIP Reader newsletter** here:
Substack: Stay Up All Night

or her **Urban Fantasy** list here:
Magic & Mayhem

SPECIAL THANKS

Immense gratitude to my readers
whose loyalty, support, and generous reviews
give me the courage to face the blank page
over and over again.

I wouldn't be able to do this without you.

I hope you enjoy this new magical adventure!

- Janita (JT Lawrence)

CHAPTER 1
A BRAWL WITH A VAMPIRE
ASHA

If Lilian Black was the only one who knew who my parents were, I needed to keep her alive. I knew it, and she knew it—it was written all over her smug, bloodsucking face.

"Besides," the silk-skinned vampire said, "if I die, this pocket realm dies with me." She gestured dramatically to the lines of unconscious girls in their white hospital beds. Black definitely had a god complex ... and she knew she had me in her grip, the tyrannical pythoness. Hex, I hated her.

I ran through my options. Weapons: none. Wand: negative. I had my skeleton key from Ferra, which wouldn't be very handy in a brawl with a vampire. I guessed that security would arrive soon, and I was sure that Black had some kind of panic button along with that little blade she kept hidden in her 1800s widow's dress.

Thank the goddesses that Mercury was awake and alert. The girls whose IVs I had dialed down were waking up. I didn't take my eyes off Black, but I could hear them moaning and moving. Of course, they would be in no state to fight, but at least they would be conscious for our escape—the escape I had no idea how to implement. I swallowed hard, but it didn't remove the lump of anxiety that was lodged in my throat.

I knew I couldn't do this on my own. I wished so hard that I had my team with me. I knew they had my back, no matter what. Without even realizing it, they consistently chipped away at my abandonment issues.

"I remember you," said Black. "You were at the market a few weeks ago."

"Yes," I replied. "You tried to kill me then, too."

"Oh," the vamp chuckled. "I'm not going to kill you, Asha, dear. You are much too important for that. You're worth far more alive than dead."

"So, we're at a stand-off," I said. "I can't kill you, and you can't kill me."

"Indeed," she replied, seemingly happy with the status quo. I kept my eyes trained on her, hoping she wouldn't turn her head.

Out of the corner of my eye I saw one of the girls sit up. Black did not notice. I also saw that Mercury's bed was empty. I needed to keep the vampire talking so that they could leave before security showed up. I said the first thing that popped into my head.

"Why do you only use virgins?" I asked.

Black furrowed her brow. "Excuse me?"

"Why do you only select female virgins for this bleed farm?"

The vampire scoffed. "I'm surprised you need to ask. Virgin blood is pure, unadulterated. Magical people have known this from time immemorial."

Sure, I knew that. "It's never been scientifically proven, though, has it?"

Lilian looked at me in a way that expressed disappointment that I was less smart than she had given me credit for. "Science can only prove so much. It is we, the arbiters of magic, who know the truth, because we feel it."

Another girl sat up in bed. I thought it might be Dusty, but I kept my eyes glued to the vampire's. Mercury seemed to be shepherding the weak girls out of their beds and down the corridor. I kept waiting for the medical machines to bleat their alarm calls, but the sound didn't come.

"Well," I said, as if we were having this debate at a book club instead of in a macabre pocket realm with the clock ticking, "I've always thought purity was overrated."

Black hissed in disagreement, which made the retreating girls jolt.

"Firstly," I said, "the very idea that having sex can make you *impure* is ludicrous. And even if it were true, which it certainly is not, what is the point of being pure? There is no *power* in purity. Power comes from experience, from pushing your limits. A woman who knows what she wants is dynamic. Pleasure is empowering."

I saw no more movement behind Black, so I could call off the bizarrely timed exchange of philosophies. As it was, she was staring at me as if I had sprouted an extra head. Perhaps she had mesmerized so many girls with the *"puritas antedecit"* nonsense that she had inadvertently brainwashed herself.

"It's imperative that the ingredients of the Æternal elixir are pure." Her eyes were dead when she said it. It was clearly a well-rehearsed line. Yep, she definitely sounded indoctrinated.

Lilian Black reached for her blade. "You're going to come with me."

I shook my head. "I'm not going anywhere."

The steel knife glinted under the harsh hospital lights, lending it the appearance of sheer menace. "I might not be able to kill you, my dear "—*Ugh, I hated how she called everyone* dear—"but don't be lulled into a false sense of safety. What I can do to you will make you beg for the relief of death."

What Lilian Black didn't know was that I had been through the wringer in the past couple of weeks, defending myself against all kinds of monsters, and winning. Plus, I too knew how to use a blade.

The fact that security had not yet showed up was unnerving, making each second that went by feel like the ticker of an undetonated time-bomb.

"Asha Viridian Rook," the vampire said, her irises darkening into black whirlpools, "you will come with me."

My brain shouted "No!" before my mouth did. Something inside me refused to be hypnotized. Black looked confused; she clearly wasn't used to people being immune to her magical manipulation. She tried again, and this time as I shouted back, I lunged for her blade and grasped it, wrenching it away from her and slicing my palm in the process.

"Asha," she scolded, as if I was a naughty puppy with a new slipper. "Give that back."

I switched hands because of the pain in my injured palm. The blood made everything slippery and I couldn't get a good grip on the handle. Where was the Celestia security? I knew I had to defuse Black without hurting her, but I didn't know how.

"Asha," she warned again. "Give the blade back."

It was my turn to furrow my brow, because the knife began twitching in my hand as if it had a mind of its own. It began to raise my arm in the vampire's direction. I pulled it back down, but it rose again and started to escape my fingers, no matter how hard I tried to keep them coiled around the handle.

"Why haven't you called security?" I asked.

As self-satisfied as ever, the vampire replied. "I'm perfectly capable of taking a witch down on my own."

I sensed that was not the whole truth. She may be capable, but I surmised that it would reflect badly on her if her boss knew about what had happened. After all, Lilian Black had unknowingly brought a troublemaking interloper into their pure, precious pocket realm. This would probably be a fireable offense, and I knew how much this vampire liked her fat paychecks.

The knife continued to unfurl my fingers, ready to fly back to its mistress, and my hand muscles began cramping with the effort of holding on. I bit down on the aching sensation, knowing that pain didn't matter. All that mattered was getting the girls home, and to do that, I had to put the vampire out of action—while keeping her alive. My arm was now stretched out in front of me, and the knife was almost free. I tried again to clench down on the handle, but the force of it was too strong — as if it was being pulled away by a powerful magnet, which, I guess, was what Lilian Black was.

CHAPTER 2
THE CRAVING
ASHA

My fingers no longer had strength in them, and my right hand was dripping blood on the white floor. Lilian Black looked at the crimson liquid and her nostrils flared, reminding me that she was indeed a vampire, a murderous creature that hid well beneath the elegant Victorian fashion. Despite her wealth and her status, she was as much a vampire as any lowly street vamp sniffing around alleys for unsuspecting victims. Her money didn't make her immune to her bloodthirsty instinct. I narrowed my eyes at her, waiting for her to pounce, but as I did so, the knife finally gathered enough momentum to leave my hand and fly into hers, but not before flipping in the air to arrive hilt-first.

"That's a good trick," I said. *I must learn how to do that.*

She hissed again, and this time there was desire in the sound. Before, it was pure annoyance, but now I heard the hunger in it, the craving. She showed me her fangs and blurred toward me, almost snapping my neck sideways in her haste to puncture my neck. The vertebra made a crunching sound, and I thought I might pass out.

"No!" I yelled, trying to push her away. Despite her lithe figure, she was exceptionally strong. I used all my strength to keep her fangs away from my skin, but the tussling made the scent of my blood stronger, and Black lost control of the carefully constructed facade she usually wore. Gone was her ramrod posture, her strict but calm countenance, her measured movements. I was losing strength in my arms as my fatigued muscles failed. Keeping her fang-face away was like pushing away a boulder that was about to crush me, and I knew I was losing the battle.

Damn it.

"Don't ... do ... it," I panted at her. "You need me ... alive."

Her hold on me eased a fraction as she remembered that I had more value as an asset than as a late lunch.

"The ... blood tests ... remember?" I pressed. I still had no idea what the results had been, but I knew that Black thought they were important. I needed to appeal to her other greedy side, the one that craved money instead of my blood.

She eased again. I was still firmly in her grasp, but the tension between my hands and her head as I kept pushing her away became easier to bear. When she looked up at me, her irises were so terrible, so frightening, that I gasped and drew back further. Inky veins writhed underneath the skin around her eyes like tiny, venomous adders. Her skin was gray. The only color in her face was the bright blood around her mouth, which frightened me, because I thought it was mine, until I realized she had punctured her own lips in her frenzy to drink from me. Seeing the two small black holes made the hair on the back of my neck stand up. My palm had stopped dripping blood, which I was grateful for. If only I could get rid of the coppery smell in the air, I was sure Black's sudden savagery would end. She was still holding the knife, and I could feel the point of its blade poking into my breastbone.

"You need me alive," I whispered again. This time the message seemed to get through. She kept the blade in position, but took a shaky step backward.

Not taking her terrifying eyes off mine, she wiped her bloody mouth with the back of her hand as the black capillaries beneath her skin faded. I could tell by the ravenous way Black was looking at me that she was still fighting the animal inside her urging her to devour me, no matter my ancestry or monetary worth. While her internal battle raged, I knew it was now or never. I snatched at the vampire's knife, trying to turn it again. The resulting battle over the blade cut my palm again, letting more blood, which was the last thing I wanted.

"*Rumpis*," I said, and the knife became desiccated, falling like sand between our hands. I put my bloody palm on her chest and whispered, "*Fiat fulgur.*" I expected the lightning spell to shock her and fling her backwards, but the magic didn't take. I repeated it, this time with more volume, but she was a wet wick. Her lips turned up in a ghoulish grin, revealing bloodstained teeth. That's when I noticed the opal amulet on the choker she wore was glowing a fiery orange. Similar to the tanzanite ring I had which glowed when I was in danger, hers seemed to have an added perk: a protection spell to ward off menacing magic. I tried to snatch it but she was too quick for me, grabbing my wrist and twisting it so that I cried out in pain. I tried to step back but her grip on my hand was so strong that it only hurt me more, and I couldn't help yelling again. Her blood-lust seemed to have given way to anger. It seethed out of her, her fury at me for daring to touch her, daring to attempt to steal her amulet. I couldn't use my magic on her, and I had no weapon. I had regular human strength, she had vampire power. Despite her delicate build and ridiculously tiny waist, she could pick up a dozen of me and we both knew it. The odds were not in my favor.

CHAPTER 3
BLOOD-SCENTED BREATH
ASHA

If I couldn't use my magic against her, I'd need to come up with something else. The destruction spell had worked on the blade, so I tried it again, this time targeting the protection amulet. I breathed in deeply to ground myself and gather my magic—which wasn't easy in a room with no plants—and when I felt sparks in my fingers, I went for her choker again.

"Rumpis!" I yelled. There was a grinding sound, and I screamed in agony. Instead of crumbling, the magical stone had reflected the spell and crushed my hand. My fingers hung limply. I stumbled backwards, trying to see through the tears blurring my vision.

Lilian Black looked especially pleased. *This is what happens,* I could imagine her thinking. *This is what happens when a witch is arrogant enough and stupid enough to infiltrate vampire territory.*

The pain was incredible.

So, that didn't work, I thought. *Best come up with a new plan.*

"Don't even think about it," said the vampire, in her blood-scented breath. "Unless you really want to hurt yourself."

An idea popped into my head that was so left field that I didn't even know if I should take it seriously. It would still involve magic, but not against the Victorian vampire—not directly, anyway.

I tried to push the pain out of my mind to make space for the spell, but I realized without enough greenery in the vicinity that I'd need the pain to feed the magic. After one deep inhalation, I went for it. Not wanting to make Black suspicious, I chanted the conjuring spell in my head. As I did so, I could feel the magic spreading throughout my body.

By the mysteries of the deep

By the flames of the wild

By the power of the east

And by the silence of the night

By the holy rites of Hecate

I conjure thee, HENRY HOLDEN

Present thyself here

And answer truly my demands

Evoco et excito, nunc et semper, res ac mortales

So mote it be!

"What are you doing?" asked Black, eyes narrowing.

I didn't see the point in answering her. I looked around —rather optimistically, I'll admit—for the small phantom, but I didn't see a hint of him. I waited for the signature drop in temperature, or goosebumps, or that poltergeist smell I had come to recognize. I knew it took a lot of spectral energy for a ghost to appear, so I didn't expect a full show, but I was hoping for some kind of help, especially seeing as Lilian Black had been the woman who ensnared Henry and his sister, causing them untold suffering in the Taranath cellar. I repeated the spell again, this time really trying to become one with the pain, trying to embrace its power. When nothing happened—apart from the vampire twisting my wrist as far as she could without snapping it—I really worried that nothing I could do would save me. The girls were probably hiding somewhere, waiting for me to get them out of this cruel cult, and I was losing … or had already lost.

Had I gotten the words wrong? Had I mixed up conjuring spells? Or was Henry just living his best ghostly life somewhere and not taking calls?

A breeze blew in from nowhere, hard enough to tousle the sleeping girls' hair and ruffle their sheets. As the wind picked up, bits of paper came sailing down the long hall. Lilian Black frowned, and it was clear to me that something unusual was happening. She let go of my wrist and glared at me, wordlessly asking what I had done.

"Curas vulnum," I whispered to my hand. I felt my knuckles click back into place, and the terrible ache in my broken hand subsided a little. I was no healer mage, but my magical first aid would do for now. She stood there in front of me, arms lifted at her sides, trying to work out what was going on.

Suddenly the vampire gasped, and my eyes darted around, thinking she had seen Henry, but when I dragged them back to her, I saw she had been looking at me all along. The wind dropped completely, and there was utter silence. Lilian Black's jaw went slack, her eyelids slid closed, and she fell forward into my arms.

It was instinct that made me catch her. If I'd had time to think about it, I probably would have let her fall on her face. As she collapsed into me, I saw a syringe pinning a hastily written note into the vampire's back. I laid the deadweight vampire on the white tiles and pulled out the tranquilizer. It was plunged deeply into her back, and the needle was so large it made me shudder. Not that the vamp deserved any sympathy. I picked up the note and immediately dropped it, as if it had burnt me.

CHAPTER 4
GHOSTLY PASTURES
ASHA

"APOLLO NEEDS YOU," said the note. It was signed by Henry.

The words didn't make sense. They scrambled my thoughts. I was confused, but knew I had to keep moving. My mind working like crazy, I shoved the note into my pocket and lifted Black's body onto the closest empty bed, which turned out to be Mercury's mattress. I covered her with the starched hospital sheet so that she would look like she belonged, but I already knew there would be no hiding what had happened. After all, there would still be four empty beds when Sister Vena did her next rounds. I hated the idea of leaving the vampire there. I wanted to take Lilian Black with us, wanted to interrogate her until she told us everything there was to know, but I knew it would never work.

I was worried that while the three girls and I traveled home to the Realm, Black and her evil company would abscond with the whole of Celestia. I searched for a pair of scissors and eventually found a scalpel, which I used to cut the vampire's choker off. I tied it around my wrist. The amulet would not only offer protection against harmful spells, but would also be a handy portal key when I was ready to come back for the girls. Even if the pocket realm moved, which I was sure it would, I knew Lilian Black would stay with the Celestia sisters. She was attached to them—she cared for them in the way a wolf might care for a flock of sheep that he doesn't want to share.

"APOLLO NEEDS YOU."

Weird, I told myself, *I am the one who needs Apollo.*

So Henry had not yet moved on to greener ghostly pastures. Perhaps he had stayed to act as a guardian angel to his skeletal sister. Knowing how much he cared for her, it was a distinct possibility. But where did the pickpocket fit in?

I took one last look around the white hall. I knew I needed to go and find my girls, but it was difficult to leave the others behind. How many of them would die before we came back for them? My ribcage ached with sadness for their families. At the same time my stomach roiled with hatred for vampires. No wonder Jax hated them so; no wonder she had spent her life striking them down. From the outside it perhaps appeared like an unhealthy obsession, being a vampire-hunter, but I understood it. Maybe, now that I had been cut loose from the Starfall coven and was no longer Soleil's hired wand, I could join forces with the female wizard once she was back at work. Dusty could be our apprentice; we'd be a fang-busting squad.

"Asha!" came a fierce whisper. "What are you *doing?*"

I looked up and saw Mercury at the entrance, waiting for me. Damn it. I had been lulled into a daydream by the puzzling note and the amulet. I needed to wake up.

"Sorry," I said, as if I were the child and she, the grownup. I shook my head to clear it and ran toward her. "I had to deal with Black, and ... never mind. Where are the others?"

"We think we found a way out," Mercury whispered. "But we can't open the door."

"Excellent," I said, thinking of the magical key tucked into my bra. I quickly felt for it to confirm it was there and was relieved when I felt the hard metal. I was aware that opening a door wouldn't get us home, but if we could escape this building, it would be a start.

I saw a conduit on the wall that had been sliced clean through, and realized that was why the security had never arrived. Even if Black had pressed her panic button or the medical machine alarms had been triggered, the signal would never have reached the guards. Mercury grinned at me. She really was something. Beauty, brains, *and* bravery. I wondered if she would consider joining our imaginary squad, too.

We ran down a passage, knowing it wouldn't be long until the nurse discovered her unconscious boss in the bed. When we reached the other girls waiting at the locked door, I almost sobbed in relief.

"Dusty!" I cried. "Abi!" Dusty's eyes were so full of affection and solace that I felt her gaze deep in my heart. We rushed to hug each other, and Abigail joined in.

"Don't be angry with me," Dusty begged. "Please, Asha."

"I'm not angry with you," I said into her hair. "There is no anger here," I squeezed them both tighter. "Only love."

I felt her sigh and begin to weep. I let go of Abi and gripped Dusty's shoulders but held her at arm's length so that we could see each other's faces. "There's no time to cry, Dust."

She sniffed and nodded. "Let's get out of here."

Zaleria was watching me with fascination. She still looked pale, but being out of bed and off the sedatives seemed to have given her some color. "What about the others?" she asked. "We can't leave them here."

I inhaled sharply around my own guilt. "We'll come back for them."

"We can't leave them here," she repeated. Her dry lips were the lightest shade of pink, and her breathing was uneven. "They'll die if we do."

I shook my head. "No. I won't let them. As soon as you girls are safe, I'll return with backup. We can't do this on our own."

"They won't be here when you come back," Zaleria said. She spoke with no emotion, and I hoped it was temporary because of the drugs in her system, and not a permanent condition due to the trauma she had endured. Blonde hair, pale skin, emotionally comatose —she was like a ghost of her formal self.

Ghost.

Henry.

Apollo needs you.

I ignored the irritating thought and brought out my skeleton key. I exhaled and murmured the spell under my breath as I tried to unlock the door. It worked.

CHAPTER 5

OLD CABBAGE
ASHA

Before leaning on the handle to open the door, I worried that if we crossed the threshold we might accidentally tumble into space, like the coyote in Road Runner when he looks down after darting off a cliff. I needn't have worried. There was another corridor beyond, one that looked identical to the one we were standing in.

I let go of the breath I was holding. "Let's go."

We sped down the new passage but I soon noticed that Zaleria was not with us. Turning back, we called for her in urgent whispers.

"Zaleria," called Mercury, eyes wide with fear. "Come! They'll be after us!"

"We can't leave them here," Zaleria protested for the third time. I had the sudden urge to hit my head against the wall. I admired her empathy, which everyone in the Realm knew ran through the Chalice family's veins, but my instinct was yelling to get out of there or we'd *all* end up like Maxine Malachay.

"Please," beseeched Mercury. "Asha's right. We can't help them from here. We need to get home before we can recover them safely."

Zaleria shook her head, which made me feel like screaming in frustration. Instead, I gritted my teeth so hard I almost cracked a tooth. Collectively, we were Schrödinger's cat, simultaneously alive and dead. Dead if we stayed, alive if we escaped, yet we were standing still, straddling the line between breathing and not ever breathing again. I wondered if Chione would appreciate our predicament.

"Zaleria," I said, approaching her cautiously, worried she'd back away. "Your parents are so very worried about you."

She blinked at the mention of her folks.

"They tracked me down and begged me to find you," I said. "Your mom can't eat; your dad can't sleep. They're out of their minds with worry. Come with us, let them see that you are okay. Please."

She closed her eyes, and I could see there was a battle raging within her despite her cold countenance. I slipped behind her, quietly slotting the key back into the keyhole, and turned it, locking us away from Lilian Black and the bleed farm. Zaleria's eyes flew wide open as she realized what I had done. It was a sly move, maybe unfair, but necessary. I shot her a look of apology, and she nodded and finally followed.

We jogged down the hallway, nerves jangling, with no idea where we would end up. As far as I was concerned, as long as we were putting distance between ourselves and the vampires, we were heading in the right direction. The corridor was long and there were no doors—or anything else—so it felt like one of those dreams where you keep running but get nowhere. It reminded me of the stone passage in the Obsidian Castle which had been hexed with various optical illusions to keep intruders from escaping. We did finally reach the end, which took the form of yet another locked door. Breathless, I opened it, thanking Ferra for the key she had made from Adrather's wand. I did rather enjoy the knowledge that the Dusk Reaper's potent wizard magic

—which he had tried and failed to kill me with—was coming in so handy.

Again, anxiety about what lay beyond spiked, and again, there seemed to be nothing to fear except the white ceiling, tiles, and walls of yet another corridor.

"Is it a trick?" asked Dusty.

Zaleria was pale again, and I wondered how long she'd be able to keep up with us.

I shook my head. "There's only one way to find out."

I kept going, and the girls followed me. We moved more cautiously than before, not sure if we were running away from danger or straight into it.

How would Henry possibly know Apollo? Unless the sneak thief was ... dead? My heart lurched at the prospect. Without the portaler we would be well and truly hexed.

No, he's not dead, I told myself. *He's too important. Directress Copperfield said so.*

I wished I had never even thought it. It became another cloud in my head, obscuring my thoughts, as worries do. Apollo was not dead. There would be a perfectly reasonable explanation as to how the child phantom knew him.

Suddenly something changed. The white passage looked the same, but something was different. The light? The energy? No. I sniffed the air. It was the smell. A smell I knew better than I'd ever wanted to. Old cabbage, dead rat, blue cheese ... it was *eau de Orc*.

CHAPTER 6

VILE AND VICIOUS
ASHA

I sniffed again. "Do you smell that?"

The girls stopped and scented the air like police dogs.

"The smell of freedom?" Mercury quipped.

I smiled at her, despite our situation.

"Ew," said Abigail, scrunching up her face. I saw her disgusted expression ripple out onto the other girls' faces as they caught a whiff.

Zaleria looked like she was about to hurl.

"What are orcs doing here?" I whispered. The question was aimed mostly at myself, but I didn't have an answer. I knew the Xarlugs were in cahoots with the

Smaragdes, but I didn't expect them to be involved in the bleed farm operation.

"Why not?" asked Dusty. "They're on the same side, right?"

"I guess so," I replied. I wished I had brought some of those tranquilizer syringes. All I had was a skeleton key and a scalpel, and I really wasn't in the mood to fight the savages. Just thinking of Alyndra Sybil's sadistic orc goon made my heart race and my eyes water. I touched the monocle, and pushed my fear down. Either way, it would be a battle. If we turned back, we'd face Lilian Black and her cultish vampires, and if we went ahead, we'd have to fight orcs.

"Keep together," I told them. "Take care of each other. And if there is any chance at all of escaping, you go for it. You run faster than you've ever run in your life. Do you understand?"

Four frightened girls looked back at me and nodded.

"Even if it means leaving me behind," I said. "Got it?"

Dusty and Abigail shook their heads.

"No way," said Dusty.

"Not gonna happen," said Abi.

"I'll be okay," I assured them. "I've lived through far worse than this."

They didn't look convinced. "You've *got* to make it out of here," I insisted. "The rest of the girls need you to."

I was worried that my magic would be weak because there were no natural green things to draw from, and I didn't have my wand. But the odor was getting stronger. We needed to move.

The passage veered left, next we turned right. There were no choices to be made or options for other routes —just the white walls that seemingly went on forever. What started off as a subtle scent turned into a smell, and later a stench. When we heard something, a rasping and gurgling, we knew we were close. A little farther on was a corner, and I knew they were behind it. I motioned for the girls to wait while I padded up to the corner and very cautiously peeked around it. I needn't have been so careful, because the two orcs I could see were fast asleep. They were in the same security guard uniforms the Xarlug thugs had been wearing in the SubRealm, which made my skin crawl. Vile, vicious creatures. They looked almost comical, sitting in chairs too small for them, legs and arms splayed, in deep slumber. The one closest to us was drooling, while the other one's head had rolled back and he was snoring. I was happy that we weren't sharing a row of seats on a plane—a silly thought, because orcs don't like flying. Apparently, it makes them nervous, plus they're charged extra for their bulk. The room they were in looked like a laboratory, but I didn't see anyone in a lab coat.

A loud siren made me jump, and my heart stuttered. I caught the scream in my throat just in time, slapping my palm over my mouth in case. Sister Vena must have found the empty beds.

Damnation!

We'd only needed a few more moments to sneak past the guards, but now they were up and on their giant meat-slab feet.

I looked back at the girls and gestured for them to stay calm despite the tsunami of adrenaline flooding my body. When I returned my gaze to the guards, I was surprised to see that they had not reached for their guns —in fact, they were looking decidedly unruffled. They seemed to be treating the siren as nothing more than a wake-up alarm. They grunted some unintelligible words at each other and approached a conveyor belt I had not noticed. Drooler hit a button, turning the belt on, while Snorer snapped on some black latex gloves and waited for the merchandise. It took a while for anything to appear on the conveyor belt, but when it did, it was in neat white medical-grade cooler boxes taped up with red bio-hazard tape. A dozen identical packages zipped along until Drooler hit the button again, causing the belt to slow to a stop. He looked at an electronic clipboard I hadn't seen him pick up.

"Twelve?" he asked his colleague.

"Twelve," confirmed the orc, nodding.

Drooler tapped his screen to confirm the delivery, put it down, and pulled on his own pair of gloves. Together, working slowly and carefully, they slit open the red tape on all the boxes. I could see by how they worked together that this was not their first rodeo. It was so well choreographed that I almost forgot they were orcs. Drooler took the first box off the conveyor belt and moved it to the pristine lab counter, reached in, and brought out what looked like a bag of blood, along with a test tube of the same. My PTSD was in full force, making my breathing labored as I watched them. It reminded me so much of my experience in the cage that I felt I was back there. I could even smell the blood and vomit and pink paste. I held down the bile in my throat just as I had tried to do back then, and was grateful for my empty stomach. The last thing I consumed had been

"Chef Pablo's" protein shake over twenty-four hours ago.

While the bags of blood were individually weighed, the test tubes were placed into a large machine that began whirring once the lid was closed. After a minute or so it beeped, and a green light came on.

"All good," said Snorer.

"All good," agreed Drooler.

The guards retrieved the tubes, matched them back to their bags, and bound each pair with a green band. These went back into the white cooler boxes which were re-sealed, this time with green tape. I thought they would put them back on the conveyor belt to transport them to the next station—whatever that would be—but instead they carried them to the opposite side of the lab where there was a large channel built into the wall. It looked like a sophisticated version of a laundry chute in a hospital, with a fancy oven door—one that you might find in the home of an elf.

The girls behind me were getting restless, so I silently asked them to wait just a little longer.

Drooler opened the hatch. It was dark inside. I heard the chinking of a buckle and guessed that the orc was strapping the box down to secure it for its journey to who-knows-where. He closed the door, toggled a blue knob, and there was a loud *whooshing* sound. When he opened the hatch again, the white box was gone.

I watched them do it again, but this time it was Snorer. They took turns in their smooth and practiced way. It was time to make a move ... I just didn't know which move to make.

An ear-splitting siren wailed, and it was obvious to everyone that this time it was not a delivery signal.

CHAPTER 7

SUDDEN DEATH

ASHA

The siren was so loud I couldn't help covering my ears. There was nothing in the corridor or the lab to absorb the shrieking, and it felt like it was reverberating throughout my entire body. It was hard to think. I would take on the orcs and the girls should ... wait? Climb on the conveyor belt and hope for the best? Hex, I really couldn't think above the soul-piercing screeching.

Copperfield's voice came into my head. *The universe supports action, not thought.*

With that, I took a breath and crept around the corner. There was nothing to hide behind so I just took my chances and rushed at Drooler—or maybe it was Snorer —and smashed the gun out of his hand. He was so surprised to see a combative witch in pajamas that he didn't even react until the gun went flying out of his hand and skidded over the tiles, clattering into the corner. He lunged at me, but I was quicker than he was, and he lost his balance and almost fell over thinking he had grabbed me when I darted past him. The other guard aimed his Glock at me and gave me a look of warning. *Don't do it,* his eyes were saying. *Don't pick up that gun or this will end very badly for you.*

Even as the action was unfolding, I felt some of my fear fall away. I had survived violent orc assaults. I had survived a Dusk Reaper's bullet. I would survive this.

Drooler caught up with me as I reached his gun, grabbing my ankle and pulling me away from it. I wondered why Snorer had not yet shot me in the back.

Action, not thought.

I flipped onto my back and pretended to aim a gun at Drooler. He instinctively let go of my twisted ankle to protect his face from my imaginary bullet. He was only fooled for a split second, but it was enough. I kicked my way backwards and grabbed the gun, aiming it at his temple. He put up his hands in surrender. I switched my aim to Snorer so that we were in each other's sights. Drooler took the opportunity to lurch at me again, but I was so hopped up on adrenaline that I didn't even think to pull the trigger—my finger automatically did it.

The bang wasn't loud, but it was ugly. A dark aperture appeared between the guard's eyes and he listed to the side.

Despite my profession, I'd never enjoyed violence. Seeing the damage to the orc's skull made me feel sick, but I didn't have time to think about it. I stared down the barrel of my stolen gun and into the barrel of my enemy's. He didn't seem that shaken by his colleague's sudden death despite the fact that they had clearly worked well together and had only each other for company.

I couldn't talk him out of shooting me—the siren was still blaring like a frantic foghorn—so we glared at each other past our guns, fingers on triggers.

"Put the gun down!" he shouted, and gestured in case I didn't hear him.

"Rumpis," I said to his weapon, but it didn't self-destruct. *"Rumpis!"* I yelled. Nothing.

I took a steadying breath and pulled my trigger. Snorer's eyes and mouth stretched wide, but no bullet hole appeared. He pulled his trigger, but there was no gunshot. Perhaps the destruction spell had worked, but not in the way I was used to. With so little magical energy available, I guess it did what little it could—jam the firing mechanisms of both firearms. The orc grimaced and tossed the Glock away. He came for me, and I closed my eyes, covered my face, and braced myself, having had intimate prior experience with what it felt like to be crushed by such a creature. I felt the ground quake beneath me, but the impact I was expecting did not happen. When I opened my eyes again, Snorer was out cold on the floor, a trickle of blood spilling from his shaved head. Dusty stood in his place holding the scale.

Without spending a second in self-congratulation, she dropped the instrument and helped me up. I did a quick mental scan of my body and found I was uninjured, apart from a smarting ankle. Knowing the orc wouldn't be unconscious for long and that more guards were most certainly on their way, we knew we had to find a way out. Dusty grabbed the other girls, who looked horrified at the bodies on the floor. Sometimes I forget that normal people aren't used to facing death, despite it being all around us, all the time.

I searched the room for an escape. The conveyor belt would presumably take us back to the lab where the technicians tested the blood. The chute might take us to some kind of factory floor—that's *if* we survived the trip. It certainly didn't look like it would pass even the laxest safety regulations for human travel, safety belt notwithstanding. But I thought it was our best chance.

"You're kidding," said Abigail, when I ran over and opened the door. At least, I think that's what she said. I've never been good at lip-reading, but I'd have to practice it in future, because I was sure the constant blaring of the siren was deafening me.

I shook my head. Not kidding. I held the door open, feeling like the evil forest witch in Hansel and Gretel. *Time to get in the oven, my lovelies. It will keep your chops nice and warm.*

We all knew it was the only way out, yet we all hesitated. I assumed it would be safe, because the product they usually used it for was extremely valuable. But I also knew that inanimate objects had different molecular structures from human tissue and bones, and I had no idea what technology they were using to vacuum the boxes up the chute. We could come out mangled on the other side, or brain dead ... or just plain dead. The landing location was also a mystery: it might deliver us directly to our enemies. Despite these terrifying thoughts whirling in my head, my instinct was pushing me to do it. I would have to trust it and deal with the consequences.

Yikes.

I motioned for Abigail to get in. She shook her head. I tried Dusty, who looked apprehensive —her lips crimped in fear—but her trust in me won her over. She took a deep breath and climbed into the dark space. I gave her a thumbs-up.

You'll be fine, I told her telepathically, and she nodded.

I shut the door and toggled the blue knob as I had seen the orc do. I didn't hear the whooshing sound this time, but there was a light vibration on the handle, and when I opened it again, the chute was empty. I exhaled in relief, and motioned for Zaleria to get in. Shaking and wobbling, the poor girl needed help to crawl in. Thumbs-up. Silent whoosh.

Abigail nodded that she was ready. She scrambled in quickly before losing her nerve and she was gone. I knew Mercury wouldn't hesitate—the girl had ovaries of steel, as Ferra would say—but I was wrong. She refused.

"Get in!" I yelled at her. I could feel the danger in the air. It lingered like spicy orc B.O.

The evil forces were so close I could almost feel their black talons reaching for us. Mercury shook her head and motioned for me to get in. It was only then that I grasped the major flaw in my escape plan. Someone had to be outside the chute to toggle the bloody button.

CHAPTER 8
SELF-CARE FOR ASSASSIN WITCHES
ASHA

"Get in!" I yelled again. I would stay behind and battle the vampires.

Mercury shook her head again and gestured desperately for me to go, pointed at the dial, motioning that she would turn it.

"They won't hurt me," she shouted into my ear. "I'm an asset."

It was my turn to shake my head. "We can't risk it! I won't risk your life! I can fight!"

"No!" she shouted. "You need to rescue the other girls. All of them. Only you can do that!"

Oh, goddess. I was flung back to a magical morals philosophy class where Professor Tramway told us that sacrificing one life to save many was the correct thing to do, ethically speaking.

"Go!" shouted Mercury, banging the wall in frustration at how long it was taking.

Zaleria told me I have a destiny, Mercury had said earlier.

"I'll be back for you!" I shouted.

She nodded and slammed the door shut. I fussed with the safety belt, fear dulling my fingertips. I couldn't get a good look at the buckle in the dark. The chute was blessedly silent compared to the noise in the lab, and I was finally able to fasten it. I was vacuumed up the tube like the gluttonous German kid in *Charlie and the Chocolate Factory*—which isn't quite as much fun as it sounds—and the pressure all over my body reminded me of portaling through the Void ... until I realized I was, in fact, portaling though the Void. It was like being in a compression supertube and my ears ached but my heart sang, because we had made it out of Celestia alive. Yes, we'd be landing somewhere in a vampire stronghold, but at least we'd be back in the Realm. I felt emotional, a heady mix of guilt for leaving Mercury behind, and intense relief for getting my girls out.

The Celestia cult seemed like a dream now, so bizarre had the experience been. Being in someone else's body always made situations seem surreal, but the "finishing school" was by far the uncanniest glamour experience I'd ever had, which was really saying something, as I was at that moment being vacuumed through space via a glassy rollercoaster tube. I tried to relax my body and focus on my breathing, to give it some kind of rest. I had been on high alert for hours now and I needed some serious grounding. But how does one ground oneself when you're being slingshotted through space? I closed my eyes and imagined I was in my jungle garden, my ducks around my bare feet. Feeding Jemima the strawberries she loved so much. Harvesting potatoes. Gathering seeds. Pruning the espaliered fruit trees. I breathed deeply, slowly, until my heart hushed. I made a mental note to do this more often. Self-care for assassin witches. When I'd finished in my garden, I imagined I was at the Copper Cog & Ale with Ferra and Sam. We'd be joined by Savvy, Abigail, Nilve SaltySnap, Chione, Captain Morgan, Stoker, and Rick. And they all looked rested and healthy and happy. The drinks looked golden, the food sumptuous, and we talked and laughed and cried together, remembering the bad times and how we had survived them all. After dinner, Sam and I would leave the pub and go home to a candlelit bath and then to bed, where he would pull me so close to him that every part of our bodies touched, including our scars, and our warm skin would transmit our love for one another.

My forward motion slowed and the pressure gradually released me, telling me I was almost at my destination. My meditation had worked, and now it was time to be on guard again. This time I welcomed my raised pulse and adrenaline injection, because I knew I had to be in top form for my landing. In theory I should arrive around half a minute after the others, and I hoped they hadn't got into too much trouble in that time. The tube went dark, and I assumed I was being delivered via a channel chute similar to the one in the Celestia dispatch lab.

The landing was gentle, and as soon as I came to a stop, the hatch door opened, and I saw Dusty's face light up at seeing me.

"You okay?" I asked her, and she nodded while she helped me out of the shaft.

The other girls looked safe, too. I didn't see anyone else in the room, so I guessed the alarm that had sounded at Celestia had not sounded here—yet. Hopefully Mercury would tell them we escaped via the conveyor belt to buy us some time. Besides, no one would be crazy enough to climb into a product delivery chute, right?

"It's a warehouse," said Abigail.

"Thank the goddesses," I replied. "Where are the guards?"

"Haven't seen any yet," answered Dusty.

"Someone will be here shortly to receive this shipment," I thought aloud.

I looked around for some kind of plant to draw magic from, but there was nothing in the minimalistic space apart from white cooler boxes and bigger brown cardboard ones. A delivery cart looked packed and ready to go—but where were the workers?

Suddenly I felt afraid. From what I had seen, the Smaragde blood business ran a well-oiled machine. There should be operators here, packers and carriers, yet the room was empty and quiet.

"You haven't seen anyone?" I asked. The girls all shook their heads, their expressions reflecting my anxiety. Had we just been extremely lucky? Somehow, I doubted it.

"Maybe they're in a ... staff meeting?" suggested Abigail.

I couldn't help chuckling. Nervous laughter bubbled up at the idea of a dozen orcs sitting around a polished boardroom table discussing objectives and incentives.

This made the girls look more worried, so I swallowed it down. I looked around for more clues as to where they could be—there were no half-drunk mugs of coffee, no open drawers, so I surmised they hadn't left in a hurry. On the contrary, it was as neat as a pin. My focus landed on the closed double door. Dusty saw me looking and said, "We haven't tried it yet. We were waiting for you."

"Can you hear anyone's thoughts from here?" I asked.

She shook her head. "It sounds empty to me."

I exhaled sharply, gathering my courage. We'd have to make a break for it. I wished I'd had enough magical energy to cloak us all in invisibility, but when I tried to get a simple tingle going, it didn't work. I doubted I could even sling the most minor of spells.

"Ready?" I asked the girls.

"Ready," said Dusty and Abigail. Zaleria gave a subtle nod, and I could tell she still wasn't feeling well. We'd need to take her to Darick for healing once we were out of this creepy warehouse. I just hoped she'd be able to keep up.

CHAPTER 9

TRUNDLE TRUNDLE

ASHA

Still suspicious of the silence, I soft-shoed to the door—which was easy, seeing as I was wearing Celestia-supplied slippers. Unfortunately, the skeleton key wouldn't work, as it was a keycard system. Paranoia surfaced again—were they keeping us locked in here? I looked up at the ceiling and saw the camera in the corner. Of course they'd have cameras in every room of the factory.

"Fiat fulgur," I whispered, rather optimistically. No lightning bolt came.

I swore, cursing Alyndra Sybil for muting my powers, and hexing the warehouse workers for not having a potted plant in the room. No wonder their souls were smirched.

I'd have to get creative. I had no weapons, three girls I had to protect, and an odiferous army of orcs against us.

Non forsit, as our Latin instructor used to say. No problem.

Dusty suddenly piped up. "Someone's coming."

"Hide!" I whispered.

The girls looked aghast. In the minimalist set-up, there was nowhere to hide.

"In the boxes!" I hissed. Dusty and Abi quickly obeyed, and I helped Zaleria into one. I sprang for the roll of tape on its dispenser and taped up their lids, flinching at the sharp sound it made, and quickly hopped into my own box, closing it as well as I was able from the inside. It felt like a harebrained idea, but I didn't see an alternative. The plan was to hide until the coast was clear, climb out and think of a better plan. Of course, that didn't happen. The door beeped and opened, and at least two orcs trudged inside. Like Drooler and Snorer, they didn't talk. I guessed they knew what they had to do, so there was no need for chit-chat. There was no urgency in their movements, signaling they had not yet been alerted to the intruders, but I knew it was just a matter of time. If we were really lucky, the guard watching the CCTV footage would be a close relative of

Snorer or Drooler, and was watching the screens with his eyes closed.

I swallowed my shriek as the box I was in was lifted and placed on what I assumed was the cart. The worker grunted—presumably at how much heavier the box was than normal—but didn't investigate. It wasn't his job to think, just to move product, and for once I was glad of the lower IQ of the race.

I was moving again, this time in a smooth forward motion, and I could hear the wheels trundling beneath me.

Okay, I reassured myself. *That is one way to get out of that locked room.* All I could do was hope that the other merchandise would follow suit. My mind flashed back to being inside the cage on wheels in the SubRealm. I really needed to get some counseling for that, or the memories would haunt me forever. I'd see Dr. Gilbert when this ordeal was over—and not forget to thank her for warning me about Garrett's attack, which had probably saved my life.

Trundle, trundle, went my PTSD, my brain flaring at the perceived danger.

Dead witch rolling.

It would be over soon.

Going by the long trip I was taking, the warehouse was huge. The blood bags would be taken to yet another lab, I was sure, for processing. I looked down at Lilian Black's purloined protection amulet, still fastened tightly to my wrist. It was glowing in the dark. I unpinned the artifact from the choker and made a small spyhole in the side of the box, widening it with my fingernail. I pinned the amulet back securely and looked out of the opening. For a factory this size, it seemed empty of workers, and I couldn't figure out why. The cart suddenly jolted, and I had to slap my palm against my mouth to stop my gasp escaping. The driver grunted, reversed a couple of inches, and kept going. Finally, I caught sight of another orc in overalls. They looked more like prison overalls than factory wear, but who am I to fashion-police orcs—especially as I sat curled up in my cotton pajamas. I looked down at his boots and saw the ankle cuff he was wearing. The orc may be working in the factory, but not of his own volition. He was a prisoner.

I could recognize that ankle cuff from a mile away. The Scorpions had a room full of them. Some were simple probation cuffs, for tracking criminals out on parole or on house arrest. Others made use of more advanced magitech, and could send an alarming number of volts up the leg of the wearer via remote signaling. These came in especially handy at the penal colony camps where the Council regularly sent wrongdoers. The most sophisticated cuff of all short-circuited the wearer's magic, which Morgan told me proved quite helpful in the dungeon at HQ when the suspects down there awaited trial. I didn't know who these orcs were, but they were being kept prisoner and made to work for the Smaragde clan. I was also pretty sure they were not convicts, but slaves.

Why the orcs ever trusted vampires was beyond me. The way the arrogant bloodsuckers treated them was truly repulsive, and yet when asked to join them in battles, the answer was always an affirmative. Seeing the ankle cuff changed our mission slightly, because while I was ready to kill as many Xarlugs as I needed to, these weren't neo-Nazis. These were ordinary orcs that had been captured just as Rick had been. This was both a good and a bad thing—being slaves, they probably wouldn't feel the need to kill us, but we should not hurt them, either, which made me wonder how we'd ever get out.

Trust in the Void, I heard Directress Copperfield say.

I trusted Copperfield, but to be honest, trusting in the Void had seen me truly messed up in the past. What was a witch to do?

Eventually we came to a halt in what looked like a storage room. The temperature dropped. I was lifted off the cart and placed on the floor, ready, I assumed, to be unpacked and shelved. I hoped the girls were close by, and worried that they'd been left in the delivery room. I also hoped the orc about to unpack me didn't have a heart condition. I mean, it would make my life easier if he keeled over in fright when I jumped out, but it wouldn't be fair to him. The best I could hope for was that he fainted, but chances of that happening were slim to none. I didn't even know if orcs could faint; they seemed far too sturdy for that kind of drama. I heard that panic-inducing trundling sound again, but this time it was moving away from me. The orc was leaving. It seemed that he was not an unpacker, just a carrier. I exhaled a shuddering breath. Maybe I should be worrying about my own heart rather than the orc's. A scraping sound next to me made me jump. It was out of sight of my little peephole.

"Asha?" came a weak voice.

I cautiously put my hand up through the top of the box

and waved, then opened it and stood up, limbs stiff from crouching.

Zaleria stood in her box, looking ready to pass out. "Where are we?"

Two other boxes opened. My girls. I smiled at them. "In cold storage."

It was fortunate; all refrigerated storage rooms had a safety-mandated mechanical handle inside, because if you ever got stuck in one without your key card, you could die.

It was frosty in there. A rather crude witch-themed simile came to mind, but I didn't voice it.

"What now?" asked Abigail. She was already shivering.

I made my way to the door. "Now we get the hell out of Dodge Town."

CHAPTER 10

NO SUCH THING AS JUST A WITCH

ASHA

With the girls crowded behind me, I opened the door a crack and tried to make out what was happening beyond the storage room. As before, there were hardly any workers in sight. We had joked about the staff meeting, but I did believe they were gathered somewhere—perhaps the company cafeteria for breakfast or lunch. I had no idea what the time was, not having seen a clock or the outside world for what seemed like an interminable amount of time. I needed to get outside, breathe fresh air, feel the sun on my face, touch the earth ... and if I wanted to draw magic, I'd need to find some greenery. It was a chicken-and-egg problem.

I waited until the coast was clear, and we rushed out of the fridge and into another room where we had a better view of the factory floor. We all hid behind a counter and watched the orcs in overalls go about their mundane jobs. It was quiet inside the warehouse, but we could hear a commotion outside. A peek out of a small window showed us six skinhead orcs in guard uniforms. Their AK-47s were casually slung over their shoulders as they stood chatting and smoking cigarettes. I wasn't surprised to see a Xarlug tattoo on the neck of the orc with his back to us. When I craned my neck, I saw a huge group of workers, standing clustered together. I thought they may be protesting, until I saw another guard addressing them. I couldn't hear what he was saying, but the speaker was spouting vehemently, reminding me of old clips I had seen of Adolf Hitler addressing the nation. Face stern and shouty, I could imagine his spittle flying, and immediately felt sorry for the prisoners standing in the front.

Although I couldn't make out his words, it was clear that it was a political speech. He might have been trying to convert them to Xarlug ways. His technique was not as effective as Lilian Black's. He was not capable of mesmerizing his victims—and his clear lack of charisma was also a disadvantage. The crowd didn't seem very interested in his rhetoric, but watched calmly. I assumed anyone stepping out of line would be instantly tased by their ankle cuff.

Dusty watched the speaker intently. "He's telling them the war has started. They need to join the army. If they agree to be soldiers, they'll be set free after the war."

"The workers here are prisoners," I told the girls. "They've been captured, just like you were. We need to help them."

"*Help* them?" demanded Abigail. "They almost killed us back there."

"Those were Xarlug members. They're affiliates of the Smaragde clan, same as those guards out there in uniform. The vampires have promised them wealth and power if they work together to seize the Realm. But the prisoners here are innocent orcs who have refused the aggressive neo-Nazi philosophy. They're being used against their will—just as you girls were."

Bums and pacifists, Rick had affectionately called them.

Dusty frowned. "But you killed most of the Smaragdes. And a lot of Xarlugs."

I nodded. "I'm sure they see me as enemy number one. Hence the ridiculously large bounty on my head. This certainly isn't the safest place for us to be."

"So let's get out of here," said Abigail.

"Yes," I agreed. "You need to leave."

Dusty's forehead creased. "*We* need to leave? What about you?"

I shook my head. "I can't leave them like this. Enslaved."

Abigail looked at the guards' automatic rifles. "But there are lots of them, and they're armed! And you're just a witch," she said.

"No such thing as *just* a witch," I replied.

We had to move before the group outside were all sent back in to work, but I didn't see a way out without the guards spotting us. If my magic was available to me, I could have made us invisible or turned us into vapor. Or jammed the guns of the guards. The girls watched me, waiting to hear the plan I didn't have. I looked out the small window again to see where the guards were.

That's when I saw him.

CHAPTER 11
INVISIBILIS FACTUS
ASHA

e looked different, but I recognized him. Gnrok.

"Holy Hecate," I muttered.

"What is it?" asked one of the girls behind me.

"There's an orc out there—someone I know. A good man. He's saved my life before."

It felt like a lifetime ago when I was in trouble at the Grackles pub.

I turned to face them. "This is why I need to stay," I said. "And you need to go."

Dusty looked annoyed. "I don't understand how you think you're going to fix this," she said, gesturing at our bleak surrounds. I understood her frustration, but I knew what I had to do.

Where there's a witch, there's a way.

I pulled her in for a hug. Her body was stiff with resentment, but she soon softened, and I planted a kiss on her head. She would always be my witchling, no matter what.

I had felt a hint of greenery outside, despite the rocky barren landscape, so I knew that I could at least siphon some magic—but I needed more. I wished I'd had my orc glamour vape, but no such luck. An invisibility spell would have to do.

"Dusty," I said. "The time has come."

Her frustration gave way to confusion. "For what?"

"For you to harness your power."

"What?" she spluttered. "How?"

"We both know that you have magic inside you," I said. In fact, everyone who had been standing in the parking lot that day outside the family court had seen it. If the girl had enough power to flip a car with her mind, she had what it would take to get us out of Dodgetown.

Dusty was shaking her head. "No way! I don't know anything."

"You want to be my apprentice, right?"

"Yes," she stated without hesitation.

"Your apprenticeship begins today. Now. I need your help."

Her eyes bulged, and she shook her head again. "I'm not ready, Asha."

"You are," said Abigail, and I gave her an affectionate smile. "We'll all do it together."

I nodded. Abi was not my goddaughter for nothing.

"Now, remember when you girls outsmarted that horrible cop at Ferra's house?"

They both nodded.

"It's going to be as simple as that. I can probably draw enough energy from outside to make myself invisible, but I won't have enough for all of you, so you'll be responsible for your own obscuration. And you're going to have to work together, because Zaleria isn't well."

Abigail and Dusty nodded. Zaleria looked like she might throw up.

"Once you've breached the perimeter, make your way home as quickly as you can. The military has already been deployed. It's not safe out there. Just because you've escaped Celestia doesn't mean you are out of danger. Abi, your mom is at my house. Find Sam, Stoker, and Rick. Cast a protection spell around the house—Savvy can help you. I'll be right behind you."

Three pale faces stared back at me. "You'll be fine," I assured them. They nodded, but I could see they were as scared as hell.

I found a half-dried-out marker and drew a circle around us. We held hands and closed our eyes.

"Infinite Void, hear our prayer," I said, and the girls repeated after me.

"This is the orbit of the wayward woman

Who knits with stars and stones,

The Wild, the wanderer, the wasp, the witch,

This is the course of the wayward goddess,

A flame, a stone, a stitch.

Infinite Void, Wisdom of the Wild,

We seek your power and protection."

"So mote it be," chorused the witchlings.

"And so it is," I said, sealing the spell, and we opened our eyes. *"Tenebrae obscuratio. Invisibilis factus!"*

I immediately felt the warmth of the invisibility spell wash over me. You would think becoming invisible might feel cold, like chilled water, but in my case, it was always a cozy, comforting sensation.

"Invisibilis factus!" chanted the girls, and they all shimmered out of sight.

"Good work," I said, feeling like a proud mama. "Now sneak out carefully, and I'll be right behind you."

They said goodbye and set off together, and I spent a moment feeling overwhelmed by emotion. Fear for their safety, pride in their magic, and anxiety for what I had to do next.

Invisible, I stole out of the room and into the cavernous warehouse, where the prisoners were gradually trickling back in after being shouted at by the bald zealot. I had lost sight of Gnrok. I moved slowly and cautiously, not wanting to bump into anyone and inadvertently alert them to my presence. Before making a plan to free the slaves, I needed to find out everything I could about this operation. I knew it was run by the Smaragdes, but who was controlling the vicious clan? I'd bet every last koin I owned that the mastermind was the powerful witch who had been controlling Sirilla Voltane's corpse. A strong instinct told me that I needed to find this high witch, that only I could put a stop to her evil. Being in the warehouse, as vastly unpleasant as it was, put me in a unique position to discover her identity. The Void works in mysterious ways, and I was here for a reason.

I couldn't help observing the shambling orcs in their ankle cuffs. Faces downcast, tree-trunk legs shuffling along, they looked broken in spirit. I couldn't believe the clan was getting away with this. How many lives were they content to ruin, just for the sake of money? All the stolen girls at Celestia, all the enslaved orcs here. I stuck to the back wall, edging along and watching carefully, looking out for clues and looking down at my hands every now and then to make sure the spell was still sticking. The workers were getting back into their various roles, and soon the production line was humming along. I knew that the blood arrived from Celestia via the insta-portal chute we had traveled through and moved to cold storage, but where did it go next? I watched as an orc pushed a cart out of the refrigerated room and headed to the north side of the warehouse, and I followed him.

CHAPTER 12

THE ÆTERNAL ELIXIR OF YOUTH

ASHA

As I followed the worker to see where the blood would be taken next, I tried to take in as many details of the factory as possible. We walked past a busy enclave with a roaring furnace. It seemed to be a glassworks section, judging by the number of vials, tubes, and bottles stacked up there. Next was the labelling section, with a huge printing machine running like a newspaper line, gluing the fresh labels to the vials. I could smell the smoke of the furnace and the ink of the printing machine. It looked like the company manufactured all the elements of their products, keeping everything in-house. This, together with free labor they were exploiting, meant they were sure to be making a huge profit. The high witch certainly knew how to make money.

On we went. A mountain of coal was being slowly eroded at its base by the men with wheelbarrows who shoveled and wheeled it away, presumably to the furnace. The same went for a mountain of silica. There were storerooms for paper and ink supplies, and a cafeteria that smelled like rotten onions and tripe. A sign for dormitories pointed downwards, below ground, indicating where the prisoners slept and showered. The orc I was following slowed slightly to let another worker pass in front of him. I almost walked into his back, but he picked up his pace a little and made his way through a swinging double door. I quickly tailgated.

The atmosphere on the other side of the doors couldn't have been more different from the busy factory we had left behind. It was like stepping back into Celestia. Everything was white, clean, and perfect. The lights were so bright they made my eyes ache. My mark was the only orc in sight, and he stood out like a sore thumb in his dirty overalls and grubby skin, because the only other people working in this section were vampires. They wore lab coats instead of their usual black capes, and their fangs were neatly tucked away in their mouths, but I could see from a mile away that they were dracs. Pale skin, red lips, and intense, hungry eyes. The high witch obviously didn't trust orcs with the more technical part of the process. Lab equipment took up a lot of the space: spinners, mixers, microscopes. The orc and I reached a nifty conveyor belt on which he began placing the boxes. Once he had unloaded his cart, he kept his gaze down and left the laboratory space. I stayed behind to investigate, but I knew I had to be quick because I was now far away from my energy source and had no way of knowing how long my invisibility would last. I watched as the boxes slowly made their way toward the lab coats, who unpacked them one by one, electronically noted which had arrived, and began processing the blood. Being a potion-maker myself, I recognized some of the equipment they were using and was rather envious of it. *If I had a lab like this, I could make a lot more money to buy food for the Thomas Harvey Conservation Project.* I shook the thought from my head and told myself to concentrate. What exactly were they making and where were they sending it? If I could discover that, it would surely lead me to the high witch. Having watched the vampires work in an amazingly focused way, I followed the line to see where the finished product ended up. There were a lot of stages to the process, and what I saw at the end was a golden serum. A large stainless steel machine pumped the luxurious-looking liquid into the small vials I had seen at the glassworks. A different conveyor belt shuttled the tinkling glass receptacles out of the side of the lab we had entered from, delivering it back to orc territory and the labelling machine. I squeezed back through the double doors and hoped no one would notice the door swinging of its own accord.

Following the filled tubes to the printing machine, I watched as the labelled vials were packaged in an even more luxurious-looking box. White—obviously—edged in gold, with a beautiful logo embossed on the front. I swiped a box, hid it under my sleeve, and hurried away with it, hoping to find the truck they would be transporting it in. I could eat two peas with one fork if I hitched a ride out of here *and* managed to find out where the product was destined to land up. Progress. My spirits lifted, but before leaving I had to disable the shock-emitting ankle cuffs on the slaves.

While I was thinking, I hid behind a corner so that I could look at the box without making people suspicious. It was a truly beautiful design. The logo was a ligature of the letters *A* and *E*, and the resulting *Æ* was interwoven with decorative lines that made it look classic and contemporary at the same time. I ran my finger over the embossed design, admiring it. Beneath the logo it read "ÆTERNA" and beneath that: "The Æternal Elixir of Youth" with a trademark sign. I turned the box around to read the text on the back.

The Æternal Elixir of Youth (TM) *is the first of its kind, and the only serum you will require to live a truly long and healthy life. Made with only the finest ingredients combined with care,* **ÆTERNA** *delivers this top-quality vitality-extending elixir that will surely change your life. For more information, please visit www.æterna.com*

It was all the confirmation of my theory I needed, and now I had the company name. This was the corporation that had paid Shadow Snow, AKA Lilian Black, to kidnap the girls and make sure they didn't ask difficult questions at Celestia. She had previously done the same thing for old man Taranath, who used the kids' blood for his own personal elixir. It was the same crime, but on an industrial scale. I had disposed of the evil elf, and, so help me Void, I'd do the same to the high witch. I would kill the owner of ÆTERNA if it was the last thing I ever did. I'd break all her curses, all her spells, free all her blackbirds. I would end her in every way.

CHAPTER 13
REVOLT
ASHA

I couldn't use the *rumpis* spell on the ankle cuffs, because it ran the risk of hobbling the orcs. I racked my brain trying to come up with some-thing. I studied the box as if it held the answer. Spoiler alert: it didn't. But I did start to see a flicker of the skin on my hands, and felt the warmth of the obscuration spell fading. I needed to act fast. I remembered Soleil's words in the first "yoga" lesson I attended after my head injury.

May Mother Earth work through us and guide us in every-thing we do. May we recommit ourselves daily to righting the wrongs we see in the world around us.

"Please guide me, Mother Earth," I whispered. "I don't know how to free the slaves."

Leave, came the reply.

Surely not, I thought. *What about righting the wrongs?*

Leave now, said the voice in my head. I understood the reasoning behind leaving; I could, in theory, be more effective if I came back with a plan, weapons, juiced-up magic, and a team. Or I wouldn't need to come back at all if I chopped off the head of the snake, because her cruel imprisonments would come undone. But leaving now would mean that I had sent the girls out on their own for no reason, and it meant leaving Gnrok behind, which I couldn't abide.

Leave. Now. My feet were now visible, and my arms were beginning to glimmer.

Fine, I capitulated, even though it was not fine. My fading invisibility was forcing my hand.

I scampered through the busy factory floor, hoping the orcs were too out of it to notice my bare feet. And if they did notice, perhaps they would ignore them, or think they were going crazy—which wouldn't be unexpected, given their terrible circumstances. I zipped past the coal mountain, the furnace, the various storerooms, and was almost at the door that led outside, where the neo-Nazi skinhead had been irrigating the crowd. I would just need to get past that Xarlug guard, and I'd be home free. The guard's face twitched, and my heart kicked around in its cage.

Damnation! So close to fresh air!

There was a panicked gurgling and a crashing sound behind me. Without thinking, I stopped and turned. An orc had dropped to his knees, and in doing so had knocked some boxes over, shattering the glass inside. The guard had seen it happen, hence the fancy face-twitch. He beelined toward the gasping orc, and I had to jump out of his way to avoid him. It was perfect timing to give me the escape route I needed, but I couldn't help looking back at the orc on the ground.

"You useless piece of—!" shouted the guard. He took out his baton and began beating the struggling orc as well as every worker who tried to help him. "You can't break stuff in here!" He hit the orc across his back, and he splayed out on the floor, blood spattering from his mouth. "Clumsy!" Smack. "Stupid!" Smack. Any orc who tried to help the now-unconscious worker was hit just as hard. They kept coming to assist him, and kept getting beaten back. More and more prisoners put down their tools to see what was happening. The guard fiddled on his belt for his remote control and began zapping the orcs who approached him. The voltage of the cuff must have been set to lightning bolt because as soon as they were tased they fell like trees, and there was the terrible odor of singed hair and burnt flesh. All the guard had to do was point at his target and push a button and the slaves were completely debilitated. The ones who were still conscious lay groaning on the floor, their eyes rolled back. Yet more workers approached, anger in their eyes, ready to wrest the remote control away. The guard frantically zapped as many as he could, but he was outnumbered. He called for backup and looked up at the CCV TV cams, but they seemed to be on the blink. I suddenly realized that the coup had been orchestrated. No backup arrived; no siren sounded. I didn't have to save the orcs because they were saving themselves.

I turned away from the gory scene—the slaves were now pulling the guard apart—and ran for the door, but a huge meaty hand grabbed my shoulder. I yelped in fright and spun around, ready to explain that I was on their side, only to find there was no need.

"Asha," said Gnrok, blinking as if he had been in the dark and I was a bright light. "Is that really you?"

"Gnrok!" I exclaimed, and threw my arms around him. "I'm so glad I found you! We've been so worried!

Morgan's so anxious about your disappearance. I even went to your house to look for you."

"I've been trying to find my brother," he said despondently. "He's not here." His grief was tangible. The ruckus behind him was getting more and more bloody. The taser remote was smashed beneath the boot heel of a particularly solid-looking slave.

"You planned this?" I asked, lifting my chin in the direction of the revolt.

Gnrok nodded. "This is just the beginning."

"Come with me," I said, knowing that he wouldn't.

He shook his head. "Sorry, witch. My place is here. We need to raze this warehouse."

"There are plenty of orcs here to do that job," I said. "If you come with me, you can join my team and we can find and destroy the witch behind all of this."

His eyebrows shot up. "Witch?"

Having rent the Xarlug guard apart, the workers headed toward the vamps in the laboratory section. I imagined the splashes of blood on the lab coats and perfect white walls.

"The owner of Æterna," I replied.

He smirked without humor. "You think that's going to be easy?"

"No," I replied. Nothing of value ever was. "Being easy has nothing to do with it."

He looked back at his crew, returned his gaze to me, and gave a slight nod. "Okay."

CHAPTER 14

NUCLEAR SORCERY
ASHA

We heard screams as we stepped out of the door, and I shuddered. I hated those vampires in there as much as anyone, but imagining the orcs tearing their bodies apart was still horrific.

"Is there a truck?" I asked. Gnrok nodded. We tore around the outside of the building, heading toward the loading dock. The air was hot and dry. As we approached, I got a distinctly uneasy feeling and slowed down.

"Something's wrong," I said.

Gnrok shot me a sideways puzzled look. This was not news. Everything was wrong.

I put my hands out. "There's an energy here ... I don't know what it is."

"Doesn't matter," grunted the orc. "We're leaving."

I shook my head. The hair on the back of my neck rose. There was something, or someone, here that was very disturbing. I felt it all the way down to my gut. I breathed out, thinking if I could see my breath, it was probably a ghost, but found there was no spectral chill in the air.

"We need to go," urged the orc.

I wanted to, but my instinct was shrill. I looked around, trying to calm my breathing.

What the hell was it?

"Maybe you can just sense the evil in this place," Gnrok reasoned. "They did not treat us well."

"Maybe," I said. I began to move forward again, slowly. The feeling got stronger, and I gulped.

As we rounded the corner, just yards away from the truck we were both longing to climb into, she appeared, wand outstretched in our direction.

"Freeze," the witch said, her snarl showing off her

ruined teeth. They were so brown it looked like we had caught her eating chocolate.

I had only met her once before, but I recognized her instantly. Mildred Malachay. Her presence here did not make sense. Captain Morgan had told me she had escaped from the asylum, but what was she doing *here*?

I put up my hands in surrender. "We're on the same side."

She hawked and spat at Gnrok's feet. "Wrong."

"We are, Malachay. The reason I ended up here is because I'm busy saving the girls."

"I don't see any girls," she sneered. Her hair hadn't been brushed in a long time. It was so matted I didn't think she'd ever be able to get a comb through it. She would look even scarier with a shaved head. I knew that the disappearance and subsequent death of her daughter had driven her insane with grief, but if she was intent on obstructing us, I'd have to take action against her.

"I know where they are now," I said. "The missing daughters. I just need my team to help me rescue them. There's a talented portaler—"

The witch started shaking her wand at us.

"The werewolves told me the truth, you see."

She had spoken to the wolves? "I thought you hated them," I said. "I thought you blamed them for Maxine's death."

She flinched at her late daughter's name. "Of course I did," she replied. "Because that's what the police report said, didn't it? But it was all one big lie. It wasn't the wolves at all. Palefang told me everything."

I did a double take. "Palefang?"

"He broke me out of the prison. Him and his people. He told me about this place and gave me the tools I needed to destroy it."

"Wait, what?"

She ignored my question. "You all say I'm crazy, that I'm a conspiracy theorist, but guess what? It *is* a conspiracy. This whole thing." She motioned at the factory building. "This whole thing. I've seen the *real* autopsy report. The one that was covered up to frame the werewolves. I've seen it with my own eyes!"

"It wasn't covered up," I said, but I knew that arguing with her was pointless. We needed to leave.

Her eyes were wild. "You think you know what is going on, but you have no idea."

Okay, I didn't have time for this.

"Malachay, we're getting in the truck. Come with us."

"You think this is about some missing girls, but the plot runs deeper and wider than that."

"Come with us," I urged her. "You can tell us everything." I would even make her a tinfoil hat.

"It was the vampires and the orcs all along," she said, baring those awful teeth again. "They want to destroy the entire country. They want to raze the Realm, and they've got the weapons to do it. I'm talking nuclear sorcery. I'm talking a dark magical bomb that's beyond imagination." She pointed her wand at Gnrok. "They took my girl's life. My girl! She was the only person in the Realm that I cared about. Violent vamps, disgusting orcs. I'm going to make them pay for it."

My head started to ache. "You're right," I said. "The dark forces are conspiring. But not all orcs are evil, and there's a whole warehouse of imprisoned orcs under Smaragde forces back there. Gnrok and I are doing what we can to stop the vampires and save the girls, so please get out of our way."

Before I could stop her, she muttered a spell under her breath and sent an electric current toward Gnrok. I leapt in the air in front of him, using the purloined protection amulet tied around my wrist to block the spell. It absorbed the magic perfectly, and I felt a thrill of power as it did so. A new wave of magic flowed beneath my skin, making me realize that not only did the magical artifact protect one from attack, it also siphoned that power and turned it over to its wearer. It would come in very handy indeed.

Malachay clamped her mouth shut and her eyes glittered with anger. "You're *one of them?*" she asked, wrinkling her nose in disgust.

"No!" I yelled, even though I hadn't meant to.

"You didn't save Maxine," she said. "No one cared about Maxine."

"I do," I insisted. "I care about Maxine and I care about you. But killing the orcs inside will not further our cause. They hate the Smaragde clan as much as we do. We need them on our side."

The mad witch blinked at me, thinking it over.

I narrowed my eyes at her. "When you said Palefang's

pack gave you what you needed to destroy this place, what did you mean?"

The witch's eyes became shifty, and I got a very bad feeling. She began backing away from us, but I knew I couldn't let her get away.

"Malachay," I warned. "Stop." I put out my hand to show I was serious.

She grinned, her brown smile sending shivers down my spine. She continued edging backwards, toward the warehouse. "If you so much as send a spark my way," she warned, "we'll all be blown to bits." She opened her witch's cloak to reveal her torso, packed with criss-crossed wires and blue dynamite sticks.

I heard Gnrok's throat make a strange noise. We both knew how destructive blue fire was.

"I'm dying either way," she said, eyes sparkling with zeal. "But you don't have to."

CHAPTER 15
IMPEDIO
ASHA

My mind whirred with ideas for spells I could use to neutralize the threat. Fire magic would not do, but I could perhaps use water or ice. Would a frozen bomb still explode? Too risky. I didn't know the chemical composition of blue dynamite so I wouldn't know how to disarm it.

As I was desperately thinking, the mad witch continued pacing backwards. She knew it was only a matter of minutes before the orcs began streaming out of the factory and toward their freedom.

"The guards and the vampires are dead," said Gnrok. "You'll be killing innocent people."

Malachay snorted. "No such thing as innocent people."

There was no reasoning with her. I drew the magic I had absorbed via the spell she slung at Gnrok and, without warning, I cast it in her direction. *"Impedio!"*

She froze instantly; even the horrid expression on her face stayed, as if the wind had changed direction. *Impedio* magic never lasted long, so it wasn't a permanent solution. At best it would buy us a couple of minutes.

"Neat," said Gnrok.

"It's temporary," I replied. "Very temporary."

Hearing a buzzing sound, we both looked up. A drone was hovering above the compound. I didn't know if it belonged to the Smaragdes or the Palefang pack, but either way it meant trouble. If it was a vampire spy cam, they'd be sending backup. If it was the wolves…

"Remote trigger?" I guessed. A way to detonate the bomb in case Malachay was taken out.

"We need to get the orcs out of the building," I said. Gnrok nodded. We ran back to where we had come from.

It was absolute mayhem inside. Not satisfied with killing their captors, the slaves were destroying every part of the infrastructure. I couldn't say I blamed them.

Bottles were being smashed; metal tools were being thrown on conveyor belts to jam the machines. Scientific equipment was being hurled into the furnace.

Gnrok tried to corral them, but their newfound mob mentality wouldn't allow it. He had opened the large exit door at the other side of the warehouse and was yelling, "Get in the trucks! Get in the trucks!" but no one was paying him any attention. I had to do something, but I knew that if they weren't listening to him, they certainly wouldn't want to hear what a puny human had to say.

I averted my eyes from what was left of the Xarlug guard who had tased the orc, walking around the dirty puddle of crimson and picking up his AK-47, which was oily with blood. In the chaos, it had been mostly covered by a cardboard box, but the gun's metal had a certain glint that caught my eye. I pointed it upwards and pulled the trigger, shooting a generous round of bullets into the high ceiling.

In the split second of near-silence that ensued, Gnrok yelled "Run!" and the orcs didn't hesitate. They stormed out so loudly I had to cover my ears as I ran after them. I followed the freemen toward the trucks where Gnrok was directing them and they all piled into the trailers. As chaotic as their violence had been inside the building, they were now acting like soldier ants—following each other instinctively and without a hint of aggression. Engines began to roar, and the first of a dozen trucks began barreling down the narrow road, like they had done so many times before. This time around, instead of transporting illegal elixirs, they were saving lives and delivering orcs to their freedom.

A second truck, then another, sped off. Gnrok, happy that everyone was on their way, joined me in jogging to the last truck of the fleet. The drone was still zipping above us like an irritating mosquito. I felt the urge to shoot it down with my new automatic assault weapon, but resisted. We clambered in, with Gnrok taking the driver's seat. He pushed the ignition button and put his foot down, and we quickly caught up with the rest of the fleet where they were whipping up the dry sand on the roadside. I was just about to exhale the longest sigh of my lifetime when there came the most almighty *BOOM* behind us. The force of the explosion smacked our truck sideways and we went plowing through a small sandy hill. Gnrok recovered control of the vehicle and got us back on the road. Only then did I look at what we were leaving behind. The huge building was almost completely leveled, and a huge wall of blue flames were hungrily devouring the remains. Another explosion shook our truck, and by the time the third one exploded we were just far away enough to feel safe. I looked down at the AK-47, switched the safety on, and leaned back against the seat.

Holy hex, talk about a close one.

"That blue dynamite packs a pretty punch," said Gnrok.

I laughed, mostly in relief, then remembered Mad Witch Malachay and my smile faded. At least she would be able to rest in peace.

CHAPTER 16

MUTINEERS

ASHA

The ride home was, thankfully, uneventful. The built-in walkie-talkie system allowed us to communicate with the other drivers, and a meet-up point was agreed upon. Gnrok, who I knew was not the best driver, especially when he was emotional, delivered a smooth and easy trip, and dropped me off on the outskirts of the city where I had asked Sam to collect me. I had an irrational fear of e-hail cabs ever since my skirmish with Alyndra Sybil, and the huge truck would not have an easy time navigating the leafy suburb I lived in. Besides, I was dying to see Sam. I missed him, and most of all, I craved the feeling of safety I got when I was wrapped up in his arms. I hadn't felt safe for a long time.

When I asked Gnrok to come with me, he demurred. He wanted to be with the rest of the orcs so that he could debrief them. They needed to know that the war had begun and that they may be free, but they were not safe. Weapons, bunkers, and strategies would be required, and Gnrok felt that he was the one who ought to lead them, just as he had planned the slave rebellion. They should trust him after the success of the coup and the way he had moved them out of harm's way at the now-flattened warehouse.

I agreed it was the right thing to do, and he revved the truck and left me inhaling exhaust fumes. I ran up to Sam's car, which was parked on a gravel patch off the highway. He was leaning on the trunk and watching me with affection. We met in a long hug, and he only pulled away to kiss me. I was back in his arms. Cars flew by, some honking their horns at our embrace.

"God, I was so worried about you," he said into my hair. "The girls are home safely."

I lifted my eyes and saw the sleep deprivation on his face. Dark circles, puffy eyes, although he was still one hundred percent gorgeous.

"It's been a ride," I said. How did I even begin to tell him everything that had happened in the last forty-eight hours?

"I saw your ride," he said. "Hitchhiking with truckers now?"

"I wasn't hitching," I replied. "And that wasn't a trucker."

"Okay," he said, loosening his grip on me. "Time to get you home. You can tell me everything once you've recovered."

I shook my head. "There's no time to recover."

"There bloody well is," he argued. He opened the back door for me, and when I frowned at him, he said it was so that I could lie down and rest. I nodded and climbed in. He had packed a chilled water bottle and a sandwich for me, both of which I inhaled.

"You make excellent sandwiches," I told him, and twenty minutes later he was rubbing my arm to wake me.

"We're home," he said gently. "The girls can't wait to see you."

As soon as I stumbled through the front door I was almost overrun by the girls. Dusty and Abigail hugged me so hard I couldn't breathe. It felt so good to have them home and safe.

Savvy pushed them away. "My turn!" she exclaimed, and hugged me just as hard. Her embrace began joyously, but within moments we were both weeping. "You did it," she sobbed, over and over again. "You did it, you did it. You saved my baby."

We both ugly-cried for a while, only stopping when Sam brought us steaming mugs of tea. It was the best tea I had ever tasted, and I told him so. Soothed by being home, seeing the girls, and the warm tea, I no longer felt like crying. My bed was calling me, but I needed to tell everyone what had happened and what it meant for us. I also had questions of my own.

"Zaleria?" I asked.

"At home with her parents and their family doctor," replied Dusty. "He said she'll be fine once her shock wears off. She keeps asking for Mercury."

I winced.

"They left a rather generous check for you when they picked her up," said Savvy, with a twinkle in her eye. "Suffice to say, you'll never have to work another day in your life."

"If only that were true," I sighed. I felt like sleeping for days, weeks, months. I envied Snow White. Still, I was extremely grateful for the money. It would go a long way in keeping the conservation project afloat—feeding the animals, paying Chione a salary. And we'd need the financing for other things—wars don't come cheap.

"Chione wants you to call her," said Sam. "She said it was urgent, but wouldn't tell me anything else."

I nodded. "I'll do that. How did you girls get home so quickly?"

Abigail sat up. "The obscuration spell worked super well. No one stopped us leaving. We followed the road until we got to a highway and jumped on the back of a pickup truck that had pulled to the side. We stowed away on the back and he brought us all the way into the city. We jumped off at a traffic light and borrowed a kind lady's phone to call my mom, and she and Rick picked us up in the monster truck."

I shook my head. "You girls are amazing. I'm so proud of you."

Letting them leave the compound on their own had been a difficult decision to make, but it had been the correct one. They both beamed at me.

"Stoker?" I asked.

"Still with the pack," replied Sam. "He said to call him when you got back, to align planning with Palefang and because he wants to be by your side."

"Salty?"

Sam shook his head. "Haven't seen her."

"And Rick?"

"Went to buy groceries for us," said Dusty. "We were starving when we got home."

I imagined Rick filling his tank-like monster truck with bags of food and it gave me a warm and amused feeling.

"I'm going to cook you a welcome home feast," declared Savvy. "All the trimmings!"

Abigail and I shook our head in unison. "No, thank you," we said.

She gasped and looked offended.

"You're a wonderful, wonderful friend and mother," I said reassuringly. "You can't be good at everything."

Savvy's mouth fell open. "Mutineers, the lot of you."

"I'll make you a deal," said Armstrong. "Once Asha has slept, I'll take you all out for dinner at the Cog."

"Yay!" cried Dusty. Not only was it her favorite place to visit, but her half-siblings were there.

It was an oddly poignant moment. We felt like a family, a *real* family, and despite everything, my heart soared.

"But first, tell us everything," said Abigail. My happiness ebbed. The other girls were still out there. Henry's note had said that Apollo needed me, and I needed Apollo to portal us back to Celestia. We couldn't risk using Salty or the magical carwash; the security on the pocket realm was too tight, and we'd have to bring over a hundred girls back with us, which was beyond the talents of my favorite slimeball and her brethren.

My eyes started to close, and I realized I was no use to anyone unless I rested, no matter how urgent the situation was.

"You've gone pale," said Sam. "Let's go up."

The girls looked disappointed, as did Savvy. They were dying to know what had happened.

"I'll tell you everything at dinner," I promised, and trudged away from them and up the stairs to my bedroom. Despite being desperate for a bath and to tear the Celestia pajamas off my body so I could burn them, I did no such thing. I don't even remember putting my head on the pillow, but when I stirred for the first time hours later, I felt Sam's body cradling mine, and tumbled back down into somnolent bliss.

CHAPTER 17

A NEW WITCH

ASHA

I woke up with no idea what time of the day or night it was. Part of me wanted to keep sleeping forever, but the other wanted the dinner Sam had promised me, and time to sit and plan what to do next with my favorite people. I felt different knowing where the abducted girls were—more confident that we could save them, and hopeful for a good outcome. Before, I had no idea where they were or even if they were still alive. I didn't have a clue. I didn't have a protection amulet or a loyal team. Hell, right at the start of this mission, I didn't even have access to my own memories. But things were changing, and I felt ready to take on the world—or rather, take on the high witch who had caused all this suffering in the first place.

Things were going well for the moment. Dusty and Abigail were safe, Garrett was out of the picture, Savvy was not drinking herself into an early grave, and we finally had the funds we needed to keep Harvey's animals fed and looked after. For as long as I had the monocle, my eyesight was mostly restored, apart from fleeting moments of blurriness—which may have been caused by emotion rather than the aftereffects of physical damage. Detective Sam Armstrong was the man I never knew I needed, and he seemed to return my feelings despite us being a terrible match on paper. Goddess knows I didn't want to jinx myself by being too optimistic, but things did seem on the upswing.

I rolled out of bed, stripped off the white pajamas I hated and promised myself I'd burn them in a sacred ceremony when time allowed. I thought of all the girls stuck at Celestia in the same pajamas, untroubled and carefree, unknowingly being groomed to end up as Æterna fodder. I would build a bonfire—like I always did at the winter solstice to burn away what no longer served me—and I would see the pajamas flame and smoke and turn to bitter ash. Fire cleanses. *Puritas antedecit.*

A quick shower instead of my regular long, deep,

candlelit bath followed. Clean clothes, and a hint of makeup. I felt like a new woman. A new witch.

"Wow," said Sam when I came down the stairs. I saw both desire and tenderness in his eyes as he took me in. I realized he had seen me in all manner of states, but mostly dirty, injured, and anxious. He had seen me at my most vulnerable. He had seen me bruised and naked. He had seen me blind.

"You clean up good," said Rick, who I hadn't registered was there.

"Hey," warned Sam. "Don't flirt with my woman."

Rick put his baseball mitt-sized hands up in surrender. "Just stating the facts, man."

Savvy had borrowed one of my black dresses. It was an understated look for her—usually she was groomed and accessorized to the nines—and she looked like she might have been in mourning if not for the smile on her face. Nails unpainted, face clean of makeup, no bling whatsoever. She reminded me of her teenaged self, when we had made an eternal pact to be blood-sisters. I suddenly felt a tsunami of affection for my best friend and pulled her into a hug.

"I love you," I said.

Her eyes sparkled. "I love you, too."

We piled into the tank, as it was the only vehicle that would accommodate the whole gang. There were six of us, and after a few phone calls it was agreed that Chione, Stoker, and Salty would meet us there.

"I can't wait to eat Ferra's roast potatoes," drooled Dusty.

"I'm craving the ginger beer," said Abigail.

Savvy and I exchanged soft glances. It warmed our hearts to have the girls back and see them get on so well, like sisters. Like we had been, like we would always be. Sam looked out of the window for most of the trip, seemingly lost in thought while he absent-mindedly stroked my back, giving me waves of goose-bumps whenever he touched my bare skin.

The trip went quickly, mostly due to Rick's driving skills and heavy foot on the accelerator, and before we knew it, we were climbing out of the monster truck in the front of the Copper Cog & Ale.

As always, walking into the gastropub felt like coming home. I would never tire of the place, and I would certainly never tire of the fantastic Fernaks. The exposed brick walls, the copper piping, the steampunk touches, the ticking clocks, the floating fires ... they were all cues that it was time to let my guard down, relax my body, and just enjoy the time spent there. Fighour was behind the counter, and when he saw us, he gave us that look that passes for a smile—a kind of grumpy acknowledgment that life wasn't always terrible—and waved us over. He was polishing a beer glass. He held it up to the light to inspect it before putting it on the shelf.

"You're in the private dining room tonight," he said, tilting his head in that direction. "Ferra's there, sorting it."

"Ooh," I replied. "We're VIPs now."

"You've always been a VIP," he replied, winking. He picked up another glass and held it over the teapot to steam it.

"Very Irritating Person?" quipped Dusty.

I elbowed her for being corny, even though I loved that she was feeling confident enough to rib me.

"Something like that," replied Fig, a glint of amusement in his eye. He was good with kids, always had been, despite his gruff demeanor. "What will you be drinking?"

We put in our order: cold pints of lager for Rick, Sam, and I, and Ferra's fiery ginger beer for Savvy and the kids. I denied the urge to look twice at Savannah when she chose a non-alcoholic beverage, and we moved as a group toward the private room that still, unfortunately, reminded me of Mordecai.

CHAPTER 18

SHADOW MENU
ASHA

When we entered the dining room, four cheerful faces turned to greet us.

"Asha!"

"Rookie!"

"Dusty!"

They stood to hug me and I accepted each one gratefully.

Ferra, Chione, Salty, and Stoker had all been waiting for us to arrive. "Ah," I murmured in pleasure at seeing them all, happy and healthy. "It is *so good* to see you lot."

"I can't believe you found them!" said Ferra, then

quickly corrected herself. "I mean, I *knew* you would. But excellent work! Dinner is on the house."

Sam gave her an unimpressed look. *That wasn't the deal,* he seemed to be conveying. She just grinned at him. Little did she know that I had a check to the tune of a million koin in my pocket.

"You must tell us everything," said Stoker, eyes intense.

"Good work, witch," acknowledged Chione. "Where's the money?"

"Give her a chance to sit down, will you?" said Stoker.

"But you did get the money?" asked the grimalkin.

"I got the money," I confirmed, not able to suppress my beam. It was such a great feeling to know that the conservation project was saved.

"Gimme!" she said, and made grabby hands. She was only kind of joking. We had agreed that I'd put it into the project's bank account and she'd need my permission to withdraw funds. We both knew that grimalkins were not to be trusted with shiny things.

We sat down and the drinks arrived. I didn't bother looking at the menu, knowing that Ferra would have asked Chef to prepare something special for me. The girls ordered cheeseburgers, Savvy, a chicken salad, and Stoker, a filet steak cooked ultra-rare.

"Just enough to frighten it" were his words, and I couldn't help chuckling.

We drank and caught up. By the time the food arrived, I had already told them everything they needed to know about Lilian Black, the Celestia cult, and the Æternal elixir.

"Æterna?" echoed Chione. "*The* Æterna?"

I shrugged. I had never heard of the company before.

"Witch," she explained in a way that would benefit a toddler, "it's, like, the richest corporation on the continent."

"Nah," I said. "I would have heard of it."

"It's a basket of companies," explained Stoker. "Extremely successful brands. You know them all— just not that they're all owned by one mega-corp. Verrrrry happy stakeholders. They pretty much print money."

"You remember how rich the Sybil twins were?" asked Chione. "The Sybil Corp?"

I couldn't help shuddering. "Yes."

"Owned by Æterna," she said.

I almost choked on my lager.

"Go Solar. Shocklit. Liscious. ALL the bottled water businesses. Most of the luxury hotel chains …"

"Okay," I nodded. "I get the picture. They own everything."

"And Platelet, of course," added Ferra.

"Platelet," I said slowly. I knew there was something sinister about that brand. They were everywhere. "That's how they're distributing the blood. And the elixir."

"A shadow menu," said Ferra.

Abigail looked up. "What's that?"

Ferra straightened her Viking helmet. "It's when there's a secret menu at a place that only a select few customers know about."

"Do *you* have a shadow menu?" wondered Dusty, asking the question that had popped into all our minds.

Ferra tsk-tsked her. "Now, skunk, it wouldn't be a shadow menu if you all knew about it, would it?"

I was sure I wasn't the only one who noticed that she had not answered the question.

We all dug into our delicious dinners, the girls wolfing down their burgers as if they hadn't eaten in days.

"Slow down," I told them. "You'll give yourselves a stomach ache."

As the words were out of my mouth, I recognized that it was something a mother would say. Chione raised an eyebrow at me. *Look at you, acting all maternal.*

Stoker's bloody steak disappeared even faster than the burgers did. He wiped his lips with a napkin and gave me a long, hard stare. "So, what's the plan?"

"I was hoping we could come up with one together," I said past a mouthful of gloriously crunchy thrice-fried sweet potato.

"But you do have an idea," he pressed. "I can see it."

"You're giving me too much credit," I replied. When he didn't smile, I continued. "Okay, I was just thinking that there will need to be two prongs to this attack." *Two peas, one fork.*

Ferra stopped dishing up more sides for the girls. "Attack?"

"Yes, *attack*," affirmed Stoker. "Otherwise we're just sitting ducks. Attack is almost always more successful than defense."

"I can see you've been spending time with the Palefang pack," Rick commented.

"And what's wrong with that?" demanded the werewolf.

"Nothing, nothing," said the orc, shaking his head. "Just an observation."

Stoker turned to face me. "The time is now, Asha. Now, or it will be too late."

I put down my cutlery, suddenly having lost my appetite. I rubbed my face. I knew he was right.

"Yes," I replied. "The time is now. But a sound strategy is worth the time it will take to plan it."

He exhaled sharply through his nose and sat back, crossing his arms.

"Two schemes," I continued. "Both are imperative. The first, obviously, is to fetch the girls before they make them disappear again."

"What if they've already moved them?" Abigail asked, wide-eyed.

I shook my head. "From what I experienced there, the realm is far too elaborate to move quickly. It will require time and a great deal of magic to transport that … illusion, never mind the real logistics of moving the high-tech lab and bleed farm. They've invested an absolute fortune, so I don't think they'd risk damaging it. The security alone—there are so many layers to it—is going to be a cluster headache to transfer. I think we have at least another twenty-four hours, maybe more. Also, Lilian Black knows that I have her protection amulet, so she knows we'll be able to portal to her wherever she is."

"So that's the first thing," said Rick. "The other things we need to do are to find Apollo, safeguard the magical painting, and rescue the girls." If only it were that easy.

"Where do we start?" asked Sam, who had been quiet for most of the dinner.

"Locate the high witch," I replied. "The one who started all of this in the first place."

CHAPTER 19

A SPECIAL GUEST

ASHA

The skunks automatically knew when to come and clear our plates, and Ferra gave them each an approving wink. Fig brought a huge tray of coffees and Ferra helped hand them around. There was a platter of sweet treats that reminded me of my Copperfield days: ginger snaps, toffee bombs, fireballs, volcanic chocolate. Recalling the names made me realize how violent they all sounded. Salty refused dessert for the first time ever, and I wondered if mixing those magical milkshakes had anything to do with it. I had never seen a goblin turn so green.

Ferra returned from the front of house. "Rookie, you have a special guest."

I looked up from my coffee, no idea whatsoever who it could be.

Ferra stepped out of the way, and Madame Copperfield strode in. A hush fell upon the room, reminding me how well-respected she was everywhere in the Realm. Her titanium hair was radiant against her dark skin, like a halo of bright ash.

I automatically stood up. "Directress," I said. "I didn't expect to see you here."

I had, in fact, never seen the headmistress anywhere but the magical academy.

"We have matters to discuss," she stated, "and I didn't want to summon you. You don't have time for that."

Dusty scurried off her chair, offering it to Copperfield, who thanked her warmly and sat down, her long skirt sweeping the floor.

"There is good news," she said. "And bad."

Couldn't someone just have good news for once? "I'm all ears," I said.

A young dwarf's head popped up next to the directress and placed a cup of tea before her.

"The bad news is that Apollo has taken the painting. Again. Craic Blackloth was apoplectic. I was afraid he may spontaneously combust. Luckily, Virvaris was able to calm him down."

Argh! I knew it. The *weasel.* My hands curled into fists and I gritted my teeth. So much for the pure-hearted pickpocket. Little piece of—

"Now before you denounce the lad," continued Copperfield, "I believe he did it to save Haryk Virvaris's life."

"You give him too much credit," I seethed. He was probably trying to sell the artifact on the black market as we spoke.

"Asha Viridian Rook," she scolded. "I would appreciate it if you watched your tone."

Chastened, I unfurled my fingers. Sam's reassuring hand travelled to my lap.

"I apologize, Directress," I said. "I just feel—"

"I understand your suspicions, Asha, and you are entitled to them. You have not yet met the man, and you did not know his courageous and selfless parents. But discounting Apollo will hurt us all. In your own words: Apollo is the key. Don't let him get away."

I rubbed my face again. I hoped it wasn't becoming a tic.

"Yes, Directress," I replied. Henry's note had—kind of—vouched for Apollo, too, so I reminded myself to be open-minded. "I'll find him, I promise." Even if I didn't want to, I didn't have a choice. "He's the only one who'll be able to portal the missing daughters back home."

Seemingly satisfied, she nodded, and took a sip of her tea.

"The good news?" asked Savvy, tentatively.

Copperfield finally relaxed enough to smile. "The good news is that we think we know where young Apollo is."

I dropped my teaspoon and it clattered on my side plate, making Savvy jump.

Sorry, I mouthed, as if we were both reduced to schoolgirls in the Copperfield dining hall.

"Where?" Stoker asked. "I'll fetch him."

"Given his coordinates," said the directress, "I don't think it will be quite as simple as that."

I groaned inwardly. I didn't want another difficult trip. I didn't want to travel to some terrifying pocket realm again. I had barely survived Oblivion, then Obsidian, *then* Celestia. Tears pricked my eyes.

Madame Copperfield correctly read the expression on my face, because she put down her cup of tea and took my hand. "You poor thing," she said. "It won't be as difficult as the previous journeys."

"How do you know?" I asked.

She smiled, and didn't break eye contact. "Because you have a friend there."

A friend? I thought. I couldn't figure out who she could mean. All my friends were in the room.

"Put me out of my misery," I said. There was enough mystery surrounding this case without making me guess the answer to things we already knew.

"My apologies," the headmistress said. "I didn't mean to make things more difficult. Here is the good news: the very clever Haryk Virvaris put a tracking spell on the painting, just in case someone was able to pilfer it again. So when Apollo stole away out of Blackloth's memory palace with the artifact, the elf was able to locate him." Copperfield didn't bother to hide her amusement. "In doing so, I daresay he's won the eternal admiration of the cantankerous librarian, a near-impossible feat."

Dusty nodded, lips downturned, also seemingly impressed.

Belly full, beer drained, I felt tired again and wished we could just cut to the chase. "Can you give us the coordinates?"

"Of course," replied Madame Copperfield. "I thought you'd never ask."

When I narrowed my eyes at her, she gave me a cheeky wink. "I sent the location pin to your phone when I arrived."

I pulled out my phone and saw the notification. "Thank you."

"Thank *you*, dear Asha. You continue to make me proud."

I thought she might stay to finish her tea, but she said she had "much to attend to" before sweeping out of the room.

When I looked around, the team looked a little dumbfounded.

"So, to be clear," ventured Sam, "Apollo is *not* in a dangerous pocket realm?"

"Correct," I replied. "Probably because that's where everyone would expect him to go."

"So…?" asked Rick, leaning forward.

I tapped my screen to open the Forage Maps location pin, but it was locked, with a timer that was counting down. Eleven and a half hours to go before it unlocked, with a message from the directress: "Have a good night's sleep, Asha. You'll need it."

Chione pulled me aside as we were leaving. Frown lines rippled her usually smooth forehead.

"What is it?" I asked. I hadn't often seen the grimalkin worried, and now that we had money for the animals, I couldn't understand why she was troubled.

"It's Rap," she said.

I was taken aback. "What? Why? What's wrong?"

"He hasn't been himself. His feathers are fading, falling out. He's tired all the time. He was like a puppy before, always wanting to eat and to play. Now he just lies there, listless. His eyes are dull."

"We need a vet," I said. "An animal mage. Immediately."

Wanted: dinosaur bird whisperer.

"Are you crazy?" she scoffed. "We'd be brought before the Council for having an illegal creature."

How could any living being be called illegal? I wanted to challenge the law, but I had to choose my battles.

"Well?" I demanded, as if it were her fault that the dinosaur bird would get us thrown into a penal colony. "Do you know anyone who could help?"

She shook her head. "Not unless you can bring Harvey back to life."

"Don't tempt me," I replied.

"I've tried everything," she said. "His favorite food, favorite toy. He just blinks at me with those dull eyes and goes back to sleep. I think he's lost his fire, too. I haven't seen so much as a spark. He's deteriorating quickly."

It could be anything. Homesickness. A common cold. A magical disease that only affected rainbow-feathered hollow-limbed Sickle-Claw Sauroraptors.

"Damn it." I couldn't help swearing. Together, Rap and Chione had saved our lives by flying us out of the Smaragde pocket realm. "There must be something we can do."

"I've already asked everyone I trust," Chione replied. "I'm out of options."

"The Void knows I have zero medical or veterinarian expertise," I started. "But how about beginning a course of antibiotics? And hydration. A saline IV with broad-spectrum antibiotics." If nothing else, it would rule out most infections. "And keep him warm."

The grimalkin nodded. "Okay. That sounds good. There's a whole room of medical stuff for animals. I'll have a look, and if I can't find anything, I'll get some."

"Spend whatever you need to," I said. "I'll deposit the check ASAP and release the payment. And for food, obviously. And your salary, with back-pay."

Chione nodded again. "Consider it done."

When I approached the register to pay for the dinner, Fig shook his head. "Sorry," he said, not looking sorry at all. "Someone beat you to it, plus a rather ... bounteous tip."

"Sam?" I asked.

"Nope," he responded. "The Chalices. They put a handsome sum into an account for you here. Your tab will probably run out in ..." He frowned at his screen, as if doing some mental math. "2082. Unless you make a habit of ordering that fancy champagne again. Then it'll only last you into the late seventies."

I laughed, but Fig didn't. Turned out he wasn't joking. The Chalices were obviously delighted to have their daughter home.

We hugged everyone goodbye and agreed to meet at my place in the morning as soon as the map pin unlocked. Savvy and Abigail wanted to stay with us, and Rick insisted on driving us home. I was disturbed by the news of Rap's condition, and Sam held me close.

"I just wish there was something I could do," I muttered, looking out of the window into the blackness of the night.

"I understand," he said. "But you can't save the world."

But he didn't understand. It was literally my job to save the world.

CHAPTER 20

BERGAMOT

ASHA

I arrived at Auric Bank the minute it was due to open, which was an hour before Copperfield's message was ready to unlock. The security guards were not keen on letting me enter.

"Call the receptionist," I told them. "Agreement."

After a quick radio call into the building, the man with the walkie-talkie nodded, and the other guard allowed me to pass through the revolving door. Agreement stood on the other side, gold name badge glinting.

"Hi again," I said, smiling.

She did not return the friendliness. "Your fingerprint is not registered on the system, which means you are not one of our clients, which means you are not welcome here.”

I ignored her terse tone and continued smiling. “I’d like to open an account.”

Her expression of annoyance gave way to a rather patronizing look. “I’m afraid we have strict criteria for new clients.”

I knew what she was getting at. “I have two million koin to deposit,” I said. “I’d like to do it immediately. I have business to attend to.”

Agreement blinked, not sure whether to take me seriously, understanding she might have to err on the side of credence or risk losing a valuable client. I handed her the checks to speed things up. I had places to be. She looked down at the luxurious stock the checks were printed on, recognizing the feel of genuine Auric products. When she noted the accountholder, she stared at me.

“You,” she whispered.

I plastered the smile back on my face. “Me,” I replied.

“You were the one who—”

"Yes," I nodded. "Can we make the deposit? I have to be somewhere."

"I should be angry with you," she whispered. "I should call security."

"No," I replied. "You should help me deposit the checks."

"First you try to impersonate Mrs. Chalice, and now you're trying to steal from her."

"No," I said again. "You can call Sabine. It's all above board."

She took umbrage at me using Chalice's first name. "I *will* call her."

"Good," I said. "But can you make it snappy?"

After Sabine Chalice passed the security questions on the call and said the checks were not forgeries, Agreement had no choice but to help me. I opened two Auric accounts, one for the conservation project, and one for my personal use. It still felt surreal to have so much money.

"You used to be the receptionist," I said later, when we were sitting in her new office.

"I was promoted." She stopped typing as the penny dropped. "It was *you*."

"Nah." I shrugged.

"Halfpint was promoted, too. On the same day. It *was* you."

"I appreciated you two not handing me over to the Metro Realm Unit. And I thought you were both brilliant at your jobs. You deserved the promotions. By the way, how is Davis?"

"Better," she drawled, trying to figure me out. She stared at me with her gold irises.

"What?" I asked. "You're not going to offer me any bergamot tea?"

CHAPTER 21
CARPE THE DAMN DIEM
ASHA

I got back home just in time to make coffee for the team before they arrived at the appointed hour of nine a.m. I made a mental note to get their bank details so that I could pay them for the work they had done so far. I never thought I'd be in a position to do that, and it made me happy.

"You beat me to it," said Sam, taking the hot mug from me, his face still crumpled from sleep as he wrapped his warm arms around me. He wanted to keep me close but I had too much nervous energy.

I picked up my CARPE THE DAMN DIEM mug and was ready for action. Even before taking a sip I was activated. When Dusty and Abigail appeared they were giggling and dressed like superheroes.

I shook my head. "You two are staying here, safe and sound."

"Noooo," they both chorused. "The directress said it wouldn't be dangerous."

"I'll be the judge of that," I declared.

The others all arrived within minutes of one another. It seemed that everyone was ready to carpe. We chugged back more coffee than strictly necessary while we waited for the blasted timer to reach 00:00:00 and unlock the live location pin. The magical tracking spell was nifty, and the fact that there was an app for it was amazing. I loved it when magic and tech mixed.

"You're in a disgustingly good mood," remarked Savvy.

"Why wouldn't I be?" I asked. Everything was going right. Then I understood the error of my ways: if everything was going right, it meant that something bad would happen. Soon.

Savvy sighed and pulled me into a one-armed hug. "Just kidding. You deserve to be happy."

My phone buzzed with the notification that the message had been unsealed, and I quickly grabbed it off the kitchen counter and opened the Forage Maps.

"Where's this?" I said aloud. Stoker offered to take my phone to have a closer look, so I gave it to him.

Madame Copperfield was right—it wasn't in a pocket realm. It was in a weird gray area on the regular map that I had never heard of.

"It's an abandoned coal mine," said Stoker after a minute. "Dangerous."

"Like the SubRealm?" I asked. Rick and I looked at each other in fear. We'd had enough of mining shafts and the explosives therein, thank you very much, and we still had the PTSD symptoms to prove it. It would take a lot of convincing for us to travel underground like that again.

"No," said Stoker. "The shafts are all closed. But there's a ghost town there. The perfect place to hide a magical artifact, right?"

A ghost town didn't sound bad at all. The fear left my body, and I began feeling optimistic again. I could picture this pickpocket living his best life in an abandoned settlement while Touched folk traversed the Void, searching for him high and low. Was I starting to like the guy? I didn't know, but I would find out soon enough.

"It's over four hours' drive from here," I said. "Salty, could you portal us to save time?"

"Sure thing," she said through a mouthful of something I assumed she had found in my kitchen.

"Your skills are back, right?" I asked.

"*Ja*," she replied, spraying crumbs everywhere. "Hundreds."

"Stoker, please seek out Kieron Palefang and get updated intel. You can tell them their ploy with Mildred Malachay worked out, but now we're all in the high witch's crosshairs."

Chione looked at me expectantly. I gave her the debit card for the new Auric account and her eyes flashed when she saw the logo. "Fancy," she said.

"You'll be looking after Rap, right?"

She nodded. Savvy was standing next to her.

"Savvy, look after the girls."

"Asha!" moaned the girls. "We wanna help!"

"You can help by staying here," I said. "On second thoughts, no. Go over to see the Belore twins and see if you can find the identity of the owner of Æterna. We're looking for a witch with power potent enough to colonize the body of a vampire queen."

They both nodded, eyes wide with excitement.

"So, in other words, more power than we've ever seen."

"Yes, Asha," said Dusty. She couldn't help smiling.

"Savvy will make sure you don't get into trouble."

"Yes, Asha," Savannah said, and mock saluted me. I gave her the middle finger in response, which made the girls collapse into a pile of giggles.

"Sam, Rick, Salty, we've got a ghost town to visit."

Cloak, dagger, wand, protection amulet. One more cup of coffee, and we were on the road, or, rather, hurtling through space-time and having the sensation of our spleens being squashed and our eyeballs being slurped out of our heads. A smooth landing had us all thanking the talented goblin.

"Gratitude doesn't pay the rent, you know," she complained.

"Don't worry," I said. "I'll buy you a magical milkshake. A couple different flavors."

She dry-heaved, making me feel bad, but she didn't seem down about it.

"This is cozy," said Rick, looking at the gray desert landscape. The mine dust was so fine it was in our lungs within seconds.

"We should be wearing masks," I said, unhelpfully.

"Pssh," replied Nilve. "It's a bit of dust. You'll survive." She sneezed, it wasn't pretty. I blessed her anyway.

We walked in the direction of the broken-down buildings. It seemed wholly abandoned, and I could imagine tumbleweeds blowing across the landscape, even though there were none. The air smelled sour, and the breeze was cold. I always expect a desert landscape to be sweltering, but of course they get freezing at night. Not that this was a true desert, but it did look like a manmade one.

"People drown here," said Sam, reminding me that he was a cop. Or used to be cop, anyway.

"In the sand?" I asked, not understanding.

He shook his head. "The abandoned mines fill with rainwater. There are no fences or warning signs, so the local kids use them as swimming pools."

I grimaced. A recipe for disaster.

"And it's not just drownings," he said. "When the ore comes into contact with water and air, it produces sulfuric acid. It poisons the water, the soil, everything. A toxic legacy. No wonder the sand is dust. No wonder it's a ghost town."

So it wasn't my imagination—it smelled sour because of the acid in the air. Salty sneezed again.

"Bless you," I said, but she ignored me. I didn't take offense. Goblin culture had different manners than we did. Besides, who was I asking to bless her? Which god or goddess? There were so many to choose from.

"Look," said Rick, and we all stopped and we strained our eyes. There was movement up ahead.

"What is it?" I asked.

Salty sneezed again. "More like *who* is it."

Their sing-song voices floated toward us on the acid wind.

"Children," I said. Children living in the ghost town.

CHAPTER 22

GHOSTS WITH CLOSURE
ASHA

"We need to warn them," I said, and Sam agreed, but Salty shook her head.

"It's too late," she said.

"Don't be ridiculous," I admonished. "We'll tell them about the danger right now. Send them home."

"It's too late," echoed the goblin, and I finally understood. It was too late. This place was literally a ghost town.

I needed a minute.

"You okay?" asked Sam, touching my elbow.

"Yes," I replied. "I just ... More dead kids, you know?" It's like I was a dead-kid magnet, and I didn't like it.

I took a breath. *They're already dead,* I told myself. *So there's no point in freaking out. No point in being sad, either, because it's done. They're not sad. They're playing and laughing and having a whale of a time. They're stuck in a perfect eternal childhood. What could be better? They don't need to eat or drink or sleep, they can just play and sing and not worry about safety or bad parents or drowning or anything. Don't let it upset you.* But I couldn't help it. I was upset.

It was interesting that Apollo had chosen this of all places. My heart softened. Did he identify with these kids? Did he feel abandoned, like I did? At least he grew up with parents he thought were his own. That's something. I was the child who no one wanted.

Strange things happen when she is in the room.

For the first time, I felt a connection to the pickpocket. I grew less suspicious, and had more empathy. Perhaps no one had told him that his parents had died trying to defend the Realm, trying to defend honor and decency, but on a deep level he would have known. He would have been able to tell the difference between the untouched couple who adopted him and the parents he lost to the dark forces. Deep down he must have always known. Okay, we had things in common; that was good.

We were on the same side. Perhaps I could use it as leverage to get the painting back.

As we approached, a few of the children looked up at us, and ran away. I was not sure why phantoms would be scared of us.

Maybe they're not scared, said my paranoid brain. *Maybe they've gone to get weapons.*

After visiting Oblivion, I realized that phantoms could be just as dangerous as living beings.

Oblivion.

Ghost children.

APOLLO NEEDS YOU.

I finally grasped how Henry knew Apollo, and why I could summon him—because he hadn't moved on to wherever it was that ghosts with closure go. Despite his satisfaction at my having freed his sister from the cellar, he was not yet done with the material world. My guess was that he wanted everyone dead—and by "everyone," I meant Gordon Taranath (check), Sirilla Voltane (check), Lilian Black, and the high witch of Æterna. Their evil deeds had bound the boy to our world, and not even breaking the curse by killing Taranath had set him free. He was living here with the other spectral children, and Apollo had recently moved in.

"Okay," I finally said. "I think we're safe here. I think Henry lives here."

I thought they would ask who Henry was, but they all seemed to remember him. He had caused such havoc, he was hard to forget.

Henry Havoc Seeks Total Vengeance.

Two kids came into sight. Young teens, both dripping wet. They must have, as Sam had explained, used one of the rain-filled collapsed shafts as a pool. My anger flared at the incompetence of the government to enforce simple laws such as closing off abandoned mines, if not rehabilitating them. A decent fence and a danger sign would do, especially after the first few drownings, but they couldn't even get that right, never mind mitigate the acid mine drainage that was poisoning the environment. A dark part of me wished the dripping ghosts would go after the people responsible for such things. Haunt them with that drip-drip-dripping sound all day and all night until they finally did the responsible things and closed up these abandoned coal mines for good. And they could lay down some compost and plant some bloody trees for good measure. I wondered if Merlin would have a suggestion for the correct kind of fungi that would help clean up the mess. I remember him telling me that certain fungi neutralized polluted soil and water by changing it to a less toxic form. The children stood and watched us, drenched.

"Hello," I called, and waved.

They looked uncertain, perhaps wondering if we were there to somehow trick them.

"We're looking for *Henry*," I called. "He's a friend."

They conferred and shook their heads.

"Henry's my friend," I repeated. "You can ask him. My name is Asha."

They stopped discussing. "Asha?" they called.

I nodded and shouted "Yes!" in case they didn't see.

"Asha?" they yelled again, as if they recognized the name.

"Yes!"

I looked at my phone screen. We were getting close to the painting. It was definitely somewhere in the dilapidated town.

"Come!" they called. "Come, come!"

Well, I thought, *if they're inviting me into some kind of death trap, at least they're being friendly about it.*

CHAPTER 23

THE BREATHING ONE

ASHA

The four of us loped up to the drowned children. They reminded me of Henry with their bloodless skin and haunting eyes, and I wished I could help them. I denied the urge to ask them what had happened, and what I could do to allow them to move on from the limbo they were stuck in. We didn't have time to solve the complaints of all the young ghosts in this strange place, but perhaps I could come back when the dust had settled and help a few of them out. No child deserved to be stuck in purgatory. As we watched them, water continued to drip from their hair and faces, and the especially dry landscape that surrounded us made it unsettling indeed.

"You're Asha!" said the smaller boy. "Henry told us all about you."

The older one nodded. "You're a hero around here."

"Am I?"

The small boy nodded enthusiastically. "You saved Henry's sister and the other kids."

I smiled at them. "I couldn't have done it without Henry. He was the hero."

I heard Salty groan as if to say *can we please get on with it?*

"Do you all live here?" I asked, gesturing at the abandoned houses, most of which were in ruins, or on their way to becoming so.

They nodded, and I felt a splash of water, even though I knew it wasn't real.

"It's a nice place to live," said the smaller boy. They looked so similar that I assumed they were siblings.

I was surprised. "Is it?"

The boy nodded. He was very cute, and it made my heart hurt. "It's better to live here where there are no living people."

"Except the *zama-zamas*," corrected his older brother.

"They're the mining pirates," said the small boy, his eyes lighting up. "They dig for gold."

Illegal miners risked their lives daily in these kinds of abandoned mines—it was a large and dangerous sub-culture in South Africa.

"Why is it better to live where there are no living people?" I asked. Sam nodded as if to say he also wanted to know.

"Living people are always *panicking*," said the younger boy.

The teen nodded. "Panicking about money, panicking about relationships—"

"Panicking about ghosts," added the child, and they both laughed.

"It's much calmer here," he continued. "We are sensitive to energy, to vibrations. There is nothing here. Only the occasional pirate or visitor, which is enough to keep us entertained."

"When you're breathing, life is hard. There's lots to make you worry. But when you're a ghost," said the smaller boy, "you understand that nothing is worth panicking about."

"You make death sound very inviting," I joked, and they grinned at me.

"You're looking for Henry," said the teen phantom.

"Yes," I said. "And Apollo."

"The breathing one," the small boy said. "He has been keeping us entertained."

I imagined the pickpocket showing the ghost kids magic tricks with koin.

I heard Salty's tummy rumble. When I looked at her, she placed a hand on her belly. "I'm starving," she said. "I'm gonna be hangry soon."

I cursed myself. Why hadn't I brought snacks for the goblin? Despite Nilve being an adult, she was notoriously bad at catering to her regular—and intense—hunger attacks.

"Damnation, Salty," I scolded. "Can't you just keep a protein bar in your pocket? Is it that difficult?"

"I do, witch!" she hissed, showing me her dirty needly teeth. "But I keep eating them, don't I? It's not a magical pocket! It doesn't keep making snacks for me!"

I sighed loudly. Being a ghost town, there was obviously no food in sight. "Come on," I said. "Let's get this over with so we can get back and feed the goblin."

"I can't portal when I'm hangry," she moaned.

I glared at her. "You will if your life depends on it."

The phantom boys led us through the town. Some of the higher-spec buildings still had their bones—we saw evidence of what used to be a grocery shop, a hardware store, and some kind of church or hall—but most of the houses were completely flattened.

"Where are you taking us?" I asked. They were still dripping wet and I wondered if it ever bothered them. It didn't seem to.

"The old school," said the teen. "It's where most of us stay. They have the right sized chairs, and an old projector that still works."

"We watch movies," said the little one. "And sometimes we act out our own stories, especially about how we died."

Impressed, I nodded. That was niche entertainment, right there.

We walked by some old burnt-out car carcasses and a gasoline station that was past its best-by date.

"There are no trees here," I lamented. "No plants at all."

"The soil is dust," said the older boy, echoing my previous thought. "It's the acid. It kills everything."

"Except us," said the smaller boy, smiling. I smiled back, despite the gloom I felt.

We approached the school, which was in better shape than I had expected. No roof, but most of the walls were still in place. There was definitely a more joyful energy, and I could hear children laughing and playing, even though I couldn't see them.

"Why can I see you two, and not them?" I asked.

"Because we want you to see us," said the older brother. "You'll never meet a ghost who doesn't want to be met."

The little phantom took my hand. "Apollo's probably on the stage," he said. "It's his favorite place to be."

Sure enough, within moments we heard his bad poetry.

"But soft! What light through yonder window breaks?

It is the East, and the specter is the blizzard.

Arise, fair sun, and kill the envious wizard

Who is already sick with evil—"

"Boo!" shouted a ghost. "Boo!"

"Boring!" heckled another.

"All right, all right," muttered a young man on a stage that was in such disrepair that it looked like a death trap. "Tough crowd." He adjusted his newsboy hat, took a pencil stub from behind his ear and scribbled in the notebook he held. He tapped his sneakers on the floor.

"Too depressing!" called someone in the small phantom audience.

"Poo!"

Apollo cleared his throat loudly to get their renewed attention, and the antsy crowd settled down.

"Inky pinky ponky," he started. There was some encouragement, so he rolled on. "Daddy bought a donkey. Donkey died, Daddy cried. Inky pinky ponky."

There was an immediate rush of applause and whistling. The crowd was bigger than it had first appeared, as phantoms showed themselves to stand and clap.

I thought the man might get angry that they preferred the latter poem, but he did the opposite. His face lit up at the applause and he bowed and thanked the audience.

What a very strange person, I thought to myself.

"Thank you, thank you," he said, "You are too kind."

"Encore!" yelled a little ankle biter.

"Too kind," murmured Apollo again, while trying to navigate his way off the stage without losing a leg. As soon as he was on safe ground, he took his book out again and made some notes. Totally lost in his thoughts, he jumped when we appeared before him.

"The breathing one," said the dripping ghost, as way of introduction. I guess it was more polite than calling him *the terrible poet.*

"Apollo," I said. "You have no idea how hard I've been looking for you."

CHAPTER 24

GRIMALKIN GIRL FRIDAY
ASHA

He blinked at the three of us, looking slightly alarmed. I got the distinct feeling he might run. I put up my hands.

"I liked your poem," said Salty, trying to break the ice. I think. Maybe she really did like it. There's no accounting for goblins' taste.

He looked at Salty and appeared more alarmed than ever.

"We're on the same side," I said.

Salty nodded. "Definitely on the same side."

I elbowed her, hoping it would stop her from acting weird.

"Ouch!" she yowled, and gave me a hurt look.

"How did you find me?" Apollo asked.

"Oh, don't worry," I assured him. "You're safe. No one knows you're here."

"Well," said Sam, "no one but Haryk Virvaris and Directress Copperfield."

"And the rest of our team," added Salty.

"We're *all* on your side," I said. I introduced myself, Salty and Sam.

"What do you want?" he asked.

"It's rather complicated," I replied. "Is there somewhere we can talk?"

The dripping boys stayed to play with their friends in the schoolyard littered with rocks and rusted roof sheeting. Apollo, still slightly wary of us, took us to the old staffroom. There were some chairs in need of a good cleaning standing on a burnt carpet. Gingerly, I sat down. In a way, I was glad there was no roof, so there was nothing to collapse on us.

Apollo stared at me as if he couldn't take his eyes off me, but not in a good way—more like rubbernecking a car crash.

"What?" I had to ask.

Realizing he had been staring, he flinched and shook his head. "Nothing!"

I pursed my lips in annoyance. "There must be *something,* or you wouldn't be looking at me like that."

"You just," he began. "You just ... remind me of someone."

I was not convinced, but decided not to pursue the matter. There were more urgent issues in play.

"We can help each other," I said. "In fact, we *need* to help each other."

"No, thanks," he said.

I opened my mouth and closed it again.

"No offense," he said, quickly. "I'm just out of the game. Retired."

Salty scoffed. "You're a teenager, you can't *retire.*"

"I'm twenty-seven!" he replied. "I can't help it that I have a youthful face."

"What?" I asked.

He looked at me. "What?"

Nilve SaltySnap's stomach growled like a lion in heat.

"I'm not asking you to steal for me," I said. "I need your legendary portaling skills to get to an extremely secure pocket realm. Urgently."

"Sorry, I can't help you," he replied. "I'm going to be living here for the foreseeable future. I've had enough of wizards and gateway magic and pocket realms."

"You don't understand," I said. "It's not for me. It's not a job. It's to save the lives of over a hundred girls who have been abducted by vampires."

He laughed until he realized no one else looked amused. "Wait. You're serious?"

"In return, I will break the curse hanging over your head."

"How do you know?" he asked, skin paling. "You can see it?"

I shook my head. "Ferra told me about it."

He looked at me with renewed interest. "You're not that witch, are you? The *cursebreaker?*"

"Finest cursebreaker in the entire Realm," bragged Sam, crossing his arms.

Apollo's face became more animated. "And you know how to break a Kill Your Darlings spell?"

"I do," I said. "If you can tell me who cursed you."

He nodded in an agitated way. "I can."

"Would you be able to take me to her?" I asked.

Apollo gulped. "Is that the only way?"

"Not necessarily," I replied. "But we'll get to that. Are you going to help us?"

He was about to agree, but I watched him deflate right in front of us. "I would," he said. "I swear I would, but there's this thing I'm looking after—"

"We know about the Marquis Mirror," I said. "That's how we found you."

The young man pushed his chair back, the steel legs scraping the burnt floor. "You're here to take it back," he whispered.

"No," I shook my head. "That is not what is happening here."

"They sent you to take it." He didn't seem to have heard my words.

"Apollo," I replied. "That is not what is happening. Madame Copperfield is happy for you to be the guardian of the painting ... for now."

"For now?" he asked.

"Until we find a more secure location," I said. "But all the while you are protecting it, your life is in danger, and that is not an acceptable state of affairs."

Apollo was still processing the implications. "Copperfield knows about me?"

"Do you really think it was a coincidence that *you* were the one to steal the painting?" asked Salty. "You humans really have no idea about how the Realm works, do you?"

"I guess not," he said, taking off his hat and rubbing his hair.

What could I say? I felt the same way. "You've been in contact with Henry Holden," I said.

Apollo was surprised. "How could you possibly know that?"

"It's a long story," I said. "Henry and I are ... connected. We help each other."

"Neat," he grinned. "Having a supernatural assistant."

If he was going to put it that way, I guess he was right. I also had a goblin portal agent, a werewolf bodyguard, an orc chauffeur, and a grimalkin girl Friday.

"Henry said you needed me," I said. "And Copperfield gave me your coordinates."

He was staring at me again, blinking, trying to understand.

Sam, who had been quiet since we had landed in this strange deserted place, took control of the conversation.

"Here's the thing," he said, leaning forward. "This all seems very complicated, but it's not. Not really. We are meant to be here, meant to find you and help you. But first, we need *your help* to get the girls, because their time is running out."

Apollo put his hat back on and sighed. He sat back, as if resigned. "Okay."

I did a quick double take. "Okay?"

Apollo nodded. "I'm in. Where do we start?"

"Somewhere that sells food," said Salty. "I need a plate of tacos."

CHAPTER 25

NOT EVEN A WEED
ASHA

I was thrilled, but also a bit dubious.

"You're sure?" I asked. "It's going to be dangerous."

Apollo sighed again. "I know," he said. "But I can tell when something is inevitable."

"We're dealing with vicious vampires," I continued, "and a cutthroat high—"

I felt a sharp pain in my shin, and when I looked at Salty, I realized she had kicked me to shut me up. Her eyes bulged. *Are you trying to put him off?*

I changed tack. "Thank you," I said. "You really are our only hope to save these girls."

He shrugged. "If Henry trusts you, I do, too. Plus, Ferra said you're brilliant."

"I don't know about that," I replied.

"Oh, don't be so modest," hissed Salty. "It doesn't suit you. And it's irritating."

"Fine." I stood up.

"I'll get the painting," said Apollo.

"We'll come with you." There was no way I was letting the man out of my sight after having finally—and rather miraculously—found him. We'd get the painting and return to the team to prepare for our final rescue mission. I felt anticipation nipping at my insides. We were so close!

"It's a short walk," said Apollo, and we followed him out of the post-apocalyptic school grounds and down what may have been the old main road. The hot, sour breeze was back, and the environment was so toxic that not even weeds grew there.

"You were really planning on staying here?" I asked.

Apollo shrugged. "For now. I figured they'd think I'd go to some exotic locale, so I tried to do the opposite, to keep the painting safe."

"So you know how important the mirror is," I ventured.

He nodded. "I do. Virvaris and Blackloth told me."

"It's a huge responsibility," I said.

"Yes, well, I need the karma points."

We approached a tumbledown house with newspaper over the broken windows. It was the only building I had seen so far that had a roof—or mostly had a roof, anyway. The walls were stained and crumbling, and a layer of mine-dust covered everything in sight.

"Home sweet home," Apollo joked, narrowly avoiding shards of glass on the broken concrete path. "Welcome to my humble abode. It's got a bed and everything."

I looked up and down the street, making sure that no one was watching us, and saw only decay and disrepair.

"The li'l ghosties let me have this house," he said. "It's the warmest on the block. And when it's not warm enough, I make a little fire. It's one of the only magic tricks I know." He pushed open the front door, and its hinges complained bitterly. When we hesitated to enter, he said, "Oh, don't worry. It's not as scary as it looks."

But it was.

There was something about it. Not the decrepitude, nor the smell. There was something else that was wrong. The last time I felt this way, I was right to listen to my instinct. Mildred Malachay, the mad witch, had been wearing a corset of blue dynamite, about to blow up the Æterna warehouse.

I shook my head.

"No," was the only word that escaped. I put my arms out, stopping Sam and the goblin from going inside.

Apollo waved off my concern. "It's safe," he said. "I swear."

"Who knows about the tracking spell on the mirror?" I thought out loud.

"Just us," replied Sam. "And the directress. And the billionaire elf."

"Can we trust the elf?" I asked.

"Well, he has safeguarded the mirror for decades, so I'd say yes."

"Plus, he's a billionaire," added Salty. "So he probably wouldn't sell out for money."

"You obviously don't know what billionaires are like," I replied. I have a T-shirt that says TURN BILLIONAIRES

INTO COMPOST. I wore it until it was threadbare, and I still garden in it.

"Haryk Virvaris is trustworthy," said Apollo. "I watched him get beaten to a pulp for that mirror. He was ready to die for it."

"Everyone on our team can be trusted," I said.

"You're a hundred percent sure about that?" he asked.

"Yes!" I replied, annoyed. *He* was the renowned thief, after all.

"Well," said Salty. "Grimalkins are notoriously greedy for material wealth. We've seen how Chione will destroy people's lives for money."

"Nilve SaltySnap!" I scolded. "Chione redeemed herself. She's proven her worth and loyalty over and over again. She'd never sell us out." Besides, I could say the same about the greedy reputation of goblins.

The goblin pursed her rubbery lips. "If you say so."

"There's no time to argue," I said. "There's someone here who means us harm."

Apollo frowned at us. "Is she always this paranoid?"

The bad juju escalated. I took an involuntary step back. We couldn't go inside, but we couldn't leave without the painting.

"Look," said Apollo. "You guys stay out here; I'll grab the mirror."

"No," I said, shaking my head. "You're too important."

"So are you," said Apollo.

"I'll do it," volunteered Sam.

Salty sighed in relief. When I glared at her, she shrugged and said, "I'm too short to do it!"

I inhaled sharply, looking at Sam. "I don't want you to." I felt the danger as if it were tangible, giant black burrs sticking to my skin.

Armstrong squeezed me. "I'll be fine."

"I don't have any magic here," I said. *Not even a weed.*

"He'll be *fine*," assured Apollo. "No one knows I'm here."

"Someone does," I replied. I knew it with every sparkling molecule of my body.

Sam took my shoulders and looked into my eyes. "We need the mirror," he said. "We need the mirror or this is all for nothing."

I couldn't stand the intensity of my emotions. I screwed my eyes shut and nodded. He was right. I opened them again and returned his anxious gaze. We weren't going anywhere without that hexing mirror.

I'll take the arrow, he'd said at Obsidian Castle. But what he didn't understand was that I didn't want to live this life without him. I loved him too much. He was a part of me. I blinked back my tears.

"I used to be a cop, remember?" he quipped, and touched my cheek.

My instinct was screaming, *Don't go in!*

"It's sewn into the bottom of my mattress," whispered the pickpocket.

Sam began advancing toward the house.

"No!" I shouted, and stumbled after him. I would not let him sacrifice himself. Not alone. We would go in together.

"Humans," muttered Salty, and I was sure it was accompanied by an eye-roll.

Apollo looked concerned, and perhaps confused by the notion that he was "important."

I could tell that Armstrong felt strongly about me staying outside, but he knew better than to argue once I had made up my mind. Besides, we stood a better chance if there were two of us.

I took my knife out of its sheath. Sam and I gave each other a slight nod and we padded into the broken building. It was dark inside, little light filtering through the windows papered over with faded discount specials on frozen chicken pieces and trampolines. The wooden floor was in as bad a shape as the school stage had been, and we had to watch where we put our weight. Sam wanted to go in front, but I showed him my wrist, reminding him that I had the protection amulet on Black's choker. The smog of evil that I had felt outside was thicker inside, and reminded me of the black mist that I had experienced at EverShade the first time I had met Lilian Black.

You don't belong here, she had taunted.

Ugh. I shook myself, trying to dislodge the mantle of fear that had attached itself to my body. My ring flashed, telling me what I already knew. I pushed myself forward, down the narrow passage. My eyes began adjusting to the dim light, and I was able to find the bedroom. Sam was so close on my heels that I could hear him breathing. We tread softly into the room, eyes on the mattress. Sam helped me turn it upside down, and I quickly found the package with my fingers, using my knife to cut it free. It was smaller than I had expected. When an artifact plays such an important role in protecting the Realm from darkness, you expect it to be … slightly bigger. Sam gave me an encouraging nod and we turned to leave.

I knew all along that it wasn't going to be that easy, so I expected something to go wrong. What I didn't expect was the evil I sensed to have a face that, even in the dark, I recognized.

CHAPTER 26

TWIST THE KNIFE

ASHA

"Fancy seeing you two here," said Wilkinson. "I thought I had shot you both."

I had truly never hated a man more. I looked at him with pure loathing, standing there in his heavy wizard's cloak, evil rolling off him in waves.

"When are you Dusk Reapers going to give up?" I asked. "I'm tired of taking you out. My bedposts are running out of space for notches."

I had stolen the imagery from the stories about Jacquelyn Denna Knight—it was probably made up, but according to the lore, she had a notched bedpost, not of the lovers she'd had, but of the scores of vampires she'd killed.

"Decided not to wear your uniform today, Inspector?" asked Sam. I could sense how stiff his body was.

"Ah, that," replied the dark wizard. "The Metro Realm Unit's salary was peanuts compared to the bounty on your witch's head." He looked at me with a kind of hunger, then switched back to Sam. "I kept the badge, though. I like it. Comes in handy."

"I didn't keep my badge," said Sam. "I did keep a couple of other things, though."

"Like the gun you stole from the evidence room?" asked the wizard. "The one you thought we wouldn't notice."

"How did you find us?" I asked.

Wilkinson laughed. "Oh, I wasn't looking for *you*. You're just a bonus. An extremely *large* bonus. I'm here for the painting, and you're the cherry on top. The very ... delicious ... cherry."

He said the word "delicious" in such a lascivious way that I cringed.

"You're not getting the painting," said Sam.

"Oh, but I will," replied the wizard. "Because that mirror is the key to the empire."

"The *empire?*" I scoffed. "How grandiose. And you'll be the emperor, will you?"

"Someone far more powerful than I will reign. It's a shame you won't live to see it," he said. "It's going to be quite something."

"Your imagination is quite something," I sniped. "The dark forces will never win."

"Witch," he sneered. "The dark forces have already won. Now it's just a matter of installing the correct royalty, and *you* and that *boy* keep on getting in the way."

I assumed he meant Apollo, and I bristled. "If you touch him, I swear I'll kill you."

Wilkinson laughed again. It grated me.

"You think I'm going to let *any* of your little friends survive?" he asked.

"I'm guessing that's a rhetorical question," I countered.

He looked thoughtful for a second. "I like your sense of humor. We could have been friends—you know, in different circumstances."

It was my turn to scoff. "You couldn't be more wrong if you tried."

Wilkinson stuck his hand out and motioned for us to hand over the painting, as if it would be that easy. In Ferra's words, he must have been smoking his socks.

"Look," he snapped. "You're going to die anyway. Just hand it over and I'll make it quick. Painless. Don't make me torture you in front of your ... boyfriend."

Sam took a step forward.

"I'm surprised you're still with this witch," Wilkinson goaded. "Since she's broken, now."

I felt a flash of pelvic pain where he had shot me. Where the bullet had forever damaged me.

"She's not broken," growled Sam.

"If anyone is broken, it's you," I said.

"Ah, you know what I mean, Armstrong," pressed the wizard. "You've always wanted to be a family man, right? You're wasting your time with her."

Sticks and stones, I told myself. *Sticks and stones*. But his words still hurt, because they were true.

Sam took another step forward, fingers curling into fists.

"And you," jeered the wizard, turning his unwelcome attention to me. "It's time you let your pet human go. It's not fair to him, is it? To drag him on all your capers. Destroying his career, putting him in danger, wrecking his virtue. He was squeaky clean before you came in to his life."

"Shut up," I said. It wasn't the best comeback, but I had nothing else lined up. He really knew how to twist the knife. "You're wasting your breath."

"The hard truth is that you'd be better off without one another."

"What do you care?" I demanded. "You're planning to kill us anyway."

He shook his head. "I never said that. There's no bounty on Armstrong's head. Besides, if I kill him, I won't have a bargaining chip."

I started to understand his plan. The painting in exchange for Sam's life. His foot was tapping, showing his impatience.

"Ah," he exclaimed in mock congratulation. "You've got it now."

He pulled out his gun to move things along, pointing it at Sam. We'd heard this song before.

"You're saying you'll kill Sam if I don't give this to you."

He pretended to think it over. "Correct. And you know I mean it after what happened last time ... I think you'll recall that I didn't hesitate to pull the trigger."

That was true. He was as cold-blooded as they came.

"Put down the gun," I said. "And I'll put down my knife. We'll settle it in the proper way."

"And why would I agree to that?" he asked. "You're the one who brought a knife to a gun fight."

I tilted my head as if I had just realized something. "You're scared of my magic."

"Of course I'm not," he snapped, annoyance written all over his weaselly face. "And I know what you're trying to do. It's not going to work. So stop wasting my time and let's get on with the exchange."

"It's not really an *exchange* if I end up dead," I said.

"But your pet will remain alive, which is what you want, no?"

If only I had enough magic to jam his gun!

"You've wasted enough of our time," said Wilkinson, pressing harder on the trigger.

"Our?" I asked. "*Our* time?

"I'm counting to five, witch. And if you don't give me that mirror, you'll be to blame for the noble detective's death."

Counting to five? What am I, a toddler?

"One," he said, making sure he had perfect aim. "Two. And don't think of jumping in front of him like last time. Three."

"If I give you the mirror, all hell will break loose because you'll let the Septics out. They have the power to kill every last civilian and animal in the Realm."

In a way, the ghost town had been an eerie premonition of what the Realm would be like if the dark forces were able to take over. Ghosts and dust and sour wind.

I decided the time for banter was over. I moved as quickly as I could, giving the gun a high kick. I landed badly and ended up on the floor, contorting awkwardly to avoid smashing the painting. The kick wasn't hard enough, and the weapon remained in Wilkinson's hand. He fired a shot into the wall. The sound must have alerted the others, because I heard hurried footsteps. Wilkinson aimed down at me and pulled the trigger, and I only just managed to roll out of the way in time.

He growled in frustration and pointed the barrel at Sam instead.

"No!" I shouted, and bit his ankle so hard that I heard a crunch under my teeth.

The wizard screamed in agony and fell over. Sam moved to help me. The gun went off again. It sounded louder than the previous shots, and there was no ricochet. Sam fell, and I felt the reverberations when his body hit the wooden floor.

"Sam!" I shouted. "Sam?"

Wilkinson turned the gun on me. We were both on the floor.

"Give me the mirror," he demanded through gritted teeth.

"Never!" I shouted back. "Never, you piece of—"

He fired again. I felt a sting in my periphery—my ear?— but the noise was worse than the pain. It blew my head sideways, confusing my body and my brain.

"Asha!" exclaimed Apollo from the doorway. He caught sight of Wilkinson, gun glinting, and automatically put his hands up. He gasped when he saw Sam.

"I should have known you were here," grumbled the wizard.

Blood dripped from the top of my ear onto the floor as I crawled to where Sam was lying. "Sam? Sam!" I felt the gun aimed at my back, but I didn't care. "Sam?" It came out as a sob. Wilkinson was right, I should never have dragged him into this. Untouched humans didn't belong on these kinds of missions beyond the Veil. I had taken a human who was pretty close to perfect and I had destroyed him.

CHAPTER 27

DEATH BY SAUNA
ASHA

I roared in fury and distress. Why was there so much evil in the world?

"Wilkinson," said Apollo. "What have you done?"

"What I should have done weeks ago," snarled the wizard. "Only this time I'm going to make sure they stay dead."

When I turned to see him through my tears, I looked up into the barrel of his gun.

"I hate you," I gritted. "I hate you with the intensity of a thousand suns. I hate everything about you. What are you waiting for? Shoot me! SHOOT ME!"

"No," he replied, without emotion, like I had offered him a sandwich.

"No?" I yelled.

"Now that the pet's dead, it makes more sense to keep you alive."

I screamed and lunged at him, animalistic and savage. I wanted to claw his eyes out, tear open his face. I wanted to rip him apart like the orcs had done to their slave-masters. Just before I reached him, I felt arms around me, pulling me back. I railed against Apollo, trying to get free.

"Asha," he was saying. "Asha. You can't die."

"I don't care!" I shouted. "I want to die."

"You can't," said Apollo. "You can't. If you die, the Realm will die with you."

"I don't care," I sobbed, feeling some of the furious energy leave my body.

"You do care," he said, still holding me. "Think about your friends. Think about the missing girls."

"You save them," I cried. "I've had enough." There was too much pain, I couldn't cope. I had learned early on that it was a cruel world. I had spent my life trying to right the balance in the Realm, but the evil kept coming. No matter how hard we tried, what we sacrificed, it just kept coming, like the tide of a black sea. You can't beat back the water forever. Everyone has their breaking point, and this was mine.

It's time you let your pet human go, Wilkinson had said. It's not fair to him, is it? To drag him on all your capers. Destroying his career, putting him in danger, wrecking his virtue. He was squeaky clean before you came in to his life.

What had I done? What had I done?

My heart ached so brutally that I screamed. I had to let the pain escape somehow. My body sagged in Apollo's arms.

"It's okay," he said, gently. "It's okay."

"It'll never be okay," I sobbed. Apollo didn't understand the connection that Sam and I had. It was a once-in-a-lifetime bond.

He brought his mouth closer to my undamaged ear. "Don't react," he whispered so softly that I wasn't sure I had heard correctly. He squeezed me harder. "Sam's alive."

I denied the forceful urge to look at Sam and instead cried harder; it wasn't difficult. My emotions were still overwhelming.

Sam's alive, I told myself. *Sam's alive.* If it was true, I could go on. I could fight. I would fight with every fiber of my being.

"This is the last time I'm going to ask you, witch," said Wilkinson. "Give me the painting."

I turned and looked Apollo right in his eyes. "You have magic," I said to him.

"Not much, I'm afraid," he said.

"Trust me," I urged. "You have powerful magic. There are things you don't yet know about yourself."

"Stop that whispering," snapped the wizard. "Give it to me or I'll come and get it."

"I'll trust you," Apollo murmured. "But now you must trust me."

Still weeping, I nodded.

"Oi!" yelled Wilkinson. "Enough of that!"

"Agreed," said Apollo, giving Wilkinson a death stare. "Enough is enough. And I've had more than enough of you." He put out his hand, aiming it at the floor. "*Ignem exquiris!*"

A fireball of silver flames smashed into the floor, igniting the old splintered floorboards and resulting in a pale silver fire in the middle of the roofless bedroom. The acid wind blew, feeding the fire.

"Amateur tricks," derided Wilkinson. "You could never be a true wizard, so don't embarrass yourself by trying."

The fire grew bigger, hotter. Sweat prickled on my skin. I could smell the wood burn.

"So this is your plan, then?" sneered Wilkinson. "Death by sauna?"

"Something like that," replied Apollo.

It was easy for Apollo to take the painting from me. I didn't even realize the pickpocket had it until I saw him toss it in the fire.

I gasped and tried to dive into the flames to rescue it, but Apollo stopped me, and Wilkinson beat me to it.

CHAPTER 28

FIERY GYRE
ASHA

I struggled to get free, but Apollo was stronger than he looked. Wilkinson's cloak caught alight as he fumbled in the flames. Smoke rose from his burning clothes. He shouted in frustration and pain, then triumph as he finally found the painting and lifted it up toward the sky. It was on fire, and so was he.

"You don't understand," I yelled at Apollo. "If the painting is destroyed, the Realm will implode."

"*You* don't understand, Asha," he said, calm as anything. "The painting is being destroyed, but the mirror is safe."

Wilkinson was yelping, trying to brush off the flames, but it was too late. He could have sacrificed the painting, dropped and rolled, but his greed made him hold on to it despite the hungry flames that sought to devour him. The heat quickly became unbearable, reminding me of the great hall in Obsidian Castle with all its braziers blazing away to keep the corpse warm enough to function. Apollo slowly let me go, and I stumbled away from him. Wilkinson's yelps turned to screams, then shrieking. As much as I hated the man, I couldn't bear to watch him burn. I looked to the side, but that didn't stop the smell from reaching me, and I fell to the floor, gagging and choking. The fire soon stole his voice, and the screeching stopped. With my head turned away from the heat and the horror, I heard his body collapse into the fiery gyre.

We needed to get out of the tinderbox. My skin felt blistered by the heat, but when I reached up to touch my cheek, it felt healthy and warm. I grabbed Wilkinson's gun and I crawled under the smoke to Sam's motionless body. He was unconscious, but I couldn't see any blood. I put my hand above his mouth and felt his breath on my palm. A sob escaped my throat. Sam was alive. Apollo appeared next to me, and we began dragging Armstrong's hefty body out of the room. I was confused by what had happened, but grateful. I wouldn't have been able to do it myself—not in time, anyway.

We pulled Armstrong out of the room and down the narrow passage. He would probably wake up with cuts and splinters from being dragged over the fragmented floor, but at least he would wake up. We got to the end of the hallway and through the front door. Its screeching hinges did not seem so loud anymore. We dragged him out onto the front steps and onto the desert dust in what used to be the yard.

Before I could wonder where Salty was, I saw her running toward us with a score of little ghosts in her wake. It was really something to behold. She gaped at us, taking in the fact that we were safe despite the burning house behind us. The goblin stopped sprinting and her tongue lolled out of her mouth like a thirsty pug. Panting and heaving, she rested her hands on her knees. The ghosts kept advancing, watching the fire, oohing and aahing as the beams gave way, falling to the ground and feeding the furnace. I expected to see Henry, but he was not there.

Salty came over, cheeks flushed and extra slimy with sweat. "Mister Cop?" she asked.

I looked down at Sam, and saw the bullet hole in his shirt. I lifted the cotton fabric up and saw the reason there was no blood. The bullet was cozily wedged into his police-issue bullet-proof vest. He had learned his lesson from the last time. I laughed; I couldn't help it. My relief was so enormous. So that was what he had meant when he said he had kept a couple of things from his old job.

The sound of my laughter woke him up. He grimaced and brought his hand to the back of his head, which I assumed he hit pretty hard when he landed. Again, thankfully, no blood. He looked at me, eyes narrowed against the light. "Wilkinson?"

"May he rest in peace," I said, and crossed myself backwards.

"Ah, thank god," he said, and dropped his head back, which must have hurt, given his further grimace. "You're incredible, you know that?"

"It wasn't me," I replied. "Apollo pulled out some serious *ignem.*"

"Apollo," said Sam, his voice hoarse. "Thank you."

"No sweat, Bernadette," he said.

"I thought you were dead," I said to Sam around the lump still in my throat.

"I thought we were all dead," he replied, holding my

hand. "But as long as you're living, you're not going to get rid of me that easily."

More of the house collapsed, and the ghosts whistled and clapped. Salty had joined them. I guess she was used to being around phantoms, given her previous death and adventure in Oblivion.

Sam hauled himself up into a sitting position. "The painting?"

Oh Hades, I thought, looking at the collapsing house. *Apollo has some serious explaining to do.*

CHAPTER 29

EXCITABLE WRAITHS
ASHA

"What?" demanded Sam, eyes fully open now. "The painting's in there?" He made as if to get up, but we held him back. It was a good thing, too, because his legs were weak, judging by the way his knees buckled.

"Take it easy, tiger," said Apollo. "I'll explain everything."

"Looking forward to it," I snarked.

More crashing down of burning timber, more cheering and celebration from the excitable wraiths.

"Let the fire burn out," Apollo said, walking away. "And then I'll be able to show you."

"Where are you going?" I called.

"To get us something to drink," he replied, and I couldn't argue with that.

"What's he going to say?" asked Sam.

"Maybe that he switched the painting with another parcel?" It was the only explanation I could come up with. "Maybe he's on his way to fetch the real thing."

"Nope," said Salty, lumbering up and dropping next to us on the fine sand.

"How do you know?" I asked.

Salty shrugged. "Goblins know things."

"Like what?" asked Sam.

"Goblins are expert liars and sneaks," she said proudly. "We have built-in lie-detectors. Deception radars. As far as I can tell, Apollo has not been dishonest."

"So, you're saying that Apollo took the only magical artifact in the Realm that matters, the only thing that's keeping the dark forces from destroying everything ... and *burned* it?"

"Yup," said the goblin. "I hope he comes back soon. I'm so thirsty. The ghosts don't understand concepts like hunger and thirst anymore."

We sat like that for a long time, watching the house burn until there was hardly anything left. I gave Wilkinson's gun to Sam. It was mesmerizing to watch first the furious flames, the collapsing of the bones, the embers smoking. By the time the house was gone, it was getting dark. The ghosts waved and made their way back to the school, and I started shivering. Sam pulled me toward him to keep me warm.

"Sorry I took so long," said Apollo. "It's not easy to find a drink in this place." He passed us a scuffed bottle of water and coffee-flavored evaporated milk. Salty got a green can—a cream soda energy drink—and Apollo had already drunk his.

We thanked him and gulped down our past-the-sell-by-date drinks.

"Ready?" he asked, and we nodded. I was freezing and exhausted, emotionally and physically. Sam helped me up.

Apollo lifted his chin at Armstrong. "How's the pip?"

Sam frowned at him. *Non comprehendo.*

"Your head," explained Apollo. "I expect you have a concussion."

"Probably," said Sam. "I'll be fine."

"Just don't pass out again till we get out of here," he said. "I can't portal non-consenters."

We walked over to the smoldering coals. *It's incredible how destructive fire can be,* I thought. *There used to be a building standing here, and now there is not.*

Apollo found a plank that had fallen away from the heat. It was black and singed, but mostly in one piece. He tossed it toward the origin of the fire and used it as a gangplank so that he wouldn't melt his sneakers. With a stick he probed the coals and ashes, trawling for what was left of the package.

"Got it!" he yelled.

I was too busy looking at Wilkinson's blackened bones to celebrate. I dragged my eyes away from the grim sight of the wizard's unplanned cremation and looked at what Apollo was pointing at. All I could see was more smoking ash. He tried to pick it up, but there was a hissing sound as he burned his fingers. He cursed and shook his hand, then blew on it. He took his jacket off and used it as an oven mitt, picking up a dark rectangular object that looked very much like a destroyed painting.

Hex, I thought. It was burnt to a cinder. I was sure that the evil Septic members would appear at any time and *rumpis* us all the way to Oblivion and beyond. Hope drained out of me. We had been so very close, hadn't we? I thought back to how optimistic I had felt just hours before, how things had really seemed to be working in our favor. And now I was standing with my ash- and tear-stained face watching a pickpocket hold up a useless charred husk, feeling like my life was over.

"Chin up, Rookie," said Sam, making me think of Merlin and realize how much I missed him. Eccentric, generous, and sage. I needed more Papa Smurf in my life.

"Asha!" exclaimed Apollo, beaming. "It worked!"

Was this young man delusional? He may as well have been holding up a burnt wall tile while grinning like a madman.

What have you done? I thought. I wasn't sure if it was directed at Apollo or myself. Either way, I felt like crying again, but didn't have the energy. Sam reached for my hand, and we waited as Apollo walked the plank back to us.

He put the black rectangle on the ground at our feet and scooped the cold desert-like sand onto it, using it to cool the object down. Using his scorched jacket, he began wiping it down.

"When I saw you for the first time," Apollo mused, "I knew you looked familiar, but I couldn't put my finger on it. Which is dumb of me, really, because it's not like I get out that much. At first, I worried that you had been one of my past clients. I worried even more that you had been a past victim."

"That would have been awkward," said Salty, downing the last of her energy drink and burping like a college freshman.

"But then I realized that *you* were the girl in the painting."

"Er," I said. *What now?*

"I know," he replied, a slight chuckle in his voice. "It's impossible, right?"

"Yes," I agreed.

"After all," he continued. "It was painted when we were babies."

"Yes," I said again, not very helpfully.

"And now I can't even show you because the painting no longer exists. But I promise you, it was you in that painting. Your eyes—"

"The painting no longer exists," I echoed. So what was all his grinning and waving about? Why was he saying *it had worked?*

"The thing about me spending so much time in the banned books library," Apollo said, still polishing the vitrified rectangle, "is that you absorb a whole lot of knowledge that you don't even register."

"Like ...?" I prompted.

"*Like*," Apollo said, his stupid smile plastered all over his face, "how to remove magical artifacts from enchanted paintings."

"I thought only the billionaire elf knew how to do that," said Sam.

"Same here," said Apollo. "I was convinced that Haryk Virvaris was the one and only Realmer who knew the secret, because he was the one who placed the mirror in the painting in the first place. So I thought it would be like a bespoke word key, or a complicated spell, or a mathematical puzzle combination safe. But it wasn't!" His eyes glinted, giving him the look of someone who was not quite sane. "Because Virvaris is smarter than that. He knew that if something happened to him, the mirror would be lost."

"But ..." thought Sam out loud. "Why would that be a bad thing? Wouldn't that be the safest thing?"

"No," said Apollo. "All the years the Septics have been stuck in there has given them time to plan and strategize and scheme. To practice their magic and grow their power."

"I still don't follow," I said.

"Lost means lost," said Apollo. "Not gone forever. If the mirror is merely mislaid, it can be found. It can end up in the wrong person's hands, and therefore the Septics would have a chance to be free, but this time they're more calculated and more evil than ever before, because that's what being trapped does to you."

"But the wrong person wouldn't be able to release the mirror from the painting," said Sam. "So isn't that a moot point?"

"They wouldn't be able to do it *on their own*. But they could find and torture a person who knows how to release it."

I was beginning to understand, but still had so many questions. "So you're saying that the spell Virvaris purposefully used was one that could be reversed by someone else."

"Not just someone else," said Apollo. "Not just anybody. It had to be *me*."

"But Virvaris cast that spell decades back, and he didn't even know you existed until a few days ago ... until you stole the painting. And, anyway, no offense meant, but why would he trust you with it, given that you're a ..."

"A thief," said Salty, who didn't seem to mind insulting anyone, ever.

"I still don't understand why you thought it was a good idea to take the mirror out of the painting," said Sam. "It was safer when it was magically locked away."

"Because it's a loaded gun," said Apollo. "It's an enchanted loaded gun floating around the Realm, ready to fire at every man, woman, and child."

I finally got it. "We need to take the bullets out of the gun," I whispered.

We thought that we needed to keep the Septics locked away to keep the Realm safe, but Apollo was right. They would find a way out eventually. The only way to win this war, as Stoker liked to remind us, was to take the offense, not defense. The ramifications were terrifying.

CHAPTER 30
THE MIRROR
ASHA

When Salty's stomach growled again, we decided to leave the ghost town for the comfort of my home, where we could be warmer and more comfortable while we discussed the finer points of the revelation, and the plan going forward. Salty's portal skills were excellent, but Apollo took it to another level. There was no discomfort, no overwhelming pressure, no strange creatures watching us from the abyss. And it was all over in a moment.

"That was like traveling business class," I said, and was rewarded with a stink-eye from a scowling Salty.

Abigail and Dusty threw their arms around me and made googly eyes at Apollo. I guess he did have a nice face. I introduced him to everyone.

"You found him, Asha," said Dusty, hope and admiration in her gaze.

"We can thank Haryk Virvaris for that," I replied. "It was his tracking spell that led us to the ghost town."

"What's that under your arm?" asked Abigail, but before Apollo had the chance to answer, Savvy came around the corner, wearing an *apron* of all things.

"Just in time!" she enthused. I peered suspiciously at her. I would bet my Chalice check that she had never worn an apron in her entire life.

"Just in time … for what?" I asked. The last thing I needed was food poisoning before going off to rescue the girls.

"Just in time for the food order to arrive."

My relief must have shown on my face, because Savvy snapped a tea towel at me. "I'm not *that bad* at cooking," she said, and Abigail and I roared with laughter. It felt good.

"Savannah's wearing an apron because she's been testing some potions," Dusty volunteered.

"Not in your potions lab, dear heart," Savannah quickly said. "Not even I am that brave."

"What kind of potions?" asked Apollo.

"Just a few simple ones that I hope will help us in the coming battle. *Invisibilis, impedio, curas vulnum.*"

Apollo tilted his head. "Can you say that again in English?"

"Apollo never went to Copperfield," I told Savvy. "Not officially, anyway."

"Invisibility, halt motion, healing potion," she explained, and turned her attention back to me. "The girls said you couldn't access your magic while you were rescuing them, because there was nothing to draw from."

"You're a hedge witch?" asked Apollo, looking at me.

"A green witch, we say now," chirped Savvy. "It's more PC."

"You draw power from nature," he said.

"Plants and trees, specifically," replied Dusty proudly. "Sometimes soil, but only if it's healthy, and mushrooms. It has to be living, though. She can't just pin a flower in her hair."

"You should see her garden," said Abigail. "It's like this amazing edible jungle."

"There wasn't a green leaf to be seen where we've just come from," I said, inspecting Savvy's work. "So these will come in really handy if that happens again. Thank you."

"I'll make as many as you need," she said. "Just put in your order."

"Do us muggles get some, too?" asked Armstrong.

The girls giggled. I gave the ex-detective a sad smile. We'd have to have a grave discussion later, and I wasn't looking forward to it. I took a deep breath. "Let's make some tea," I said. "We've got a lot to talk about."

"The tea can wait!" came a voice from the front door. It was distinctly orc-ish. Rick marched in with a dozen white plastic bags.

"Razor clam soup?" I joked.

"Asha!" he cried. "You're alive. Welcome home. Tell us everything."

Over an unusual mish-mash of Chinese, Indian, and Japanese fast food, we filled the others in about what had happened, and what it meant.

Dusty dropped her chopsticks. "You took the mirror *out* of the painting?"

"I know," I said. "I also thought it was a terrible idea at first. But it's the only way we'll get rid of the Septics forever."

"The longer we leave them in there," added Apollo, "the stronger they get."

"Leaving the mirror locked up is only delaying the inevitable," said Sam. "Your generation, or your kids' generation, would have to deal with it. Best to nip it in the bud."

"Nip it in the bud," chortled Rick in a bitter way. "You make it sound like it's an easy thing to do. To kill the Septics. May I remind you that they are by far the most powerful wizards in the Realm?"

"I didn't mean to make it sound easy," said Sam.

"Can we see it?" asked Abigail. "The mirror?"

Apollo wiped his lips with the flimsy paper napkin and stood up. "It's not a toy," he warned them. "I don't need to tell you what will happen if this mirror breaks."

"I'm not touching it," said Dusty. "No way."

Apollo walked over to my bookcase, where he had laid the mirror when we first arrived. He picked it up carefully and brought it over to the table. Everyone stopped eating to look. It was the first time I was seeing it in decent light. An intense, overwhelming feeling of déjà vu hit me right between my eyes, harsher than if I had been struck by lightning.

"Holy hex," I murmured. It came out sounding like a curse.

"Asha?" said Sam. "You're white as a sheet."

"What's wrong?" asked Dusty and Abigail.

"Mister Cop is right," said Salty. "You look like one of those ghosts."

My thoughts swirled around, disjointed and confused.

How could it be?

"For Persephone's sake," said Savvy. "Tell us what's wrong."

"That's the mirror," I said.

"*Cor-rect,*" drawled the goblin, implying I had the IQ of a potato.

I shook my head to clear it. "That's the mirror I saw in the hut. When I was a baby."

Sam looked concerned. Salty looked like I'd just spoken in tongues, and Savvy stood up. "Right. Time for everyone to leave. Asha needs to rest."

I shook my head again. "I know it sounds crazy. But I know that mirror. I was the baby in the mirror." I realized I was just making it worse, making my friends worry that I'd finally snapped, like Malachay.

"Give her a chance to explain," urged Sam.

I shot him a grateful look. "I know this sounds deranged," I started, hoping it would stop them from thinking I was one fry short of a Happy Meal. I scratched my eyebrow trying to find the right words. "When I took that mushroom. The Purpurea. It allowed me to access the spiritual world." I stopped to think for a while, to arrange my thoughts in a non-nutso way.

"Yes?" prodded Rick.

"Part of that weird hallucinogenic journey was about me. I got to, I don't know, go back in time? No, that's not right. I was able to ... *observe* what happened to me as a baby."

All eyes were on me. I pushed my carton of soy-stained noodles away and touched my temple as if it would help me think. "So, it was black and white, everything was black and white. Like an old movie. There was a hut, in the snow. There was a baby."

I decided to leave out the traumatic birth I had witnessed—the even earlier event when I saw my mother cut me out of her belly. I also left out the wolf who had cared for me after my mother had abandoned me.

"I saw this baby, and I realized I was looking into a mirror. The baby I was looking at was *me.*"

"And you think this is the same mirror?" asked Apollo.

"I know it is," I replied. "It feels the same."

"You mean it looks the same?" asked Savvy.

"That, too," I said. "But mostly it's a feeling."

"What does it mean?" asked Rick. "This dream?"

I shook my head. "It wasn't a dream. It was real. I was that baby."

"Your personal records show that you were abandoned in the forest," said Sam. "So that adds up."

My ring shone. It wasn't a flash, like it did when I was in danger. It was more like a confirmation of what I was saying. "This ring," I continued, frowning at the newfound memory. "I found it in the forest. I was older —old enough to walk. There was a couple there. They ran away from me."

"They ran away from a toddler?" asked Dusty. "They should have helped you!"

I took a sip of water. "They were scared. I had power. I had all the power of the forest. It was all I knew."

Sam supported me the way only a man with police experience would. "If they reported the incident, there'll be a file. We can corroborate it." It was his way of telling me that he believed me, and we would be able to prove that what I was saying was true.

"They did report it," I replied. "I saw it in my file at Copperfield. That's why I was taken from the forest and put into foster care." I looked down at the tanzanite ring, then at Apollo. "I still don't know what it means."

He didn't break eye contact. The gaze of his mismatched irises traveled deep into mine. "We'll find out," he promised.

CHAPTER 31

MOSTLY DEAD

ASHA

The only person at the table who was able to finish eating their dinner was Salty. No surprise there, not even when she helped herself to everyone else's remainders. She didn't mind mixing sushi with naan, and curry sauce with sweet and sour pork. I was really glad I wouldn't be sharing an enclosed space with her in the foreseeable future.

We cleared the table and Sam switched the kettle on for tea, even though I would have killed for a large whisky.

"My head is spinning," said Savvy. "Can we spend a moment summing up what the hell we need to do now?"

"Good idea," I replied, pushing my chair back to give me some extra breathing space—extra thinking space.

"Apollo has agreed to portal us to Celestia, where we'll destroy Lilian Black, get the girls, and portal them back."

"That's really nice of you," said doe-eyed Dusty, looking up at the sneakthief. I could sense the beginning of a very large crush.

Apollo shrugged. "Don't think too much of me. In return, Asha has promised to break my curse."

"You don't look cursed," said Abigail, with equally affectionate eyes.

Oh, boy.

Apollo turned back to me. "Who's this Lilian Black?"

"One of the evilest vampires I've ever met," I replied. "Smaragde clan. She's the one who's been kidnapping the girls. I assume she has her eye on the leadership position now that Sirilla Voltane is ash."

"They lost their leader recently," Rick said to Apollo with a wink at me.

Apollo noticed. "I don't suppose that had anything to do with you?"

"It was a team effort," I said. "She was mostly dead, anyway."

He looked like he wanted to ask more questions, but I pushed forward.

"Bring the girls home, destroy Black," I reiterated. "After that we can move on to finding the high witch."

"The who?" asked Apollo.

"The high witch," I repeated. "The evil force behind the bleed farms."

Apollo's forehead creased. "I thought that was Lilian Black."

"Lilian Black is a vampire," I reminded him. "Don't get me wrong, she's as villainous as they come, but in the grand scheme of things she's just a pawn."

"Got it," he said. "Get Lilian Black, then the important witch."

Everyone nodded.

"Wait," said Apollo. "How do you know it's a witch who's behind all this?"

"It's a long story," I said, wanting to get on with planning our strategy.

"I'll give you the short version," said Rick. "When we got to the Smaragde stronghold, Sirilla Voltane was a meat puppet. She was like a corpse on marionette strings. It's a unique kind of spell possible only for powerful witches."

"Got it," said Apollo, shuddering.

"What's up?" I asked.

"Nothing," he replied. "I've just met my fair share of powerful witches. Enough to last me a lifetime."

"Your curse?" asked Abigail.

I saw real pain in his eyes. "Yes," he replied.

"Don't worry about it anymore," said Dusty. "Asha is the best cursebreaker in the Realm."

Apollo smiled. "So I keep hearing."

"Once we've taken care of the bloodsucker, we'll move on to the Septics."

"I feel exhausted just thinking about what needs to be done," said Salty with a barely concealed yawn. Her hand lay on top of her overstuffed belly, and her eyes were closing.

"Sorry, Nilve," I said. "There's no time to rest, not until the girls are safe ... Nilve?"

She didn't reply. When I looked closer, I saw she was already asleep.

"Give her ten minutes," said Sam. "A power nap will do her good. We can have another cup of tea and be on our way."

I exhaled. The lump in my throat was back, and my eyes stung.

"Guys," I said to the team. "While you're getting ready to leave, Sam and I are going to have a quick word outside."

Armstrong didn't attempt to hide his surprise. "Why? What is it?" His subtle smile made me feel worse. He murmured, "Don't get me wrong, I'd never turn down an opportunity to be alone with you."

"Can we talk outside?" I asked, as gently as I could. Despite being at home and safe, my heart was racing, and I felt like I couldn't catch my breath. This was going to be one of the most difficult things I'd ever had to do.

CHAPTER 32
TART DECAY
ASHA

"You're making me nervous," Armstrong murmured, catching my hand and kissing it. I took it away. We were sitting outside in the jungle, on the bench under the mulberry tree. I could smell the tart decay of the fallen berries. I knew that particular scent would, from then on, forever bring me heartache.

"Did I do something?" he asked. "Say something ... to upset you?"

I tried to breathe, tried to hold back the tears, but it was impossible.

"Asha!" he exclaimed, distressed. "What is it? Whatever it is, I can help. We'll get through it."

Stomach in knots, I forced myself to stop the infuriating rush of tears. I felt like I could weep for days, weeks, years.

I got the feeling he wanted to shake me in frustration. "Tell me!"

"Wilkinson was right," I said, and fresh tears erupted.

"What?" Anger and confusion abraded his voice. "What are you talking about?"

"We both know it's true," I cried. "Wilkinson just put it into words."

He shook his head. "No."

"Sam," I cried. My beloved Sam. "I wouldn't be doing this if I didn't love you." I took off the ring he had given me in that wonderful ceremony in Ferra's garden.

"No," he repeated. "You're not thinking straight. You've been through so much. You need some time to—"

"I am thinking straight," I said. "For the first time since I met you. I should never have pursued a relationship with you. It was stupid and wrong, and I'm sorry."

The lump in my throat was a hot coal.

"How can you *say* that?" he asked through gritted teeth. "Asha! We are meant to be together. We were always meant to be together." He took my hand again, and this time I didn't resist. He put it on his chest. "I know you feel it."

I sobbed and shook my head. "It's not right," I said. "It's not right to put you in danger like I have. I love you too much." I clenched my jaw, trying to get a handle on my emotions.

"You think I care about right and wrong?"

"You do!" I cried. "You always have. That's one of the reasons I love you! Because you're so *good*."

"But you've taught me that it's not as black and white as that."

"That's the problem," I said. "Look what I've done to you. Wilkinson was right."

His anger flared, and he let go of my hand. "You think you're that powerful? That you can break a man's moral compass?"

"It's not about power," I whispered. "It's about love."

"It's about love? That's why you're ending our relationship? Is this what you want?"

Another sob rose up in my aching throat. "It's not about *what I want,*" I wailed. "It's about what is *right.*"

I was saving the man's life. My love's life. It was the right thing to do, even though my whole body insisted otherwise.

"No," he said. "I'm not letting you do this. You're making a mistake."

I shook my head. "The biggest mistake would be taking you into battle and losing you forever."

His gaze was as intense as I'd ever seen it. "Asha. What you don't understand is that I don't want to live a life without you. I'd rather die fighting with you than live in a world without you."

I laugh-sobbed, and wiped my eyes. "You are not making this easy."

"Good," he said, pulling me closer, squeezing me against his strong body. "Do you feel that? Do you feel me?" He turned my face up to look into his eyes. "This is us, Asha. Bonded and unbreakable. Do you feel it?"

Against my better judgement, I nodded. My face began pulling into an ugly moue but Sam brought his mouth down to mine and kissed me so tenderly that my tears retreated. After a while I had to pull away to breathe. He was still squashing my body against his, as if he thought that if he let go, it would be forever.

"You were abandoned," Sam said, and his words made my heart ache even more. "You didn't deserve it then, and you don't deserve it now." He put his ring back on my finger. *"I will never abandon you.* Do you understand?"

I nodded, weeping silently, throat aching, his shirt wet with my tears.

CHAPTER 33
STARDUST SPECKLED
ASHA

"Hey, love birds!" called Rick. "Let's get the show on the road!"

Sam finally released his grip on me, but not before looking into my eyes again to make sure I had received his message loud and clear. We nodded at each other, and he helped me up. I don't know how he knew I had jelly knees. We held hands as we walked through the jungle and up onto the patio. Seeing the rest of the team ready to go and thinking of the Celestia girls gave me my strength back—although I did feel shaky, my emotions running high.

Wand, knife, choker, potions. I was ready—or at least as ready as I was ever going to be.

"Hey, Slimer," I said to Salty. "Time to rise and shine."

Her eyes opened mid-snore. "Wha?"

"Come on," I said. "We're off to put that vampire out of her misery for once and for all."

A silver thread of saliva broke as she sat up straight. "Vampire?"

"Give her a minute to adjust," I told them. "She's probably been dreaming of waffles."

"Everyone else ready?"

"Yes, ma'am," said Apollo.

Savvy lifted the old bow and quiver she'd uncovered in the garage.

"I'm wearing my lucky socks," said Sam, and I smiled at him.

"We're ready," said the girls in unison.

"We've already had this conversation," I told them. "You're staying, end of story."

Dusty looked at me beseechingly. "But Asha, we know the pocket realm. We can help."

"Plus," said Abigail, "You'll need as many hands on deck as possible. There are so many guardians there."

"The Void knows I love how brave you two are," I said. "But you're staying here."

They knew better than to keep arguing, but both fixed their baleful eyes on me.

Salty, finally awake, hopped off the kitchen counter stool and looked ready for action.

"I've just had a thought," said Sam, and we all looked at him. "How did Wilkinson know where we were? An old mining ghost town would not be anyone's first guess. How did he know exactly where we were?"

"The tracking coordinates," I said. "It's the only way he could have known."

Sam nodded. "Who else had that information?"

"No one," I replied. "No one but the directress and Haryk."

"Madame Copperfield would never have betrayed us," Savvy said.

"Nor would Virvaris," said Apollo. "I've seen him tortured for information, but he didn't say a word."

Sam looked at me suspiciously. "What?" I asked. Then I realized he was looking at my phone.

I dropped it on the counter with a clatter as if it had burnt me.

Within a minute, Apollo had taken the phone apart, and Sam had identified the spyware.

"That weasel," I said. How had Wilkinson got hold of my phone?

Apollo removed the alien parts and put the phone back together, but I wasn't sure I wanted it. I decided to leave it at home.

"What if they've moved the girls?" asked Savvy.

"It won't matter," I said, showing her the choker I had wrapped around my wrist. "The portal key will take us to Lilian Black." I would put all my money on the fact that wherever she was, she would have the girls with her.

We all stood in a circle.

"Are you sure you're up for this?" I asked my best friend. She hadn't done any magic in a decade.

I saw burning determination in her eyes and I knew what that meant. She would have stayed out of the various battles if they hadn't taken her daughter. But once they grabbed Abigail, the gloves came off. Savvy was going to make it her personal mission to find Griffin and finish him, and anyone else who played a part in kidnapping the missing girls. Together, we would make sure that this would never happen again.

Apollo nodded at me, and I put my arm out. He touched the choker and we immediately vanished. It was the most bizarre feeling, like someone had brushed a roller of invisible paint over me. My house disappeared and I was flying through the stardust-speckled Void space.

We landed so smoothly that Salty glared at Apollo, no doubt wondering how he managed it. I would have suggested he give her lessons but knew it would make her sulk even more.

As unwrinkled as the trip had been, Apollo was pale. "I've never seen security measures like that on a pocket realm before," he said. "It was like trying to get through magical barbed wire with trip switches everywhere I looked. There was a moment I thought we weren't going to make it."

"Well done," I said. "And thank you."

As expected, we were in a white room. It looked and felt like Celestia. I gave Apollo the thumbs-up.

When Dusty and Abigail popped into the room, I felt a bolt of anger.

"Apollo! Girls!" I whispered fiercely. "I specifically—"

He put his hands up. "Wasn't me! They must have stepped into the circle."

I frowned at him, then at the girls. "This is *not* okay."

"Don't be cross with us," pleaded Abigail. "You need us here. We'll prove it to you."

Dusty nodded. "We know this place. We know Miss Black."

I glowered at them, my mouth a thin hard line. "Dusty, if you ever disobey me like this again, you will no longer be my apprentice. Do you understand?"

She shrank back. "Yes, Asha."

The youth of today! I gave Savvy a look, thinking she would be just as angry as I was, but she tilted her head at me, silently arguing, *At their age, we would have done the same thing.* She was right, of course, but I didn't enjoy the feeling of having so many of the people I cared about in this kind of situation. I have heard mothers say that once you have a child, it's like a part of your heart is just walking around exposed, vulnerable and raw.

That's what it felt like having the girls and the team—I cared deeply for every one of them. They were at the same time my weakness and my strength.

"This is the hospital wing," said Dusty. "I'll take you to the girls."

CHAPTER 34

GAME ON

ASHA

"Take out any vampire you see," I told them, "except Lilian Black. We need her alive." Only once all the guardians and vamps were taken care of would we be able to safely portal all the girls home. Again, I found myself wishing for Jax. No one ashed vampires like that wizard. I gestured for Dusty to lead the way, and we followed her. Being back in the white corridor made me feel like no time had passed at all since I had last been there. I may as well have been wearing those white cotton pajamas.

"What is this place?" asked Apollo. "I'm getting a strange feeling from this building."

"Me too," I replied. I could practically smell the blood they were harvesting. "Wait until you see the grounds."

I followed Dusty, feeling nervous but bold. The moment I'd been waiting for was finally here.

Apollo shook his head as if to dislodge something.

"You okay?" I asked.

"Yes," he replied. "It's just this place. My instinct is telling me to get out."

"Understandable. I hope we won't be staying long."

Just as I was beginning to think we were stuck in one of those Escher enchantments again, the passage opened up to a large room with a handsome staircase.

"This is it," whispered Abigail. "The girls will be down the stairs—in various rooms and outside in the grounds."

We readied our weapons.

"Where are the guardians?" asked Apollo.

"Dotted all around, hardly visible."

We kept moving as we whispered, down the magnificent staircase carpeted in rich maroon and gold. When we got down to the landing, the reception area was empty. There were no guardians behind the front desk, and not a Celestia sister in sight. Dusty, Abi, and I frowned at each other.

"Where is everyone?" I asked in a low voice.

The girls shook their heads.

I looked into a few rooms—the crafting room, the sewing hub, the art studio. All empty. We moved outside onto the perfect emerald lawn. No one.

"They were expecting us," said Sam.

"We're too late," said a stricken Savvy. "They've moved them."

I disagreed. "I don't think Lilian Black would risk sending them somewhere. She'll stay with them. They're her golden ticket."

"But they knew we'd come back for them," said Savvy. "And they know the warehouse has been destroyed. They've made some kind of plan for damage control."

"Yes," I replied, but I still believed that Black would be with the girls, and the choker portal key had shuttled us to where she was. "We just have to find her."

I wished Stoker was here, positive he could have sniffed the vampire out.

"But where would you hide a hundred girls?" asked Rick, scratching his head.

"The dining room?" I suggested. They could hide there for days with access to food.

"Dining room, hall, or somewhere outside," said Abigail. "The garden goes on for miles."

"We'll split up and search. When you find the girls, send up a flare." As soon as I said it, I remembered not everyone in the group had the magical powers to do so. "Or, just ... retreat and find us."

They nodded and set off. Savvy and Abigail went into the building in the direction of the dining room. Rick and Apollo went outside. Sam, Dusty, and I made our way to the hall. Despite my reluctance to have the girls with us, it was coming in handy. I hadn't even known there was a hall.

We moved quickly along the west side of the building, passing all manner of sports equipment and the stables, which smelt of hay and horses. Eventually a separate building came into view. It was starkly white and beautiful. It looked like a church, apart from the bold Celestia symbol punched into its facade. I found myself wishing that Mad Witch Malachay was there with her blue dynamite.

I took back that thought immediately upon spying through one of the windows. It looked like a refugee camp inside, with thin mattresses on the floor and groups of girls huddled in various clusters. Guardians lined the walls and doors. Even the sedated girls were there, and I was simultaneously relieved and worried to see that Mercury was one of them.

Sam and I looked at each other with wide eyes.

I breathed in some energy from the prolific garden and sent up a silent flare. Savvy and Abigail wouldn't be able to see it, but the others would. Judging by the sudden noise in the distance, I assumed some patrolling orc guards had, too.

"Game on," I said, with more courage than I felt.

We traced the perimeter of the hall, ready to deal with the Xarlugs when they arrived, and found a neat little concrete bench we could hide behind. Soon enough, the lumbering orcs arrived—only a pair of them, for now. Sam's breathing was louder than usual. He was looking at Wilkinson's gun as if summoning the courage to use it. I took out my wand and nodded at him, and he nodded back. We stood up and both began firing at the same time, Bonnie and Clyde style, Sam with bullets, I with lightning bolts. Sam's aim was spot-on, and they both fell within a second of each other, my bolts arcing over their bodies. The gun had a silencer, but the shots still seemed loud. We didn't know if the guardians had heard them. Dusty peered into one of the small windows and gave us the thumbs-up. Three more Xarlugs came running, and I took two down with electrocution by wand while Sam shot the other. I had mixed feelings seeing Sam kill. It went against his nature, but you'd never know because he was so good at it. The Sam I knew was not a killer, and yet his aim was medal-worthy.

We didn't have a lot of time before the guardians noticed the rather large uniformed corpses strewn on their perfect lawn. Sam gathered their firearms and dumped them behind the bench where we had taken cover.

We waited a while, and no more orcs came, but neither did any of our team members.

"There are seven vampires that I can see," whispered Dusty. "So, maybe double that."

I nodded. "Can you see Black?"

"No."

We needed backup if we were planning on taking out more than a dozen vampires. I was also wary of collateral damage.

"No guns around the girls, okay?" I said.

Sam hesitated, and holstered his weapon. I knew what he was thinking—how were we going to win the battle without firepower?

The hairs on the back of my neck stood up, as if Henry was standing behind me. When I looked, no one was there.

"Do you feel that?" I asked.

Neither Dusty nor Sam did, but my phantom-radar was in the red. There was definitely some spiritual energy going on around us. If not for my experience with Henry, I might have been scared, but he had taught me that ghosts were like humans—good and bad, and mostly a bit of both.

"Miss Black!" whispered Dusty. We peered into the hall and saw her in all her gothic Victorian glory. She was standing at the front and speaking to the girls, but we couldn't hear what she was saying. The girls watched her attentively, nodding. I could see by their slack jaws that she was mesmerizing them en masse.

"Should I fetch the others?" asked Dusty. It was a good idea, but I didn't want her going alone. Sam read the concern in my eyes. "I can go with her," he volunteered.

I looked through the window again. Black was still hypnotizing her charges.

"Okay," I said. What I wanted to say was, *I don't want to be here alone!* But seeing as I was wearing my big girl undies, I let them go. I watched their backs as they went into the main building to find Savvy and Abigail, while I could practically hear the ticking of the clock before someone noticed me or the bodies on the lawn and all hell broke loose. Ticktock. I watched Lilian Black speaking to the girls, every single one of them stolen from their previous lives and brainwashed into being happy prisoners. Stockholm syndrome had nothing on Shadow Snow. My ring flickered.

Mercury was still passed out, along with another ten comatose girls. I noticed with regret that Frankie was also one of those girls, and was sure she was there because she had asked too many questions. I recognized a few other girls in Black's audience from my brief stay at Celestia. They were looking at the vampire with nothing but acceptance in their eyes. I shivered.

I felt a cool breath on my neck. I turned on my heel, expecting to see Henry, but it wasn't him. It wasn't any kind of ghost. It was a young blonde girl in her pristine Celestia uniform. She had a daisy crown on her head. When she smiled at me, I knew I was in danger, felt it right through my bones, but it was too late. All the thoughts came too late, because she had already stabbed me.

CHAPTER 35
A SEARING BRIGHT PAIN
ASHA

I felt the knife puncture me just under my rib cage, a searing bright pain, but I didn't believe it until I looked down and saw the blood on her blade.

Still smiling, she tried again, but this time I grabbed her wrist and smashed her arm against the building, forcing her to drop the blade. We both exclaimed in pain. I took her down with a judo move and knelt on her back, causing her to cry out again.

"*Impedio,*" I said, directing the spell at her mouth, so she would not be able to yell for help. The rest of her body was also paralyzed. I felt another presence behind me and gasped, but saw it was Sam. He took over, dug a cable tie out of his pocket, and bound her wrists with it. He looked satisfied until he saw the bloody blade on the grass and took in the girl's unharmed body, then scanned mine. I was holding on to the wound, blood seeping between my fingers.

"It's not deep," I said. I hoped.

I heard a growl in his throat. "Should never have left you." He pulled up my shirt and looked at the knife wound. My shock was keeping the pain at bay.

"It's bleeding a lot," he said. He picked the knife up off the grass and cut a swath of material off the girl's dress. He wrapped it around my torso so tightly that it constricted my lungs until I learned how to breathe past it. Turned out the faux yoga we used to do at Starfall came in handy after all.

Sam looked down at the girl again. "I don't understand."

"It's Black," I said. "The girls are under her control. She medicates and mesmerizes them. They'll do whatever she says."

The ramifications hit us both hard, and we stilled, processing how this would change our strategy. We thought we'd be up against a dozen guardian vampires and around the same number of Xarlugs, but now their army included a hundred girls instructed to kill us—

knowing very well that we would not, under any circumstances, harm the innocents.

My jaw tensed with anger. Black was so wily, so evil, so hexing clever, and always seemingly one step ahead of us. My wound was starting to sting in earnest, and I hoped my usual quick healing would rise to the occasion.

"Where's Dusty? We need to warn the others."

"We found Savannah and Abigail," he replied. "So the three of them went off to find Apollo and Rick."

I saw something—someone—in white behind Sam. "Behind you."

He whirled around and saw her. A Celestia sister standing next to a dead Xarlug guard on the ground. She hadn't found his weapon so gave up and beelined toward us.

"Don't hurt her," I said, even though I knew it was unnecessary.

This one wasn't smiling. She had caught sight of the blade in Sam's hand and pounced at it.

I jammed my wand into her back. *"Fiat fulgar!"*

Her slim body trembled under the onslaught of electricity and she fell down, unconscious. I felt bad, but not that bad. I looked at Sam. "Hope you brought a lot of cable ties."

We decided warning the others took priority—who knew how many of these Stepford students were roaming about the school grounds? Little Trojan horses in their pretty white dresses and daisies in their hair.

They are not the enemy, I reminded myself past the pain radiating from the knife wound as we darted away from the hall and into the gardens to look for the rest of the team. I worried that the grounds were so large that we wouldn't find them in time, but within a few minutes we spotted them in a copse, all striding toward us. They seemed unharmed, and I was relieved. Salty was perspiring—it must be hard to keep up with people who have legs four times as long as yours.

"What happened?" asked Savvy, aghast at seeing my fashionable tourniquet.

"One of the sisters," I said, my hand traveling toward the gash. "I'm okay."

Dusty gasped. "One of the *sisters?* That doesn't make sense."

"Yes, it does," said Abigail, paling. "Miss Black controls them."

Rick frowned. "But the meat puppet spell is only available to witches."

"It's not that spell," I said. "When I was here under the guise of a young girl, I saw how Celestia chemically and magically indoctrinates them. Black is a powerful vampire, and her mesmerizing skills are potent. They are all completely under her control."

Abigail was especially upset. "So we can't win," she murmured. "Not with all of them against us."

"We'll find a way," I assured her. I had Sam, I had my team, and I had my magic. "The difficult part will be subduing the girls without hurting them." We would also need them conscious to consent to the trip back home. It wasn't going to be easy, but the last few weeks of my life had all led up to this moment, and I was going to get every single one of them to safety, or die trying.

Sam handed out some of his cable ties, and we all checked our weapons while summoning our courage.

"They're all in the hall," I said. "Or most of them, anyway. They'll soon notice that the guards are down, and that two girls are missing."

"So, what do we do?" asked Dusty.

I wished I had the answer. Our plan of taking out the guards and vampires and being greeted by grateful girls desperate to go home was history. "We'll have to make it up as we go," I said. "Rick, please guard Dusty and Abi. Stay with them no matter what."

He saluted me. "Yes, boss." The girls, despite their bravado, looked relieved.

Sam and Savannah turned to me for instructions, but I had none. "I guess we need to get back to hall and just take it from there."

I was racking my brain for some kind of brilliant strategy to magically knock everyone in the hall out, like a kind of chloroform gas bomb spell. Unfortunately, our potions master had not covered that at Copperfield. The sleeping spell wouldn't work; it took too much magic to keep one person under, never mind a hundred. Although ...

"The hospital wing," I said to Dusty. "You know where it is, right?"

"Of course," she replied.

"Go and look for anything we can use to overpower them. Chloroform, sedatives, anything."

The girls both nodded, and Dusty looked pleased to have something to do.

"We'll all meet back at the hall," I said. "Try to stay unnoticed. Use your invisibility spell if you have to, but try not to use too much magic. We're going to need it."

They rushed off, leaving Sam, Savvy, and me to head back to the hall.

"What do you think Black's plan is?" asked Sam. "To just keep them all in there?"

It was a hostage situation, except the hostages were all programmed to kill you if you freed them. Honestly, I didn't see a way we could win this, but that was often the case with these kinds of missions. I remembered being locked in the cage in the SubRealm, and how hopeless that situation seemed, but Rick and I survived it. This would be the same. This had to be the same.

"How did they know we were coming?" asked Apollo, who had been very quiet. "This realm is so secure—it was practically impossible to enter."

Salty gave Apollo that envious look again, her naturally green skin adding to the effect. "But you're so good at portaling it was easy for you, right?"

He shrugged. "Sorry."

"They knew because they're Smaragdes. We destroyed their stronghold, and their factory. We shouldn't fool ourselves. They know who we are, and they need us dead if they have a hope of continuing their business and ascending to power."

I agreed. Why else would she be so obsessed with Æterna? Rule the money, rule the Realm.

"That vampire will be especially intent on killing us," said Apollo. "Good to know."

If they were able to kill us, their problems would disappear. As if on cue, a group of three girls in white appeared in the distance, their eyes trained on us.

CHAPTER 36

ANTIPSYCHOTIC VARIETY
ASHA

They had come from the hall, given their direction. Would Black keep sending girls out until we reached some kind of impasse? I thought they'd be too valuable to her to sacrifice, but I understood that narcissists will do anything in their power to preserve themselves. She'd save as many as she could, of course, because she needed them. But if most were to die, well, no one was as good at getting fresh fodder as she was.

The girls marched toward us like robots—no expression, no idea of who they were or what they were about to do—brainwashed soldiers ready to kill on demand. They had black straps over their shoulders. Anxiety made my stomach burn and head buzz. I heard Salty whimper, so I reached out and touched her shoulder.

It'll be okay, I told her through my skin.

I needed magic that would temporarily incapacitate them without hurting them. Easier said than spelled. I willed my witch's intuition to come up with something, but before I had the answer, the girls swung their borrowed AK-47s forward. They had found the weapons cache at the hall, and were using them on us. I took out my wand. They lifted the automatic rifles and aimed.

"Arma ignifera volas!" I yelled, and swiped my wand, cutting through the air in a dramatic upward motion. The guns obediently flew up into the air above the girls, who stood looking confused. They had probably never seen a levitation spell, never mind a troupe comprising a witch, a goblin, a gruff ex-detective, and a Peaky Blinders pickpocket. It was probably making their mesmerization short-circuit. The rifles remained in the air, twitching like they didn't know what to do next.

"Contendis!" I shouted, and they arced toward us. I drove them neatly into my stunned teammate's hands. Salty looked especially bizarre, and I was sure I'd remember that image for a long time, standing there goggle-eyed with an automatic weapon that was as long as she was tall resting perfectly on her potbelly.

Unarmed, the girls seemed far less dangerous, but they were still advancing.

"Savvy," I said. "I can take two. *Impedio.* You take the other?"

"I'm so rusty," she said, but agreed. We stretched out our hands and gathered some last-minute magic, then together called, "*Impedio!*"

A cool blue stream flowed out of us and into the girls, stopping them in their tracks.

"Quickly, Sam, I can't hold it," said Savvy.

Armstrong bound the girls' wrists and ankles in record time, and we let our spells go. One of the sisters tried to bite him, but he dodged her jaw. He was no stranger to cuffing people.

"That seemed easy enough," quipped Apollo. I could hear the nervousness in his voice.

"We need another way," I said, hoping Rick and the girls would be back soon bearing gifts of the antipsychotic variety. "There's a lot of magic here to draw on, but not enough for a hundred girls."

We all took a collective breath and pressed on toward the hall. The garden made our mission seem completely surreal—crowds of flowers bobbing so beautifully in the breeze, as if it was an ordinary day in the sunshine.

"We're just going to leave them lying there?" asked Apollo.

"For now," I replied. "Unless you have a better idea?"

"I could try to talk to them," he suggested. "I understand human psychology. That's what made me a good sneakthief."

"We're not talking about wallets and watches, Apollo," I said. "They've been subjected to—"

Of course!

"What?" asked Savvy. "You've got an idea. I can see it."

I blinked at her. Yes, I had an idea. "Apollo. Take one of the girl's watches."

"Huh?" He tilted his head at me. "They're tied up, Asha. It's hardly a challenge."

I must have glared at him, because he quickly did as I asked and brought over the Celestia watch I knew every sister had to wear. I turned it over in my hands, inspecting it while the others hovered around me, wondering if I had lost the plot.

"They all have to wear them," I said. "It's part of the control. I just don't know what or how."

"Spyware, like on your phone?" asked Sam. "Or tracking software."

"Or both, and more," I replied. I put it in my pocket until I knew more.

We reached the hall with no more trouble. I kept taking the watch out and looking at it, trying to figure it out. I wished Ferra was with us. She'd crack it open and tell me exactly what it was capable of, and how I could use it to my advantage.

CHAPTER 37

SLEEPING MIST

ASHA

Rick, Dusty, and Abigail were waiting for us behind a tall hedge, looking optimistic. Dusty gave me a thumbs-up. They had found something. I made grabby hands to show how happy I was to have some medical reinforcements.

Rick, meanwhile, looked at the new AK-47s and whistled quietly. "Nice accessories."

Dusty was out of breath. She pushed her hair out of her face; it was damp with perspiration. "No sedatives, but we got some tranquilizers." She showed me a bag of loaded syringes with needles attached.

"Excellent work," I said.

"That's not all," chirped Abigail, who held another bag. "We also found anesthetic. Like, *lots* of anesthetic." I peered into it like a child looking into Santa's bag. *Oh, yes. That's what I'm talking about.* At least a dozen large bottles of medically guaranteed sleep tinkled merrily within the bag. That magical cloud of chloroform became a more realistic option.

"You girls are brilliant, you really are."

Wide-eyed, they both smiled at me, on edge with fear and uncertainty.

We handed out the syringes to the team. I took the anesthetic from Abigail and moved closer to the hall with Rick, whom I asked to blockade the doors. I looked through one of the small square windows and saw the sisters all standing at attention, facing Lilian Black. She must know that we had arrived, because the previous easy atmosphere was gone, and the sisters now reminded me of the old photos of the blond, blue-eyed kids in Nazi Germany—the so-called Aryan race. Not because they were all pale-skinned; it was the expression on their faces, as if they had been bred to follow orders.

I shuddered and crossed myself backwards. *Please,*

Mother Earth, I thought. *Protect these girls, and protect my team.*

I unknotted the strip of fabric that Sam had tied around me to stop the bleeding. It, combined with my rapid healing, had worked well. There was still a dull pain, but the cut had already scabbed over. I found an area on the fabric that was not dyed crimson and tied it around my head, to cover my mouth and nose.

"Why do you look like a confused Karate Kid?" Salty asked under her breath. I hadn't realized she was behind me. I spun round.

She shielded her eyes. "Whoa," she whispered. "I take that back. You look hardcore. I wouldn't mess with you."

I peered through the window again. Rick gave me a thumbs-up from outside the window on the opposite side of the hall, indicating that he had been successful. I nodded back.

"The mask is for the gas," I said to Salty.

"What gas?" she asked.

Holding a bottle of anesthetic in my left hand, I smashed the window with the hilt of my dagger and threw the bottle into the hall like a canister of teargas.

The guardians jolted at the sound and all turned to look at the window I had broken, and the broken glass glittering on the polished timber floor.

"Nebulum!" I chanted, narrowing my attention to focus wholly on the transparent liquid on the floor of the hall. I saw it sparkle and rise up—an airborne silver puddle —before dissipating into vapor. I didn't waste a second throwing the next one in, then the next, *nebulum, nebulum, nebulum,* until every single bottle of anesthetic had been aerosolized to create a sleeping mist—a potent soporific haze. I watched as the first girl dropped. Her sisters looked concerned for only a moment before they fainted away themselves. The guardians began rushing around, shouting orders. One came up to the shattered pane and tried to grab me through it. I gripped her arm and sliced it along the jagged edge, cutting it clear to the bone. She shrieked and pulled back, causing more damage. I couldn't help looking away. It was bloodcurdling, but she was a murderous vampire and deserved some pain for what she had done. Her suffering fed my magic—as pain sometimes did—and I glimpsed why evil witches and dark wizards did what they did, because that hit of power was so heady and exhilarating that I could imagine how they could become addicted to it.

Once the screeching vampire had fallen back onto the unconscious girls at her feet, freckling them with her blood, I could see the rest of the hall once more. Most of the girls were asleep, reminding me again of the fairy tale of Snow White. The inverted story was playing out before us: instead of a good Snow White being put to sleep by an evil witch, we had Shadow Snow who had to be put to sleep by a good witch—and there would be no Prince Charming to save her.

Strange, silly thoughts to be having when so many lives hung in the balance, but perhaps there was a hidden meaning I had yet to grasp.

The vampire guardians and Celestia sisters who were still conscious saw what the vapor was doing and moved away from it, but could not escape the hall, thanks to my favorite orc who had sealed the exit. They panicked, perhaps thinking the gas was deadly, and began smashing themselves against the door with all their might. One of the vamps grabbed a candlestick and began breaking all the windows to allow the mist to escape, but succumbed to the anesthetic, melting to the floor before she was able to finish the job.

In all the chaos, I couldn't spot Lilian Black. Under the haze, the floor was a surreal landscape of motionless white-clad bodies, some spattered with blood, and the occasional black-clad guardian, but I couldn't spot Lilian amongst them. Nor was she one of the remaining souls trying to break down the door. I knew she hadn't been able to escape the hall, so it made me nervous. Was she hiding, ready to pounce as soon as we let down our guard?

"Go!" I shouted. "Go, go, go!"

I heard my team echo my words. The door opened and the guardians ran straight into Rick. Apollo, Dusty, and Abigail snagged a girl each, who were confused, weak, and easy to subdue. Savvy was ready with her bow and arrows, and made short work of the five vampires trying to flee. The blessed wooden arrows, like spear-shaped stakes, turned them all into fireballs, and there was a sudden heat and a flurry of ash that settled on our shoulders like snow.

CHAPTER 38
VAMPIRE-FLAVORED FIREWORKS
ASHA

We dealt with the stragglers, binding the wrists of the rest of the girls who escaped the hall and smoking the vampire guardians. Still, there was no sign of Lilian Black. Had she somehow escaped? Vampires were powerful, but as far as I knew, they couldn't walk through walls.

"We have to find Black," I declared, and entered the building, careful not to trip over any bodies. I looked at the stage, where the bleeders had been sleeping, but all the beds were now empty. That didn't make sense.

There was another fireball in my periphery, and I saw Savvy making her way through the hall, identifying vampires and mercilessly putting arrows in their backs. It was difficult to think with all the vampire-flavored fireworks being detonated in the enclosed space. Shattered glass, stained tunics, smoke and blood. I was looking forward to fresh air, but first I had to find the vampire who had kidnapped so many innocents.

I got that feeling again, that shiver, and the hair on the back of my neck rose. I wished the phantom would reveal itself. This was not the time to be coy.

"Henry?" I asked. "Henry? Are you here?"

The ghosts in the mine dump ghost town had said that Henry was on important business. I couldn't think of anything more important than dealing with the woman who had stolen his life and destroyed his sister's. If he was here, he could help me again, just like he had done when I was trapped in the bleed farm.

"Henry?" I called. I felt something cold touch my arm and flinched. "Is that you?"

There was so much noise reverberating in the place that I wouldn't have been able to hear his answer even if he did reply. The cold touched me again, this time with more urgency. It was a hand. I nodded, and it began to guide me. It started pulling me on stage, where Black had been standing before. It was darker and quieter at the back of the platform. Colder. I saw a hint of the phantom, a sliver of gray, and my own white exhalation of breath. It wasn't Henry.

"Who are you?" I whispered.

"That is not important," came the reply. The voice was young, female. A victim of Celestia.

"Maxine?" I guessed. "Your mother blew up the Æterna factory in your honor."

"Who do you think led her there?" replied the ghost. "Henry helped me. He teaches me things. How to communicate through the wall. How to make bad things happen. You need to be angry enough."

"I'm angry enough," I replied. "I want to make bad things happen to Lilian Black."

"Lilian Black is merely a pawn," whispered Maxine.

That didn't stop me wanting to kill her.

"You need to keep her alive," said Maxine, as if she had read my mind. "Celestia is her invention and creation. If the creator of a pocket realm dies, the realm dies with it. All the sisters will be lost."

"I know," I said. "But she needs to pay for what she has done."

"She will," assured Maxine. "The Void knows. She will."

"The hall is secure," yelled Rick in my general direction. "We're going to collect the other girls and bring them here."

I nodded, and my team disappeared outside. Knowing him, he would throw a girl over each shoulder and carry another in his arms. They'd all be back together in no time. When I looked back to where the phantom had been, I got a shock. In her place stood Mercury, her previously glowing brown skin now gray and lifeless.

"Mercury! I'm so glad you're okay." I felt like hugging her, but her energy was the antithesis of welcoming. Dead eyes stared back at me. "Mercury," I said. "It's Asha."

"I know who you are," she said through lips chapped and dry.

"You're not well," I ventured. "I can see you're not yourself."

I noticed a glint of metal and knew before I looked down that she had a knife just like the other sister had stabbed me with. My wound ached in apprehension.

"Do it," came a sinister voice from the shadows.

Mercury kept her dull eyes trained on me, but she did not obey.

"Kill her!" commanded Black, who I couldn't see.

"Mercury," I said carefully. "Marielle misses you. Ms. Hammond wants you back at Woodhaven."

She blinked for the first time.

"You don't have to do what the vampire tells you to. You have a robust mind, an independent spirit. You are stronger than her."

"Shut up, *witch,*" sneered Black.

"Zaleria's safe at home with her parents now. She's home and safe because of you."

"Zaleria," repeated the girl in a trance.

"Zaleria Chalice," I said. "You saved her life. They gave me enough money to send you and Marielle to university and have your own place, like you wanted."

"Don't listen to her," purred Black. "She left you behind, remember? They all left you behind."

Mercury's brow creased, and the blade glinted. It was true. We had left her behind, even if it had been her decision. And her time since then had clearly not been easy.

I pushed harder. "Zaleria told you that you have a destiny, remember? This is your moment."

"This is my moment," she echoed.

"Mercury!" snapped the vampire. "You will obey me, and me alone! Kill that witch!"

"Destiny," I insisted.

Mercury began moaning, and I didn't know what to do.

"Mercury!" yelled the vampire.

The moaning got louder. She was fighting the mesmerization, battling to regain her agency.

Lilian Black finally stepped out of the shadows. Her presence seemed to take up the whole stage. More powerful than ever, she shone with vitality, and her skin was luminous. It wasn't just her body that seemed stronger and rejuvenated; she had an aura of dark potency. Her gothic Victorian dress looked like it had been redesigned for a dramatic debut on a catwalk. Tighter waist, billowing shoulders, layers and layers of black satin and lace.

"Been dipping into the merchandise?" I asked her. "I'd cut down on that elixir if I were you. Not good for your mental health."

She hissed at me, showing her bright white fangs.

"Look around you," I said. "You've lost."

"I don't *lose*," she replied.

"My team won't hurt you," I said. "You'll be coming back with us."

Black laughed. "Such naiveté," she simpered. "You really don't understand the grand plan at all, do you?"

"I know that you've been supplying Æterna with virgin blood for their elixir. I know the elixir makes them billions, but more importantly that it keeps the likes of you alive for as long as it will take to destroy the Realm. That it increases the power of evil while making good people despair as you kidnap their future." I remembered Maxine's words. "And I know that you are merely a pawn."

The vampire hissed again, and took a step closer. I could smell blood on her breath and it nearly made me gag. She struck my cheek so fast and so hard that I spun to the ground, just catching myself in time before smashing my face on the floor. Mercury did not move.

"Insolent witch," she spat. "I'll teach you who really rules the Realm."

Lilian Black was usually so ladylike in her actions that I didn't expect her to climb atop me. I was surprised by a hailstorm of slaps and punches as her sharp knees and elbows pinned me down. I fought back, but had forgotten how strong vampires were. It felt like there were ten of her as her limbs blurred while beating me. Just as abruptly as it had started, it stopped. Black gasped and lost her grip on me. I wrestled her still body off mine, and saw the knife in her back.

"Oh no," I said. "Oh no no no."

Mercury's previously blank expression turned worried and confused. She looked down at her hands, perhaps looking for blood. Perhaps wondering what she had just done.

With a grunt I shoved Black off, kneeled next to her, and inspected the knife wedged just under her shoulder blade. It was a small knife, but the entire blade was embedded. I put my ear to the vampire's mouth and heard the labored dragging in of breath.

"Collapsed lung," I guessed.

I got the chills. Maxine was clearly not happy.

I inhaled deeply to gather my magic, and soon my hands felt warm. I laid one on the vampire's back and the other on the dagger, slowly easing it out as I chanted.

"Curas vulnum. Curas vulnum. Curas vulnum."

Her breathing sounded worse than ever.

"What did I do?" asked Mercury.

"Don't think about it," I said. "You were under her control and you fought it. It's not your fault."

The hall began to shake, worse than if an earthquake was rumbling through the ground. A crack appeared in the white wall. I swore. A wooden beam landed with a bang on the stage, just a little way away from where we were standing. The sedated girls, still prostrate all over the hall, would have no chance of surviving if the building collapsed. Another huge crack zipped its way up to the ceiling.

CHAPTER 39

THE TROUBLEMAKERS
ASHA

"*Curas vulnum!*" I yelled. Black was motionless.

I remembered the extra potions I had and quickly rooted in my pocket.

Invisibility.

Distraction.

Protection.

"Ah!" I exclaimed as I saw the label of the healing potion. I pulled out the stopper with my teeth and began pouring a thin trickle over the gaping wound. It bubbled and hissed like peroxide, and the meaty, smoky smell was awful. The vampire moaned in pain and lashed out, trying to stop the source of the agony. The irony was not lost on me that I was using a precious healing potion on my worst enemy.

Mercury looked on in fear and confusion.

"If she's in pain, it means she's alive," I said. I looked at the shuddering walls. "We need to get the girls out of here."

But there were so many of them, and just two of us. I would need twenty Ricks to clear the hall in time, but I only had one, and he wasn't here.

"We can wake them up," said Mercury.

I shook my head. "How?"

"Miss Black has a remote control," she said. Her face was starting to look better—the dullness had dissipated, and her eyes were bright.

"A what?" I was sure I'd heard wrong. Then I remembered the remote control the Xarlug guard had used on the slaves at the Æterna warehouse.

I remembered the watch Apollo had taken off the girl at my request. "The watches?" I asked.

Mercury nodded, and got down on her knees on the other side of Black. She used the bloody knife to slice open

Black's bodice to reveal her corset, which had been specifically designed to hold a small tablet. Mercury tapped the screen a few times, picking up Black's limp hand to use her fingerprint to unlock the interface, then forced open an eye for the iris scan. It beeped in the affirmative.

"We have to be careful with this thing," Mercury said. "It has a kill switch."

Ice ran down my spine. "A what?" I asked, even though I knew what a kill switch was.

"I heard her talking about it to the nurse when I was pretending to be sedated at the bleed farm. She was saying how tempting it was sometimes to just flip the switch on some of the girls—the troublemakers—and Sister Vena just laughed. You can choose an individual, or all of them."

I gulped. "What else can it do?"

"Mostly medical stuff. Temperature, heart rate, sleep quality, glucose level, BMI. Other readings and tests. It's how Dr. Bianca knows what to put in our supplements. It's got a tracking device, obviously. And a tasing function."

"How does the kill switch work?"

"I'm not one hundred percent sure. Something about short-circuiting the heart. A small but deadly detonation."

"Okay," I looked at the motionless bodies. "Hopefully a little shock will wake them up."

We grimaced at each other. I obviously didn't want to hurt the girls, but we had to get out of there before Black fell off her perch. Things weren't looking good for her, but at least the ground had stopped shaking.

Rick appeared at the door and saw us kneeling over the vampire. "You okay?"

"Debatable," I said. "We need to get the girls conscious and out of the hall."

"But you said you wanted them—"

"Black is badly injured. If she dies, we all die with her."

He looked at the cracks in the white walls, the timber beam that had fallen on the stage, and nodded. "Yes, ma'am. We've got about a dozen girls out there."

I nodded, and Mercury activated the taser function. It asked her for confirmation and she tapped yes. We both held our breath as she clicked the final button. Within the blink of an eye, a collective spark sounded—a hundred of them in unison—and the girls' bodies arched as if they'd been zapped by a defibrillator. There was gasping and groaning.

"You need to tell them to go outside," I said to Mercury. "They don't know me. They'll trust you more. Apollo is waiting out there to take us all home."

Mercury gave me the tablet and stood up. "Sisters," she called. "Sisters, this realm is about to be destroyed."

The poor girls. Pale, drowsy, confused. Some crying. But they paid attention to Mercury, gazing up with bleary eyes.

"We need to get out of this hall." She gestured at the damaged walls. "And onto the lawn outside. There is a man there who is going to take us to a safe place."

"What happened to Miss Black?" asked one of the sisters.

"She's hurt," said Mercury, avoiding the real question. "But we are helping her."

A new quake rumbled under our feet, and the girls cried out. It was good timing, and backed up what Mercury was saying. They began standing and helping each other up. The ceiling growled, and soon gray sky was shining through the rip in the roof.

"Hurry," called Mercury. "We don't have long!"

Rick, Savvy, Salty, Abigail, and Dusty rushed in to help the girls get out in time. I couldn't watch, terrified that the building would fall on them. They made quick work of shepherding the sisters out of the deathtrap.

"Lilian," I said to the limp-bodied vampire. "We need to get you out of here."

She didn't respond. I checked her wound—it looked better, and the terrible soggy lung sound was gone. The healing potion had definitely made a difference. Mercury stepped forward to help me lift the vampire off the ground. She was lighter than she looked, or maybe the adrenaline coursing through my body just made it feel that way. When I looked up, I saw that almost all the sisters had left the hall. One girl remained on the floor, unconscious.

"Frankie," we gasped in unison, wide-eyed with worry. I was worried she was dead, but I saw that she wasn't wearing a watch.

"You go and help her," I said. "I've got Black."

Just as I said that, the vampire's knees buckled and she felt heavier.

"You sure?" asked Mercury.

I nodded. "Go!"

A new split in the ceiling, and the western wall crumbled. Rubble smashed down, destroying anything on the floor beneath it.

Close one.

Mercury couldn't wake Frankie up. She tried to pull her immobile body but was struggling. They'd both be dead if they didn't leave immediately. I balanced Black unsteadily and looked at the screen of the vampire's tablet.

I called to Mercury to catch the watch I was throwing toward her, and she did, bless her. She pressed the back of the face to Frankie's wrist and I sent a magical pulse through it. Her body curved like the others had, and she groaned. Mercury shook Frankie by the shoulders and spoke to her, and they finally hobbled out of the hall.

I released an exhalation of relief, even though my problems were not yet over. As I turned to look at Black's face to gauge her responsiveness, I felt a sharp pain in my belly where Wilkinson had hurt me. I didn't understand until Lilian Black smiled at me. I doubled over, taking us both down.

The pain was incredible, as if she had thrust her hand into a deep open wound and twisted my insides.

I screamed and hit her. I didn't know what else to do. She hissed at me and let me go. I grabbed her head and smashed it on the stage floor, hoping to knock her out, but it just slowed her down. Again, the screeching pain from my belly. I dropped the tablet, and Black pounced on it.

"No!" I shouted. I climbed onto her and tried to wrestle the tablet from her.

A sharp elbow crashed into my chest, then my face, as she tried to dislodge me. I lunged for the tablet, but she moved it out of my reach as soon as I touched it.

"Give it to me!" I demanded.

"Over my dead body," she replied, knowing full well that I wouldn't kill her.

I roared and grabbed at it, pushing Black down and hitting the hand which clutched the tablet.

"You're not taking them away!" she yelled.

"*You're* the one who took them away," I said. "I'm returning them."

She had the screen open on the collective kill switch.

"You wouldn't," I said.

Despite the pain and blood and fear swirling around us, the vampire seemed amused. "You think I *care* about them? They're a means to an end. Do you think a farmer thinks twice about killing a cow for money? They're *fodder*. That's all."

"You disgust me," I rasped, and reached for the tablet, but I grabbed it one second too late. Lilian Black had already tapped the kill switch. There was a flashing red light on the screen, and as I read the word "Activated," there was screaming and an explosion outside.

CHAPTER 40
MONOCHROME DYSTOPIA
ASHA

I felt like dying. Everything was lost. How, how, *how* could I have been so close to saving them and fail right at the finish line? Grief overwhelmed me, but I was too shocked to cry.

"Poor witch," pouted the vampire. "So close."

"I should have let you die," I snarled.

"Too late for that," she replied.

Another earthquake shook us, and the back wall of the hall disintegrated.

"Asha!" shouted Savvy from the door. "It's falling apart out here; we've got to go!"

Lilian Black reached into her corset pocket and pulled out a small vial. I recognized it immediately. I was right—she had been drinking the merchandise. She tipped it into her mouth and swallowed, and seemed immediately stronger, but the building kept shuddering. Perhaps her pocket realm wasn't fooled by the life-extending effect of cruel and illegal elixirs.

"I should have killed you the moment you appeared on my radar," Black said.

"The feeling is mutual," I replied. I wrenched the tablet from her, even though it was too little, too late.

"Bloody Mordecai," she spat.

Mordecai? Another shot of adrenaline, like a fuel injection into my blood. "What?"

"Nothing."

"You said Mordecai. Bloody Mordecai."

"He told us not to kill you. Special orders."

Mordecai had refused to tell me who he was working for. "Special orders from who?" I asked.

"None of your damned business."

"Tell me!" I yelled.

"Go hex yourself," she replied, and I had to use every ounce of self-restraint to not punch her in her fangy face.

"Get out," the phantom whispered in my ear. "Get out now."

"What's the use?" I replied. I had failed the Realm on a spectacular scale.

The vampire frowned at me. "What?"

"I wasn't talking to you," I snapped.

She gave me an uncomfortable look. Most of the ceiling collapsed, crashing down with an almighty force. I heard screams from outside. The others must have thought it had landed on me, but the stage remained relatively unscathed.

"You speak to ghosts," Black said, seemingly out of nowhere.

I didn't reply. She was looking weaker again, and I thought that no matter if she was downing serums like tequila at a frat party, she wouldn't live for long. Especially not if I could help it. Maxine was right, I needed to get out. I edged away from Black.

"You speak to Henry," she said.

That stopped me. "What do you know about Henry?"

I had assumed she wouldn't know any of the children's names years after kidnapping them.

"Henry haunts me," the vampire said. "You led him to me. He can't kill me, so instead he'll haunt me till the day I die."

"Well," I replied. "Today's his lucky day."

The vampire looked at me with a mixture of uncertainty and dread. She followed my gaze behind her to where Savvy stood like the goddess Artemis, arrow nocked in the bow and aimed at Black's heart. Grin and Frolics aside, I'd never been happier to see my best friend.

"Get out," whispered Maxine. "*Now.*"

I dragged myself up off the floor, still hurting. "Got to get out," I told Savvy, limping to her.

She nodded and began moving backwards alongside me, eyes and arrow trained on the vampire. The steps leading down from the stage were covered in debris, so I picked my way through it while Savvy covered me. Beams and bricks fell, smashing into the already-quaking floor. My mind was as chaotic as the falling building. A yard from the door, I heard a wrenching sound from above, the only remaining part of the celling. As I looked up, I knew it was too late. It would smash my skull to smithereens. Just as I'd accepted my fate, a powerful push from an invisible source behind me propelled me forward. My feet barely skimmed the floor as I flew forward, the heavy wooden pole ramming the floor behind me.

Thank you, Maxine, I thought. *I couldn't save you, but you saved me.*

Savvy rushed to me and hoisted me up by the back of my cloak. Again, I felt like I was flying, until she dumped me unceremoniously on the lawn outside.

A storm was gathering. I assumed it was the first time Celestia had anything but perfect weather. In my short experience there I had never felt too hot or too cold, and the sky was always blue. Now, threatening storm clouds quickly approached—so fast that it looked like dragon smoke—and impossibly bright lightning skewered the sky. The combination of the dread in my chest and the pain in my belly, the destruction all around us, and the roiling clouds made it feel apocalyptic. To add to the feeling, a huge bonfire reached toward the darkening sky. I tried to make sense of the fire, my thoughts muddled. I averted my eyes from the ground, not wanting to see the dead girls, but when I lifted my gaze, I saw my team grinning back at me, and I didn't understand why. Yes, Savvy and Maxine got me out of the hall in time, but—

I saw them. The Celestia sisters, all standing in a crowd of dirty white tunics like a choir stuck in a war zone. They were scared and weeping, but they were alive. The explosion, the bonfire. I would learn later that Apollo, at the behest of Abigail and Dusty, had quickly relieved the girls of their watches and thrown them into a pile. Black had tapped the kill switch just as the final watch was artfully taken off the last girl's wrist.

They're alive, I told myself. *They're alive.* My dread dissipated, especially when I saw that all my friends were there and unharmed. I hadn't understood their grins before, but now I had one of my own. Apollo had begun the portal spell as soon as he had seen Savvy and me escape what was left of the hall, and as I reached them, the girls were already stepping through the shimmering gateway. I felt a cold slimy fish in my palm and flinched, but I needn't have. It was Nilve SaltySnap holding my hand. The lawn was black, as if killed by frost, and the trees and plants were dark and skeletal. A monochrome dystopia, apart from the warm hues of the bonfire and the swirling blue magic of the portal.

The girls were all through, so it was time for the rest of us to go. Savvy still had her back to the team, arrow aimed at the wreckage that entombed Lilian Black's body. I turned to look at the destroyed stage just in time to see the vampire stand up. The destruction of the plants had weakened my magic, so the healing spell I had used on her had snapped. I knew she was still dying because the pocket realm continued crumbling around us. The school building was in ruins, and the few parts that still stood hurtled down as we looked at them.

Everyone was through the portal, apart from Apollo, Savvy, and I.

"Come on," I said to Savannah, but it was like she didn't hear me. She was completely transfixed by the vampire who had just emerged from the wreckage. The vampire who had kidnapped the girls. A lone figure—still elegant, against all odds—with ash and smoke boiling around her.

"Savvy," I said, touching her arm to get her to listen. "Time to go."

"Yes," she murmured. "Time to go."

She walked toward the bonfire where the weaponized watches burned, sparked, and popped, and lit the front of her arrow. Calm and strong, she again took aim at Lilian Black and released the flaming arrow. It sailed through the smoke-scented air and hit the vampire in the chest. Her eyes protruded; her mouth open in a roar as she was engulfed in an instant inferno. Apollo grabbed Savvy and me, breaking our fixation on the deadly fire, and the three of us fell into the shrinking gateway and whirled away as the pocket realm crumbled behind us.

CHAPTER 41

A CURSED TINDERBOX
ASHA

It was a rough landing, but no one seemed to mind. We all lay on the grass like dolls, feeling the firm ground beneath us. We were safe. The feeling of relief and pure joy made the air seem clear— or maybe we could all just breathe properly for the first time in hours. With Shadow Snow finally dispatched to whatever hell she belonged in, and no watches or mind-controlling "supplements" to manipulate the sisters, their trance was broken, and they were disoriented and confused.

I sat up. The pain was gone. "Where are we?" I asked Apollo. My voice was hoarse from the shouting and smoke inhalation.

"You don't recognize it?"

I blinked and looked around. Of course. It was the hockey field of the Copperfield Institute.

"I didn't know where else I could put a hundred girls," he said, and smiled.

I looked into his mismatched eyes. "You know, I wasn't sure about you," I said. "But the directress was right. You're good."

"The directress?" he asked. "I think you're confused. Maybe you hit your head. The directress doesn't know me."

Smiling at him, I could only say, "That's what you think."

I felt Sam's hands on my shoulders and turned to him. We hugged for a long time, then he looked at me with shining eyes. "You did it."

I nodded, and blinked back my tears. "We did it," I said, and we embraced again.

My ritual knife did a good job of cutting through all the cable ties. The girls thanked me and rubbed their wrists where the plastic had chafed their skin. Dusty and Abigail had run to fetch Madame Copperfield, and when I saw her striding toward us in her thick long skirt, her platinum walking stick glinting in the sun, I couldn't help feeling consoled in the way a daughter might feel when seeing her mom after missing her.

"Well," Copperfield said rather breathlessly once she had reached us. "I see your mission was successful."

"It was close," I replied. "But we made it."

The directress nodded, appearing exceptionally pleased. "I knew you would."

"I didn't," I said, and laughed. "It was seriously touch-and-go."

"And you, young man?" she addressed the pickpocket.

"I, er—"

"We couldn't have done it without Apollo," I replied. "He was able to get through all the magical barbed wire and trip switches on the way in. And no one I know could have portaled so many people out."

"Excellent work, all of you." While she wouldn't take any credit for the mission, I could see the pride in her expression at her alumna's success. "I have informed the captain of the Scorpions of the rescue. She has someone phoning parents to fill them in, and is sending various teams over to evaluate the girls."

"Doctors?" I asked.

"Yes. And psychologists specializing in deprogramming."

"Deprogramming?" asked Dusty, who had sidled up to us.

"Helping escapees of a cult, basically," I said. "Healing the damage done by the indoctrination."

"Were they hurt physically?" asked Copperfield in a low voice.

"Not as far as I know," I said. "The Smaragdes were careful to take good care of their fodder."

She nodded, a grim expression creeping onto her face.

The matrons arrived with large bags and began erecting gazebos on the field. Sam, Rick, and Apollo helped them while the rescued girls chatted quietly amongst themselves. Half an hour later, the field was abuzz with activity. Ambulances, police vans, mysterious black SUVs. Sirens and flashing lights. Medics rushing about, parents shouting in relief and wonder that their daughters were home, and alive.

While we sat on the field to rest and catch our breath, mulling over the past events, I couldn't help but think of *The Missing Daughters of Evaron*. I relayed the story to Sam.

He shuddered. "Fairy tales beyond the veil are more bone-chilling than ours," he said. "That's a particularly brutal one."

"Copperfield mentioned this story after loaning me the book," I said. "The directress said that we shouldn't be surprised if an evil witch is behind the kidnappings, because it's a centuries-old trope. Of course, she's right."

Sam picked a blade of grass and chewed it. "I'm sensing a 'but.'"

"But people get the morals of stories wrong, you know. Well, not wrong, I guess, but everyone has their own interpretation of the story. They think the only villain is the witch, but it's not one hundred percent true."

"Go on."

"*Jack and the Giant Beanstalk,* for one. Readers are led to believe that it's the big stomping giant who is the villain, but in fact it's Jack who steals from him on multiple occasions, despite having more gold than he can spend, and kills him and destroys his home. Just because the giant likes to recite a rhyme about bones and bread doesn't make him the bad guy."

Sam nodded. "I never liked that story."

"The village of Evaron forced the witch out of the only home she'd ever had, and continued to make her life hell with their pitchforks and flaming torches. She was made to live out her days in total isolation in a dark forest, for Void's sake! She was benevolent until they drove her to evil."

"So, totally understandable then, that she ate some of their children."

"I'm not saying it's okay for witches to eat children. Also, there was no proof that she actually killed them."

"Their bones were found in her hut."

"Wild forest witches will decorate their huts with animal bones and other objects imbued with energy. Mostly for protection. I'm not saying she didn't eat the children—I'm just saying it was not proven. She is the villain of the story, but there is a bigger villain."

"I'm listening."

"In my mind, the true villains are the girls' fathers. They let fear get the best of them. They chained their kids up, for hex sake. The girls were so desperate for freedom yet their pleas were ignored."

"It was to save their lives, though."

"At the expense of their liberty? That was not a deal the girls were willing to make. Their agency was taken away from them, their choice, and it was their own blood who did it. It was fear that caused the trouble. Fear made the villagers drive out the witch and imprison their own daughters."

"And all of this, over a peasant story told to scare children into good behavior and not go into the woods alone."

"Not in my case," I said. "While other parents were trying to keep their kids out of the forest, mine literally left me there."

"You turned out pretty well, though."

"Thank you." *I guess.*

"And you still have all your fingers."

He meant it as a joke, but I had seen witches with half a pinkie finger. It was a constant reminder of freedom for the descendants of the Evaron daughters.

We fetched some bottles of water and chugged them down.

Sam rubbed the small of my back. "Look at all these relieved parents. Does it feel good?"

"Yes," I replied, leaning into him. "Thank you for coming with us."

"I told you that you wouldn't get rid of me so easily." He winked at me and pulled me closer. "What do you say to grabbing some food and a shower?"

"Great idea," chirped Salty. "I'm ravenous."

I chuckled. "You're always ravenous."

"Today I'm extra-ravenous," she said.

"Our mission isn't over yet," I reminded them. We still needed to stop the Realm from descending into chaos. But first, a long hot bath. Food. Coffee.

Savvy and Abigail were also ready to go home.

"You proud of your clever daughter?" I asked Savvy.

If Dusty and Abi hadn't asked Apollo to take the watches off the girls, they'd all be dead.

"Not as proud as I am of my mom," replied Abigail. "Did you *see* her?"

I nodded, and smiled at my best friend. "I thought you'd be rusty with that bow and arrow."

"I've still got it!" Savvy boasted, tongue-in-cheek. "True talent doesn't wither."

She had single-handedly ashed at least a dozen vampire guardians in the hall, never mind delivering the coup de grace to Black at exactly the right moment.

I walked over the field to say goodbye to Captain Morgan.

"You little gem, you," she gushed, and kissed me on the cheek. "When Copperfield called me, I thought it was a prank. No way did you save all the girls."

"Well, it's nice to know you had faith in me," I snarked.

"Getting those girls back was a pipe-dream and everyone knew it. Only you were crazy enough to think you could succeed."

"Wow. You're full of compliments today," I deadpanned.

She laughed and hugged me. Captain Morgan was not a hugger.

"What's happening out there?" I asked, gesturing at the city beyond.

"It's a cursed tinderbox sitting on the edge of a precipice," replied the captain. "Wolves, orcs, vamps, all armed and ready to pounce."

"Anything from Shagar?" I asked.

"Nope. But there is a new Xarlug flag hanging outside the Or'Capone."

"Damn it," I swore. I had hoped she would have come to her senses, especially after hearing about the Smaragde slavery of her people at the factory. "I was really hoping to have her on our side for the final battle."

"Me, too," said Morgan. "The Realm may believe they don't need orcs, but the opposite is true. Orcs can win the war. It's a pity they're not on our side."

CHAPTER 42
IMAGINARY BIRDS
ASHA

Morgan organized transport for us, and soon we had our own blue light brigade of those dark, shiny SUVs careening toward my house. Three black cats greeted us at the door, and I thought I was seeing things until the slinkiest feline stood on her back paws and transformed into Chione.

"Where the hell have you been?" she asked. "Circe and Odysseus don't have kibble."

"I left plenty," I argued, going so far as to point out the half-empty bowl.

"Cats like a *full* bowl," Chione replied.

"Apologies," I said to all three of them, and opened a can of tuna to seek their forgiveness. I drained the brine and shook the stinky shredded fish into two new clean bowls. When Salty began salivating, I opened a can for her, too, and a jar of vegan mayonnaise, which she sniffed suspiciously and treated with caution.

"I'll order food," said Sam, and took out his phone. After a moment I heard him chatting with Ferra, and he promised to collect the food himself and tell her "everything."

Apollo avoided the indifferent gaze of the cats. Chione told me that Rap was still ill. Despite the happy atmosphere, my heart sank.

"Make yourselves at home," I told everyone, and filled the grimalkin in on our progress.

"So, let me get this straight," she said, looking impressed for the first time since I'd known her. "You killed Wilkinson *and* Lilian Black?"

"Technically, Apollo killed the wizard, and Savannah ashed Black. But, yes. They're done. Two down, one to go—and at least we now know where to find her."

"Where?" asked Salty, spraying flakes of fish on the kitchen counter.

"Æterna," I replied.

Apollo spat his coffee out, making Savvy snort in amusement.

Chione rolled her eyes. "Melodramatic much?"

His eyes resembled a nervous guppy's. "Æterna?"

"What?" I asked. "What do you know?"

"Æterna, as in … the mega-corp that owns the coffee and synth blood business?"

"I guess?" I replied. "I don't know much about the holdings of big businesses. But how many Æternas could there be?"

"Shut the front door," he said.

"Are you going to tell us why you're so emotional?" asked Chione. I could tell she found the pickpocket irritating. She was too cool for him.

Apollo smiled, grimaced, then smiled again. "So here's the funny thing," he began. "You know how you're going to break this curse of mine?"

"Ye-e-e-s?" I drawled.

"It looks like you're going to kill two birds with one stone."

Chione got a hungry look in her eye. I should have given her some tuna, too.

Two peas with one fork, I corrected him silently. There was enough violence and brutality in the world without killing imaginary birds with imaginary stones.

"You're saying the high witch ... the owner of Æterna, is the one who cursed you?"

I found it difficult to believe, but I couldn't say why. Perhaps I thought the young man-boy Apollo wasn't important enough to catch the attention of the most powerful witch in the Realm, but I remembered what the directress had said—that he was so important they couldn't allow him into the school. He had to be kept in the dark, and hidden amongst the nonmagical folk.

I took a deep breath, which made Apollo look even more nervous. It was time to have a proper conversation. Savvy handed me a cup of coffee. I thanked her, and turned to Apollo. "It's a good thing you're sitting down."

He scrubbed his hair nervously. "If you're trying to put me at ease, you're not doing a very good job."

Sam cleared his throat. "Okay, you lot. I'm going to the Cog to pick up food. Who's with me?"

No one replied.

"I'll rephrase that," Armstrong said. "Everyone but Asha and Apollo, get in the car now."

I gave him a grateful look, and he winked at me. After some moaning and scraping of chairs, Apollo and I were alone.

His sneakers beat a tattoo on the floor while he looked at me with apprehension. "Why do I get the feeling that you're going to tell me very bad news?"

"It's good and bad," I replied. "What do you know about your parents?"

He scoffed in a bitter way. "Funny you should bring them up."

I wrapped my hands around my mug, grateful for the comforting warmth of the ceramic, and waited for him to go on.

"The last time I was home ... they didn't know I was there because I portaled in. Before I could announce my presence, I heard them arguing."

I nodded for him to go on.

"My parents never argue," he said. "So that was weird, and I paid attention ... and heard what they were fighting about." He stopped tapping his feet, and the silence was deafening. "My mom wanted to tell me the truth, but my dad said it wasn't the right thing to do. That they had promised the Council to keep it a secret. Mom said I deserved to know."

Even though I knew the answer, I asked the question. "To know what?"

My heart went out to him. I could see the knowledge had hurt him deeply. "That they weren't my real parents."

"I'm sorry," I said. "That must have been very difficult to hear."

Like him, I had been guided by well-meaning surrogates, but I had always known that Ferra, Soleil, and Copperfield weren't my real parents. He must have felt betrayed when he learned the truth.

"Don't be too hard on them," I said. "They volunteered to adopt you and keep you safe. They are the good guys."

"But to live a lie like that ... How can I ever trust them again?"

"They had no choice," I replied. "It was the only way to keep you safe."

His forehead creased. "From what?"

"From *who*," I replied.

I told Apollo what Madame Copperfield had told me. He sat with a gaping mouth, astonished to hear that his parents were talented mages who lost their lives defending the Realm from the Septics during the Starless Time, and that he owed his life to the people who had brought him up, because they had kept him anonymous and safe.

"Until now," I finished. Because it was clear that once the high witch knew who Apollo really was, he'd be dead meat. "Tell me about Æterna."

While I made us another round of coffee, he told me about how Ms. M, the owner of the wildly successful corporation, had hired him to steal the Matahandi book on elixirs, and her vortex of fury when he had refused to return the stubby pencil, which he showed me.

"It's a portal key," he said. "To the banned books library in Blackloth's memory palace."

I finally understood the dead bird in the library, and the rat. RIP.

"She knew I loved animals," he said sadly, "so that's what she took from me."

"How convenient for us," I replied warmly, squeezing his arm, "that the high witch was the one who cursed you."

"Yes." He sat up straight, as if making up his mind to cheer up. "Convenient, indeed."

I took out the Marquis Mirror, and we stared at it for a while.

"How did you know how to get it out of the painting?" I asked.

"I told you, I spent a lot of time in that library," he said.

"But how did you actually *do* it?"

Apollo's cheeks reddened, and he shrugged. "Good luck, I guess."

I gazed at him for a while, trying to figure him out. "You may be a good thief, Apollo, but you're a terrible liar."

CHAPTER 43

SILVER SPARKS IN THEIR SKIN

ASHA

"All right," he said, clearing his throat. "So there was this theory put forward in one of the books—"

"A theory," I said, feeling my own cheeks redden, for different reasons. "You risked the Realm on a *theory?*"

"It's not like we had much choice, remember?"

That was true. I suddenly felt exhausted, and found myself fervently wishing we hadn't emptied all the gin down the drain.

Apollo must have seen my expression, because he quickly explained himself. "So this book. It said that if someone ..." He trailed off.

Feeling impatient now, I was a little snappy. "Yes?"

"I don't know how to explain it, because I'm obviously not pure of heart."

"Wait, what? Pure of heart?"

His face was redder than ever. "I know, right? Impossible, really, given my … checkered past."

"Not impossible," I said, as the realization dawned on me.

He looked at me for an explanation.

"It doesn't matter what you've done."

"I don't follow."

"Nothing can reverse your purity."

"Now I *really* don't follow."

Puritas antedecit. Purity above all. Except that Lilian Black had got it all wrong. The "purity" of the girls she bled did not translate into better-quality serums. But the purity of the person who would put an end to Ms. M's elixir empire did matter, because it was inviolable and irreversible. This kind of purity didn't come from one man's actions, but from the gift he inherited when his mage parents sacrificed their lives to save the Realm. Apollo's real parents had guaranteed him a pure heart always, and now he was given the chance to live up to that, and to continue the legacy they had left him.

"How did you know?" I asked. "How did you figure out that you were pure of heart?"

"The book said if you can make silver fire …" He trailed off again. "And the spell Virvaris put on the painting called for silver fire for that reason. He used ancient magic to make sure that no evil person—or even a morally gray person—would be able to remove it. I quote, but not verbatim: *only a person with silver sparks in their skin is able to say they're truly without sin.*"

"Shadow Snow thought she could use the purity of the innocent girls to lend potency to the serums, but she was wrong. She didn't know what real purity was. But you have it."

Apollo shook his head. "I don't deserve it."

"It's not about what you deserve," I replied. "It's what you were given by your folks."

His chest swelled, his nostrils flared. "I'm going to make them proud. Well, you know what I mean. I'm going to live up to it."

"And I'm going to help you," I said.

•   •   •

Apollo and Asha.

The cursed and the cursebreaker.

The pure of heart and the one who corrupts hearts.

We heard the car pull up.

"We'll eat and get some rest," I said, getting up. "And tomorrow we'll save the Realm."

I hoped I had enough coffee in the house.

CHAPTER 44
FAR FROM PERFECT
ASHA

Sam and the others arrived with a veritable feast the likes of which only Ferra could supply. A whole roast chicken for Nilve, various roast meats, spuds and veg for the others, with a truly delicious gravy, and the most beautiful, comforting vegan lasagna I had ever tasted. The biggest, greenest, crunchiest salad with a fresh herb and black pepper balsamic vinaigrette cut through the creaminess of the pasta, and I had three helpings of it while Sam looked on approvingly. It looked like it was too much food, but Rick and Salty easily hoovered up all the leftovers. I would never know how goblins managed to eat their own body weight in carbs, but it was a trait I admired. My dwarf fairy godmother had even included a brand-new crossbow for Savvy, a note for me, and a bag of spice cookies.

Dear Rookie,

I knew you could save those girls, and you did it!

I've never been prouder.

Ferra

The simple note made me feel ridiculously emotional. I would remember those eighteen words forever. It was the closest I'd ever been to having made a parent proud. Of course, my immediate reaction had been to say that it wasn't just me, and I couldn't have done it without my team—which was one hundred percent true—but something in her note made me spend a moment thinking of the role *I* had played and an unusual warmth bloomed in my chest.

So this is what it feels like, I thought, *to make a mother proud.*

It meant everything to me. I looked over at Abigail and Dusty, misty-eyed, and promised myself to make sure they always knew how much I loved them, and how proud I was.

While the others ate dessert—a marvelous cobbler made of homegrown peaches with vanilla bean ice cream—I went to sit outside in my jungle garden with Jemima. I sat on the damp grass with a bowl of salad greens I'd saved for her to peck at. Once she had her fill, I put her on my lap like a cat, stroked her, and wondered how poor Rap was. I told Jemima that I'd get her some new friends once the war was over. Perhaps some baby chicks—I loved tending the little peepers, and it would be good to have some fresh young ones in the house after all the death and destruction we had seen. I would never be able to have my own biological children, but that didn't mean I couldn't have babies of the furred and feathered variety. And of course there was Dusty, who I had, in my mind anyway, already adopted. I didn't need the legal papers, I just wanted to be the mother to Dusty that neither of us had ever had.

Sam ambled out into the garden after I had been there a while, his face lit up by the fairy lights. He had two tumblers of aromatic whisky, and he handed me one. He held a finger to his lips—a suggestion to not tell Savvy that he had saved a bottle of something-something and kept it well hidden. Jemima the hen decided three was a crowd, so she hopped off my lap and went into the coop to perch. Sam sat down next to me, handed me a glass, and chinked his to mine.

"As if I could love you any more," I said. "Stop being so bloody perfect."

Armstrong chuckled. "I'm far from perfect."

"He lies!" I told the sky. "At least he lies."

"In which case, I'm not perfect," he reasoned, to which I had no rejoinder, witty or otherwise. "How are you feeling?"

"Tired," I answered. "Dirty. Grateful."

"Same," he said. "I've run you a bath. I was going to light some candles, but I didn't know which ones to use. I didn't want to inadvertently cast a spell."

I laughed. "Didn't want to turn yourself into a frog?"

"Or worse."

I nodded. There were certainly worse things in life than being turned amphibian.

Sam didn't laugh.

"What is it?" I asked.

"Nothing. I just wanted to tell you how proud I am of you, but I don't know how to say it without sounding patronizing."

"Thanks," I said. "And thanks for not leaving when I asked you to."

We spent a quiet moment drinking our whisky.

"You're an amazing woman, Asha Viridian Rook."

I laughed, but Sam remained serious. He took my hand and touched the ring he had given me before kissing my palm.

"Let's get into that bath," he said. "And then I'm taking you to bed."

CHAPTER 45

PROMISE OF SOLACE

ASHA

I woke up happy. Yes, I was also scared, nervy, and bruised, but I couldn't help being in a good mood. Dinner the night before had been wonderful, and spending quality time with Sam had healed and restored my body and psyche in a way I hadn't known was possible. If it had been my last night on this earth, it had been a night well spent.

We'd had a deep rest and we had a plan. I was ready for it.

I let Sam sleep in while I stole downstairs to make tea. Dusty and Abigail were still fast asleep on the couches in the lounge. Always the protector, Rick had chosen a mattress on the floor nearby. Salty had slid down the wingback and was half on, half off, and snoring like a rusted chainsaw. I heard movement behind Savvy's closed door, assumed she was awake, so took two mugs out of the cupboard while the kettle boiled. I yawned and looked at the kitchen. The guys had cleaned up, but there was still evidence of their dinner dotted around the room—a pile of unused paper napkins, salt and pepper grinders on the counter, and soggy paper cartons crowding the trash can. I had lived alone for so long that I still found it strange to have so many people in my house. I loved being alone in my own space, but I had to admit to myself that having friends there was a really good feeling. I had grown up lonely, so I guess it made sense.

When the tea was ready, I took it to the guest room where Savvy had been staying and knocked gently. "You awake in there?"

The movement inside the room stopped.

"Savvy? Are you okay?" I asked.

"Er ... yes," she replied. "I am okay!" She didn't open the door.

It was a weird response, but who was I to judge? "I'm leaving tea here for you," I said.

"Thanks," she said. Only when I heard a muffled giggle did I figure out that she was not alone in there. It looked like I wasn't the only one who had some healing work done last night.

I went outside into my jungle, said good morning to Jemima and the ducks, tried to avoid looking at the mound of earth topped with its blessed stone, and sat on the bench with my tea. I pulled out my phone—now stripped of its spyware—to check the blizzard of messages I had received. When I was still getting used to my blurry vision I increased the font size to make for easier reading, but I found I could reduce it now with no problem. It looked like the magical monocle and I were getting used to each other. It was such a relief to be able to see, especially when I thought I'd be blind forever.

The tea was warm and comforting in the cool morning breeze. I looked up at the leaves above me and watched them whispering. I breathed in their freshness, their green energy, their promise of solace in a chaotic world. In Japan they call this "forest bathing"—so perhaps I was jungle-bathing to the soundtrack of the fluttering leaves and occasional quacking of the pekins. Hearing, sight, health, fertility, mobility, magic, love ... all the things we take for granted until they're taken away.

"Thank you, Void," I breathed. "For your many blessings."

It may have been coincidence, but the breeze picked up for a moment as if in response. I watched the dappled light on the ground moving—Mother Nature's disco lights—and felt completely supported by the earth and its protection and gifts. I surrendered to the wholesome bliss I felt flowing through my body, so different from the magic I was used to, which was at its most powerful when I was angry or afraid. I closed my eyes and tried to remember the feeling. I would need it later.

Once I had bonded with the leaves, breeze, soil, and sunlight I felt restored in a new way. The mission ahead, while most probably fatal, seemed less impossible to me. I had great people, I had my magic, and the Void had my back. Jemima clucked in agreement. Or perhaps she was just delighted to find a blackberry revealed by the disco lights.

Returning my attention to the phone, I first saw a message from Merlin.

Rookie! Sorry I haven't popped by. Word on the street is you've been through hell. I'm tied up at work right now but will make a plan to see you ASAP. I won't forget the hot chocolate for the wizardling! If you need me, I'll bunk my lectures and come straight over. Let me know!

The avuncular mycologist was definitely one of earth's blessings.

I replied *Thank you Papa Smurf*, and added a mushroom and a heart emoji. He came online and began typing.

Just checking that you still have your amulet?

At first I thought he meant Lilian Black's protection amulet, but he meant my cyanide tooth—the vial of mushroom poison I kept on my necklace. My way out if things got too bad. He had made it for me: the essence of Death Cap.

I do, I typed. *Thank you.*

He gave me an emoji thumbs-up. *Take care, Rookie. See you soon.*

Next was a message from Captain Morgan. *All the girls you brought home have been reunited with their insanely grateful parents and caregivers. They'll all undergo intensive therapy and deprogramming. Ya did GOOD.*

That's why you pay me the big bucks, I replied, which was kind of a running joke between us, because the free-lance fee I was paid by the Scorpions was peanuts. But then I remembered I actually *was* paid big bucks by the Chalices, so the quip was less funny.

Come in when you can to get your gifts from the parents before my hay fever kills me.

What now? I replied.

I obviously didn't give them your home address, but they insisted on buying you things. My office looks like a florist shop.

Oh! I really hadn't expected any gifts.

I may have eaten a few boxes of chocolates, she went on. *Because you're vegan. I was doing you a favor. Good quality merch.*

Eat as many as you want, I typed. *And please hand the rest out to your staff.*

Don't you want some of it? Supply lines are dicey because of the conflicts. There may be a shortage of wine and chocolate soon. There's a veritable mountain of treats here, including some good gin.

I remembered Sam pouring my gin down the sink to protect Savvy. *Keep a bottle for us. We'll drink it together when the war is over.*

It may be well-aged gin by then, she replied.

Good. It'll match our well-aged spirits.

Done, she promised.

The rest of the messages were a bizarre mix of thanks, well wishes, government warnings to stay indoors, and a little spam. I took my last sip of tea, put the device away and stood, ready to begin the day.

CHAPTER 46

POLLEN AND PERFUME

ASHA

I could smell the coffee before I entered the kitchen.

Sam looked up at me, his face still furrowed by sleep. "I'm making coffee," he said, unnecessarily.

I kissed him, kind of wishing we were back in bed. "I couldn't love you more if I tried."

"Try harder," he said, and grinned.

The aroma of the coffee seemed to crack the hibernation of the others, and they staggered into the kitchen looking for their share. Apollo ambled in with the mug I had left for Savvy, and I gave him a knowing wink. He blushed and avoided eye contact.

We gathered around the kitchen island, perching on barstools and leaning against walls. I noticed there were still some glints of the shattered glass underfoot from Garret's attack.

"Right, boss," said Rick. "What's the plan?"

"We're off to kill the wizard," piped up Salty. "I mean, the witch. The high witch."

"Correct," I replied. "Apollo says she goes by the name of Ms. M."

"Ms. M sounds like a Skippy shop milkshake brand," said the goblin, and Apollo agreed.

What flavor would she be, I wondered. Evil Elderberry? Vanilli-Villaini? Killer Kiwi? Or Felonious Fruit Punch – the flavor that's always in stock but that no one wants.

"Where does this witch live?" asked Sam.

Apollo shrugged. "I only saw her at work."

"Which is where she'll be," I guessed. "She's a billionaire running the biggest corporation in the country. She probably lives in her office."

"The biggest corporation in the country?" asked Sam. "And how are we planning on getting in there? The security will be iron-clad."

"Luckily, I have some friends who know about security protocols," I replied with a grin. "They'll meet us there."

"Where?" asked Rick. "Where does this Ms. M work? I'm assuming it's going to be a booby-trapped old castle in some dark, hard-to-find pocket realm?"

"Nope," replied Apollo, cheerfully. "It's here in the Realm. A fifteen-minute drive."

Sam frowned. "Say that again?"

"Sandton," I replied.

Sam did a double take. "Sandton? Are you sure?"

Sandton is the richest square mile in Africa. It's known for its constant construction, deep pockets, bling, luxury sedans, and diamonds—not villainous witches brewing illegal elixirs.

Hidden in plain sight.

"Apollo's been in her skyscraper," I said.

"The penthouse," he added.

"You've *met* the high witch," said Rick. "And you didn't think to mention it to us as soon as we met?"

"I didn't know," Apollo replied. "I didn't know she was the high witch. I didn't know about Celestia. I thought

Ms. M was just a regular morally corrupt billionaire witch."

"Understandable," I said.

"Is it?" Apollo asked, grimacing. "I mean, I saw first-hand how cruel she was. I should have guessed that I wasn't the only recipient of her brutality. But I couldn't report her to the Council because of my involvement in the theft of the Matahandi book."

"How did you find her?" asked Sam.

Apollo shrugged. "I didn't. She found me via my ... business associate."

I guffawed. Calling Skippy a business associate was like calling the high-heeled lady across the road his PR manager. He shot me a look and I had to bite my lips to stop laughing.

"So, does she know?" asked Salty. "That you're, you know, important?"

"I doubt it," I mused. "Or she would have killed him instead of cursing him."

We poured more coffee.

"Let me get this straight," said Savvy, whose hair was more tousled than usual. "We're just going to walk right into the lair of the most dangerous person in the Realm?"

Everyone looked at her, nodded, and murmured in the affirmative.

"Yes."

"Yep."

"Sounds about right."

Savvy gave me an unimpressed look. "You know that's not going to work, right? She's going to be up to her eyeballs in security. And not just any kind of security—billionaire magitech security."

"I know," I replied. "But look at what happened at Charybdis, at Obsidian Castle, at the ghost town. Every time we set out, we thought it would be a losing battle, and every time we won. Sometimes you just need to trust the Void."

"Trust the Void?" she spluttered. "The same Void that took my daughter?"

"The Void didn't take your daughter," I said gently. "A vampire did."

She crossed her arms and gave me a hard stare.

"Or maybe," I ventured, "if you can't trust the Void, you could trust me?"

Savvy uncrossed her arms. "Oh, Asha, of course I trust you."

"Good," I replied. "I'd like you to stay here with the girls while we take care of the high witch."

"No," she said. "Nope. No way."

"I need them to be safe," I said.

"Then we'll hire a bloody babysitter," she snapped. "Because I'm coming with you. I'm fighting by your side."

Apollo was obviously on Savvy's side. "You saw her with that bow and arrow."

I did. And she was kick-ass. But I needed my best friend to be safe. Having a good team made me stronger, but having people I loved too much with me would be a weakness on the battlefield. Or in the penthouse, or wherever we would face off with the high witch.

"Sorry, Asha, but it's not your decision," said Savannah.

"It *is* Asha's decision," said Rick. "She's our leader."

"And it's my body," Savvy retorted. "And *I* decide what I do with it."

Rick's mouth turned down at the edges as he nodded. *Fair enough,* he seemed to be saying.

"Are we portaling in?" asked Salty.

Apollo shook his head. "Unfortunately not. After last time, Ms. M barred me."

The goblin sat up straight. "Barred you?"

"Blocked my gateway magic," he explained. "She didn't want me coming back to the Æterna premises."

"What about Salty?" asked Sam. "She's great at gateway magic."

Nilve gave him a look of pure adoration.

"We need to reserve her portal energy," I said. "In case we get into a tight spot and need to escape."

"But Apollo could do that," said Rick, and was met with a sad silence. Judging by his next expression, I think he realized there was no guaranteeing anyone would survive this mission, so counting on only one person to get us out was too risky.

My phone buzzed. Thinking it might be important, I looked at the latest message. It was a voicemail from Captain Morgan. I excused myself to listen.

"I gave away everything in the office," she said. "Every flower arrangement, every teddy bear, every chocolate, every bottle of wine. Cleared the whole place out. I went to grab a coffee with the leprechaun. I came back to my office and ... you guessed it! It's full again! I have zero desk space and a nose that won't stop running. The office is literally overflowing with blooms. It's like a pretty version of the little shop of horrors, but instead of wanting to eat me, it wants to suffocate me with color. And pollen, and perfume. Send help."

I decided I'd respond later. Perhaps she could donate it all to a hospital, and pick up a box of antihistamines on the way out.

I slipped my phone into my pocket to join my other devices, magical and otherwise.

"Okay, team," I said. "It's time."

CHAPTER 47

HOPE EVERYONE IS WEARING THEIR LUCKY UNDERPANTS

ASHA

The doorbell rang, and I ran outside to the pedestrian gate to see who it was. I could smell smoke in the air. I was hoping the visitor was Chione with good news about Rap, but when I saw who it was, I wasn't disappointed.

"Merlin!" I said, hugging him. "We've got the team together inside; would you like to come in?"

"I'm on my way somewhere," he said. "But I wanted to give you something."

Merlin adjusted his round glasses and looked down at his car keys. He spun the steel ring around and removed the fob—a cute toadstool keyring—and placed it in my hand. He looked into my eyes without blinking. "Use this," he said. "Whenever you need me, no matter what, you can summon me with this. Do you understand?"

I nodded. I appreciated the gesture, but there was no way I was going to bring Papa Smurf into battle.

"Rookie," he said in a stern voice. "It's not an *if* you need me, it's a *when*. I'll be ready and waiting." He tipped his mushroom leather hat. "Oh, and I'll come back in a little while to look after the girls, if you want."

"Thank you," I said through the lump in my throat. "For this, and for always being there for me."

For being my surrogate father.

"You've got your Death Cap," he checked, looking at the vial around my neck. "Good. I'll bring the antidote when you summon me—just in case."

I nodded. He clasped my hands and we took a deep breath together. We hugged again and he jumped into his little car and tooted cheerfully as he drove off.

The team began spilling out of the house. I put the toad-stool keyring into the same cloak pocket as the Traitor's Doom seed. Savvy gripped her new crossbow, and Apollo had the Marquis Mirror in his backpack.

Rick jingled his car keys in his hand. "It's not pretty out there. Just a warning."

"What's it like?" Apollo asked.

"Yesterday was bad. Today will be worse."

"That's not very helpful," he replied.

"You want details?" Rick asked. "Remember the Hammerskin coup?"

We all nodded.

"It's pretty much the same as that. Tanks and trucks rumbling over the highways, soldiers with automatic weapons on every corner. The bombs are the worst. They come out of nowhere."

"Bombs!" said Salty. "Who is shelling?"

"Xarlugs. They're more aggressive than ever. It's like they've been given instructions to destroy every part of the Realm."

"Only because the Smaragde clan have instructed it," I said. "Once we take the high witch out, the rest of the system will crumble."

"And they know that," Savvy said. "So they're not going to let us get anywhere near her."

I nodded. "I never said it was going to be easy."

We piled into the monster truck. I gave the incense-smoking Hanuman a wink.

"Everyone got everything?" I asked, kind of hoping that we'd have to wait for someone to go back inside. I was more nervous than I realized. "Hope everyone's wearing their lucky underpants."

My street did not yet look like a war zone, but judging by the helicopters flying over, I was sure that the city was in bad shape. There was smoke in the distance.

Rick switched on the radio.

"... government warns citizens to stay at home if at all possible, and not to panic. If you do venture out, please do not buy more than you need. Think of your fellow citizens."

"*Ja*, that's not going to work," said Salty. "They'll start looting soon."

The news anchor continued. "... There have been reports of arson and looting ..."

"Ha," crowed the goblin. "Humans are so predictable."

"And goblins aren't?" asked Rick.

"I never said that," replied Nilve.

"War brings out the worst in everyone," I said.

"Not everyone," said Sam, and held my hand.

The neighborhoods closest to my house were eerily quiet, but as we approached Sandton it grew busy, and there was a manic feel in the air. People were waiting for something big to happen. We were able to get within three blocks of the Æterna building before being gridlocked. Rick parked on a sidewalk and we climbed out. We threaded through the honking cars and minibus taxis. Hawkers, apparently not put off by the threat of war, still sidled up to cars to sell mobile phone chargers, cold drinks, and neon toys for kids. Lycra-clad cyclists still zipped along. I shook my head. *What a strange thing it is to be alive at times like this.*

A loud blast quaked the ground. We all exclaimed and covered our ears. Rick wasn't wrong about the bombs. Once the asphalt stopped shuddering, we looked at each other, dumbfounded.

"Hey," called a skinhead orc in a black uniform. "You're not supposed to be here."

It was not the first time I'd heard that phrase, and I'm pretty sure it wouldn't be the last.

"Yes, Officer," I said, and kept my gaze down. Apollo also avoided eye contact. We backed off, only to walk around the block and try again. This time we got past the first Xarlug agent, and the second, but it was soon clear that the skyscraper was surrounded all around the base by an army five orcs deep. When we looked up, we saw an additional band of guards on a ledge. Vampires.

"This was expected," I said, more to myself than anyone else.

The black-clothed skinhead faction threatened people with their AK-47s and tried to disperse the traffic. We edged around the building, trying to stay together and out of sight. I was worried when I couldn't spot what I was looking for, but soon it appeared. A brand-new delivery truck painted red and branded with the Platelet logo.

"There it is," I told the team. We scurried over. I banged on the back of the van and heard it unlock. Rick opened the vehicle's double doors and we climbed inside.

"Hi, Halfpint," I said. "Thank you so much for helping us today."

The dwarf smiled. "No problem, Asha."

The tinted screen that separated us from the driver turned transparent, and I saw that Agreement was driving. "Howzit, A.G.?"

She nodded curtly and rolled the screen down. I introduced my team and they all greeted each other.

"According to my calculations," Agreement said crisply, "we'll be snail-pacing for the next half a kilometer to the entrance. It should take around thirteen minutes."

"Perfect," replied Halfpint. "It gives us exactly the right amount of time to prepare." He rubbed his hands together.

"What have you got?" I asked as he dragged a large duffel bag out from under the bench he was sitting on.

The dwarf grinned and zipped it open.

"It's beginning to feel a lot like Christmas," sang Salty.

He took out a Xarlug uniform for Rick, replete with automatic weapon accessories, and red overalls for the rest of us. Savvy complained that there was no waistline on hers, and Salty that hers was too big, but in a kind of tongue-in-cheek way, so the dwarf did not seem offended. I didn't want to go in without my cloak, so I made it invisible and wore it over my overalls.

Another nearby blast rocked the van. Salty swore in goblin vernacular, which was a certain kind of talent and got her impressed looks from us all.

"Now," said Halfpint. "May I have your monocle? I've been itching to see it."

"It doesn't come off," I said. "It fused as soon as I put it on."

"Incredible," he said, peering at me. "Well, I suppose I can do it while it's attached."

"Do what?" asked Sam, immediately protective.

"Just a quick upgrade," I assured him. "Nothing major."

I scooched up, getting nearer to the dwarf. Halfpint already had his miniature toolkit open. He took out what looked like an eyeshadow clamshell and opened it, revealing a contact lens. With a tiny pair of tweezers he picked the lens up and lifted it to my monocle.

We all exclaimed as the van lurched forward, causing him almost to drop it.

"Sorry," called Agreement from the front.

"Gearsplitter," cursed the dwarf under his breath. He steadied himself and tried again. This time as soon as he brought the lens close, it whipped onto my eyeglass like a magnet. I gasped, but it didn't hurt.

"You okay?" he asked.

"Yes," I replied. "I was just surprised."

"Does it feel any different?"

I blinked and looked around. "Not yet."

He nodded. "Good."

Halfpint handed out contact lenses to the rest of the team.

"Why do we get lenses?" asked Apollo.

"Biometric security," said Agreement. "You'll get matching fingerprints, too."

We peeled the 3D-printed thumbprints off the cards we were given and stuck them onto our thumb pads.

Halfpint looked us all up and down in satisfied approval. "Luckily, the hiring policy of Æterna is progressive. They have a multi-species quota to fulfill—a fair ratio of orcs, goblins, and dwarfs—so you shouldn't stick out too much."

We reached the delivery entrance perfectly on schedule, and Agreement used her own false biometrics to get through the boom. They dropped us off at the elevator and wished us luck.

"I'm so grateful," I told Halfpint and Agreement. "I owe you."

"Nonsense," Halfpint replied. "This is the most exciting day I've had in ages!"

"We're in," murmured Salty, as if she were not expecting the plan to work at all.

"I told you I had clever friends," I replied, nudging her.

It was a surreal moment, standing in the dim depot, everyone but Rick dressed in red. It reminded me of the heartless "red ants" that the cops used to demolish shacks in informal settlements. I hoped we would demolish this entire corporation.

The offloading depot was crammed with boxes, and I could smell the coffee beans destined for the Platelet café on the ground floor that Apollo had told us about. The biometric security on the elevator button recognized my silicone thumbprint and soon the door pinged open. We planned to bypass the restaurant and take the elevator as high as it would let us go.

I stared at myself in the mirror of the service elevator as we ascended, noticing how I had changed over the past weeks. I was more muscular, and more scarred. I had a gray streak highlighting my hair. Of course, the monocle was the most obvious modification. In the beginning, I didn't like seeing it in the mirror—it reminded me of what I had lost—but it was growing on me. Without it, I'd be in darkness forever, and not able to fulfill my duty to the Realm. I saw it now not as a trigger for remembering my trauma, but a magical artifact to be grateful for. Add to the mix Halfpint's upgrade, and the eyepiece became an extra tool to help me track down the high witch.

Our elevator shuddered, and I wasn't sure if it was another blast outside, or just a wobbly lift.

No one spoke. The door pinged again, and we exited onto level sixty-six.

The workspace was deserted. Open-concept offices revealed empty chairs and half-drunk cups of coffee. It was clear they weren't on a day off—they had been evacuated.

"We already guessed she knew we were coming," I said. "What we don't know is which kinds of traps she's set."

"How do we know if she's even here?" asked Salty. "If I were her, I'd be on a tropical island somewhere, not holed up in a skyscraper amidst a civil war."

"Me too," I replied. "That's the difference between people like us and people like her."

The goblin looked perplexed. "She doesn't like coconuts and rum?"

"She likes power and wealth more. Besides, I know she's here. I can't explain it, but I can ... feel it." Perhaps she was giving off some kind of evil energy, like radiation.

The service elevators only went up to floor sixty-six. "What floor is the penthouse?"

Apollo shrugged. "I don't remember. I was a bit dazed by the wealth on display and the utter scope of the building. Remember, I didn't know what I was getting myself into when I arrived."

"Fair enough," said Rick, looking restless. "Shall we risk the main elevator, or take the stairs?"

"Stairs are probably safer," I replied, and saw Salty slump.

"You forget that goblin legs are short," she whined. "I can't climb all those stairs. I'll die!"

"Come on," said Rick, offering her a hand, and within seconds Salty was sitting on his shoulders as if they were at a Grateful Undead concert. Savvy used her contact lens and silicone print to open the door to the fire escape, and gave us a thumbs-up.

"How do you know those security people, anyway?" She asked me. "The woman and the dwarf?"

"It's a long story," I said. "I'll fill you in when we next frolic."

We made our way up four flights of stairs before having to rest. After the next three, the stairs came to an end.

"It's been walled off," said Sam, inspecting the wall with his fingers.

I sighed. My legs were burning. "Of course it has."

We all nodded grimly. Rick swung Salty off his shoulders, which she didn't look happy about. It was time to face whatever hellscape the high witch had planned for us. We had no idea what was waiting for us on the other side of the door on level seventy-three. Savvy put her hand on the handle, ready to push it open.

"Hang on," I told her. I focused on the door, and nothing happened. I understood my mistake and attempted to focus on what was past the door. *"Monstras,"* I whispered. *Reveal.* My vision turned cyan, and then blue, as if had downloaded a TikTok filter. I tried to blink past the color to see better, but the door turned semi-translucent, enabling me to see past both the cold tint and the door. I was delighted by my newfound X-ray vision, but not at what I saw beyond.

Adrenaline flooded my already tense body. "Holy Hecate."

CHAPTER 49
BLAST CHAK GA GRUM
ASHA

"What is it?" asked Sam.

When I didn't answer immediately, Salty piped up. "I'm guessing it's not good news."

I exhaled with force and shook my head.

"It's a whole hexing army," I said. "The worst kind." Beyond the door stood no fewer than fifty heavily armed skinhead soldiers. There were five of us.

"Rick," I said. He turned to me, awaiting instructions. I took out my wand. "Forgive me."

I pointed it at his hair. *"Caput capillus rumpis."* Destroy.

The orc stood stoically as his hair fell out and turned to dust before it hit the floor. Salty sneezed.

"It'll grow back," I said, hoping it was true. Orcs had notoriously hideous hair, but Rick took good care of his and had the best orc locks I had seen. If he minded, he didn't show it. He steadied himself and pushed carefully through the door and joined the army on the other side. My blue filter faded.

"Now what?" whispered Savvy.

"I don't know," I replied. "We're winging it until we find her."

"It's not the best plan we've ever had," said Salty.

Five minutes later, Rick was back, and exceedingly cheerful. "So, they've been given orders to shoot first and ask questions later."

"Good to know," quipped Sam.

I narrowed my eyes at Rick. "Then why are you grinning like that?"

"Because they're not real."

"What now?" asked Savvy.

"It's a conjuring trick," he said. "Watch this."

Without telling us more, he flung open the door again and marched through, leaving us exposed. Had he lost his mind along with his hair?

We stood back, frozen. The sheer volume of firepower in the Xarlug hands was enough to take out a small town.

"Come on," Rick called, gesturing for us to follow. "It's an illusion." When we still didn't move, he said again, "It's not real."

"The guns look pretty damn real to me," murmured the goblin.

Rick chuckled at our reticence. "Okay, I'll prove it to you."

Alarmed, I shook my head. "No!"

"Oh Na-zi-s," Rick cooed. "You're so ugly, your momma had to tie a pork chop around your neck so the dogs would play with you!"

I braced for an attack.

The Xarlug soldiers, however, ignored Rick, and carried on with their chatting, smoking, and card-playing.

"Xarlugs!" said Rick, emboldened. "You're so ugly your momma had to turn off the lights to breastfeed you!"

Salty snorted.

"Okay," I said, still nervous. "You've made your point."

We filed through the entrance toward Rick. Being surrounded by soldiers was nerve-racking, even if it was just an illusion.

"Don't get too cocky," said Savvy. "This looks more like a projection than a conjuration to me."

We all looked at her for an explanation.

"The details," she said, pointing out a cigarette pack with a design was so precise it looked one hundred percent real. She indicated an untied shoelace of a boot, and the chin of an orc with a small shaving nick. "They're too realistic. It would take months to conjure up so many men at this level, and an enormous amount of magic."

"So you're saying they *are* real," I replied. "They're just not on this floor. Their image is being projected here."

She nodded, still inspecting the scene. "It's a lot easier and efficient to project what already exists."

"Pork chop," sniggered Salty. "Good one."

"Why would Ms. M do this?" asked Sam. "Why not just put the real soldiers here?"

"She's trying to scare us," I said. "Trying to put us off advancing any further."

"Almost like a warning," added Rick. "In 3D technicolor."

"Well, it's working," said Savvy. "If this is what awaits us up there, we're dead."

"Not necessarily," I replied, with more optimism than I felt. Turning to face Rick, I said, "We've taken out more than a hundred orcs before, right?"

"Right," he said. "But that entailed a phoenix feather bomb that took out the Charybdis Harbour and half of the SubRealm. Do you have any explosives on you?"

I patted my cloak pockets as I scoured my brain for an idea. "Nope."

"Why did you say that about shooting first and asking questions later?" asked Savvy. "If you didn't talk to them?"

"It's engraved on their AK-47s," he said, and showed us the clumsily etched slogan. I assumed it was in pidgin Orcish. *"Blast chak ga grum,"* he read. "Directly translated it says, 'Blast, then ask.'"

"Charming," she replied.

"We could use this to our advantage," I said. "If this is the army that we'll face, any intel we can gain now can help us. There are about fifty or sixty of them, right, and six of us. So if we can each take out around ten soldiers each, we'll be fine."

"Ten?!" exclaimed Salty in a high-pitched voice. "Have you seen the size of them?" She walked up to an orc to illustrate her point. At her full height, she came up to the orc's black utility belt.

"Some of us will be able to take on more than others," I acknowledged. "Just do your best."

"Do my best? *Blast chak ga grum!* I'm a dead goblin walking! I wish I could still turn invisible."

"You can," I said, and pointed my wand at her.

She put up her hands as if afraid it would hurt. "Ow!" she yelled, before I'd even cast the spell.

"*Invisibilis factus,*" I uttered, and she shimmered into water and mostly disappeared. "Hang on. I can still see a hint of you."

"We can't," said Savvy. "It must be your fancy new lens."

"Oh, good," I replied, returning my gaze to the goblin. "That means I can keep an eye on you."

"I'll cause as much havoc as I can," Salty promised.

"What else can we learn?" asked Sam, looking closely at a particularly large Xarlug specimen. "Presumably they have ammo in their backpacks. A handgun in their holsters. There's something small in their shirt pockets, top right. They all seem have it."

I joined him to look. There was indeed something in there, a very slight bulge in the fabric, but what it was, was anyone's guess. "I suppose we'll find out soon enough."

CHAPTER 50
ELECTRIC WAND
ASHA

We had no option but to the take the elevator. We argued about it first, that it was a terrible idea and that we may as well use the company's intercom speaker to announce our presence, but no one had a better plan. We argued again about which floor to choose. We weighed up what would be better—fighting enemies one floor at a time, or going straight to the penthouse which we saw on level eighty and risking them all converging on us at the same time. We decided one floor at a time would better our chances of survival.

The next three levels were empty. Level seventy-seven was not.

As soon as the doors opened, we knew we were in deep trouble. The pinging sound the elevator made did not help our cause. As soon as the Xarlug squad saw us, they snapped to attention and opened fire.

Luckily, this wasn't my first rodeo. Magical muscle memory from our battle at Charybdis kicked in.

"Clipeum glaciei!" I shouted, and a wall of ice sprang up to shield us from the bullets. I did it fast enough that only one shot had made it through before the shield was up. It just barely missed Savvy, embedding itself in the metal door above her head. Horrified and angry, my magic grew more powerful. The ice wall thickened and remained sturdy despite the spray of bullets hitting it. Feeling the power of the frost, I knew I had more where that came from. I struck the floor with my wand like Gandalf on the bridge and turned the tiles below to ice. *"Glaciem exquiris!"*

The Xarlugs began slipping and sliding on the new ice rink beneath their feet. Despite losing traction, the orcs kept firing, which led to a couple of own-goal casualties on their side of the insta-winter wonderland.

"Ventum exquiris nix blizzard!" I shouted.

Snow and icy wind pumped through the space, freezing the orcs' hands and faces. I knew that orcs hated the cold. Many dropped their weapons, but those who still had fingers capable of pulling triggers, did. I pushed harder, creating more snow, more wind, more ice, until my own fingers turned blue and I knew I had to stop or lose them to frostbite. I gave Savvy the go-ahead by nodding at her crossbow, and she set to work taking down the orcs who could still fire, using the end of the ice wall for cover after every shot. Rick began mowing down the shivering orcs, and when he ran out of bullets, he picked up a frosty replacement and kept going. Salty, emboldened by Savvy and Rick, scampered around the wall and picked up her own automatic rifle and joined the fray, using her shoes like ice skates and blading like a pro. Her experience as a roller derby skater was paying off. It was a curious sight to behold—an AK-47 gliding through the air at knee height, shooting at anyone who frowned at it.

Our subzero wall held up despite the barrage of bullets. I looked around the edge and saw a gun being lifted by a grounded orc. It was pointed at Rick.

"Fiat fulgur!" I yelled, and an intense current ran through my arm and into the wand, transforming into a bolt of electricity that speared the wounded orc where he lay. He dropped the gun.

Quickly darting behind the wall again, I narrowly missed a retaliatory bullet. No longer able to hold my electric wand with my freezing hand, I cried out and dropped it. Sam scooped it up for me and put it in my pocket, then took my hand and blew warm air into it while I grimaced at the pain.

"You're okay," he said. It was an assurance, not a question. I nodded.

The gale died down, and the snow stopped. As the final dusting of snow fell, the firing stuttered to a halt. We heard a thunderous crack.

"Get back!" I yelled. We retreated just in time to escape the wall falling on us, and landed on our backs and elbows. The massive sheet of ice shattered as it made contact with the floor. One of Savvy's bolts was released and hit the light above us, showering us in thin glass and golden sparks.

"That's a handy trick," said Sam.

"Almost killing the whole team with a giant slab of ice?" I joked. "My talents are numerous."

We helped each other up off the floor. "That they are," he replied.

Still nervous, we cautiously surveyed the space. Rick and Salty stood amongst the dead bodies, a sea of frosted black uniforms. I approached the corpse closest to me and unbuttoned his top pocket. Inside was a vial that I recognized immediately. A flash of anger made me want to smash it on the floor. Hex the Smaragdes, and hex the high witch. Not only were we outnumbered by these savages, but they had an unfair advantage.

"What's that?" asked Savvy, clipping her crossbow onto her back, her cheeks red from exertion.

"The Æternal elixir," I replied. "They've supercharged their army."

My hand was still burning from the frostbite and electric current, but when I flexed my fingers, my hand still seemed to be working okay. I'd switch over to my left for the next attack.

Adrenaline still pumping, I was ready to advance to the next level.

"It's like a computer game," said Salty. "Hope there are gemstones and gold coins waiting for us at the top."

"More like vampires and black magic," I said. And one soon-to-be-dead billionaire witch.

"Good work, team," said Rick, wiping some blood spatter off his neck.

We were about to get into the elevator when we heard boots thundering above us. It got louder. They were marching down the stairs, walled off or not. A bomb went off nearby and rattled the windows. An axe came through the wall.

"Hide!" I said to everyone except Salty. Rick, still in Xarlug uniform, just lay down and played dead. Savvy, Sam, Apollo, and I hid behind a metal storage unit.

The leader of the new wave of Xarlug soldiers was the biggest orc I'd ever seen. I felt my mouth drop open; my heart raced. He must have been chosen for his build, I thought at first, but the others barreled in and they weren't any smaller. Savvy and I looked at each other with wide eyes. This platoon had clearly been taking the elixir for longer than the first lot.

"Cheeses, merry and Josephine," whispered Apollo. I agreed. I could feel my blood thudding. Sparks all over my skin. My power was pushing through my veins.

"They're here," said the leader, and the other savages hawked and spat phlegm on the floor. Their cruel beady eyes searched the massive space. "Find them. Boss Lady wants the witch and the mage alive. You can kill the others."

The soldiers grunted back, not happy with their instructions. They wanted to kill all of us.

Why? I wondered. *Why would she want Apollo and me alive? Didn't it make more sense to execute us before we did any additional damage?* Something was not adding up.

"Six people, Muroth," said one of the soldiers. "Six people did this?" He nudged a dead body with the steel toe of his boot.

"No ordinary people," sneered Muroth. "Powerful people."

"Not as powerful as us," bragged the soldier, opening fire on the dead bodies that carpeted the floor before them. I'm not sure what he was trying to prove. Firing at cadavers—especially cadavers of the men on your team—wasn't the bravest move I'd ever seen. Out of the corner of my eye I saw Rick flinch. I clutched my wand, ready to defend him if they noticed, but they didn't. I heard Apollo exhale in relief.

"Find them," growled Muroth. "Search every corner."

CHAPTER 51

A STUMBLE, A SNEEZE

ASHA

The huge orc comrades marched in and began searching for us. There were around forty of them, from what I could tell. Less than the previous group, but so much larger and vicious-looking.

Forty, I told myself. *We can handle forty. Even with my compromised hand.*

But more tromped in, and more, until the whole floor was filled with despicable greasy orcs turning over tables and smashing cardboard boxes. I raced through our escape options—staying to fight these monsters would be signing our own death warrants.

I could nebulize the team—turn us to vapor and we could rise to the next floor. Or turn everyone invisible and sneak through the destroyed wall of the fire escape.

Both would take a considerable amount of magic, which would leave me with less for the final showdown. Then again, if we didn't survive this, there wouldn't *be* a showdown. I risked a glimpse at Rick, who was still playing dead. I could hear the orcs coming closer, the way they sniffed and grunted and spat. Their breathing seemed phlegmatic and labored, and I wondered if their lungs weren't up to generating enough oxygen for the freakishly sized bodies they had developed.

I could freeze them all for a couple of minutes, but that would drain all my power. I could destroy the ceiling, but that would risk our lives, too. In the end, I decided that being temporarily invisible was the way to go. Although it required a lot of energy, it was an economical spell compared to the alternatives, and I wouldn't have to hold it long.

I got the team's attention—apart from Rick who couldn't see us, and Nilve who was already invisible—and pointed at the stairs.

"Up," I mouthed. "Up the stairs."

They nodded. I had to tell them where to go, because as soon as we were all invisible, we wouldn't be able to see each other.

I incanted, and felt the familiar warmth of the *invisibilis factus* magic. I saw the others turn transparent. I could still see shimmers of them, but a pair of regular eyes wouldn't be able to. We moved slowly, knowing that a misstep would give us away. A stumble, a sneeze, and we'd be riddled with lead. I knew their orders were to keep Apollo and me alive, but orcs aren't the sharpest crayons in the box. Plus, they had *"Blast chak ga grum"* engraved on their gun metal and in their smaller-than-average brains.

We minced along the floor, careful not to stand on the cold bodies.

"Salty," I whispered. It was the quietest whisper in the history of whispering. I was standing close to her, but she didn't hear. I tried again. "Salty." Her face turned to me, although she couldn't see me. "Up," I whispered. "Stairs."

Unnerved, she nodded, and began moving in the right direction. I exhaled as quietly as I could, then made my way over to Rick, who hadn't yet noticed he was transparent. I gave him the same message, and he very slowly stood, but didn't know how to get through the mire of bodies at his huge feet without giving his position away. I'd need to distract the orcs.

I looked at the farthest corner of the space and pointed my wand at it. All we needed was a neat little explosion there and we'd be able to sprint to the stairs. I trained my attention on the empty chair there and whispered *"Rumpis."* I didn't give it too much energy, all I wanted was a small distraction, but the chair had other ideas. It acted as if I'd soaked it in nitroglycerin before taking a match to its legs. A deafening blast reverberated through the space, and the orcs yelled in surprise, covering their faces to protect them from flying debris and fire. The noise and the smoke proved the perfect cover, and we were able to stop teetering and sprint for the fire escape, dodging the orcs as they hurtled in the opposite direction.

Up the stairs we flew in a chaotic jostle of invisible limbs, and I dropped the spell to avoid a possible collision, quickly counting heads to see if we had all made it out. We had. We'd escaped the brutes, but I had no doubt that they'd be hot on our heels as soon as they realized we were no longer on their floor. We had the advantage, but only for a slim window, and we needed to make the most of it.

"How much farther?" I asked Apollo, my lungs protesting.

He shook his head. "I don't know. I think we're near the top."

Now that we were above the orcs, we needed to seal them off to stop them from following us. I just didn't know how.

"We could flood it," said Sam. "You could send a tsunami down there."

"It would destabilize the building," replied Rick, who had Salty on his back again. We didn't want the skyscraper falling down—not while we were still in it, at least.

"How about knocking them out with something," suggested Savvy. "A sleeping potion in the air conditioner?"

"We don't have enough," I replied.

Apollo sighed. "Well, we'll just have to beat them to the top."

We all grimaced. The last thing we wanted was the threat of a platoon of nazi orcs on our tails while we were dealing with the most evil witch in the Realm.

I shook my head, more at myself than anything else.

There must be *something* we could do to keep them from ascending.

"Let's keep climbing," I said, hoping some kind of solution would present itself before we reached the top. Not the best-laid plan, but the only one I had.

"Wait," hissed Sam, grabbing my wrist with such urgency I almost cried out. I looked at him for an explanation, but his eyes were trained on the flight above us. We were silent, ears pricked, stomachs in knots. I didn't hear anything, but I trusted Sam. His sense of hearing would certainly be better than mine, given the blasts my eardrums had endured over the past weeks. He confirmed his suspicion to me with a finger pointed up, and an anxious nod.

I heard it. Army boots on metal steps. Too many to judge how large the company was.

Hex!

We turned to bolt back downstairs, but as soon as we did so we saw the orcs waiting for us on the platform below, sharp gray teeth staring at us as if they were sharks and we were their lunch.

CHAPTER 52

ORC SOCK

ASHA

ithout discussing it, we collectively decided we'd rather take our chances with the enemy above us because they seemed farther away. We spun again and began galloping up the stairs, but as soon as we reached that level, we saw the boots above us and knew there was no way out. We took the gap afforded to us by the mezzanine, happy to get off the stairwell, but it didn't change the fact that we were well and truly trapped. I had my wand out, Savvy, her crossbow, and the others had their borrowed automatic assault weapons. We were ready to fight, but we all knew there was no point. We'd be killed in the battle, even if their orders were to keep us alive.

I put my wand away and lifted my hands in surrender. At least if we capitulated, we'd—probably—stay alive.

We'd still get to the high witch, just on her terms instead of ours. The others put their weapons down, too, and Savvy clipped her crossbow to her back. Apollo was paler than I'd ever seen him, probably worried about the mirror they'd find when they took his backpack.

The first dozen arrived, shouting at us to stay still. Muroth followed shortly, swaggering in and looking exceptionally pleased to have captured us. His sheer size was panic-inducing. I noticed I was shaking. He nodded to the orc next to him, who held a bag. He had a squint and a terrible haircut, and I could smell him from where I stood. I found myself wishing that the trauma I'd been through had weakened my sense of smell instead of my hearing. As the oily mullet approached us, I had to breathe through my mouth to keep from gagging. He opened his bag of tricks and I cringed, not knowing what to expect but certain it would be horrible. He pulled out a pair of high-tech ankle cuffs—the ones they had used to enslave their orc brothers in the factory.

"You have *no shame*," I spat at Muroth. "Using these on your own kind, and now us. You're despicable."

He strutted up to me and angled his head, as if I were an unusual creature he wanted to take a closer look at.

Before I knew what had happened, I heard and felt the most vicious slap I'd ever experienced. It was so hard that I involuntarily pirouetted to the floor. Vision once again reduced to stars, I feared he'd broken my monocle, but when I touched it, it was fortunately still in one piece. Warmth spilled out of my ear and nose. I couldn't see it, but I knew it was blood. I heard the others tussling; perhaps Sam had tried to defend me. They were soon subdued by the front line of the army, and when I could finally see past the galaxy in my vision, I saw that we'd all been fitted with the ankle cuffs I so reviled. I knew before I looked at my ankles that mine were on, because the magic had disappeared from my skin.

Muroth towered above me, enjoying my shock and pain. "Just because our orders are to not kill you, it doesn't mean we can't have a little fun."

Needing no more encouragement than that, a soldier with a scarred face kicked Savvy in the ribs. She yelled in pain and curled up to protect herself from further blows. Usually my magic would kick into high gear seeing someone I loved being hurt, but the cuffs cut me off completely.

"You'll pay for that," I growled.

Scarface chuckled, then set his sights on Salty.

"Don't you *dare*," I warned him.

He sniggered. A fat bully in a schoolyard.

"I am warning you," I said through gritted teeth, as Salty whimpered in fear. "If you so much as touch any one of us again, I will rain vengeance down on you."

Scarface acted confused. "How are you going to do that?" he asked, feigning curiosity. "Your magic is gone."

My jaw was so tightly clenched that I thought the bone might crack.

"Besides, she's just a goblin," he said. "Why do you care what happens to her?"

The obvious answer was *because she's my friend,* but I didn't want to give them more reason to hurt her. I could play the reverse psychology game and lie. *Do what you like,* I could say. *I don't care about her.* But I knew they wouldn't believe me, and if we survived this ordeal, Salty would never forgive me. I decided to keep my lips zipped and instead just stared at him in defiance, hoping that my glare and promise of revenge would put him off hurting her. I was wrong.

He took her hand. I winced and shut my eyes. "No!" I shouted. "Leave her alone!"

Rick, Savvy, and Apollo all yelled at the sadistic soldier. "Stop it!" "Leave her!"

I opened my eyes only to see abject terror in hers, then came a stomach-churning crunching sound as the orc snapped the goblin's wrist. Salty howled in pain and shock, her hand hanging limply from her wrist.

I completely lost it. I forgot about our mission, the kidnappings, the enslaved orcs, the Smaragde clan, the high witch. I forgot about everyone and everything apart from that revolting specimen with his disfigured face who had just tortured my loyal friend. I could hear Nilve wailing, but it sounded far away. There was a fury rushing through my body and in my head that I couldn't control. I was yelling as I launched myself at him. He was more than twice my size, but the furious force of my leap took him to the floor. On his chest, I punched his face so hard I heard my knuckles fracture. I didn't care. I used the new shooting pain to fuel my attack, hitting him again and again. There were hands on me, beefy orc arms lifting me off the savage and into the air where I kicked and punched and screamed.

"Take it easy, squirt," came the voice of the orc with the bad haircut.

"Hex you," I cursed. "Hex you, and every generation forth. May your bloodline be eternally cursed."

Orcs were naturally superstitious, and he dropped me as if I had burnt him. My knuckles smarted as they hit the tiles.

"Take that back," he demanded, eyes ablaze.

"A hex on you!" I hissed.

"Don't worry about her," said Muroth. "Her magic is gone."

"And curse you, too," I spat, looking up at the lead orc with pure hatred. "May your daughters be born blind, and may your sons be born without testicles."

The leader looked a little less smug than before. "Shut up," he said.

"I have a lot more in my arsenal," I replied. "Hurt any of us again and you'll find my wrath in your unborn baby's eyes."

"We should kill her before she does any more damage," said Squinty, gripping his gun.

"Gag her," ordered Muroth.

A thick piece of stinky fabric—an orc sock?—was balled up and forced into my mouth. I retched. I heard the crackling sound of duct tape being pulled from its roll, and felt rough, clumsy hands wrapping it around the back of my head and over my mouth. It took me a while to adjust to breathing solely through my nostrils, but I soon calmed down enough to be comfortable doing it. I still felt the seething rage, but outwardly I made sure to appear calm.

"Attention!" yelled a soldier from the back where the stairs were. The men quickly reacted by standing up straight with their arms at their sides and shuffling their boots to the correct position. I straightened my spine, trying to get a look at who was coming, but I couldn't see past the Xarlug army until it started parting for the apparently important newcomer. The squadron parted neatly in the middle, like the Red Sea, and down the middle swept the army general, epaulettes bright against the uniform's black fabric. I had to blink a couple of times to make sure I was seeing right.

"At ease," the general said, and the men relaxed their stance, but didn't move or talk. Sugar Shagar looked satisfied, but her face was hard. Being in an army commander's uniform certainly suited her.

CHAPTER 53

QUEEN HITLER

ASHA

"I see you were successful in your operation," a satisfied Sugar Shagar said. "I am extremely pleased." I would have gaped at her if my mouth wasn't stuck together with duct tape.

"Yes, General Shagar," replied Muroth. "Alive, as per your orders."

"Excellent work," she said. "Your company will receive a generous bonus."

"Thank you, General," he replied, not taking his narrowed eyes off mine, probably wondering if my curse had taken hold.

I dragged my gaze off him and watched the orc godmother inspect the soldiers nearest to her. I couldn't believe she would stoop so low. I mean, I could believe it, because she had told me she would in her own words the last time I had seen her, and I had practically self-incinerated with rage, but this was much worse. It was such a terrible betrayal, not just of me, but the entire Realm. It was no secret that the Xarlug army wanted to bulldoze the Realm. The Xarlugs were the ones who had enslaved her people. The Xarlugs had literally ground her citizens up into pink pet food, yet here she was, commanding them like a bloody Queen Hitler.

"Were you able to follow my second order?" she asked.

"Yes, General Shagar," he repeated. "Every single Xarlug member in the Realm is in the building."

Some in better shape than others, I thought, thinking of the frozen corpses below.

"Bring them in," she ordered. "I want every man here to witness this."

My blood ran cold. Execution was one thing; execution as a public spectacle was far worse.

He nodded, grabbed the walkie-talkie off his belt, and issued the command. Soon the number of orcs in the space had tripled, and even more streamed in. There must have been five hundred soldiers packed in there, and there was much excitement in the air. The combination of so many orcs in an enclosed space, and me only being able to breathe through my nose, was truly retch-inducing. It was a novel kind of torture.

Don't hurl, I told myself. *Do. Not. Hurl.* The last thing I wanted to do was drown in my own vomit.

There were smirks and smug expressions everywhere I looked, and it just made me feel more nauseated. Sam caught my eye and lifted his eyebrows, asking if I was okay. I nodded. I wished the duct tape would come off so that I could curse the hell out of Shagar. I can't believe I bought her baby that floofy monkey toy. I wanted it back.

"They're all here, General," reported Muroth.

Sugar nodded. She snapped her fingers at a platform alongside the wall, and two men quickly picked it up and brought it to her, helping her up onto the podium so that everyone could see her speak. The army fell silent and stood at attention. Sugar straightened up and lifted her chin.

"Comrades," she began. "At ease."

There was a collective sigh as the orcs relaxed.

"This is not a time to be formal," she projected, holding her clenched fist up in the air. "This is a time to celebrate our victory!"

A happy roar broke out, and the beasts beat their chests and slapped each other on the back. Sugar waited for them to settle down a little, and continued. "From the beginning," she said. "From the *beginning*, the only thing on my mind was the ascension of the orc race."

More cheering and whooping, stomping and smacking.

"People told me," she said, gesturing toward me, "people told me that the Xarlugs were evil. That the Xarlugs didn't care about the orc race. That the Xarlug would fall."

Booing and hissing arose at the sentiments, and at me.

"But I knew," she continued. "I *knew* that the Xarlugs were something different. Something vital to the movement. Something *imperative* to the movement. No ... Xarlugs *are* the movement."

Cheering again, and chest thumping. *Don't vomit,* I reminded myself.

"Without the Xarlugs, we orcs are nothing. We orcs are the bottom of the food chain. We always have been! *We would always be* if not for *your* bravery, *your* strength, and *your* power."

Every second word was punctuated by applause and hooting.

"And let us not forget the clan who has helped us ascend. Sirilla Voltane, may she rest in peace, and the Smaragde vampires who have led us from the beginning of this revolt, who have funded the movement, who have paid us well, and who will keep supporting us and our families until we are given the status we deserve. The Smaragde Clan, who have given us health, longevity, fast healing, fortitude, and extra strength. The Smaragde Clan, to whom we will deliver our enemies." She motioned toward us and smiled. Roaring, clapping, whistling from the men as acid climbed my throat. Their collective halitosis was truly straight out of Hades. Apparently the Æternal elixir didn't solve bad breath.

"Turning these terrorists in is a huge victory. Once they are taken care of, things will be easier for us. We *will* ascend. And we will kill every last person standing in our way. When we leave this building, we will paint the roads red with the blood of our enemies!"

The orcs roared and clamored as if their favorite soccer team had won the World Cup. The floor vibrated beneath me from their boot stomping.

The orc mafia godmother let them howl and whistle for a while, then waited for quiet.

"Comrades, let us celebrate! Let us drink to our victory!" Sugar looked around as if someone would hand her a champagne flute, and when no one did, she smiled and unbuttoned her shirt pocket and took out the vial that was there. She snapped open the tiny bottle and held it up in the air. "Victory!"

The Xarlug soldiers followed suit, taking their elixirs out of their pockets, opening them, and chanting, *"Victory! Victory! Victory!"* and *"Kill! Kill! Kill!"*

Sugar downed the serum and smashed the empty bottle on the floor, as if this were a Greek wedding instead of a Nazi party.

Victory! Victory! Victory!

Tiny explosions sounded as the vials shattered on impact, sending shards of glass all over the floor to crunch under the orcs' heavy boots. The cheering was so loud I could hardly think. All I knew was that I hated the

Xarlugs more than ever, and most of all I hated hexing General Sugar Shagar.

I snarled at her, desperate to rip my gag off, smash the ankle cuffs to pieces, and sling the most potent, devastating spell I could muster at her in her fancy black commander's uniform. She would not deliver us to the vampires. I would kill her, and enjoy doing it, before she had the chance.

Next thing we knew, there was music, and the soldiers began humming, singing, and dancing. I wasn't sure if I could stomach this. I closed my eyes to block out their glee. Murderers, all of them. I wished they were dead.

I had never seen Shagar so bloodthirsty, and it sickened me. I hated her, I hated her, I hated her. I sat there with my gag on, boiling over with anger ... when some kind of intuition took over. A bright, beautiful thought pushed its way into my consciousness.

Sugar Shagar killed her first husband with poison.

Sugar Shagar killed her second husband and his entire wedding party with poison.

I didn't want to get my hopes up, but was it possible that she would do it again? I watched her with different eyes now, watched how she was grandstanding and riling up the troops so that the last thing on their minds was to question what was actually in the bottles. When they were all celebrating and smashing their vials, she very slowly edged her way toward us, along with the guard who had been as her side for the speech, and whispered something to him. He nodded, and roughly pulled us all up off the floor. Her beady eyes surveyed her soldiers expectantly as if counting down for a bomb to explode. Five, four, three, two, one …

CHAPTER 54

SHINY NEW SUSPICION

ASHA

It started with a few facial tics. I wouldn't have noticed them if not for my shiny new suspicion, but it became more and more obvious as the seconds marched on. A soldier began grimacing; another pounded his chest as if to beat down indigestion. Delightfully, Muroth clutched his heart, ugly eyes protruding. The jubilation fizzled out, transforming quickly into groaning and panicked gasping. One orc foamed blue at the mouth and fainted, taking down the people around him.

Indigo Violent, I thought. A master stroke.

More fell. Some fainted, some were pulled down by pain. Blood streamed from Muroth's nose, but he refused to be brought low. Confused, angry, he looked at me, wondering how I had pulled it off.

"Dirty witch," he spluttered, blood now running down his chin, teeth pink.

He was disoriented, but he still had his AK-47. He aimed it at me, and I felt my magic blast through me. It was my turn to be puzzled until I looked down and saw that Shagar's guard had removed our ankle cuffs.

I looked up again to Muroth with his finger on the trigger, smiling through his pain, happy that he was now allowed to kill me. I was brimming with power, and felt like I could send lightning bolts into every single one of them, but I stopped myself in time. I still needed to preserve as much as I could in order to win the final battle. They were dying already, I just needed to be patient—and not get shot. Muroth took aim.

"*Nebulum,*" I said. No shouting, no special effects, no showing off. Just a gentle vaporizing spell. As the orc pulled the trigger, the gun imploded into loud black smoke. He frowned and swore, trying to catch the vapor. As his weapon disappeared in his hands, he fell forward, collapsing in stages, and finally knocking his head. It made me think of being in the ambulance with the healer mage who had saved Sam's and my life. Cheating death, he had called it.

There you go, Grim Reaper, I thought. *We're paying back what we owe you, with interest.*

While I watched Muroth's demise so intently, most of the Xarlug soldiers had died. There was still flailing and groaning, but no one left standing.

Shagar sidled up to our team, and her guard ripped off my duct tape gag. "What did I tell you, witch?"

I didn't reply. I didn't care what she had told me. I was struck mute with horror—and, if I were to be honest, admiration—by her efficient mass-murdering skills.

"I told you that you can do more damage from the inside."

Apollo tipped his hat. "Did the orc mafia godmother just quote Thomas Shelby?"

"I don't know who Thomas Shelby is," said Sugar, "but I like the sound of him."

I glared at the fearsome orc. "You could have told me your plan."

She smirked. "You'll soon grow out of your naïveté," she said.

"What is that supposed to mean?"

"You're too trusting, witch. You have no idea how many enemies you have."

"My team is loyal," I replied. My team had more integrity in their little fingers than she did in her whole oversized body.

"You will be betrayed before this day is over," she proclaimed.

"How?" I asked. "Who?"

"If I knew, they would not be breathing," Shagar replied.

"Why did you do this?" I asked, looking around at the dead bodies that covered the entire mezzanine. "With the Smaragdes' help you could have ascended, exactly as you said."

"No," she said, shaking her head. "I don't believe the promises that vampires make."

"Fair enough," said Salty. Sugar looked down at the goblin as if seeing her for the first time. Wide-eyed, Salty took a step back, still cradling her broken hand.

"But killing your own men," I said, trying to process the slaughter. It's not that I wasn't exceptionally grateful, I just wanted to understand.

The orc grunted. "These are not my men. These savages enslaved my men, worked them to death, branded their bodies, killed them for profit. It was time to stop their barbarism once and for all. I want a better future for my baby. A safer, more prosperous future. Under Smaragde and Xarlug rule, the Realm would be destroyed."

Most of the Smaragdes were demolished, and now all of the Xarlugs were dead, but we still had many enemies to deal with. "There is still much danger," I said.

"Let's see what we can do about that." Sugar looked up at the ceiling, which had a few bullet holes in it. She wrenched an automatic assault weapon from the body at her feet. "Ready for the penthouse?"

I exhaled forcefully, trying to reset my nervous system. Having so many huge men wanting to kill me was not good for my PTSD. At this rate, if I survived, most of the Chalice paycheck was going to go towards my shrink sessions with Dr. Gilbert. Savvy picked up the ankle cuffs discarded at our feet and put them into Apollo's backpack. Perhaps they'd come in handy.

"You okay?" asked Sam.

I nodded. "That was hectic."

"We're making good progress," he said.

I agreed. The Xarlugs were dead, and we got to advance to the next level. Game on.

Sugar's guard passed us a couple of bottles of water. We all eyed the bottles suspiciously, making her snort with laughter and slap me on the back. Suffice to say, we declined, despite being parched, which only made Sugar laugh again.

"So, witch," she said, once she had recovered from her attack of sudden mirth. "What's waiting for us up there?"

"The high witch," I replied. "And her consorts."

"Not many of those left, though," said Sugar. "I was informed of your mission to Celestia. You did some legitimate damage there."

"The pocket realm no longer exists," I said. "And Lilian Black is dead."

"Superb. And you happened to blow up the Æterna manufacturing plant on your way home?"

"I can't take the credit for that, but yes, the warehouse and factory are gone."

"You saved my men from that prison," she said. "I am grateful."

"They saved themselves, really," I said. "There was an uprising. They got away safely, but I don't know where they are."

"I'll tell you where they are. You know those huge trucks they left in?"

I nodded.

"They're evacuating the city. We're expecting fireworks in Sandton tonight. Not the fun kind."

"Good," I replied. No one knew what the collateral damage would be, so it was best to get the innocents out of the war zone. There were already all those bombs going off. "Thank you for that."

She waved it off. "It's not just to save peoples' lives. It's to rebuild our credibility. We orcs need Realmers to trust us again if we are to be a successful race."

Of course. Shagar wasn't doing it out of the kindness of her heart. She was always playing the long game.

"So it's Ms. M and whoever she has left in her thrall," said Savvy. "And she knows we're coming for her."

"Who are you?" asked Shagar.

"This is Savvy," I replied. "And Nilve SaltySnap, Rick, Sam, and Apollo."

They all nodded and gave weak smiles, clearly nervous around the orc—and for good reason.

"Where are the rest?" asked Sugar.

I blinked at her. "Hm?"

"The rest," she said. "The rest of your team."

"Chione's looking after Rap. He's really sick. And the girls are at home. This is too dangerous for them. Stoker is with the Palefang pack. They're stalking the city, taking out vampires."

"So ... it's just you five?"

"Six," said Salty, crossing her arms. "Just because I'm vertically challenged, doesn't mean you don't have to count me."

The orc ignored her. "Do you mean to tell me that this ragtag group of misfits is your only hope of saving the Realm?"

"We're not misfits," objected Rick, but his tone was not convincing.

Sugar sighed. "Every time I begin to think you're smart, witch, you do something to change my mind."

"I'm doing the best I can," I said a little defensively.

The orc mafia godmother sniffed. "Do better."

CHAPTER 55

HOW DO YOU KILL A DEAD MAN?

ASHA

I turned to Nilve, who was still sulking. "You're an important part of the team."

The goblin pouted, but looked slightly less peeved.

"Any final words before we go up there?" I asked.

"A last meal would be nice," said Salty. "You know, like they give prisoners on death row."

"What would you choose?" asked Rick.

"Ferra's roast chicken," she replied. "No contest."

"Ha," he said. "Me, too."

"Fillet steak with mushroom sauce and a baked potato dripping with butter," said Savvy.

Apollo looked at Savvy as if he had just fallen in love with her.

"Asha would choose a carrot or something," joked Salty, and I feigned annoyance at her, even though I felt none.

"We'll have a feast," I promised them. "A huge celebratory feast for our victory."

"Just as long as Sugar's nowhere near the kitchen," said Sam, and I almost choked trying to keep my laughter in. I didn't think anyone would trust Sugar's cooking for a long time.

"Deal," I said. I could really have used a sip of that water.

I heard something, and asked the team to keep quiet. We all strained to hear it.

There were more boots coming—scores of them. I didn't understand. Dread cooled my blood.

"These are all the Xarlug men," I said to Sugar. "Right?"

"Right," she said, concern creasing her forehead.

"Then what is that *sound?*" asked Savvy.

No, no, no, no, I thought. *Not another round, please!*

"It's impossible," said Sugar. "I saw their bodies with my own eyes."

"You think it's the orcs below?" I asked. "The ones we *killed?*"

"There are no other Xarlugs left in the Realm," she replied. "It's them."

"That's impossible," I said.

"Nothing is impossible, witch. Especially with that elixir in their veins." She clutched her gun to her chest. "Get ready for battle."

"No way," said Savvy. "We need to run."

"Run where?" Sugar demanded. "Straight into the high witch's arms? We'll be surrounded." I didn't often see fear in orcs' eyes, but hers glowed with it. I guessed that, given the carnage around us, they'd be extra-hard on her for her treasonous actions.

"We'd better portal," I said. Forget saving portal energy, it was do or die. The boots were already on the stairs just outside, heavy rubber vibrating the metal stairs.

"No," said Sugar. "I need to face them."

"You're crazy," I said. "You'll die."

"If I die trying to defeat the Xarlugs, it will be with honor."

"Please don't do this," I begged. "What about baby Jackie?"

Sugar growled, as if she were a wounded animal and I had touched a tender spot.

I spun round to Salty and Apollo, both visibly trembling. "Gateway, please!"

Apollo shook his head. He was looking past me. "It's too late," he said. His eyes stretched wide. Every one of my team members looked so terrified, I was scared to turn around. When I did, I held back a scream.

They were the orcs we had killed on the level below. They still had their gunshot wounds, but their blood was almost dry. Some had Savvy's arrows in their chests. They plodded toward us, the irises of their eyes milky, their gait clumsy.

"Holy Hecate," I murmured. What was in that elixir? It was clearly not on par with the Sybil twins' famous— and famously exorbitant—vitality shakes. It was much, much more powerful.

Sugar aimed her gun and opened fire, and the rest of the team followed suit, but we soon learned that pumping lead into the zombies did nothing but waste bullets. They kept on clomping toward us. The only thing that slowed them down were the bodies of their comrades lying on the floor. They didn't seem to be able to see anything but us, like automatons with facial recognition. There was indifference in their eyes, but I knew that when they got hold of us, they would be anything but indifferent. I knew they'd tear us apart.

I stepped forward, wand out. *"Impedio!"* I shouted.

The spell stopped the white-eyed cadavers in the front, but the magic didn't reach the back, where more were lumbering in. They got impatient with their frozen comrades and pushed forward, creating a surge of dead bodies. Wary of being crushed, we backed away. Savvy uttered her own *impedio* incantation, her magic supported mine, and we were able to stop the next wave, but yet another group pushed through the door and plowed through the frozen bodies to get to us. Savvy began to waver; there were too many big bodies to hold back and only two of us. It was burning through too much magic. We had to stop, but stopping meant being ripped apart.

"Asha," Savannah gasped. "I can't hold it anymore."

I groaned in accord. I couldn't either.

Sugar was still firing into the mob, even though she knew there was no point. Maybe it felt better than just standing there, waiting to die. My power was ebbing, and I cried out. This wasn't how I was supposed to be spending my magic. Damn them. Damn the Xarlugs and double damn the high witch for her potent elixir.

"Argh!" yelped Savvy, collapsing. Apollo caught her just in time.

Without Savvy's supporting power, my spell folded. I swore and shook my hand. A creeping sense of dread told me that I had used too much and would pay for it when I most needed it.

The uniformed zombies were mere yards away, and I couldn't see a way out.

A new smashing sound reached our ears. Glass breaking, panes shattering all over as if the room had exploded and taken all the windows out. But there had been no explosion, and the glass fell to the inside. Something was smashing *in*. A wrecking ball? No. Creatures! Animals were flying in and attacking our enemies. But not any creatures.

Wolves.

It was so shocking and surreal it took us a moment to understand what was happening. The arm of a crane was visible through one of the broken windows. They were huge, handsome creatures with powerful jaws and long limbs. We watched in alarm and relief as the animals tore strips off the orcs, crunching down on bones and ripping out windpipes. The zombies didn't run away or scream—they just marched on like the braindead meatsacks they were.

An orc was getting too close to me. I backed up against the wall, hoping he'd lose interest, but he didn't. The closer he trudged, the more I pushed myself into the wall. He was so near that I was awash in his fetid breath. Before I could defend myself, a massive wolf sideswiped the orc and he went down hard. The wolf, a beautiful, rich rust-colored animal, didn't waste time putting the orc out of his misery. Huge claws slit the orc's throat in one slashing movement. The zombie gurgled and collapsed. Before leaving the body, the werewolf peered up at me and we looked into each other's eyes. I knew those eyes. Stoker. He moved swiftly on to his next victim, an orc getting too close to Apollo, and jumped up on him and went straight for his throat. Blood splattered on the tiles and on Apollo's sneakers, who was avoiding eye contact with the wolves. Within moments of our defenders arriving, the Xarlug contingent was dead—again. A dozen or so wolves walked around the bodies, sniffing out any sign of life and quickly extinguishing it. I watched their elegant bodies, muscles moving under lush fur, ears still pricked, ready to attack. I worried that the blood on their pelts was theirs, but judging by the way they demolished the orcs, it wasn't.

Kieron Palefang had said I smelled like a wolf cub, and after my *purpurea* trip I knew why. Meeting the alpha werewolf had cemented my belief that they were smart and noble creatures, not the bloodthirsty destroyers Soleil perceived them as. Getting excommunicated from the coven, though emotionally difficult, was the correct outcome. I had believed that we wouldn't win the war without the Palefang pack on our side, and seeing the mass of bodies on the floor now confirmed that conviction. I owed my life to wolves. First to the wolf who ensured my survival as a baby in the forest, and now, to the pack who had come to our aid.

A black wolf approached me, sleek and beautiful. Despite his powerful, crimson-wet jaws I instinctively put out my hand to stroke him. As soon as I touched his coat, he transformed into his human shape. Fur disappeared beneath skin, claws retracted, fangs shrank down to incisors. I recognized his handsome face before the transformation was complete.

"Kieron," I said, squeezing what was now his shoulder. "Thank you."

CHAPTER 56

WOLF SPIRIT

ASHA

The rest of the pack turned into their human versions and loped toward something—someone—on the floor. I craned my neck to see who it was, and recognized the rust-colored coat immediately.

No! I ran towards Stoker, tripping twice over the limbs of the dead in my haste to get to him. *No no no.* He was still in his wolf form, and he was losing blood fast.

"Stoker!" I exclaimed.

His eyelids were half mast, and I could tell it was an effort to keep them open. When he saw me, he smiled. "Asha," he whispered.

One of the others had her hand clamped down on his neck in order to staunch the blood loss.

"What happened?" I asked, knowing it was a useless question. It didn't matter what had happened. Stoker was dying.

"Xarlug got him," she said. I looked at her properly and remembered her face from the meeting at the caves. She was as beautiful now as she had been before.

"Bronx," I said. It came out as a wail.

Her firm grip on Stoker's neck was doing little to stop the flow. I felt panic rise up inside me. Stoker could not die. I would not allow it.

"Move your hand on the count of three," I said. She was reticent, but when I took out my wand she understood. Stoker's eyes slid closed, and my fear for his life made the magic effortlessly available to me.

"*Ignem exquiris,*" I chanted. The tip of my wand lit with fire, and without warning him against the pain, I cauterized the bullet hole. Stoker didn't flinch, which sent desperation through me. The smell of singed fur and burning flesh made us all gasp for air.

"Stoker," I said, shaking him. "Stoker!" But he didn't respond.

I dropped my wand and put my hands on him. *"Curas vulnum, curas vulnum,"* I chanted, not caring about my magic reserves, not caring about anything but saving my friend's life, but no matter how much healing energy I channeled into him, he remained unconscious.

Bronx put her ear to his mouth. "He's not breathing," she said.

The pool of blood was still growing. *Damn it!* We turned him over and saw another wound on his back. I cauterized that one, too, but there was nothing I could do about the internal hemorrhaging.

"Stoker, please," I begged him. "We need you." What I really meant was *we love you,* but words don't always make sense in such dire situations. My team had assembled behind me.

Bronx tried to find his breath again, and failed again. Her lips turned down at the corners as she shook her head at me, her kohl-lined eyes wet with grief.

"Curas vulnum," I said again, understanding it was pointless, but not knowing what else to do. A sob caught in my aching throat. I fumbled for my wand again and held it to his chest. *"Fiat fulgur,"* I cried. A blast of electricity made his torso arch. It made no difference to his condition. I sent two more rounds of

defibrillating shocks to his heart, but he remained lifeless. I was going to try again, but Bronx put her hand on my back and gently pushed my wand down.

"It's over," she said. "Let him rest now."

I shook my head, a torrent of tears overcoming me. "I can save him," I wept. I just needed to try harder. More magic, more effort. I wouldn't let him die. "I can save him," I repeated.

"No, Asha," said Bronx. "You can't. Stoker is gone."

"No," I wailed. "We can't let him die."

"He's already dead," she replied, eyes bright with tears.

Still shaking my head, I looked at his lupine face. It was peaceful. There was no pain. Sobs thundered out of me. On my knees, I crouched forward and laid my face on his chest.

"Oh, Stoker," I wept. This was not fair. He was such a wonderful being; he had been a friend and an asset. I had a flashback of happier times—of riding in the monster truck with Rick, and Stoker enjoying putting his head out the window. "He didn't deserve to die this way."

"This is exactly how he would have wanted to die," said Bronx. "He was the most noble wolf I knew. Dying in a battle to save his friends, and save the Realm ..." Her voice trailed off as she choked up.

The pack stood in a circle around us and howled, their voices whipping through me. They tried to expunge their anguish through baying and barking, and their voices intensified my heartache. Bronx and I wept together for a time, my chest empty and aching with loss. Once the wolves had finished their mourning, Palefang took a step forward.

"We need to move," he growled. "Before she gets away."

But how could we? How could we go on, knowing Stoker was gone?

The alpha wolf hauled me up like a rag doll. "You need to draw on your wolf spirit now, little cub," he said. "What's done is done. We need to push forward. It's what Stoker would have wanted."

I nodded, my mouth still being pulled down by sorrow. I knew he was right; I just didn't know if I had the strength to go on.

"Don't let his death be in vain," grated Bronx. "Let's finish this."

"We need to burn the bodies," said Savvy, and Palefang nodded.

We needed to stop the Xarlugs from reanimating again. There was no knowing how many lives they had with the elixir in their blood.

"Not Stoker," I said. "He deserves better."

There was no way in Hades I was going to let Stoker burn here in this evil place surrounded by the corpses of neo-Nazi brutes.

Kieron looked concerned. "Agreed, but we have no way to move him. We need every pack member here if we're going to stand a chance."

"I'll take him," volunteered Salty. "I'll put him somewhere peaceful until this battle is over."

She was cradling her arm, and I remembered the orc had broken her wrist. It gave me an idea. I unzipped my jeans and used my ritual knife to cut off a swatch of fabric from my lucky underpants—the sleep shorts that the healer mage from the ambulance had given me— and handed it to the goblin.

"Use this as a portal key," I said. "It'll take you to a mage who will fix your wrist. He'll help you with Stoker's body."

Stoker's *body*. I gritted my teeth to stop further tears from falling.

The goblin nodded and took the fabric from me. We gave her some space as she crouched next to Stoker and held on to him as well as she could. Salty murmured her gateway spell and an oval of golden light opened up on the floor beneath them. She gave me a last wistful glance, and they fell through the floor, the portal closing quickly behind them.

I sighed, and felt Sam's arms around me. "I'm so sorry," he said, voice gruff with emotion.

I swallowed and nodded, burying my face in his chest.

"I'll handle the fire," said Savvy. Her mascara was smudged, her lips a firm line. Rick avoided my eyes. He had been the closest to Stoker and I could tell he wasn't ready to process the loss yet. We needed clear heads for what was going to happen next. If we survived, we'd mourn properly. The orcs were a stoic bunch; we had plenty to learn from them.

"Time to go, witch," said Sugar from behind me. I nodded. We all gathered together before heading up the stairs again—stairs I had grown to hate—as Savvy siphoned power from the Void for her spell. Her breathing was hard and deep as she let the magic move through her.

I heard her mumbling to herself, a longer incantation than I would have used. Her magic had always been more sophisticated than mine. It built to a crescendo and she held out her arms.

"*Incinerare!*" she demanded.

Blue flames poured from her hands like water. When they reached the floor they acted as an ocean wave of fire, rolling over the bodies and creating a *whomp* sound as every corpse caught alight. We felt the sudden heat on our faces. They burned swiftly, as if their uniforms had been soaked in gasoline—but gasoline would have smelled better. The broken windows allowed for plenty of oxygen to feed the fire, and soon the entire mezzanine level was engulfed in purifying flames.

Whereas before we had sprinted up the stairs, we now trudged. Our bodies were tired, our hearts heavy. A part of me felt like the high witch had already won.

CHAPTER 57

TRICKERY OR TRAPS

ASHA

"Anyone else feel like they're walking into an execution chamber?" asked Apollo. No one answered, but it was clear on everyone's faces.

"No," I said, despite the pure dread I felt with every step. "We will not let her defeat us. We will not allow the Realm to succumb to evil forces." Yes, we were in grave danger, I could feel it in every part of my body, but I also felt a small glimmer of hope. We were a steadfast team with various talents, and we would do whatever it took to destroy the high witch. "We will not allow Stoker's death to be in vain."

I felt a change in emotions, from defeated to determined, and we quickened our pace.

Not knowing exactly what awaited us was nerve-racking, but one thing was certain in my mind: the high witch would be waiting for us. She had spent so much money and effort trying to kill me through the Dusk Reaper network, but had never been successful. By going to the penthouse I was pretty much offering myself to her, and this was going to be her chance to finish me off. I accepted the fact that I may lose my life, but if it meant returning balance to the Realm, it would be worth it. It had been my life's mission for so long that it was part of me—no, more than that; it was the core of me. My reason for living, and one day—maybe today—it would be my reason for dying.

I was an unlikely assassin, as Sam liked to point out. I never did enjoy killing, but this was one liquidation I was looking forward to. The Realmers deserved to live in peace. Orc families didn't deserve to live in fear of losing their husbands and fathers to organ theft and enslavement. Humans deserved to live without the constant dread of vampires snatching their daughters. And lambs like Dusty and Abigail, Valeria and Maple, Frankie and Mercury deserved to live in a world where they didn't have to fear for their innocence, or for their lives.

These thoughts galvanized and fortified me. They hammered my fear. With Stoker's spirit behind us, we reached the very top floor of the skyscraper and entered the penthouse.

It was empty.

Of course it was—or at least, appeared to be. Ms. M might want me in her lair, but she wasn't going to play the sitting duck. There was certainly some kind of deception: trickery or traps. A large window had been left open, and the breeze pulling through swept papers off her desk and made the leaves of the bouquet of black blooms on her office desk flutter. Standing in the drafty space with the whole city at my feet was a powerful feeling. I could imagine if I was as rich and powerful as the high witch, it would feel like I was queen of the world. That's probably what she saw herself as.

Eleven werewolves, Sugar Shagar and her guard, and the five of us stood in the spacious open-concept apartment waiting for something to happen. The pack sniffed the air, trying to track her scent, but it was difficult thanks to the smoke rising from below, reminding us that we didn't have much time to deal with Ms. M and escape the building before the whole thing went up in flames. I tried to focus my monocle to achieve the X-ray vision I had used before. The cyan filter returned, and I blinked a few times to get used to it. I started with the office and scanned the kitchen, lounge, and bedroom, but didn't see anyone. Doubts started niggling at me. Would the high witch really stay here if she knew we were on our way? Paranoia kicked in. What if she had lured us here so she could do her evil work somewhere else, without our meddling? What if she was building a brand-new Celestia somewhere we'd never find it? The knot in my stomach tightened. What if she was at this very moment hurting Dusty or Abigail? I hoped Merlin was with them. I noticed I was trembling again, wondering if I had been played for an utter fool.

In desperation, I looked up at the ceiling and saw a shadow. I grabbed Sam's arm and pointed up. More shadows.

"Do you see that?" I asked.

"What?" he replied, answering my question.

I was seeing through the ceiling. She was on the roof, and she wasn't alone.

I blinked back to my regular vision.

"Palefang. Shagar. She's up there."

We all looked up, as if we could see what was on the roof.

"How do you know?" asked Kieron.

"She sees things," said Rick, and drew a circle over one of his eyes to illustrate the monocle.

Palefang's generous eyebrows shot up and he looked impressed, but only for a second. "How do we get up there?"

I didn't know.

Kieron motioned for the pack to find access to the roof. It felt strange to wage war on a rooftop. My roof garden at home was my happy place: plants, beanbags, fairy lights, stars. It was a place I practiced yoga, tai chi, meditation. A place I took a book and a bottle of wine, and sometimes a lover. To kill or be killed on a rooftop would be a definite change.

CHAPTER 58
AFTERSHAVE AND BLOOD
ASHA

The Palefang pack spread out and, sniffing the air, searched for a way up to the roof. When they didn't locate one, I assumed there was a trick to it. I racked my brain.

"Savvy," I said. "What kind of magic would a witch use to get up there? With her vampire minions?"

She shook her head. "Nothing immediately comes to mind. I'll keep thinking."

"Some kind of secret trapdoor?" Sam wondered aloud, inspecting the ceiling. "With a ladder that pulls down?"

"Could be," I replied, but upon searching, we found no evidence of it. I knew she was powerful, but would she use magic every time she wanted to go up there? Or did she never go up and was only there to have the advantage of being higher than us, like soldiers on a hill, or up in a castle?

The smell of the smoke was still subtle, but getting stronger. We needed to get this done.

"She's not alone," I told the others. "I'm pretty sure the remaining clan members are up there with her."

"How many?" asked Apollo.

"I don't know. I just saw shadows. Not more than ten?"

He nodded. I couldn't help noticing there was still blood splashed on his sneakers.

"Are you okay?" I asked him. The last time he was here, it was the most traumatic event in his life—that he could remember.

"Yes," he replied. "Better than okay. Looking forward to ending this."

He had lived under the shadow of the high witch's curse for over a year, and lost precious friends to it. The Void knows I love breaking curses, and snapping Apollo's Kill Your Darlings curse would be the most satisfying one ever.

Frustrated that we didn't have a way up, we all began poking around the vast penthouse. It proved much bigger than it initially appeared, with passages leading to a private theater, a glorious library—where I was sure I'd find the Matahandi book if I looked for it—and more than one bedroom, which made me wonder who would sleep over. I couldn't imagine M had many friends, but maybe I was wrong. After all, billionaires did tend to attract hangers-on. After looking in the library—rather enviously, I'll admit, I found another narrow passage which I tentatively followed. Because the walls were glaringly white, it reminded me of the hospital wing in Celestia, which made me shudder. I imagined Lilian Black staying over here, and the two of them chatting about the initial plans to produce the elixir. How they might best kidnap virgin fodder and keep them happy and healthy in a mesmerized trance before stealing their life-force.

I glanced at my wrist to make sure I still had Black's protection amulet. How poetic it would be if it ended up saving my life.

I didn't find anything interesting in the minimalist, stylish penthouse apartment, so I turned back. At that angle I could see a vertical line on the passage wall that I hadn't seen on my way in. I examined it, and put my palm on the wall as I did so. I heard a mechanism unlocking, and the secret door slid soundlessly open.

The huge room revealed was in stark contrast to the rest of the fresh and light apartment. The walls were painted black, the soot-colored furniture disappearing against the dark. The only light was from a large black chandelier that glittered from a chain in the ceiling. A king-sized bed was covered in black satin, with a charcoal and metallic gray comforter folded neatly at the end. The pillows matched. There was no art, no homey touches, no soul, and the air was subtly scented with aftershave and a hint of blood. I sniffed, trying to recognize the fragrance. I knew it. I knew the person who was living here. A shadow fell across the luxurious sable carpet, and I spun round to see who it was.

I gasped when I saw my exit was blocked. My hand automatically flew to my chest where my heart was pounding.

"Asha," he greeted, both hands on the doorframe to signal he would block my way if I tried to get past.

"Mordecai," I replied. "Haven't seen you in a while. I thought you'd given up stalking me."

He didn't react. He looked terrible—he had always looked pale, which came with the territory when you were undead—but now he looked exhausted, even grief-stricken.

"You need a vacation," I said. "Where do vampires go on holiday?" I wondered. "I'm assuming you don't flock to the sunny beaches like most people do. Somewhere dark and rainy seems more your style."

"This is a joke to you?" he asked, real pain on his face.

"Of course it's not a hexing joke to me," I said through gritted teeth. "I've just lost a friend because of the likes of you," I hissed. "I hate you and all of your kind."

There was more hurt in his eyes, but I didn't understand why. We had agreed a long time ago that we hated each other, that we didn't want to be around each other. Why the long face now?

He massaged his temple like I was giving him a headache. "Asha. How many times did I tell you to back away from this case?"

"Your arrogance is truly something to behold," I replied, anger pushing blood through my veins. "You think you can just tell people what to do and they'll do it? Well, I'm not one of those people. I don't just lie down and let your kind steamroll over me. I will not be bullied and abused by you or anyone in your clan. The sooner you stop telling me what to do, the better for both of us."

"It's not about arrogance or steamrolling," he said. "It's about what's best for you and your friends."

"Oh, please!" I yelled. "You really want me to believe that you have our best interests at heart?" I laughed in an ugly way, incensed and bitter.

The vampire became exasperated. He raised his voice. "Asha, I have done nothing but protect you!"

I couldn't believe what he was saying. Did he honestly think I'd believe that?

"How many times have I removed you from a dangerous situation?" he demanded.

Okay, he had a point there. He had spent hours digging my coffin out of the ground when I had been buried alive. He had saved me from Sirilla Voltane by giving me an impromptu archery lesson at Obsidian Castle. He had told me which arrow to use to end Voltane's reign. There were also the countless warnings to keep out of dangerous situations ... which I consistently ignored.

"You have helped me in the past, I won't deny that," I said. "But you are still the enemy."

"You are giving me a cluster headache," he remarked, as if it was my fault that I was in the Æterna building.

"Ah, shame," I said. "Poor murderous vampire has a migraine. Shall I fetch you some paracetamol? Or perhaps you'd prefer the black magic of the illegal elixir you've been helping to produce?"

"It's not like that," he said.

I laughed again, a horrible guffaw of disbelief—and indignation that he would really think I'd believe that. My jaw was so tense I had to actively loosen it to be able to speak again. "You are literally *living* with her," I said. "You are *living* with the high witch who has caused untold suffering to the people of the Realm."

He was uncharacteristically quiet, so I pressed on. "It's funny," I said, not thinking it was funny at all. "It's funny that I thought you were better than the rest. Better than the Smaragdes that sought to kill us, better than the Dusk Reapers you so loved to warn me about. But you're not. You're worse than them, because at least they were honest about their intentions, whereas you've been deceitful and conniving from the very beginning."

We stood in silence for a moment. I could have gone on, but I wanted him to explain himself. When it was clear that he wasn't going to, I sneered. "I saw glimmers of goodness in you, Mordecai. I saw a hint of something good about you, but I was wrong. Because now I see that you have been the true enemy all along."

Mordecai shook his head. "No."

"No?" I exclaimed.

Worried, he turned his head to look down the passage. "Keep it down."

I felt I would self-implode. "Keep it DOWN? Are you for real? You're DESTROYING the Realm and you're worried that I am *speaking too loudly*?"

Pinpricks of magic stuck me all over my skin. Pins and needles made me flex my fingers to dislodge them.

Mordecai gestured for me to calm down. This man knew nothing about how to treat an angry woman. I wanted nothing more than to punch him in his lordly face.

"I am not your enemy," he murmured.

"Well, forgive me if I don't swallow your lies. I've had enough of your drivel. Now, I need to get back to my friends. They're going to start worrying. I'd appreciate it if you get out of my way."

"I'll let you go," he said.

"Your kindness is overwhelming, truly," I snarked.

"I'll let you go as soon as you understand something. I was tasked to watch over you."

"That's old news, vampire," I replied. "I know that someone was paying you to make sure I didn't get too close to finding the missing daughters. To ensure that I didn't find out who was responsible for the murders of the pacifist orcs and the ascension of the Xarlug nation. I didn't know who it was, but now the answer is obvious."

"She wanted you to stay away so that she could keep you safe. So that I could keep you safe."

"Really," I said. It wasn't a question.

"Yes. Really. Ms. M said I needed to do everything in my power to protect you."

I tried to not let the surprise show on my face. "In that case, you're all completely delusional. The only people I need protection from are you and the high witch."

"I realize it's difficult to understand without all the facts."

"Tell me the 'facts' then. I can't wait to hear them."

Mordecai sighed and rubbed his face. "You know I can't tell you."

My frustration was so intense, I thought my head would explode. I had to get out of that black room before my brains made art on the wall. I reached for my wand. "Get out of my way now, vampire, or I'll have to move you myself."

"You only remember the recent events when I saved your life —"

I wanted to roll my eyes at that, but it would be disingenuous. As much as I hated to admit it, he had saved my life on more than one occasion.

"But I've been around a lot longer than that," he said. "I introduced myself to you only because I had to warn you to stay away from Æterna." He pursed his lips. *Not that you listened,* I could imagine him thinking. "But I've always been watching you."

CHAPTER 59

RAINBOW CHEERIOS

ASHA

"Just when I thought you couldn't get any creepier," I said.

"I was with you when the Dusk Reaper cracked your head open. I called the ambulance. I was with you in the operating room and ICU. Before that attack, I was with you when you needed me, even though you didn't know I was there."

"Prove it," I challenged.

"When you were six you almost touched an exposed live wire at one of those terrible foster homes you were in."

I screwed my face up in disbelief ... but there was a hint of a memory. "The lightning took out the circuit breaker box," I said slowly. "The house went dark."

Mordecai nodded. "It was still raining when you went out to look at it."

The box had been cleaved in half by the lightning. It was smoking and sparking.

"I was alone at home," I said. Those particular foster parents had not been around much. "They would blame me for anything that went wrong in the house. So I thought I'd better fix it."

I had stretched my hand out to reconnect the main cable, but just before I touched it, I was thrown backwards into the rosebushes.

"The thorns ripped you up. But at least you were alive."

"I still have the scars," I said.

"I know."

We were quiet again. It was a lot to process. I felt slightly less murderous toward him. "How many times have you saved my life?"

He shrugged. "I stopped counting. You were a fearless child. The bane of my life."

"The forest?" I asked. "The hut?"

"Yes," he said, now with a gentleness in his voice that I had never heard before.

"Were you the one who kept me alive there?"

"It was a group effort," he replied. "Orion stayed with you. I visited when I could. I brought supplies. Orion only fed you what he could hunt in the woods."

That memory tasted like warm raw meat.

"I'd bring fruit. Biscuits. Cereal. I tried vegetables, but you didn't like them. Your favorite was rainbow Cheerios. You used to play with them. I bought you a cat food dispenser."

I looked at him in disbelief. "I ate Cheerios from a cat food dispenser."

"Ingenious, I know."

I just blinked at him.

"What?" he said. "Wolves can't open cereal boxes."

Now it was my head threatening to ache. *Wolves can't open cereal boxes.* "I don't even know what to do with that information."

"You don't have to do anything with it," he replied. "You just need to believe that I have—that I've *always had* your best interests at heart. Even though it clearly pains you to believe it."

"Orion," I said. "Who was he? Why was a wolf looking after me?"

"Because a hut on stilts in a forest is not the safest environment for a baby."

"You're avoiding the question."

"He was looking after you because your mother couldn't."

"Couldn't?" I asked. "Or wouldn't?"

Mordecai breathed out a long-suffering sigh and pinched the bridge of his nose.

"I saw her give birth to me," I said. "In a vision. She was dying. Alone and desperate in that Void-forsaken hut. Screaming because I was stuck and she knew she would die. She picked up a knife." I patted my own ritual blade. "She picked up a knife and cut me out of her, and sewed herself up again. She called me a curse."

"You're not a curse," he said, that gentleness in his voice again.

"I felt like a curse growing up." Why was I telling this

vampire my most vulnerable thoughts? "No one wanted me."

"You were too special, Asha," he said. "They didn't know how to handle you."

"Why wasn't I taken to Copperfield right away? You could have done that for me. I would have had a different life. A better life. I had to spend my childhood being shuttled from one terrible place to another, always different, always rejected. Abandoned over and over."

"Copperfield would be too obvious," he said. "You would have been in danger."

Did I have a similar childhood predicament to Apollo? "What kind of danger?"

Mordecai tilted his face at me. "It doesn't matter anymore."

"It doesn't *matter*?" I asked. "You mean it doesn't matter to *you*. I need to know. And if you won't tell me, I'll find out some other way."

I heard footsteps nearing. The vampire quickly stepped inside his room and the door slid closed.

"I beg you, Asha," he said. "*I beg you* to go home and leave this place. There is only death and heartache here."

"And then what?" I demanded. "I leave here to go home … but there is no home, because you and your vile company have demolished the city, torn down everything that is good in the Realm."

"It's the way it has to be," he said.

"Why?" I demanded. "Because you need to flatten the country so that there is nothing left, and you can have all the power?"

"There are bigger forces at play here."

"Why is it that you always talk to me like I'm a child? Of course there are bigger forces. That's why we are here. To stop them!"

"You can't stop them!" he yelled. "They are too powerful for you. Asha, please, I'm trying to help you. I've always tried to help you."

"Why? Because you're being paid? Maybe it's time for you to get a different job."

"I did it for the money in the beginning. I did it out of loyalty to the cause."

The cause.

"But we bonded. We bonded almost immediately."

"When you were feeding me cat food?"

He ignored the jibe. "You were the most … marvelous child."

I thought I might be hearing things.

"Even as a tiny baby you had those eyes … Those arresting green eyes exactly like your mother's. So alert and clever. And the way they'd shine when I visited you. It was … endearing. As a toddler, you were just so whip-smart. And affectionate. I didn't want to form an attachment, but you gave me no choice."

"You're not going to tell me that you're my father, are you?"

"No," he snapped. "No! I was there for your protection *against* your father."

My brain felt like it was short-circuiting, fizzing and smoking like that live wire box when I was six. I wanted to ask more questions, but my words were not working. Before I could formulate a decent sentence, there was a crash, and Rick stood in the doorway, having just used his shoulder as a battering ram.

He looked at us, trying to get used to the dim light in the room. "Did he hurt you?" he demanded, drawing himself up to his full height as he approached Mordecai.

"No," I replied, urgency in my voice. "He's been protecting me."

The vampire shot me a grateful expression. Not because I had possibly stopped the angry orc from crushing him, but because I had finally accepted that he had always had my best interests at heart, even though it was challenging for me to admit.

Some of the others heard the noise and came running in.

"What's going on?" demanded Sam. "We were looking for you everywhere."

"Sorry," I said. "Mordecai was giving me information. I was just about to come and find you—"

Palefang appeared, along with Bronx. "Vampire," he said. "Kill him!"

CHAPTER 60
STEP INTO THE FIRE
ASHA

"N o!" I shouted. "Don't kill him."

Kieron reacted as though I had slapped him. "Asha," he said. "He's a *vampire*. He is the enemy."

"I know it looks that way," I replied.

"Looks that way?" sneered Bronx. "Look at the inside of his cape. Not only is he a bloodsucker, but he's the worst of the worst."

"Smaragde," hissed Kieron. "Our pack will not rest until every single member of the Smaragde clan is turned to ashes." His teeth were sharp and menacing. He was ready to tear Mordecai's throat out.

"Wait," I said. "He has information."

"We don't need *information,*" replied Bronx, lupine fangs bared. "We have all the intelligence we need."

"He knows who my parents were!" There was desperation in my voice.

"Leave the past where it belongs," replied Kieron. "We don't have time for this. The penthouse is already heating up."

I could feel it. I thought it was my emotional state keeping me flushed, but the room was really warm.

"Not who your parents *were,*" said Mordecai. "Who your parents *are.*"

I shook my head. *No.* I had given my hope of having a mother to the Void. It had been the price of surviving Alyndra's attack. Even if my mother was alive, she was no longer my mother. My throat ached again. We needed to go.

"We'll take him with us," I said. "He'll take us to the high witch."

"Fine," growled the alpha werewolf, and turned to leave.

I let out a long, silent sigh of relief. In his own way, Mordecai had always been there for me. He had been the only constant in my life when everyone else had abandoned me. If nothing else, he deserved my understanding and gratitude.

As Kieron and Bronx stalked out of the dark room, another of my friends took their place. It was Savvy, and she had her crossbow trained on Mordecai.

"Savvy," I said on a sharp intake of breath. The pins and needles feeling was back. It was all over my body. My magic was fighting to get out. "Put your weapon down."

"No," she replied sharply, not even looking at me.

"Savvy, please." I looked wide-eyed at Sam for help.

"Savvy," said Armstrong in a calm voice. "Put it down and we'll talk."

She didn't take her eyes off the vampire. "I'll put it down once I've shot a bolt into his heart."

Mordecai looked at her with sad eyes. "Hello, Savannah."

"Wait, what?" I asked. "How did he know—"

Oh.

"Hello, Griffin." There was a coldness in her voice that I had never heard before. "I was hoping to see you again."

The room grew warmer still. Perspiration prickled down my neck.

"Savannah," said the vampire cautiously. "I can explain."

"I don't want an explanation," she replied. "I want revenge."

I put my hands up to get her to look at me. "Savvy, please, there's more to it than we know."

"I don't care," she murmured, and I saw the tendons in her arm tense as she grasped the stock and put more pressure on the trigger. "I know enough. I know that this vampire weaseled his way into my life, took advantage of me, and took my daughter."

"I shouldn't have done that," he said.

"Correct," sneered Savvy.

"Why the elaborate ruse?" I asked. "And why Savvy and Abigail? You said you didn't want me to pursue the case of the missing daughters, so why ensnare my best friend? My goddaughter?"

"I didn't want to do it," Griffin said. "I told them it was a bad idea. But they wanted someone on the inside. Someone to feed information back on developments."

"But you already knew everything," I said. "You put the spyware in my phone."

He looked confused for a moment. "No, I didn't."

"One of you A-holes did," I replied.

"No, Asha," he insisted. "I would have known about it."

There was no point in lying about the spyware now, so I mostly believed him. "Fine," I conceded, "but then why take Abigail?"

"Lilian insisted. She said Abigail was special ... but I think it had more to do with spite. She knew about you, knew you were on her trail. She was a vicious thing."

Sam interrupted. "The fire," he urged, watching as the smoke became visible. "It's coming."

"Why isn't the sprinkler system working?" I asked Mordecai.

"It was too sensitive," he replied. "Kept ruining the carpets when Ms. M did any kind of powerful magic. We shut it off."

"Can you turn it back on?" I asked.

Mordecai shook his head. "Wouldn't know how. We have people for that kind of thing."

Of course they do.

"Got to move," said Sam again, with a bit more urgency than before.

"I'll meet you out there," Savvy promised darkly, finger still on trigger, cold eyes still trained on the vampire who stole her daughter.

I tried one last time. "Savvy, please. We are better than this. Better than *them.*"

"Speak for yourself," she replied, and pulled the trigger.

"No!" I shouted, flying at her in a rugby tackle and taking her to the ground, but it was too late. Freshly oiled by Ferra, the crossbow mechanism worked with no resistance. There was a swift whooshing sound and a dull thud as the bolt landed deep in Mordecai's chest. His eyes flew open in shock.

"No!" I yelled again. "Mordecai!"

I gave Savvy a horrified look. How could she? *How could she?*

Mordecai made a pained sound and looked down at his chest. I wanted to be angry with Savvy, wanted to smash that crossbow out of her hands, but I knew deep down that what happened between her and Griffin was between them. As much as I wanted to, it was not for me to orchestrate peace. He had known Savvy at her best: kind, generous, foxy, vulnerable, and easy to love. In short, not someone you'd expect to put an arrow in your heart. By doing what he had done to her, he'd irreversibly changed something inside her, had transformed some soft pliable part to cold, hard flint. The vampire wrapped his hands around the shaft protruding from his chest and pulled it out with a bellow of pain and disbelief.

He had taken her child. My godchild. Despite my feelings for Mordecai, I knew it was unforgivable. My anger toward my best friend faded. I checked that she was okay, then leapt up to heal Mordecai, but it was too late. The crossbow bolts, crafted lovingly out of oak and honed to perfection, were the ultimate vampire-killers. A streamlined wooden stake. He managed to remove the shaft, but his chest was a glowing coal. He fell to his knees, and I joined him there. He'd be ash in seconds.

"Thank you," I told him. "For everything you did for me."

He looked at me with something close to pained affection, then up at Sam. "Protect her," he whispered. "She's in grave … danger."

Sam nodded.

"How do we get to the roof?" I asked him.

He sighed his last sigh, a widening hole burning in his chest. "Fire," he murmured.

The fire in his chest? The fire below? I didn't understand. I watched as he put every last bit of his energy into his next words.

"Step into the fire," he said, and his eyes closed, his face went slack.

Before he collapsed, I hugged him as hard as I could, and hoped he felt my arms around him as he died. Griffin Mordecai crumbled in my embrace, then disappeared as he turned to ash.

CHAPTER 61
FUR & FANGS
ASHA

I wanted to weep, but there was no time. Irrationally, I gathered up a handful of the warm ash and put it in my pocket. Sam helped me up, and tried to help Savvy, but she was unresponsive.

"Savvy," I urged. "We've got to move."

She just stayed there, face to the floor. Rick moved me gently aside and lifted Savvy up. He held her like a sleeping child in his arms, and we left the room.

Back in the open-plan part of the penthouse, things were dire. Scared of the smoke and uncertain as how to get to the roof, the werewolves were climbing the walls. In the middle of the space was the huge contemporary fireplace.

"Quickly," I commanded. "The fire."

If I'd had more time to consider our options, I probably wouldn't have had the guts to do what I did next. No one decides to step into a fire on a whim just because a dying vampire tells them to. I was either trusting Mordecai or my own instinct, but I knew it was the only thing to do. The heat coming off the fire was not insignificant, and I almost lost my nerve, but I took a breath and stepped into the flames. I expected my boots to burn, my cloak to catch fire like Wilkinson's had, but they didn't. It wasn't even warm in the center. I looked back at my team to tell them, but the molecules of my body had a different idea, coming apart and rising like smoke up through the ceiling. The potent instaportal spell placed me smoothly on the roof, where I felt my body come together again. It was my first taste of the high witch's power, and it scared me. I knew when someone had more powerful magic than I did, and Ms. M's ability was like nothing I'd ever encountered. It was a neutral spell, with neither good nor bad intentions, but there was no denying the potency of its caster.

The top of the building was as large as I had expected. There was no one in view. The sky had darkened considerably, filling with heavy, threatening clouds that I could only describe as doomsday-bringers. Lightning flashed in the distance. I felt lonelier than I ever had in my life, like I was the only one in a suffocating world. I clutched my ritual knife.

The air was scented with the promise of apocalypse. Fumes from the shelling of the city, smoke from the burning floors below that rose from the windows the Palefang pack had shattered. Bitter, acrid, and foul to breathe. This was what Æterna wanted, this utter destruction. This disgusting reek of death. All because of one woman, one witch brimming with so much evil that she spilled it everywhere she went, everywhere she looked. I imagined her standing in the middle of this roof garden—a slender silhouette like a vase of black ink—and it overflowed onto the roof, flooding it, covering every surface with its oily slick until it sloshes over the sides and all the way down to the ground, painting the entire skyscraper black, and the city below, until the entire Realm disappeared into her greedy black hole, like the rift left in your heart when someone you love dies.

The wind blew sour. Kieron appeared beside me with Bronx. I immediately felt stronger with their presence. The others arrived, too. Sugar, along with her guard. Sam, Rick—still holding a comatose-looking Savvy—

and Apollo. Most of the other wolves had been tasked with securing the penthouse.

"Where is she?" asked Bronx, sniffing the air.

"She'll be protected by the clan," I said. "She'll be the last person we find up here."

A hissing sound reached my ears. Vampires. I could tell the wolves heard it, too, because their bodies stiffened and they pricked up their ears. The clouds blocked out the setting sun, and it became difficult to see.

"Watch out!" yelled Rick.

I twisted around to see a bloodsucker about to plunge his fangs into my neck. Without even thinking, I brought my dagger up and thrust it straight through the soft underside of his chin. It made a terrible squelching sound, but instead of cringing, I relished it. I pulled out the knife, and as I did so the vampire turned to ash. I moved on to the vamp approaching Sam. He had the assault weapon from earlier, and sprayed his attacker full of bullets, throwing the enemy back with the power of the missiles, and I quickly crouched over him and knifed the drac in the chest to finish the job. Another vampire ashed. It was difficult to see in the smoky, over-cast light, but when I blinked to focus, a new green filter appeared through my monocle. Night vision. I knew the wolves would have a similar advantage. Palefang ripped his second assailant apart, and Bronx followed. Working together, they took on a third and made short work of him before a fourth and fifth arrived. Fur and fangs, beasts and blood. The darkness seemed over-whelming.

Rick had put Savvy down behind him so that he could fight and defend her at the same time. He also had an assault weapon, which was useful in pushing the vampires back and slowing them down, but to truly be put out of their misery they needed a crossbow bolt or my knife in their hearts. Lightning flashed, and the wind picked up. I wondered if the high witch was controlling the weather.

A leering vampire set his sights on me. Feeling cocky, I called him closer, ready to force my knife into him. I tripped over something and stumbled toward him, and he took full advantage. He sprang on top of me, sharp nails digging into my arms, fangs on my neck. I yelped, desperate to not get bitten, and used all my strength to shove him away. When he came back, I bicycle-kicked him in the chest, jumped up, and landed on him as he fell backwards onto the ground. My blade travelled easily into his heart, and I gave it a twist for good measure. I used his cloak to wipe his slippery blood off the handle just before he exploded into flames. I didn't see the next vamp who attacked me from behind. He took my head in his hands, preparing to snap my neck. I elbowed his stomach. He yelled, and his grip on me loosened, but he quickly recovered and clutched me with more power than before. The vampire's hands moved to my neck and began strangling me. I tried to throw him off, but he was much stronger than I was, and he was unyielding. I tried to take a breath, but my airways were too compressed to get any oxygen. Dizziness set in, and my night vision faded. I just couldn't catch a breath. I fumbled for my wand, but my limbs were not obeying instructions. I wasn't going to die like this. I refused. I tried to throw him off again, but he squeezed harder still. My body became limp, and just as I was about to pass out, the vampire let me go. I didn't know what had happened. I couldn't hear or see anything beyond the rushing in my ears, the sparks in my eyes. Dragging oxygen in with a wet gasping sound, I finally turned to see the vampire behind me. He had a bolt through his chest. As he began burning up, I looked beyond him and saw Savvy lower her crossbow. Our eyes met, and we both gave a slight nod.

Sam bellowed, and I spun to find two vamps on top of him. I leapt forward and shoved the dagger into the first one. The second saw me and let go of my detective to pursue me instead. I kicked him in the throat, and when he swayed back, I jumped onto him and plunged my dagger into his chest. He incinerated quickly, almost taking my eyebrows with him.

Ready for the next altercation, I crouched down and surveyed the battle scene, preparing myself for the next strike. The only movement were the flames of the small fires burning in the spots the vampires had fallen. I thanked the Void and crossed myself backwards. As far as I could see, the Smaragde vampires had been vanquished.

CHAPTER 62

STARDUST & BLACK FLAMES

ASHA

We staggered toward one another, relieved to have survived the attack but knowing that our fight was not yet over. My neck was bruised and it was painful to swallow. Sam had contusions and abrasions on his face. Sugar yelled at her guard to stop fussing, and I saw she had a large gash on her cheek.

I noted with concern that a few of the werewolves were missing. I hoped they were just hiding in the shadows, but then I saw the thing I had tripped over a moment ago was the body of one of the pack members. Bronx whispered to Kieron that two others had been flung off the roof while protecting us.

"The sooner we kill her, the better," replied the alpha wolf. I remembered that he had lost his mate a few weeks ago to the same clan. No wonder this battle was so personal to him. Thunder rumbled in the clouds above us. It sounded like a warning.

"Come out and face us!" I shouted into the wind. "You want me dead? Come and kill me!"

Sam squeezed my hand, and I squeezed back. Things were going to get ugly.

Fire licked at the edges of the roof garden. The skyscraper was fast turning into an open-air crematorium. A nearby potted tree burst into flames, lighting up the space. I saw fear on my friends' faces, as well as smudges of dirt, blood, and scratches. But most of all I saw righteousness and bravery, and that gave me courage.

"Come out!" I shouted. I assumed the queen of darkness was not often told what to do, and I hoped she'd take umbrage and appear, ready to strike me down for being so stubbornly insubordinate.

I heard him before I saw him. A dog's keening. Bewildered, I looked around, and when I turned back he was there, sitting right in front of us, regal and handsome.

The whole Palefang pack immediately bowed, gazing at the floor to show their subservience.

He was the most beautiful wolf I'd ever seen. Eyes like glaciers, a soft graying pelt that ruffled in the breeze. Everything in my body told me that I knew him. My sinuses stung with sudden emotion.

"Orion?" I asked.

He padded over to me. I put out my hand, and the wolf nuzzled my palm. A torrent of tears blinded me, and I fell to my knees and put my arms around him. "Orion," I cried into his neck. He whined in response, and I sobbed. I knew his scent so well, knew the feel of his fur against my skin. I tumbled back in time to when he brought me some small dead animal that he had hunted in the forest. It was the most intense feeling of familiarity, nostalgia, deja vu. I remembered the sensation of him licking my hair. I remembered looking in the mirror and seeing a baby cuddled up to a wolf, and watching my small pink hand grabbing his fur, the thumb of my other hand deep in my sucking mouth.

The wolf howled. The pack joined in, getting up and baying with all their might.

"Orion," said Kieron, bowing. "We are at your service."

Sam watched with growing confusion. While deep down I knew more than he did, I couldn't explain what was happening. Intense emotions were rocking me, making it difficult to think, to work out what this meant. Before I was ready to let go, Orion padded back to his original position and sat down, seemingly holding court. The tree was still burning, and it lent a dreamlike quality to the scene. We watched and waited. We remained still despite the fire that was slowly consuming the building we stood on. The smoke was irritating my lungs, and I coughed. It hurt.

The air behind Orion began to shimmer and sparkle. A human form gradually appeared seemingly out of stardust and black flames. We waited for the high witch to take her full human form. When I saw her face, it felt like my life was over.

CHAPTER 63
UNGODLY ELIXIR
ASHA

I couldn't ever remember seeing my mother's face —she abandoned me too young to have any kind of recollection—but I had glimpsed it during my trip, that scary time when the mushroom had allowed me to see past the flimsy walls that hid the secrets of the universe.

I hadn't seen my mother's face in real life, but I saw it now.

Apollo, similarly shocked to put two and two together, kept glancing from my face to the high witch's. I remembered that he had said the painting of the woman he had stolen from Virvaris had looked like me, which had not made sense until now.

"Asha," said the witch. I couldn't work out her expression exactly, but she was not surprised to see me.

I, on the other hand, felt like I'd been sucker punched.

Ms. M.

Maleficum.

Belladonna Maleficum.

I remember seeing it on the door of one of the cells at Riverside Asylum. It had been a trap.

"Mother." The word was unfamiliar in my mouth, awkward. Unlike most children, my lips had not uttered the word "mom" hundreds of thousands of times over the years. I felt Sam's body stiffen beside me. He was as dumbfounded as I was.

Kieron Palefang growled and eyed me suspiciously. "What is the meaning of this?"

"I didn't know," I replied. "I had no idea."

"It's true," said Savvy, and Rick nodded. "No one knew."

"Apart from the queen of darkness herself," said Sugar, with a decapitating glare in the high witch's direction.

"I stopped looking for you," I said.

"Apparently not," she replied. "You made Mordecai work overtime."

I mimicked her cold manner. "And now there are no more minions to keep us apart."

She understood what I had just relayed. Her loyal vampire consort was dead. Her eyes flickered with the realization, and she took a moment, turning her gaze to Apollo. "You," she sneered.

He cowered a little, but I could see he was trying to stand bravely.

She didn't hide her animosity. "You led her here."

"No," I interrupted. "Your evil led us here. Your greed and violence led us here."

My words didn't dent her confidence. She forced a smile. "You don't understand the way things are. I don't blame you. You are young and … impressionable."

"And you are the opposite," I said. "Old. And set in your depravation."

Everything about the encounter was bizarre. Standing on a burning roof high above the city, the thunderstorm wildly stirring the sky. Looking into the eyes of a woman I had longed for my entire life, and hating what

I saw. It didn't help that we looked so very similar. I could see that she used to be beautiful—if I was being honest, she still was—but the corruption of her soul was clear. There was something extremely unsettling about her appearance, like looking into a mirror of who I could be if I took the wrong path. Cruel, diabolical, and simmering with a power so compelling that she seemed to glow. An uneasy feeling, knowing that I could attain that kind of magic if I was willing to embrace the darkness within me.

"I did everything in my power to stop this from happening," she said. "To stop us from meeting."

This wasn't news, but it still hurt.

"I know," I replied. "I've had to fight all kinds of demons to find you, including Sirilla Voltane. That's how we knew a witch was behind it all. I recognized the spell."

"It's a handy one," she said with a note of pride.

"It didn't work," I replied, hating her self-satisfaction. "None of it worked in the end, because we're here, and we're going to stop you."

She smiled again, but this time it was genuine. "There's no way to stop me."

I was just about to rephrase it in a way she would understand when Kieron spoke.

"We've already stopped you," he said. "Your army is defeated, both Xarlug and Smaragde. You have no one left."

"I no longer need an army," she replied. "They performed their duties. I have what I want."

"We destroyed your business," I said. "The supply chain, the storage facilities, the factory. We brought home the girls you were farming to make your ungodly elixir."

"Factories are easy to replace," she replied nonchalantly. "And so are people. Since your visit to Obsidian Castle, I have begun talks with another clan who are very happy to help me rebuild."

"Are you really that depraved?" I asked.

"Business is business," she said.

I couldn't believe anyone would be so corrupt. To sell out everyone and everything. "So it really is all about the money?"

She chuckled in a patronizing way. "No, Asha, it's about

what money buys. Wealth is *power,* and I have the most power in the Realm."

"Power," I spat. "And what are you planning on doing with all this control you are so hungry for?"

"That's the beauty of it," she grinned. "I can do anything I want."

CHAPTER 64

CORPSES AND RUBBLE
ASHA

"Is it worth it?" I asked. "Is it worth all the lives you've destroyed?"

"That's the thing about life," my mother said. "It comes and goes. Everyone dies in the end."

"But the suffering you've caused …"

Belladonna shrugged. "It's the human condition. It has been since time immemorial."

"Your brutes killed our friend," said Bronx. "And killed Kieron's mate."

"And you killed my consort," she said directly to Savvy, as if she had seen it happen with her own eyes. Savvy took this as a threat, and raised her crossbow. I could imagine her thinking, *Killing your consort was only the beginning.*

The high witch did not worry over Savvy's threat. "Before you get trigger-happy, banished one, I'll warn you that I am immune to your arrows."

"Why would I believe that?" Savvy asked. "You look as vulnerable as anyone else standing on this roof. Shall we test your theory? I'd be happy to oblige."

"Go ahead," Belladonna taunted. "But first, a warning. My protection aura is not benign."

At this, Savvy looked a little less certain. We knew what that meant. Any attack on the high witch would be intensified and reflected back at us. Shoot a crossbow at Belladonna, get a dozen bolts in return with no effort on her behalf. While we had to preserve our magic to survive this, she did not. We may as well have been aiming our weapons at ourselves.

This made me angry, and I felt a renewed surge of magic in my veins. I had Lilian Black's protection amulet, so what would happen if I slung a spell in my mother's direction? I took a step forward.

"So," I said. "You're finally going to kill me. You've tried for so long and you're finally going to get to do it."

"You know nothing," she replied.

"You left your baby in the woods," I said. "Your first attempt on my life."

"Not true," she said. "I made sure you were looked after."

Orion watched me with his pale eyes.

"You left a defenseless baby in the care of a wolf and a vampire," I spluttered.

Her eye twitched slightly—a hint of emotion. Finally.

"It was the right thing to do," she said.

I laughed through the fresh wave of heartache. "It was the right thing to do? Your own baby!"

"One day you'll understand," she replied.

I stepped forward again. "No. Not one day. Tell me now. I deserve to know."

When she didn't respond, I pressed on. "And the bounty on my head. Sending the Dusk Reapers after me. After your own flesh and blood."

The storm clouds roiled around us.

My mother frowned. "Dusk Reapers?" she said. "You think *I* sent them?"

"Who else? You've clearly wanted me dead since the moment I was born."

"That's not true," she replied. "I left you with Orion to save your life, not take it. If I had wanted to kill you, I would have. It would have been much easier."

"You sent the wizard bounty hunters to take my life, to stop me from uncovering your despicable plans. To preserve your wealth and power."

"Asha," she snapped. "The opposite is true. I sent Mordecai to warn you about them. And he did, time and time again. But your stubbornness—"

"My *stubbornness!*" I yelled. "I was trying to save the girls. Hundreds of girls! From *YOU*. Only you could make that sound like a personality flaw."

The combination of my anger and the burning building below made me feel manic. I wanted to end it, but I didn't know how. "Who sent them?" I asked. "If it wasn't you, who put a bounty on my head?"

There was a whoosh of flames and the corner of the roof gave way. A huge chunk of concrete fell, almost taking

Sugar and her guard with it. They vaulted forward as the ground beneath them crumbled.

"We don't have much time," Belladonna said to Apollo. "Give me the mirror."

I expected Apollo to look scared, but he didn't. He squared his shoulders. "No."

The high witch's eyes flared, and sparks came off her. "Apollo!" she shouted. "Give me the mirror!"

"You'll have to wrench it from my cold, dead hands," he replied.

"That can certainly be arranged," she replied, rippling the air around her with menace.

Lightning struck nearby, and we all jumped.

"Now," said the witch, her arm outstretched to receive it. "Hand it over *now.*"

Belladonna Maleficum was clearly not used to taking "no" for an answer. With her hand that was already extended, she sent a current of red electricity through the air. Apollo tried to dodge it, but it hit him in the shoulder. The air around him buzzed, and he cried out in pain. His backpack looked undamaged. The high witch sent another current. This one struck him in the stomach, and he doubled over.

"Leave him alone!" yelled Savvy, raising her crossbow again.

"What are you waiting for?" demanded Belladonna. "Pull the trigger already!"

"No!" I shouted. "Savvy, do *not*. Don't listen to her!"

Ignoring us, the witch threatened Apollo again. "Give me the mirror!"

Still doubled over, he shook his head. The third red lightning strike was the strongest. It smashed into his body, singeing his hair and blistering his skin. Despite the smoke in the air, I could smell him burning. He bellowed in pain.

"Stop it!" I hissed at my mother, jaws so tightly clenched that my skull ached.

"I'll make you a deal," she said, that awful smile on her face again. "I'll stop AND I'll let you all go if you give me the mirror."

"That's not going to happen," said Kieron.

Belladonna blinked at the alpha werewolf. "Oh, yes, it is. Because the mirror belongs to me. It always has."

"Wait," I said. "*You* put the Septics in the mirror?"

"Of course I did. That mirror is the only thing standing between us and the complete annihilation of the Realm."

"But you're the one who wants to destroy the city," I said.

She frowned at me. "No, I don't. Why would I destroy the city I want to rule? What's the point in inheriting corpses and rubble?"

"Why?" Sam asked. "Why hire Apollo to steal it for you?"

"I didn't," she replied. "I hired Apollo to steal the Mata-handi book."

I could tell Sam was trying to puzzle out the case. "Wilkinson didn't work for you?" he asked.

She looked at Sam for a while before speaking. "Who is Wilkinson?"

CHAPTER 65

ORION

ASHA

"You put the Septics in the mirror," I echoed. It wasn't making sense to me, but Belladonna had no reason to lie. "You ended the Starless Time."

"I did what I could. Dystopia is not conducive to a good economy."

"You pretend all you care about is wealth, but I can see that's not true."

"It is true. Wealth is power; wealth gives you options. Wealth doesn't disappoint you."

"What about people?" I asked.

"People are the opposite of wealth. They make you feel powerless; they break your heart."

"You have a heart?" snorted Sugar. "Could have fooled me."

Belladonna ran her tongue over her teeth. I could tell she was growing impatient. As if to illustrate this, another corner of the roof collapsed. Apollo was still on the ground, and he still had the backpack.

"Asha," she said, "I think I have given you and your friends enough of my time."

If I didn't attack her now, it would be too late. It was a huge risk, but so was biding our time on the lip of an inferno. Best to strike while she wasn't expecting it. My nerves were shot, but that wasn't a bad thing, because my magic was so close to the surface it didn't take much effort to call it up without being too obvious about it.

"Sneakthief! I'm giving you one more chance," she snapped at Apollo, even though he seemed barely conscious.

"If you hurt him again ..." I warned.

"You'll what?" she demanded.

I was brimming with magic now; it was an effort to hold it back.

She stretched her hand out to Apollo again, and I heard her murmuring under her breath. The now-familiar red lightning shot out of her hand, but I jammed my wand in her direction and knocked her backwards with a *rumpis* spell so that the crimson bolt flew over Apollo's head.

Absolute pandemonium ensued.

My destructive spell, after disrupting Belladonna, bounced right back at me just as she said it would. Prepared, I dodged the worst of it. Only the edge of it got me, shearing my hair on my left side. It cut like a razor, and I knew that I was lucky to be alive. It seemed that Black's amulet would not protect me from my own magic. Orion growled, warning us to keep our distance from Belladonna.

There was no option but to keep at it. I slung another *rumpis* spell as two AK-47s opened fire. Savvy used her crossbow. Every missile hit the high witch's aura, and all were redirected swiftly back at us. I threw up a fire shield before anyone was hurt, designed to incinerate every projectile sent back to kill us. Because Belladonna was unhurt, it seemed useless, but we had gained ground. We all took another step forward and repeated the attack. Again, it boomeranged back, and I created a new wall of fire to protect us. It worked. We edged closer still. I wasn't a hundred percent sure what would happen when we were up close and personal, but I followed my instinct because I was out of my depth and didn't know what else to do.

Close in, attack, defend.

Belladonna started getting nervous—I could see it in the way she was moving. So confident and composed before, she retreated now, glancing back to see how close she was to the flaming edge of the roof. I didn't see fear in her eyes, only annoyance that she had to deal with us when she'd be much happier sitting somewhere more comfortable, drinking French champagne and checking Æterna's stock price.

When we got too close for comfort, she was forced to do something. "Orion!" she shouted, pointing at Apollo and hissing. "Sic!"

Orion bared his teeth, growling at the pickpocket, ready to pounce.

"No!" I shouted at him. "No! Down, Orion! Stay!"

The werewolves looked shocked. My dog training skills were sketchy at best and nonexistent at worst. I was sure I had offended the important wolf by treating him like a dog, but I wasn't going to let my old friend kill my new one just because some mad power-hungry witch commanded it.

"Orion," Belladonna warned through clenched teeth. "Get. Him."

"No!" I shrieked, using as high a pitch as I could manage to make sure he heard me.

The old wolf keened, trapped between the wills of the two humans he loved.

This made Belladonna absolutely furious. "You're a *hunter*," she sneered. "Hunt him!"

Orion whined in the face of his mistress's anger. He wasn't used to it. He'd been a loyal companion for longer than I had been alive. He padded in Apollo's direction, but I could tell there was no violence in him. Perhaps he was planning to take the backpack off him— a good compromise in the otherwise untenable situation.

"No, Orion!" I yelled. "If she gets that mirror, we're all dead."

"Attack!" shouted the high witch.

Orion looked at Apollo's slack body on the ground, burnt and bloody. Barely conscious. He sniffed the air and, perhaps surmising that Apollo was not a threat to his mistress, decided not to attack.

I wanted to shout "Good boy!" but didn't want to risk offending him again.

Belladonna's disbelief was palpable. She lifted a hand and drew a silver whip from the sky above her. Before any of us could stop her or warn the wolf, she snapped it at him, lashing his flank with an awful cracking sound. Orion yelped, then howled—his voice betraying his hurt and disbelief that his beloved Belladonna would whip him. He turned his head to look at her, and she pointed the whip's handle at him in a threatening way. "Kill," she commanded.

I wished he would turn his claws and fangs on her, but his loyalty was stronger than his pain. He set his sights on Apollo and growled a warning. He was giving Apollo one last chance to hand over the mirror. When he didn't, Orion growled, snapped his jaws, and leapt at him.

CHAPTER 66

ETERNAL OBLIVION

ASHA

"No!" I screamed. As the majestic wolf launched himself at Apollo, who was still on the ground, Apollo lifted his head. The universe seemed to shrink, and time slowed all the way down as Apollo made eye contact with Orion, triggering his terrible curse. The wolf whimpered—his high whine razoring through the air—as I tried to get to them before either was hurt.

I landed at the same time as Orion, but my landing was bouncy, and softened by my hands. His was heavy and final. Apollo's expression was grief-stricken as I gathered up Orion's lolling head, his fur as soft as ever.

"Orion," I murmured. "Orion." There wasn't much else to say.

The wolf's eyes were eclipsed, but he knew I was there. He lifted a paw and put it on my lap, his body sagged, and he stopped breathing. I buried my face in his neck, his scent so nostalgic I almost choked on it. The wolf had been my world during my formative years, and now he and Mordecai were gone.

Utterly furious, I turned on Belladonna. "YOU did this!" I shouted. "How could you?" My voice was as raw as my heart.

The high witch appeared less rattled than I expected. Orion had been her loyal companion and familiar for decades, but she didn't seem even half as devastated as I felt. I was suddenly glad that she hadn't been in my life. Being raised by a mother this cold would surely have done more damage than any mysterious abandonment. Perhaps giving up any hope of finding my mom was the correct deal to strike with the Void.

"I gave Apollo a chance to return the mirror," she said. "He is responsible for the unfortunate outcome."

I hated how she framed things to make herself seem less nefarious. I hated how similar we looked, and that we were irreversibly bonded by blood. My feet began to burn, the hard rubber soles of the boots softening with the heat of the fire consuming the ground I stood on. My emotions were just as fiery. I wanted to smash her right off the roof with an *ignem* spell.

"Take that as a warning," she said. "Nothing will stand in the way of me getting that mirror." She looked directly at me. "Not even my daughter."

"Don't call me that," I spat. "You have no right."

"Give me the mirror," she said, "and I'll let you leave. If not, I'll kill every single one of your friends."

She may not know me well, but she knew I wouldn't sacrifice my friends—even for peace in the Realm.

"I won't let you," I said.

"I'll start with your least favorite, shall I?"

Before I could respond, she slung a *rumpis* spell at Sugar's guard, knocking him up off his feet and clear off the roof. His screaming as he fell the dozens of stories to the dark streets below was terrible to hear.

"Who is next?" she asked cheerfully, as if she were handing out ice cream instead of eternal oblivion. I knew she wasn't bluffing.

"We'll give you the mirror," I said.

"No, Asha," warned Sugar Shagar. "She'll destroy everything."

"If she kills us all, she'll get the backpack anyway," I said.

"And if you give her the backpack," argued the orc, "she'll kill us all."

It was a solid point, but I knew there was no way in Hades I was going to stand back while my mother murdered my team.

A defeated-looking Rick went over to Apollo, who was still in bad shape, and got the bag off his back. He unzipped it, pulled out the mirror, and passed it to Belladonna cautiously, holding it like he was feeding a dangerous snake and didn't want his arm taken off. She snatched it from him, and he backed away.

Her body language was electric with glee. I noticed she was a great deal more excited to see the magical artifact than she had been to see her prodigal daughter. Using her black-lacquered claws she tore open the brown paper, shredding it in haste. Her face lit up when she saw it, and for a moment I pictured her as the evil witch in Snow White as she cradled her own reflection.

I looked at Apollo, hoping his spelling ability wasn't as injured as he was; hoping he'd be able to draw on his pain to magnify his magic and complete our mission.

CHAPTER 67

UP CLOSE AND PERSONAL

ASHA

"Apollo," I nudged. "Apollo!"

I didn't know what he was waiting for. He needed to trap Belladonna in the mirror immediately, or it would be too late. He looked at me and shook his head sadly. He couldn't do it. It may have been because she had hurt his ability to work magic, or that his spell was bouncing off her aura, or perhaps she had some kind of immunity to the particular spell, but the reasons didn't matter. We couldn't kill her, and we couldn't trap her in the mirror. It looked like the end of the road for us. The storm seemed to agree, because its onslaught became more violent than before, pushing us around with its gale-force wind. The lightning was closer, and it reminded me of the day I had almost electrocuted myself. I felt my scars burn with the memory of the rose thorns.

My hair was whipping around my face. "Why did you send Mordecai to protect me?" I demanded. "Why have a vampire protect me my whole life, only to betray our bloodline now?"

Belladonna's head snapped up to look at me. She blinked, as if waking up from the reverie of the reflection. "The answer to that is in your question," she replied.

I didn't understand, and didn't know where to start trying to puzzle it out.

"The Septics have been trapped in there for twenty-eight years." I had to shout to be heard over the wind and thunder. "They've had decades to plot and scheme and improve their magic. They will be more dangerous than—"

"Do you think I don't know that?" she shouted back.

"Your wealth and power won't matter to them!" I yelled. "They'll take it from you!"

Belladonna looked at me like I'd crawled out from under a rock. "I know that!"

"Then let us put it away," I urged. "We can keep it safe."

"Keep it *safe?*" she demanded. "If you had kept it safe, it would still be hidden away in Avalon."

Wait, what? All this time she had known where it was? Why hadn't she just swooped in to take it?

"You got Wilkinson to hire Apollo to steal it. That's why it's not there anymore."

Again, the look of repugnance. "Perhaps you should get that injury seen to," she sneered. "It's clearly affecting your reasoning ability. Sending Mordecai to protect you, and at the same time hiring Dusk Reapers to kill you … doesn't make sense, does it?"

"Who knows?" I replied. "Your iniquity seems to trump logic. You're the one who left your only child in a hut in the woods 'for her protection.' Forgive me if I find your strategic planning a little cloudy."

I looked at Apollo again. I had bought him some extra time to craft his spell, but it hadn't seemed to help. His expression was blank. We needed a Plan C.

I reached for the toadstool keyring in my pocket.

I whispered to the fob. *"Evoco et excito, nunc et semper, res ac mortales, Merlin."*

The summoning spell worked, and Merlin appeared, along with Dusty and Abigail.

The high witch looked indifferent to the new additions to the team. A stout man and two young girls were hardly threatening.

Savvy's mouth dropped open. "Why are you here? Who is this man?" She didn't even recognize Merlin—it must have been the shock of it all.

"Don't be angry," begged Dusty. "Merlin came to check on us at the house and we were all together when you summoned him."

Merlin shot me a look of apology, his glasses glinting as he shook his head. "I couldn't leave them on their own."

The fact that the girls were also in danger now made my mandate all the more urgent.

"I need to kill her," I whispered to Merlin. "My magic just bounces off her aura."

"Get in there and do it," he urged me. "You have what you need." He tapped at his throat, indicating that I should use the essence of Death Cap.

I nodded. My magic was no match for hers, but poison would work.

Soleil's voice came to me on the wind, a long-lost memory from when she was training me to be her wand-for-hire.

"Go in for the kill," she had said. For the purposes of our training, this phrase didn't only signify what it commonly meant. For the high priestess and me, it translated literally. It indicated that I had to get right into Belladonna's intimate space—I needed to get inside her protective aura in order to effectively strike. Up close and personal.

"The aura is impenetrable," I said.

"Portal in," suggested Merlin.

I shook my head. Apollo's magic was too weak. "My portal skills—"

He took my arm forcefully. "Rookie, you can do it. I know you can. Your magic is much more powerful than you realize."

My adrenaline jangled.

"It's now or never," said Merlin.

"Invisibilis factus," I muttered. The warm rush inside my body told me I was invisible, and I made my move. I dashed straight at her. *"Ianua sit,"* I whispered. I cringed

as I said it, expecting the portal magic to backfire. It wasn't an ambitious spell—all I needed was a doorway into her space beyond the aura. A glimmer appeared, a slice of silver. My entire body tensed as I slipped through it, hoping I wasn't going to accidentally transport myself to another place entirely. Once I stepped safely inside, I looked at the witch close-up, her expression changing from disbelief to anger. She couldn't see me, but she knew I was there in her cocoon with her.

"Monstras," she said, making me visible once again. *"Impedio!"*

I raised my wrist and Lilian Black's protection amulet absorbed the spell that would have otherwise frozen me in time. I felt my magic swell. It was time to stop being on the defense. I needed to attack.

"Fiat fulgur!" I yelled, but my wand did not respond. *"Ignem exquiris!"* I shouted. Nothing.

"You're forgetting something," said the witch. Her eyes were so dark I felt like I would drown in them. "You made a deal with the Void, remember?"

"The deal was to give up hope on you. I did that years ago," I lied. *"Fiat fulgur!"*

Nothing. My wand was impotent against my mother. I swore loudly. I could feel my magic, it was right there, within reach. Why wasn't it working?

"You see?" she preened. "If I don't exist, you can't use your magic against me."

"You're wrong," I replied. I snatched the vial of poison from my neck. She put out a hand to stop me, still clutching the mirror against her body with the other.

"Asha," she warned.

I smashed her hand out of the way and pushed her as hard as I could. She was strong, but her holding on to the mirror gave me an advantage. I shot my boot out, tripping her backwards, and she fell onto the hard, burning ground. She gasped at the heat of it, and in surprise at finding herself on her back. Before she could stand, I jumped on top of her, knees on either side of her torso. I wrestled the mirror out of her grip and flung it aside.

"Asha," she repeated. "You don't know what you're doing."

But I did. With my left hand I bound her wrists together, and with my right I emptied the poison into her protesting mouth.

Belladonna choked on the toxin, and spat out as much as she was able. It didn't matter—I knew the dose was lethal even in minuscule amounts. Her eyes grew darker, until her eyeballs were inky spheres. The skin beneath darkened, and the capillaries pulsed with purple. She coughed and spluttered, her lips pale. My heart felt like it was breaking, but it couldn't be. Not for this monstrous witch. Still, a lacerating pain cut my chest in half, and I cried out, clutching my heart as if it were dying along with my mother.

Her aura began fading, allowing the others to approach.

"Oh, Asha," said Savvy, dropping to her knees beside me. Sam did the same. They both held my hands, squeezing them, showing me there was a life and light and hope on the other side of this awful thing.

Belladonna's body was twitching, and I wished it would stop. Despite everything, I didn't want her to suffer. The whole point of a cyanide tooth was a quick, painless exit —but the elixir had made her health so robust, it was taking longer than usual.

"It's okay, Mom," I said. I was just as surprised by my words as anyone else. I let go of my friends' hands to lay them on my mother's heaving chest, trying to calm her, trying to ease her passage.

She was struggling, using all her power to fight the poison traveling through her body. My eyes burned with smoke and tears. Her pain was my pain, and it was almost unbearable. I was so connected to her in that moment, as if we were one person. I couldn't take my eyes off her contorting face, my own expression twisted by my tears. A mirror image of agony.

"Mom," I wept. "Mom."

It could have been different. It *should have been* different.

She tried to say something, but it was inaudible. I held back my sobbing so that I could hear her final words, crouching closer to her so that our faces were almost touching. Her hand traveled to my monocle. It seemed to be a gesture of affection, so I leaned even closer, and with a sudden, violent, ear-splitting lightning strike, I disappeared.

CHAPTER 68

SO THIS IS WHAT DEATH IS LIKE

ASHA

I pitched over into the Void space, my body in free fall.

So this is what death is like.

I wasn't sure what exactly had occurred, and working it out while tumbling through the stars wasn't going to happen. Still, my brain tried to make sense of it.

I had been struck by lightning, and died there on the roof. Or Belladonna had killed me—or perhaps a combination of both. I was free of pain, for which I was grateful. My body began etiolating, then fading from sight altogether, and I wondered if this was how one returned to stardust. A gentle withering; a whisper.

"Asha," said the Void. It sounded like wind on the reeds, or swishing leaves.

Asha.

I realized it was my mother's voice. It felt like dappled sunshine on my skin.

I was a small child, standing in a field of long grass. It moved so beautifully in the breeze. There was so much green, it must be heaven. The sky was an uninterrupted blue. So much color and goodness here. I was dressed in a pretty frock, my hair was brushed and smooth and held back with a headband. I knew it wasn't a memory, because I had never had clean, combed hair or dresses when I was that young—I had been a forest witchling with a black halo of tangled hair.

A woman appeared. "Asha," she purred, all smiles and wonder, her fresh blue and white summer dress flapping in the wind. She looked like me, minus my botanical tattoos. She was a purer version of both of us.

"Mom," I replied, my heart swelling. She took my hand and we walked together, giggling as the grass tickled our legs, and pointing out wildflowers. I felt so much love for her and knew hers was even greater. It was the perfect moment ... but it had never happened.

Why was the Void showing this to me? Why taunt me with what could have been, and why now? It seemed cruel on one hand, on the other, a small part of me was happy to experience it at least once in my life, even if it wasn't real.

"Asha," my mom said again. "It's time for you to see."

I remembered being on the roof with her, when she tapped my monocle. She was dying.

It's time to see.

I looked up at her, expecting the grass to blacken, the branches of the trees to strangle us, because scenes like this—walking happily in a field—are how the best nightmares begin. They lull you into a false sense of peace and joy, and then, without warning, it turns. The water you're gulping turns to ink, the cat you've been stroking turns out to be a huge rat, and the beautiful apple you've just bitten into is teeming with worms. The best horror surprises you; it takes you by the throat when you assumed an embrace, and I was certain this would be no different. But the scenery did not turn to ash. Instead, my mother squeezed my hand and we were transported to another place I didn't recognize.

It was nighttime, and we were on a deck at the beach. Fairy lights swayed from the awning above us. My mother was sitting at a table. She was barefoot, her skin was tanned, and she was wearing nothing more than a loose cotton coverall over a bikini. She was young, oozing vitality and sensuality. A silhouette—a man with a bottle of beer dripping with condensation—approached her, and she invited him to sit down. Something he said made her laugh. Later they were walking on the beach, stopping to kiss when the urge took them. She had introduced herself as Donna, but he called her Belle.

He would always call her Belle. For the rest of that tropical holiday, for the dates they went on afterwards, and at their wedding. He was eccentric, funny, and super-smart. She was beautiful and ambitious. Most of the time, their magic powers complemented each other. They were happy for a while, then the water turned to ink.

Shouting, screaming, plates magically smashing against the walls. Cupboard doors all being flung open at the same time, as if a poltergeist shared their kitchen. Paper and photographs being burned with purple fire, the same color bruises appearing from phantom punches. Once, a butcher's knife narrowly missed my mother's forearms as she held them up to protect her face. It landed in the cupboard door behind her, wedged into the wood. She removed it without a word and put it in the drawer, where it belonged, and packed her bags. When she was finished, she vomited into the toilet bowl, and her hands traveled to her flat stomach as she gazed at her reflection in the bathroom mirror. My eyes stared back.

Backwards and forwards we'd go a few times, packing and unpacking, until we woke up in a hospital where she thought I had left her, but I hadn't. When hearing the news, she cried, but not with relief. Speed healing was on her side, and we left before the staff asked any difficult questions. After that, there was no going back to him, but he found us over and over again.

On an overcast day she sat at the window watching the rain fall. We were in a rocking chair, and the motion felt good. Her belly was swollen with me growing inside it. She was wan and ill-looking, as if I was taking too much of her life force. Her movements were measured and slow. She was planning her disappearance.

That night he found us again. He was in his wizard's cloak, and scared us with his violent magic. It was a night of battling it out—explosions of their individual magic pitted against one another—until it was too much for her. I thought we'd wake up in the hospital again, but she didn't wake up for days. Splayed out on the floor, the sun streaming through the window, setting, then rising again, I wondered if she'd ever wake up. The destruction he had wrought was significant. When she did surface, she stayed down on the floor and wept.

"He has cursed me," she cried. "He has cursed me."

At first, I thought she meant his vicious presence in her life was a curse, but her hands were on her stomach, and it became clear that I was the curse. I had his blood in my veins. I was the thing that made him keep coming back.

She packed a tiny suitcase and we moved to the hut in a seemingly magical forest where a young wolf adopted us. Orion had no pack, so we became his family. We would go for long walks with him, throw sticks and give him treats as if he were our dog. We were closer to Orion than any human before him. He lay down by the fire in the evenings and slept on the foot of the bed at night. Ears always scanning for strange sounds, like he knew there was danger in the air. Every morning my mother would redraw the protective circle around the hut on stilts while incanting an hour-long safeguarding spell. She used whatever she could find—pebbles, flowers, branches, bleached animal bones—and shored them up securely so the ring was never broken. It worked, and the dangerous silhouette stayed away.

Some days were easier than others as she waited for me to arrive. Her energy was darker than ever before, and she'd stare into her mirror and think bad thoughts. The word "curse" was never far from her lips. One day she didn't get out of bed, even though Orion kept nudging her with his snout. He spoke to her in that way of his, a velvety growl of a voice.

You need to get up, he was saying. *I know you feel heavy, but you need to check the protection ring and find some food before the sun sinks too low.*

She remained on her back, staring at the ceiling, hardly blinking.

The second day of not getting out of bed was the first time Orion hunted for us. He brought a drooping rabbit in his jaws, but she just turned on her side and ignored the gift.

She had disappeared from her life successfully, and now she was disappearing altogether.

"Is that all I was to you?" I asked her. "A curse?"

But I already knew the answer.

CHAPTER 69
RELICS OF DEATH
ASHA

The colors faded. It became a black-and-white world where everything was cold and bitter-smelling. Like the story *The Missing Daughters of Evaron*, evil lurked behind the gnarled black trunks, and the rocks were jagged. Unknown creatures slithered and crawled and scurried. The howling began. A wind chime made of animal teeth chinked in the breeze.

I had been here before.

I was hovering above the nightmarish shack ringed in relics of death and broken wishes. The screams came in waves. They reached a terrible crescendo and crashed.

Even up there above the hut I could smell childbirth: earthy, salty, metallic. The scent of blood and fear. I sank down through the roof and into the hut with the stick pentagrams on the walls. Their shadows danced as a small fire burned in the corner. My mother's body, racked with pain, struggled on the bed that had become both her escape and her prison, sheets damp with perspiration and blood.

Yes, I had been here before.

She was in between contractions, resting while she could before the next round of convulsions contorted her body. Her hair was a shock of black dreadlocks and knotted threads, her face a moon behind a veil of clouds. She was teetering on the brink of oblivion.

Inside her, I was also dancing with death. I knew I had to get out or drown, but I was stuck.

"Curse," she muttered. "Curse." The contractions took hold again and the raven-locked witch arched and squalled in agony. There was another tide of blood, and she gritted her teeth and swung her body off her bed. She lurched, hunched over in pain, toward the small counter near the fireplace. She picked up her ritual knife, the blade glinting in the firelight, and dropped it into a cauldron of boiling water.

Once she retrieved the knife, she barely waited for it to cool. With a brutal slash, she opened her belly. Caterwauling rained down. After a moment, I was no longer stuck. She wrenched me into the air and I joined in on her howling.

Later, waking up nestled in soft rags, I looked into my mother's eyes. She had stopped her bleeding and I could smell the herbs of the healing potion on her breath. It was my first introduction to the magic of plants, and it would stay with me forever, along with the concept of being a curse.

CHAPTER 70
THE ANTIDOTE
ASHA

I opened my eyes. I was back on the roof of the skyscraper, my mother's twitching body beneath me. It was chaos. People shouting and coughing, the edges falling away. There was an urgency to portal home immediately or die in the flames—but I was not ready to leave.

"Mom!" I yelled, and she opened her eyes a fraction. She tried to say something, but the words would not form. Fortunately, telepathic Dusty was beside me.

"Leaving you with Orion ... she wants you to know that she did it to protect you."

"From my father?" I asked.

"From the darkness in both of them," Dusty replied. "She felt how powerful your magic was, even as a baby, and she knew the darkness would take you, would harness your power for evil if she stayed with you. It was too late for her, but not for you."

"But we could have left the darkness behind," I said. "We could have done it together."

"It was too deep and too dangerous," said Dusty. "You had to both disappear."

I closed my eyes against the acrid air and to stop the tears. I snapped out of my emotional trance. "The antidote!"

I let go of my mother and stood up. "Merlin!" I shouted. "The antidote! Quickly!"

Merlin was standing right there and had been watching me crouched over my mother as she died. He gazed at me, but didn't move.

I raised my voice, my body alight with panic. "Antidote, Merlin, please!"

Merlin finally spoke. "There is no antidote."

I stared at him. "Of course there is," I shouted. "It's in your pocket."

Merlin shook his head slowly. "Asha," he said, calling me by my first name for the first time I could remember. "Listen to what I am saying. *There is no antidote.*"

My brain fizzed out. I didn't understand. I didn't understand … and then I did, and it felt like the world was falling in on me. The skyscraper could as well have collapsed beneath us—it would have felt the same. The flames behind Merlin painted him in a silhouette.

As we watched, Merlin's shape changed from that of a portly uncle to a taller, more muscular version. His face remained similar, but when he flung the round specs I knew so well into the fire, he looked like a different person. I wouldn't have recognized him in the street.

"I must commend you on your Mason & Sons glamour potions, Asha," he said. "They work every time, without fail." He adjusted his neck and cracked his knuckles, settling into his real body.

"No," I whispered. "No." I was shaking my head, not wanting to believe it. "It's not possible."

But as I stood there denying it, all the puzzle pieces clicked into place.

Merlin had given me the phone as a gift—the same phone with the baked-in spyware. That's how they always knew my whereabouts and my plans. That's why Wilkinson knew where to find us in the mining ghost town. That's why, despite Merlin having "been in my life for years" Savvy hadn't recognized him. Why he never appeared in any photos on my walls. I did nothing but stare at him as it all started making sense.

"When I finally found you," he said, "all grown up and with my and Belle's power in your veins, I knew you were the only one who could stop me from getting what I wanted. I had to enlist the Dusk Reapers before you grew too strong. But you survived that attack, and I learned you woke up with amnesia. It occurred to me that it was the perfect opportunity to infiltrate your life. I could pretend that I'd always been part of it."

I felt sick to my stomach with his treachery. Sick, sick, sick. I felt like keeling over.

"But why?" I asked. "Why insinuate yourself into my life?"

"Because you were my ticket in." He gestured at the building, burning all around us. "I would never have gotten to Belle without you. You were my Trojan horse."

"You wanted to destroy her?" I asked. "After all this time?"

"More than that," he replied. "I wanted to take everything from her, because she took everything from me."

CHAPTER 71

JEKYLL & HYDE

ASHA

Belladonna, who only had a few breaths left in her, groaned. Dusty and Abigail were still with her. Dusty narrowed her eyes at Merlin, and I could see the disappointment in her face.

"I can't believe you," she muttered. I could hear the hurt in her voice, the betrayal, as she spoke for both of us.

"I did warn you," Merlin replied. "Jekyll and Hyde, remember?"

My mother murmured in pain.

"What is she saying?" I asked Dusty.

"She doesn't have much longer. Things are fading. She wants you to know that she loves you, that she always has. She feels her abandonment of you was all in vain now that Merlin found you anyway. She's mourning the loss of the time she could have spent with you."

The words cut deep, but with a double-edged sword. I was devastated that she was dying—that *I* had been the one to kill her—and hearing that she missed me, missed the time we could have had together—was something I'd never forget.

"She put the spell on your ring," said Dusty. "To glow when you're in danger. She tried to keep you safe."

"Enough," said Merlin, approaching Belladonna. When we protested, he swept the girls away with a spell. The hair on the back of my neck rose, my magic sparkled.

"Leave her alone!" I yelled.

He gestured at me, sweeping me backwards with a gale force like he had done to the girls.

"Belle! Reunited at last," he said to her in a low voice. He picked up the mirror. "Before you die, I want you to know that I am going to take everything from you. I'm going to take the Marquis Mirror. I'm going to take your magic, your wealth, and our daughter."

Belladonna groaned and shook her head. He placed his hands on her chest and muttered a spell. I tried to get closer to stop him, but I bounced off whatever barrier he had put between us. I watched impotently as he continued his incantation. The girls tried to get through, too, with the same result. Purple energy began traveling from Belladonna's body up Merlin's arms, and into his chest. He arched his back as if he were touching a live wire—which I guess, in a way, he was. It began as a siphoning of magic, but her power was so heady that it looked like he was being electrocuted. It got brighter and brighter until the connection snapped and Merlin was thrown backwards, leaving Belladonna's body limp.

"She's gone," said Dusty, who didn't need to check someone's pulse to see if they were alive. Apollo made a gasping sound, and when I looked at him, holding his head, I realized his curse was broken, which could only mean one thing.

My mother was dead.

My eyes flicked back to the dark wizard on the ground, hoping he was incapacitated. I was to be sorely disappointed. Merlin rose like a monstrous phoenix emerging from the ocean of flames. He was glowing with the strength he had siphoned from my mother. Now he looked twice his original size, and the glinting black magic was coming off him in waves, making the air around him shimmer and sparkle. Worst of all, he had the mirror.

I hated him with a raw force of a volcano about to erupt. Mixed in with the sheer hatred was anger, heartbreak, and an intense sense of betrayal I'd never experienced before. My own magic was amplified to such an extent that I was having trouble holding it back. It urgently needed an outlet before I spontaneously combusted.

Dusty looked at me with eyes like saucers, and I was sure she felt the same sensation.

Dusty, I said silently. She blinked to show she heard me.

We need to combine our magic if we are to have a chance at defeating Merlin.

She nodded.

Tell Abigail and Savvy. Together we'll weave our fiat fulgurs *together.*

Dusty moved toward Savvy, who was aiming her crossbow at Merlin, and gave her the message. Savvy quietly handed her crossbow over to Sugar, who had been standing behind her for cover. The four of us lined up facing the wizard: Abigail, Dusty, Savvy, and I.

Still shocked, I was tearful with the utter betrayal of it. "Why, Merlin, *why?*"

How did it benefit him to raze the Realm? I understood that he had stolen Belladonna's power and wealth, but why destroy the city?

"Do you remember when we were foraging for fungi and I taught you about the meadow-maker mushroom?" he asked.

"Yes," I replied. "*Armillaria.*" It was the fungus that strategically took down trees in areas where the soil needed sunlight and water. Pioneer plants take over, a meadow appears, nitrogen is replaced, and balance is restored to the ecosystem.

"Now, you are like a meadow-maker," said Merlin. "You realize that sometimes people need to die to restore balance in the Realm. And, like father, like daughter, my purpose is also to be a meadow-maker. In destroying the Realm, I'm opening it up to be a better version of itself. To renew itself. And as mushrooms growing on dead trees, so we will attain our energy from the destruction and decomposition below us. As you know, decay is its own form of energy. The end result will be a sweeping renewal—with me at the helm, with more power than anyone believed possible. But I will need some help." Merlin cast around.

"You," he said to Apollo. "Get the people out of this mirror."

No matter how potent Merlin's magic was, he was not pure of heart and could not remove the Septics himself.

Apollo had barely recovered enough to stand, and he looked unsteady on his feet. "No sir," he said. "That's not going to happen."

"Listen here, you witless weed," said Merlin. "You will do as I say, or you will live to regret it every day of the rest of your quotidian life. You thought Belle's curse was bad? Just wait until you see what I have in store for you."

Apollo's nostrils flared. He was nervous, but brave. He began slowly circling Merlin where he stood. "You can threaten me all you like, but I'm not freeing the Septics."

"Fool," sneered the wizard. A projectile of black electricity darted from Merlin's hand into Apollo's already-wounded shoulder. He yelled in shock and pain, spiraling back down to the ground. Merlin stalked closer.

"You can't kill me," said Apollo. "If you kill me, you'll never get them out."

"You're right," said Merlin. "But I can kill the people you love."

"You've already done that," replied Apollo.

Merlin was an imposing figure standing against the starless night sky. "Talk sense, boy," he demanded.

"There are only six dark wizards trapped in the mirror. I realized one was missing, but I didn't know who until I saw you and Belladonna together. She was the one who imprisoned them, but she wasn't able to ensnare you, right?"

"Too much history between us," Merlin said. "Her magic wouldn't allow it."

"You were the leader of the original seven Dusk Reapers," said Apollo. "Later known as the Septics, who killed my biological parents. I hoped that we'd never cross paths, but I guess it's part of my destiny. So here I am. It's time to end this thing once and for all."

Merlin laughed. "You?" he taunted. "*You're* going to finish this thing?"

Apollo stood up again. I felt a twinge of pain in empathy for him. He joined Savvy, the girls, and me in our line as we faced up to the wizard.

I looked my father in the eyes. "*We* are going to finish this thing."

Merlin looked amused, like he was the adult and we were children playing a game. "Apollo. I'm giving you one last chance to free the Septics."

"Hex the Septics," I said. "They're not going anywhere."

That's when he noticed the mirror was gone. He blinked to clear his vision, but the mirror remained missing from his hand. Sometimes, having a pickpocket on your team comes in very handy indeed.

CHAPTER 72

HOT DEATH & DECAY
ASHA

The five of us stood firm, ready to combine our magic to defeat Merlin, but the wizard had other ideas. Quick as a whip, he sent out a silver-black rope and lassoed Abigail, tugging her toward him and grabbing her. Savvy and I cried out as Abi tried to fight him, elbowing him in the stomach, but he just held her tighter. She began coughing from the smoke and being gripped so tightly.

"Let her go!" shouted Savvy. She moved forward instinctively but Merlin stopped her in her tracks by holding his wand to her daughter's temple, like a gun. Savvy froze, her eyes wild with worry, her hands shaking. Merlin muttered a spell and a ring of deadly fae fire erupted around him to stop anyone from approaching, and to stop Abi from escaping should she break free.

He smiled at Savvy. "Not so confident now, are you?"

Savannah growled at him.

"I wonder, dear witches, if you are aware of the *adela* spell."

I gulped. Savvy and I knew the black magic. In Old English the word meant liquid filth—as in, your brain becomes contaminated mud. It was the Latin root of the word "addle."

"It scrambles your mind, you see. It would be a shame if someone so young were afflicted by it. It's a lifetime of suffering, and there is no cure."

I thought of how addled Mildred Malachay's mind had been after losing her daughter. We would not let that happen to Abigail.

The girls were crying. Savvy turned to Apollo. "Do what he says," she demanded. When Apollo didn't budge, she grabbed her crossbow back from Sugar and pointed it at him. The thunder rolled; lightning struck nearby.

"Savvy!" I yelled. "What are you doing?"

"I'm saving my daughter," she said, not taking her eyes off Apollo. "Now do it!"

Abigail struggled against the wizard. Apollo put his hands up in defeat. "I'll do it," he said, then repeated himself loudly to make sure Merlin had heard. He looked at me and I nodded.

"You'll need their names," began Merlin.

"I know their names," replied Apollo. "They killed my parents."

I spoke to Dusty silently.

Calm down, I told her. *Stop crying. Abigail needs us rational and strong.*

She took a few breaths. I was saying it to myself as much as I was to her.

Good. Now I'm going to need you to use your magic. Are you ready?

Dusty wiped the tears off her cheeks and nodded.

Listen to my instructions before doing anything. No sudden movements. Don't do anything to call attention to yourself. I need you to turn yourself invisible while Merlin is distracted by the mirror. Then go to Apollo's backpack. Can you see it?

Standing where she was next to Savvy, she blinked and swept the ground with her eyes, and nodded when she found it.

There will be six open pairs of magitech ankle cuffs in there. Make those invisible, too.

Dusty's expression changed from terror to hope as she understood the plan.

As soon as a Septic steps out of the mirror, you clamp one of those babies on his ankles.

She nodded, and I winked at her. *Good girl. That's it. Do it now.*

Dusty took a slow step backwards, and another, then disappeared altogether.

Apollo looked into the mirror until he saw the surface turn to silver fire. "Malakar the Dark, I summon you to appear before us."

Lightning cleaved the air. Perhaps the Void was warning us of the danger we were inviting. My ring was going berserk, flashing and glowing.

Out of the corner of my eye, I saw Apollo's backpack moving very slightly, then it too disappeared. Black mist poured out of the mirror. It smelled worse than Sirilla Voltane's throne room—hot death and decay—and brought back the blood-curdling memories of Obsidian Castle.

The stomach-churning mist took the shape of an old man in a cloak. His corpse-like face reminded me again of Voltane. He looked a hundred and twenty in the shade. Clearly, the land inside the Marquis Mirror was not kind to its inhabitants. Maybe it worked something like dog years—one year in the mirror aged you ten in the real world.

Perhaps their degeneration was due to the fact that they had nothing to do in there apart from stewing in their evil. No amount of collagen or Botox was going to put that right.

"Malakar the Dark," I said, projecting my voice to make sure he could hear me. "We have found you guilty of treason and first-degree murder."

He snarled at me, gray lips giving way to brown teeth. His black hood covered some of his face, but I could still see him well enough to send shivers down my spine. He aimed his hand in my direction and chanted something wicked. I held up my protection amulet to counter the spell, but it wasn't necessary. The spell fizzled out before it left his palm. He looked down at his hand, trying to figure out why his spell hadn't worked,

"What," croaked the old wizard, "is the meaning of this?"

Well done, Dusty. I thought in her direction. *That's my girl.*

One threat neutralized, six to go. I prayed to Themis, the Greek goddess of divine law and order, that it would be just as easy to cuff the others.

"Malakar!" exclaimed Merlin. "What are you waiting for? Kill them!"

Malakar tried again, failed and hissed at us.

Apollo went on with his list, and each wizard was released from the mirror in turn.

"Zarek the Shadoweaver."

"Azazel."

"Nylas Blackwood."

"Malcolm Morbideus."

"Lord Vaulter."

The six stooped wizards stood there in their cloaks, reeking of their sinister history, confused as to why their previously formidable magic was no longer working. Merlin wasn't happy, either. He had expected his men to be as healthy as he was, brimming with their signature malevolence.

Dusty, I thought. *Tell Sugar what you have done, then reappear quietly and rejoin us.*

A moment later, Sugar was nodding.

"I have done as you asked," said Apollo. "Now let Abigail go."

"Why would I do that?" Merlin asked, and I felt like smashing my fist into his face. We couldn't get to him because of his fatal fae fire ring. It reminded me of the fairy rings of mushrooms we'd found in the forest that day when he took Sam and me foraging. The poignant truth was that I had loved Merlin during the short time we had together. He had known that I'd always longed for parents and had masterfully manipulated me. His illusion as Papa Smurf had been consummate, and I had swallowed the act whole. The coffees, the chats, the cash donations for the conservation project ... and the advice that almost got me killed in Oblivion. I couldn't help but to see the irony that I had wished he was my father.

"Because it's over, Merlin," I said. "You've seen how useless your once-powerful Dusk Reapers are. Your plan hasn't worked. It's *over.*"

I signaled Sugar, who gave me a barely perceptible nod. Her hand was already in her pocket.

One of the Reapers cried out in pain as his cuff sent a huge current through him.

Merlin glared at him. "What's wrong with you?" He let go of Abigail, but she was still trapped inside the ring.

"You can see what's wrong with him," I replied. "You expected them to be more powerful than ever; you thought they'd rise out of that mirror, larger than life, and wreak chaos and destruction." To be fair, it was what we had all expected, but the Void path curves towards honesty and justice.

Merlin was looking at the old Reapers as if they were vermin.

I kept on going. "His evil has eaten him from the inside. It's corrupted his body, just as it will do to you, except that you took Mom's power, too, so your decline will be rapid, and you will die a sad and lonely death. The death you deserve."

I signaled Sugar again, and another of the Reapers cried out and fell to the ground.

"Abigail," I shouted, my voice getting hoarse from the smoke inhalation and the yelling. She looked at me with utter desperation. "Remember how you dealt with Jed Harkner?"

Her pale little face nodded.

"We're going to do that again."

"Quiet, witch," sneered Merlin. "I'll be the one issuing commands here."

I could tell he was trying to strategize, trying to find the best way to kill us all, but we were not without our own forceful magic, especially when we combined it. I had successfully reserved most of my power and I was ready to use it.

I signaled Sugar, and she used her remote to blast another of the Reapers. While Merlin was distracted, I grabbed Apollo and whispered in his ear. "Do you know how to extinguish fae fire?"

"Yes," he replied.

Those days and nights of reading the banned books in Craig Blackloth's mind were really paying off, just as the directress said they would.

"But we need a gift to the fae."

My knowledge of fae was close to zero. No, I take that back. It was literally zero.

"Like what?" I asked. Perhaps I could conjure something. I hoped they wouldn't require a human sacrifice. Fae could be cruel and unpredictable.

"Gold," Apollo replied.

I had none.

"A diamond? Or an emerald?" he asked.

Merlin's attention fixed back on us. "Stop scheming or I'll send a *veneno imbuis* your way."

No, thank you. I'd had enough magical poison to last me a lifetime.

Sugar didn't wait for my signal, and another of the Reapers shrieked in pain.

"Tanzanite," I whispered to Apollo. "Will that work?"

He shrugged. "It should."

I took off the ring I had found in the forest as a wild young witchling. The picnic spot had been a favorite haunt of mine as a child. I learned that if I looked scary enough, the visitors would run away and leave their food behind. I never had to try hard. My eyes had always been an unnerving shade of green, and my hair was matted and unruly. Orion's howling added to the spooky atmosphere. I had only ever been interested in their food, and I'd share it with my familiar. But on one occasion, a couple left a ring behind. I liked the color of it, how it sparkled so blue, and decided to keep it. Years later I discovered, with Captain Morgan's help, that it was the same couple who had gone to the authorities and reported a feral urchin in the woods.

The ring had warned me of danger over the years, and now it would help to put a stop to the greatest danger of all.

CHAPTER 73

SUPERNATURAL DECAPITATION

ASHA

I gave the tanzanite ring to Apollo, who threw it into the ring of fire. It fizzed and burned a bright blue, the same hue as the stone itself. The blue looped quickly along the line of the green fae flames, extinguishing the deadly magic. Merlin lunged for Abigail, but she had already turned invisible and taken the gap. I clenched my jaw in pride. That was my fairy goddaughter.

His lethal barrier smothered, Merlin was finally vulnerable. Sugar took down the remainder of the Reapers while our line of attack reassembled, facing my father.

"Now!" I yelled. Apollo, Savvy, Abigail, Dusty, and I thrust our hands and wands in his direction.

"Fiat fulgar!" we all shouted. Our magic, all different colors and strengths streamed out of us, converging into a massive ear-splitting blast of malediction.

"Effectus adversum!" yelled Merlin, batting it straight back at us.

I hopped in front of my team, lifting my forearm with my protection amulet. *"Protendo!"* I shouted, making the ricocheted magic peter out just before it reached us. One small residual trickle hit Savvy and she gasped in pain.

That made me angry. *"Rumpis!"*

A thin blue line of vicious destructive energy flew his way, and he batted it away again, almost hitting Rick, who ducked and avoided being supernaturally decapitated just in time.

"I'd always thought you were smart," Merlin said, implying he had changed his mind. "What do you think will happen if you kill me?"

"The Realm will be a better place?" I replied.

"Debatable," he said. "What else?"

"Asha," said Sam, taking my arm.

I searched his face. To see his goodness after being immersed in such iniquity was a balm. "Yes?"

"You told me that if you kill the curser, it breaks the curse."

He let it sink in.

"Merlin cursed Belladonna with a pregnancy," Sam said. "She called you the curse."

"Yes," I said.

His face crumpled with emotion. He understood that if I killed Merlin, the wizard's curse would be dissolved, and I would die along with him.

If we killed Merlin, I would cease to exist. But the Realm would be safe, and my friends would be safe. It was a bargain I was willing to make.

"No," said Sam. "I won't let you."

"Goddess knows I love you, Detective Sam Armstrong," I said, forcing words past the lump in my throat. "And you have made me feel more loved than I have my entire life. Even when I asked you to leave for your own safety, you refused to abandon me. I want nothing more than to spend the rest of my life with you."

"Then let's make that happen," replied Sam, tears making his eyes shine. "I want a family with you. I want to adopt Dusty and the cats and Jemima. I even want to adopt Nilve SaltySnap, god help me. I want to make you coffee every morning and take you to the Cog for every anniversary."

"It sounds beautiful," I said, gritting my teeth to stop from crying. It was the most sublime fantasy—but that's all it was.

My fate was here, on this roof, in this fire. This is what I was destined to do; I was born for this. It had come full circle—I was the cursebreaker, and it was time to break my final curse.

CHAPTER 74

EQUINOX STITCH

ASHA

"There must be another way," said Savvy, who had joined Sam's side.

"There's no time," I replied. "We have to strike now. There won't be another chance."

Savvy wouldn't stand for such nonsense. Without a moment's hesitation, she aimed her crossbow at Merlin and pulled the trigger. The bolt darted to his stomach and froze right there, not making contact. It vibrated in the air, as if awaiting his command. As fast as it had arrived, it shot right back at Savvy, penetrating her ribcage just under her breasts.

Abigail and I screamed as she fell backwards. Rick caught her, cradling her in his huge arms. I wanted her to gasp or moan or make any kind of sound, but she was silent.

No no no no no!!!

It was conniving of Merlin—he was expecting us all to drop our defenses and rush to her so that he could attack us from behind. It was grim, but I knew I had to stand my ground or we'd all be done for, including Savvy. It took every ounce of grit I had.

"She's alive," I heard Rick murmur, and the relief I felt steeled my resolve. They would tend to Savvy, and I would face down Merlin. The Septics, seeing the team was now distracted and vulnerable, stealthily shuffled to attack them.

I took the deepest of breaths and summoned all my power. I had thought that I was a regular witch, but I was not. I had the blood of two of the most powerful witches and wizards sprinting through my veins. I had potential I'd never dreamed of. Every spark of magic was right there, waiting, and even when I couldn't bear to hold on to any more of it, I summoned more, siphoning it from everywhere I could: my fear for Savvy's life, my love for Sam, the high emotions all around me. My disgust towards the Reapers, the energy of the plants on the roof, the electrical storm churning above us. I took it all, and felt so charged with energy that it seemed I would soon begin floating in the air.

I lifted my arms to Mother Nature and her fury: the clamorous storm, the tumultuous wind, the lightning that was threatening to cut us down—but the Void told me that Zeus was on my side. That I should not fear the lightning, but harness it.

Arms still in the air, I called on the storm. *"Tempestas!"*

It answered me by booming so loud I thought my ears would bleed. I looked up and saw an arrow of lightning tease my palm, willing me to grab it. I plucked the lightning bolt from the darkness and hurled it at the Reaper closest to my friends. His feet left the ground, pulsating with the voltage running through him, back arched, face a mask of agony, keeled over, and burned down to nothing. The flaming ground beneath us was collapsing. I was already reaching for the next thunderbolt, and it came to me easily. I quickly reduced all six Septics to sad smoking piles of old black cloaks before they were able to touch my friends.

As I turned to Merlin, the words of the Equinox Stitch spell came to me.

. . .

She burns whole forests green to black

Turns hand-shaped leaves to dust

She caps oceans with her smoking ice

Moves mountains with fearsome gusts.

Power erupts from her like lava

Flames race along burning roots

As she knits the future with her fire

From the ashes grow green shoots.

All that burns will soon flourish

and all that flourishes must burn

Death is not the end, no, no—

The world just turns and turns.

All sleeping seeds she wakens

The rainbow is her token

The destructor's power is taken

In love, all curses are broken.

As the seasons all blow through

Our fragile destiny's sealed

Everything lost is always found

Everything hurt is healed.

This is the orbit of the wayward woman

Who knits with stars and stones

The Wild, the wanderer, the wasp, the witch

This is the course of the wayward goddess

A flame, a stone, a stitch.

CHAPTER 75
SLEEPING SEEDS
ASHA

Two of the lines stuck in my head, refusing to be dislodged, blocking my focus on the final spell I needed to kill my father.

All sleeping seeds she wakens.

The destructor's power is taken.

Oh goddess, I had it! I didn't need a huge showy spell that would probably be smacked right back, toppling me into an early grave. After what I had heard and smelled and seen, I couldn't bear to use the violence that was so often expected of me to keep the balance in the Realm. I didn't need Zeus or the squalling storm, or a complicated spell. All I needed to do was look inward, embrace the inherent power of my bloodline, and go back to what I did best. I reached into my pocket and retrieved the seed I bought from Skippy's shop.

Merlin swirled his power in his palm, a shimmering ball of murderous magic meant for me. He grew it while I stood confidently before him. The nefarious magic was reflected in his eyes as he took aim. I wished I could say goodbye to my friends, wished I could thank them for their mettle and tell them I loved every single one of them. More than anything, I wanted them to not grieve my passing, because it was, and always had been, my providence, and wishing for things to end differently would just lead to suffering. I looked into my cursemaker's eyes.

"Traitor's Doom" was the name of the magical seed, and here I was, standing in front of the biggest traitor in the Realm.

"*Ianua sit,*" I whispered to the small brown seed.

Merlin hurled his magic at me at the same time as the seed streaked toward him. I lifted my forearm as a shield, Lilian Black's amulet protecting me from most of the damage, but the force of it was still so intense that I went flying. I jumped up as quickly as I could, just in time to see Merlin grab his chest as he would if he was experiencing chest pains. Assuming the seed had reached its target, which looked likely, it would be nestled in Merlin's heart.

All sleeping seeds she wakens.

He grimaced, and took a step back. "What are you doing?"

"I'm planting a tree in your meadow," I replied. I pointed at his chest. *"Augescis!" Grow.*

He grunted, clutching over his heart harder than before, and bellowed in pain. I couldn't bear to watch, but I heard the horror unfold. The branches puncturing his skin on their way out of his body, the roots shooting down through his legs, ripping his flesh, the tree trunk destroying his insides as it widened. None of his power, wealth, or magic would help him now.

The destructor's power is taken.

The sounds were harrowing and grisly, and I cowered beneath them, eyes scrunched shut, hands over my ears, waiting for the maledictive thread that connected us to snap. Waiting for the end.

The skyscraper finally buckled, fiery rubble falling, taking us all down with it.

552

In love, all curses are broken.

CHAPTER 76

LAZYBONES

ASHA

It was so dark, and so quiet. There was no fire or smoke or danger.

"Asha," called Sam's voice. I felt him stroking my hair.

If I could hear Sam's voice, it meant he was dead, too. Had everyone died in the fall? They must have—there was no way we could have survived that.

I opened my eyes, and the light stung like lemon juice. I knew this light, I knew this room and this bed. It was where I had woken up with thirty-seven stitches in my head.

"Asha!" he cried, excitement in his voice. He let go of me

and yelled into the corridor. "She's awake! Guys! Asha's awake!"

He returned to my side.

"Let me guess," I croaked. "You're here to arrest me."

Sam chuckled and squeezed my hand. "You've been asleep for a couple of days."

"He says *asleep*," came Savvy's voice. "But you were in a coma. It was touch-and-go for a while. He never left your side."

I blinked through the bleariness and turned my head to see Savvy. She was bandaged and sitting up in a hospital bed identical to mine.

I remembered the arrow piercing her. "Are you okay?" I asked.

"Hundreds," she replied, with a thumbs-up. "Some smashed-up ribs, and minus a spleen, but the bolt missed the most important organs."

Sam adjusted the angle of my bed so I could sit up, and handed me some water. It tasted amazing. I heard a crunching sound, and saw Salty sitting in the corner, helping herself to a snack basket with a balloon emblazoned with "Get well soon!" floating above it.

"Oh, hi, witch!" she said, peanut brittle festooning her teeth.

"Hi, Salty," I replied. "How's the wrist?"

"Good as new!" she said, a piece of the confection flying out of her mouth.

Chione, Apollo, and Morgan bounced in with hugs, smiles, and gifts.

"It's about time you woke up," snarked the grimalkin. "Lazybones."

"She was literally in a coma," said Morgan. "Give her a break."

"All I'm hearing are excuses," muttered Chione. "While you've been getting your beauty sleep, I've had a *lot* to deal with."

"Leave her in peace," scolded Ferra, who had just walked through the doorway. The Belore twins were with her, carrying containers of food.

"Ferra," I said, so grateful to see her I was near tears.

"Don't look so surprised, Rookie. Do you honestly think I'd allow you to eat *hospital* food?"

"Don't worry," piped up Salty. "I've been eating her hospital food."

Ferra laughed. "And people say goblins aren't thoughtful creatures."

Everyone snickered.

"How are we alive?" I asked.

"Well," said Nilve, "the only reason you're alive is because you were wearing your lucky underpants."

I laughed, but she was being serious. "Once that paramedic mage fixed my wrist, I was able to portal back to you via the sleep shorts. It was perfect timing, because you were pretty much dead."

Not words you often hear, but there you go.

"Once he stabilized you, he fixed old boozer over there," she pointed at Savvy.

"Ex-boozer," corrected Savvy.

"And made sure the rest of us were okay."

"But ... the building," I said. "It was burning. It collapsed. There's no way anyone could have survived that fall."

"We didn't have to," said Sam. "Apollo portaled us here before we hit the ground."

"No way," I replied. "Not possible."

Apollo buffed his nails on his shirt and admired them. "Told you I was the best portaler in the Realm."

"And your curse?" I asked him.

"Broken," he said, bouncing in his sneakers. "Thanks to you. Hey, if you like, I can show you. Chione, turn into a cat."

The grimalkin rolled her eyes. "He's been doing this all morning. He may be a brilliant portaler, but he is utterly exhausting to be around."

I laughed before realizing that Rick was missing. "Where's Rick?"

Morgan smiled so widely she almost swallowed me whole. "Tureek? He's with Gnrok! They're catching up. They're obviously hugely grateful to you for reuniting them."

"They both saved my life on multiple occasions," I said. "It's the least I could do."

"Dusty and Abigail?" I asked.

"They're working on a secret project for you," said Sam. "Dr. Gilbert debriefed us all after the showdown on the skyscraper and we all had to promise to go to follow-up sessions to work through the trauma. She's the one who gave the girls the idea to make you something."

"They're at my place," said Ferra. "As soon as you're up to it, we can see them."

"I'm up to it," I said. "I've never felt better."

"Um, no," said Morgan. "I'll repeat it louder for people at the back. You just woke up from a *coma*."

"True," I said, "but I also have blisteringly fast healing ability. I feel good ... actually, I feel better than good."

Ferra perked up. "Do you think you're well enough to come over to the pub?"

"I would absolutely LOVE to," I enthused. "I can't imagine anything better. Plus, I promised the team a huge feast when this was all over."

"Excellent," Ferra replied, grinning. "Feasts happen to be my forte."

"Before we get ahead of ourselves," said Chione, "we've had to make some arrangements while you've been sleeping."

"Okay," I replied.

"So. Apollo is annoying as hell, but he's really good with animals."

"Yes?" I replied.

"I've hired him to run the Thomas Harvey Conservation Project."

"Oh, that's brilliant," I said.

Apollo nodded. "It's the most amazing job I've ever had! Plus I have somewhere to live, and plenty of money left over from my salary to stock my parents' fridge and pay their rent."

"Most importantly," said Savvy, "it means he doesn't write poetry anymore."

We all laughed, but not too loudly, so as to not hurt Apollo's feelings.

"Nathan Steiger now also has a job," said the grimalkin.

"Oh!" I exclaimed. "He's better?"

"Devka did a brilliant job nursing him back to health. He's in a wheelchair—probably for a while—but his brain is as sharp as ever. So we put him in charge of Æterna."

"What?"

"Obviously we'll need to change the name of the corporation and pivot the business model, but there's a huge and successful business waiting for you. Belladonna left it to you in her will. The distribution network alone is worth billions."

"Distribution network?" I echoed dumbly.

Chione nodded. "For example, think of how we'll be able to scale up your glamour vape business. We've got labs, freight logistics, retail outlets across the Realm. And we don't have to stop at glamour potions. Steiger's got excellent business acumen and the Chalices are guiding him on how to invest the company's profits, including a large chunk of change to be donated to the BetterRealm Foundation, but it's all going swimmingly. Devka is his assistant, and Sebastian is the company mascot. It's all worked out rather well."

"Oh," Sam chimed in. "And we poached Agreement and Halfpint from Auric Bank. We doubled their already-generous salaries as a thank-you for helping us with hacking the entrance into the skyscraper."

I beamed at him.

"One last thing," said Sam. "Now that Garrett is in jail, Dusty's mother has agreed to give up custody."

I nearly yelled in glee. "What? Seriously?"

"Yep," said Ferra. "The Belore skunks are beside themselves, knowing they'll get to see Dusty on the regular."

"What about my news?" demanded SaltySnap.

Sam smiled indulgently. "Salty and Skippy have opened up a new business."

I raised my eyebrows in surprise.

"The Lime Shake Shack," Salty said. "'Cause our skin is green, get it? And because I love lime milkshakes. It's a pop-up shop. We wanted to call it The S-lime Shack, but Chione said we'd be in business rescue within a week. She's very bossy."

I laughed. "What else did I miss?"

"The Chalices coughed up for an apartment for the girls. Zaleria, Mercury, and Marielle. Apparently, it was Mercury's dream to share a place and go to university, so the Chalices made it happen. They knew that Mercury risked her own safety to make sure Zaleria got home safely."

"That's wonderful news," I said. "Mercury deserves that."

"They also made a sizable contribution to the Wood-haven Children's Home. Apparently, they were about to go bust, but now they're going to be pretty darn comfortable."

Beyond happy, I sighed. "You guys really know how to get things done. I should slip into a coma more often."

"Don't you dare," said Sam.

I was nervous asking the next question, but I had to know. "How is Jax?"

A moment of silence betrayed everyone's ongoing concern.

"The honest answer is that we don't know yet," said Morgan. "We'll only know when the baby comes. Jax is due any day. Everyone's nerves are wrecked. It feels like the whole Realm is holding their breath."

My heart sank. "Okay. I guess there's nothing to do but wait and see."

"Talking about waiting," said Apollo, "Harvey's project —there's some good news and bad news."

"Aw," I replied. "Rap?"

Salty piped up again. "As Polly would say, Rap, R.I.P."

"Ah, no," I murmured. "I loved that hollow-boned sickle-clawed rainbow raptor. He saved our lives."

"*She* saved our lives," said Chione.

I looked at her. "She? How do you know?"

"Because she left us a gift," said Apollo, looking delighted. "I found an electric heating pad in Harvey's house—"

"The one I bought him for his back," said Morgan.

"So the egg is being kept nice and warm. It may even hatch by Halloween. Wouldn't that be something?"

My visitors left, and I was about to pull my IV out when Sam stopped me and insisted I wait to see the doctor.

"There's no rush," he said gently. "The girls need a little time to complete their project, and Ferra will need a couple of hours to prepare."

He kept me company and we shared the grapes he had brought. Once the doc gave me the go-ahead to leave, I was home free, leaving the medical man scratching his head at my miraculous recovery.

"Okay," Sam said, looking at his watch. "We still have an hour before Ferra is ready for us. We'll go home to change, and then head over."

I loved how he referred to my house as "home."

"Are you saying you don't like my outfit?" I teased, posing in my backless hospital gown.

"I like it very much," he said, and kissed me. "But I'd prefer you out of it."

I grinned at him. I pinched myself, and was delighted when it hurt.

An hour later I was clean, dressed, and ravenous. We drove to the Copper Cog in near silence.

"You feeling okay?" asked Sam. He was looking exceedingly handsome in his smart black jacket.

"Yes, thanks. There's just a lot to process."

He nodded in empathy and agreement. "It'll take a while. But the most important thing is that you're safe —we're all safe—and that Merlin and Belle are gone."

Yes.

"You did an incredible thing, Asha. I'm so, so proud of you."

"Why do you think I didn't die?" I asked, "You know, when I killed Merlin?"

"Oh, I've been thinking about that," he replied. "It's because you're not a curse."

There were tons of cars at the Cog. I craned my neck in an attempt to see why it was so busy.

"Never seen it like this before," I commented. I had seen the magical gastropub absolutely crammed before, especially due to Ferra's ability to make extra tables and chairs appear when they needed them—and sometimes extra rooms, too—but this was unusual.

"Luckily, Ferra knows we're coming," I said. "Or we'd go hungry."

Sam laughed. "No such thing as hunger if Ferra's around."

"Never a truer word spoken," I replied.

He opened the car door for me and helped me out. "You're sure you're well enough to see people?"

"Definitely," I said. "I can't wait, especially to see the girls."

He pulled me closer. I was reminded of his words on top of the Æterna skyscraper. "I love you," I said, and he crushed me in a hug.

"I love you, too," he said, and took my hand as we walked into the Cog.

CHAPTER 77

LUCKY LIPSTICK

ASHA

The inside of the pub was empty. The fire was roaring happily, but there wasn't a table, chair, or person in sight.

"Nothing to worry about," Sam assured me. "Ferra told me to expect this. Dusty and Abigail are in the private dining room."

I couldn't help being reminded of the Chalices when we went through. It's where they had implored me to help find their daughter, so it seemed a fitting place to have our celebratory feast. But when we got there, only Dusty and Abigail were present. They gasped when they saw me and ran into my arms.

"We visited you in the hospital," said Dusty.

"But you weren't awake," said Abigail. "We brought you a basket of treats too, but I think Salty ate them."

They handed me a box. It had holes punched in it, and there was a distinct peeping sound coming from it.

"That's for you, too, but the hospital staff wouldn't let us bring it in."

I cautiously opened the lid. Six of the most adorable multicolored chicks I'd ever seen were inside.

"Aw," I said. "They are the cutest! Thank you!"

They both glowed.

"Ah, my girls," I said, heart almost bursting. It was so good to feel them in my arms, and I was so proud of the pair of them. I kissed the tops of their heads, and noticed a large swath of black fabric on the table. "What's this?"

"We made it for you," they chorused.

"It's a special dress," said Dusty.

"A special *witch* dress," said Abigail. "With *pockets*."

"The Belore twins helped us."

"Oh my goodness," I exclaimed. "It's so beautiful!"

"We thought of making a white dress, but it reminded us of Celestia, so we changed it to black. Also, because it's your favorite color. And we made it sleeveless to show off your beautiful botanicals."

"Well, it's gorgeous," I replied, holding it up to admire it. "I love it. Thank you so much!"

"Will you put it on?" Dusty asked.

"Now?" I didn't want to seem ungrateful, but it was a formal dress and not really suited to a pub.

They both nodded.

"Ah, okay," I agreed, and nodded enthusiastically. It was supposed to be a party, after all.

Dusty gestured for Sam to turn his back to preserve my modesty, but he excused himself from the room to see if he could help Ferra with anything. I stripped off my clothes and climbed into the sleek, stylish dress.

The girls were totally goggle-eyed. "WOW, Asha," said Abigail. "You look AMAZING."

"So, here's the pocket for your wand," said Dusty, showing me a slim pocket running up the ribbing.

"And Ferra let us use some of her Kevlar, so the dress is bulletproof," said Abigail.

"Good to know!" I laughed. "You girls thought of every-thing. Thank you, I love it."

"It was fun to make," said Abigail. "Dr. Gilbert said it's good to use your hands and make things when you're processing trauma, plus we got to spend more time together."

"You two are just brilliant," I said.

There was a polite knock at the door, and I called for Sam to come in, but Kieron Palefang entered instead.

"Kieron!" I exclaimed. "I didn't think you'd be here."

"Werewolves are allowed to return to public spaces now, thanks to you," he said.

"And thanks to you," I replied. "We wouldn't have made it without your pack."

"Which brings me to why I am here," he said. He took a jewelry box out of his jacket pocket and gave it to me.

"What's this?"

"Open it," he said.

Inside the small box was a necklace with a round pendant attached. I held it closer to look at the sigil on the silver disc. It was a handsome wolf's head—the insignia of the Palefangs. When I turned it over, I saw the symbol of Orion, framed in an S-shape.

"We'd be honored if you'd accept this on behalf of our pack," said Kieron. "Honorary membership in the Palefang pack, with a reminder of Orion and Stoker on the back."

I was deeply touched. Tears sprang to my eyes.

"No, Asha," he said sternly. "It's not the time to cry."

"Thank you," I stammered. "Will you put it on for me?"

Kieron did so, and as I heard the clasp click into place, Sam stepped back into the room. I turned to look at him, and he looked shell-shocked.

"My god," he said, almost breathless. "You look incredible."

The girls giggled, but I was still fighting back tears.

"Come on," he said, "everyone's waiting for us."

I didn't know who "everyone" was, because I still couldn't see another soul apart from who was in the room with me. Sam led me out the side entrance to the herb garden where we had our sweet ring ceremony a lifetime ago. Just a bit farther into the garden, which was the beginning of a fairy-lit forest, a hundred faces peered back at me. I didn't recognize any of them.

"Oh, hex," I said to Sam, ducking in embarrassment. "We seem to have gatecrashed someone else's function."

"Nope," he said, catching me and steering me back in the direction of the people. "Not someone else's function."

"But who are these people?" I whispered.

"People who want to thank you," said Sam.

The crowd happily milled toward us. *Asha,* they were saying, the name rustling on their lips.

"Thank you, Asha," said the first man who reached me. He took my hand in both of his. "You saved our daughter."

"Thank you," said the woman beside him. Her eyes were swollen, her makeup long since washed away.

"You saved my sister," said a little girl.

"You freed my uncle," said an orc with pigtails. "He was in the factory."

A dwarf came up. "I just wanted to see if you were real."

On and on it went until I reached the front of the crowd, where there were chairs set out among what could only be described as an explosion of blooms. There were so many flowers, in so many colors, it looked like a spring carnival, or Mardi Gras.

"Ding, dong, the witch is here," sang a voice just behind me. Captain Morgan.

"Morgan!" I said, spinning around to hug her. "I wasn't expecting this."

"You look amazing," she said, waggling her eyebrows at me. "Just missing one thing." She took out the lucky lipstick I had bought her from Skippy and applied it to my lips. "There," she said, "Perfect."

I thanked her.

"So," she said in a low voice, "your sexy detective and I were chatting in your hospital room when you were recovering, and I was complaining about all the flowers and gifts, you know."

"Yes," I said. "The pollen."

"So … we decided to just let people know to come here to thank you instead of making my office completely uninhabitable and jeopardizing my sinuses and the safety of the Realm. We got Rick and Gnrok to bring the flowers here too, you know. In Rick's monster truck, because it's massive."

"Great idea, Morgan," I said.

"So, then, a funny thing happened," she said. "Savvy was awake when we were talking about the masses of flower arrangements, and all the chocolates and booze, and she said—hey, Savvy, what did you say?"

Savannah appeared, still bandaged, but wearing a glamorous dress anyway. "I said, we're going to have people here, flowers, gifts, and a feast. We may as well have a—"

Sam cleared his throat to get our attention. When I turned to him, he went down on one knee.

Wait, what?

"Asha Viridian Rook," he said, "I've admired you since the moment I laid eyes on you. Your bravery and determination. Your humor and your warmth. I couldn't imagine a more perfect partner in life. Will you marry me?"

CHAPTER 78

EPILOGUE: THE ROOK FAMILY

ASHA

I nodded and tried my best not to weep.

"Don't you dare ugly-cry," whispered Savvy in my ear. "You'll ruin your face for the wedding photos."

"Was that a yes?" asked Sam. "Like, yes, let's get married right now?"

"Yes," I murmured, then gave a more emphatic, "Yes!"

Sam's face lit up like a lighthouse. He jumped on the spot and yelled to the crowd. "The wedding is on! People! It's on! Get ready!"

The crowd cheered and whistled. Some of them were drinking green milkshakes with candy-cane-colored straws. When I lifted my gaze, I saw Salty and Skippy handing them out from their pop-up Shake Shack.

"Attention, attention," boomed an orc's voice into a microphone. It was Rick. I gave him a frantic wave hello and he smiled back. "I have just been informed that the lady said yes."

The audience went ballistic.

"So please take your seats," announced Rick, "and let's get this party started!"

He signaled to Gnrok, who sat beside him in a makeshift DJ station. Gnrok played an instrumental rock 'n roll version of "Here Comes the Bride," which made me laugh. Sam caught my hand and led me to the very front, where an altar was bright with green leaves and beautiful heavy blooms. Soleil looked wise and beautiful in her officiating gown, and she gave me the warmest of smiles. Everyone was seated, but something was missing.

"I need a minute," I said to Sam. "I'll be right back. Will you wait for me?"

"I've been waiting for you all my life," said Sam. "What's another minute?"

I kissed him and ran down the aisle and back into the Cog. I slammed open the double doors to the kitchen and saw a hive of cooking activity as the skunks got about their work in double-quick time.

"Weren't expecting so many guests!" said one of them, beaming. I grinned back.

I caught sight of Ferra, who was issuing instructions, tasting sauces, and mopping her brow. "Ferra!"

"Ah!" she exclaimed, "Is it starting? What did I miss?" She pulled her apron off and slung it to a skunk, who caught it easily and dropped it into the laundry hamper nearby.

"It's starting," I said. "Will you walk me down the aisle?"

She grabbed the tea towel she always kept on her shoulder and sobbed into it. I'd never seen her cry. She was wearing the brooch I had bought her at Skippy's shop: Odin's ravens, Huginn and Muninn. Thought and Memory.

"Don't cry," I repeated Savvy's words from a minute earlier. "Think of the wedding photos."

She nodded, still hiding her face with the cotton towel, and wiped her eyes with it. She took a moment to gather herself, fanning her eyes, and we marched out together, into the sunshine. When the guests saw Ferra they clapped like mad. I glanced at the altar where Sam stood, and he looked as happy as I'd ever seen him. Savvy and Morgan stood as my matrons of honor, and Apollo as Sam's best man. The flower girls, Dusty and Abigail, giggled behind us.

Gnrok started the music again, and my dwarf fairy godmother walked me down the aisle. I'd never felt more loved or happy in my life. Before she turned to leave, she hugged me fiercely—one of her famous rib-cracker hugs—and said, "I'm so very proud of you, Rookie."

Gnrok gave Soleil the microphone, and the Starfall witches in the crowd cheered and clapped. Halfpint and Agreement were sitting next to Craic Blackloth, engaged in a lively conversation. Haryk Virvaris looked dapper in a white tuxedo.

"Welcome, friends and family, to this joyous occasion as we celebrate the union of Asha Viridian Rook and Samuel Ray Armstrong. As the high priestess of the Starfall Coven, it is my honor to officiate at this wedding and witness the love and commitment that Asha and Sam share."

Sam and I grinned at each other. I spotted Steiger in his wheelchair at the front, along with Devka and Sebastian. Behind them sat Ms. Hammond, looking beautiful in a new dress, along with Mercury, Marielle, Frankie, and Zaleria. The handsome Chalice couple kept looking at their daughter as if to make sure she was still there.

"As they stand here before you, let us take a moment to honor the elements that will bless and guide their marriage. Earth, air, fire, water, and spirit."

Sam had never been to this kind of wedding, and he seemed to be enjoying the novelty of it.

"Asha," intoned Soleil, "as a skilled gardener and potion mistress, you bring the nourishing and healing energy of earth and water to this union. Sam, as a detective, you embody the quick-witted and adaptable energy of air. The strength of your determination brings heat and fire. The coming together of your like minds and hearts will be the spirit. Together, you will create a strong and vibrant foundation for your marriage, rooted in love and trust."

The people hooted and cheered. It was certainly the rowdiest wedding ceremony I'd ever attended, and it made me happy.

"It is now time for you to express your love and commitment to one another." She eyed Sam to go first. He laughed nervously, and cleared his throat.

"I, Sam, take you, Asha, to be my lawfully wedded wife. I have never loved anyone as I love you. I'm not good at witchcraft stuff, but I can promise you that you are my moon, my stars, my everything. I promise to love, honor, and protect you, and to be by your side through all the challenges and joys that life brings. And I will always take the arrow for you."

I gulped. It was my turn and my mouth was so dry. "I, Asha, take you, Sam, to be my lawfully wedded husband." It sounded so weird! "I promise to love, honor, and support you, and to be your partner in all things. With my skills as a cursebreaker, I will work to remove any obstacles that may stand in the way of our happiness."

Soleil looked pleased. "Samuel and Asha will now exchange rings as a symbol of their eternal love and commitment to one another," said the high priestess, nodding at someone at the back of the crowd. I panicked for a second. I didn't have a ring! But Sam moved closer and squeezed my hand to show that there was nothing to worry about.

Gnrok played a fun but lurching song that sounded like it should be part of the *Addams Family* soundtrack. I spotted Sugar sitting in the congregation with her baby on her lap. He was cuddling the foulmouthed monkey. Behind her sat Mason Senior Senior Senior with his oxygen tank, Mason Senior Senior, and Mason Senior. Mason Senior Senior caught my eyes and waved, then had a coughing fit. There was cooing from the crowd as a creature made its way up the aisle. I almost bent over double laughing when I saw who it was: Jemima in a pink tutu. I could have cried, but instead I chose to laugh. Highly distractible, as dinosaur birds are prone to be when everything looks like food, she took her time to make her way up to us, where Apollo threw some seed down for her. While Jemima was pecking at them, he untied the ribbon attached to her tutu, which had a ring on it, and passed it to Sam. It was the same ring he had given me in this very garden.

Sam smiled at me, and took my hand. "Asha, this is the ring I gave to you before as a symbol of my commitment. We had to cut it off in the hospital's ER, but I had it fixed. Just like the ring came back together, I will always come back to you." He put the ring on my finger. "With this ring, I thee wed."

I looked down at my hand, and saw a shimmer. Set in the ring was the protective amulet's opal. I wouldn't have to wear Lilian Black's choker anymore.

Oohs and *aahs* emanated from the crowd as three sleek black cats sashayed down the aisle toward the altar. As they reached us, Chione took her human form and Circe and Odysseus sat on either side of her as she passed me Sam's ring. It was heavier than I expected, and I must have frowned, because Chione quickly whispered: "It's made from the melted-down bullet."

I knew which one she meant. I still had the scar over my womb. The symbolism of the ring was a clear message from Sam: *we are a family no matter what.*

I took Sam's hand. He still had the shiny burn scar on his arm from when he had rescued the inmates from Riverside Asylum. "With this ring, I thee wed."

We joined hands and gazed into one another's eyes.

"Asha," said Soleil, "as a witch, you have the power to bring light and positivity into the world through your magic. Sam, as a detective, you have the courage and determination to seek out the truth and protect those in need. Together, you have the strength and wisdom to face any challenge that comes your way—"

"Stop the wedding!" shouted Madame Copperfield. She held her phone aloft with one hand, and swayed her staff in the other to get our attention. "Stop the wedding! I have an important announcement to make."

My mouth dropped open. The microphone in Soleil's hand made a squealing sound as she lowered it.

"What is it?" asked Gnrok.

"It's Jax," yelled the directress.

My stomach instantly knotted. I knew the day had been just too perfect. Morgan and I exchanged worried expressions.

"Darick's on the line," Copperfield announced. "Jacquelyn Denna Knight had a healthy baby girl! Mom and baby are doing well!"

The congregation cheered. My whole body sagged in relief. I hadn't realized how anxious I had been about it. What wonderful, wonderful news. I caught Sugar Shagar's eye and she gave me a genuine smile for the first time.

Soleil lifted the mic again. "A blessed day indeed!" We turned back to face her, and she continued on to the last part of the ceremony. "May these hands, joined in marriage, serve as a reminder of the love and partnership that you share. May they work together to bring healing, justice, and happiness to the world. By the power vested in me as—"

"Wait," interrupted Sam.

Now what?

"Please wait," he said. "Could we ... would it be possible to ... include a quick adoption ceremony?"

Soleil looked confused, but nodded. "Of course. It won't be legally binding, obviously, but—"

Sam called Dusty over. She looked like a lamb again in her flower girl dress. Awestruck, she looked up at us. "Are you being serious?"

"Of course we're being serious," said Sam. "You're our daughter, now."

Dusty's face crumpled, and she wept. I joined in. Sam's eyes didn't look too dry, either.

Soleil straightened her spine and prepared to finish the ceremony. "As a high priestess, and in accordance with the sacred traditions of the Realm, I now pronounce you husband, wife, and daughter. You may now seal your vows with a kiss."

Sam and I kissed the top of Dusty's head, then each other.

"Bollocks!" shouted Sugar Shagar's baby, and there was a ripple of laughter around them. Sugar looked as proud as punch.

"Ladies and gentlemen, goblins and orcs, werewolves and dwarfs, wizards and witches," announced Soleil. "It is my great pleasure to present to you the Rook family: husband, wife, and daughter."

The crowd went berserk. Confetti, hugging, champagne corks popping, the most delicious snacks on platters, silent fireworks, and Gnrok's unusual choice of dancing tunes. There were speeches by those I loved and by perfect strangers. There was lots of laughter, and bucketloads of tears. It was a blur of absolute bliss. I think I caught a glimpse of Henry in the crowd, but I couldn't be sure. When it was time for our slow dance, Sam hugged me tightly and whispered in my ear as we moved to the music, my heart too big for my chest. Dusty joined us, and we swayed together.

"You're the best thing that has ever happened to me," said Sam. "My wonderful witch, my wife, my curse-breaker."

"My mother," Dusty said, and I couldn't stop my tears from falling. I snuggled in tightly, and that line from the Equinox Stitch spell came into my head again.

In love, all curses are broken.

YOUR NEXT ADVENTURE AWAITS

Thank you for joining us on this caper! We hope you enjoyed reading it as much as we did, writing it.

Looking for more magical urban fantasy in the Makeshift Universe World?

**Blood Magic Series
(complete 6-book series)**

Find more awesome reads at
www.jt-lawrence.com

ALSO BY JT LAWRENCE

FICTION

WHEN TOMORROW CALLS

• *SERIES* •

(Futuristic kidnapping thriller)

The Stepford Florist: A Novelette

The Sigma Surrogate

1. Why You Were Taken

2. How We Found You

3. What Have We Done

When Tomorrow Calls Box Set: Books 1 - 3

(complete)

URBAN FANTASY

BLOOD MAGIC

(complete 6-book series)

1. The HighFire Crown

2. The Dream Drinker

3. The Witch Hunter

4. The Ember Isles

5. The Chaos Jar

6. The New Dawn Throne

STANDALONE NOVELS

The Memory of Water

(steamy psychological thriller)

Grey Magic

(witchy magical realism)

EverDark

(urban fantasy)

SHORT STORY COLLECTIONS

Sticky Fingers

Sticky Fingers 2

Sticky Fingers 3

Sticky Fingers 4

Sticky Fingers 5

Sticky Fingers 6

Sticky Fingers: The Complete Collection:

Books 1 - 6: 72 Short Stories

NON-FICTION

The Underachieving Ovary

(memoir)

The Indie Author Game Plan